The Caine Prize for African Writing 2016

The Daily Assortment of Astonishing Things

and other stories

D0543425

New Internationalist

The Daily Assortment of Astonishing Things
The Caine Prize for African Writing 2016

First published in 2016 in Europe, North America and Australasia by
New Internationalist Publications Ltd
The Old Music Hall
106-108 Cowley Road
Oxford
OX4 1JE, UK
newint.org

First published in 2016 in South Africa by
Jacana Media (Pty) Ltd
10 Orange Street
Sunnyside
Auckland Park 2092
South Africa
+ 2711 628 3200
jacana.co.za

Cover illustration: Nick Mulgrew.

Design by New Internationalist.

Printed by T J International Limited, Cornwall, UK
who hold environmental accreditation ISO 14001.

British Library Cataloguing-in-Publication Data.
A catalogue record for this book is available from the British Library.

Library of Congress Cataloging-in-Publication Data.
A catalog record for this book is available from the Library of Congress.

ISBN 978-1-78026-320-5
(ebook ISBN 978-1-78026-321-2)

Jacana ISBN 978-1-4314-2435-1

Contents

Introduction

Selected from a record number of eligible entries, 166 stories from 23 African countries, this anthology contains the five stories from the 17th annual Caine Prize shortlist, which was announced in May 2016. Two Nigerians were shortlisted this year, one of whom, Tope Folarin, is a past winner from 2013. The other, Lesley Nneka Arimah, is this year's only female contender. They are joined by a South African, a Zimbabwean and, for the first time in the history of the Prize, a Somali/Kenyan. Each shortlisted writer is awarded £500 in addition to a travel and accommodation grant to attend a series of public events in London and the award dinner in Oxford in July.

The Chair of Judges, award-winning author and academic Delia Jarrett-Macauley, praised the high standard of the entries, describing the shortlist as 'an engrossing, well-crafted and dauntless pack of stories', and remarking on 'the increasing number of fantasy fictions'. Also noted was a 'sci-fi trend [which resonated] in several excellent stories'.

She added: 'My fellow judges commented on the pleasure of reading the stories, the gift of being exposed to the exciting short fictions being produced by African writers today and the general shift away from politics towards more intimate subjects – though recent topics such as the Ebola crisis were being wrestled with.'

Of note this year too was the writers' increasingly bold approaches to both subject matter and style. The judges were inspired by 'wild or lyrical voices matching the tempered, measured prose writers,' as well as 'stories tackling uneasy topics, ranging from an unsettling, unreliable narrator's tale of airport scrutiny, to a science-fictional approach towards the measurement of grief, a young child's coming to grips with family dysfunction, the big drama of rivalling siblings and the silent, numbing effects of loss'.

The 2016 shortlist comprises:

- **Abdul Adan** (Somalia/Kenya) 'The Lifebloom Gift' from *The Gonjon Pin and Other Stories* (New Internationalist Publications Ltd, UK, 2014)
- **Lesley Nneka Arimah** (Nigeria) 'What it Means When a Man Falls From the Sky' from *Catapult* (Catapult, USA, 2015)
- **Tope Folarin** (Nigeria) 'Genesis' from *Callaloo* (Johns Hopkins University Press, USA, 2014)
- **Bongani Kona** (Zimbabwe) 'At your Requiem' from *Incredible Journey: Stories That Move You* (Burnet Media, South Africa, 2015)
- **Lidudumalingani** (South Africa) 'Memories we Lost' from *Incredible Journey: Stories That Move You* (Burnet Media, South Africa, 2015)

Joining Delia Jarrett-Macauley on the panel of judges are acclaimed film, television and theatre actor, Adjoa Andoh; writer and founding member of the Nairobi-based writers' collective, Storymoja, and founder of the Storymoja Festival, Muthoni Garland; Associate Professor and Director of African American Studies at Georgetown University Dr Robert J Patterson; and Mary Watson, the winner of the Caine Prize in 2006. Once again, the winner of the £10,000 Caine Prize will be given the opportunity to take up a month's residence at Georgetown University, as a Writer-in-Residence at the Lannan Center for Poetics and Social Practice. The award will cover all travel and living expenses. The winner will also be invited to take part in the Open Book Festival in Cape Town, South Africa, the Storymoja Festival in Nairobi, Kenya, and the Ake Festival in Abeokuta, Nigeria in 2016.

This collection also includes 12 stories crafted at this year's Caine Prize workshop, which was held in Zambia and sponsored by the Carnegie Corporation. In attendance were three local Zambian writers (Chilufya Chilangwa, Bwanga 'Benny Blow' Kapumpa and Kafula Mwila) and one Malawian

(Timwa Lipenga). They joined former shortlisted writers Billy Kahora, Elnathan John, FT Kola and Masande Ntshanga, and an unprecedented four former winners: NoViolet Bulawayo, Namwali Serpell, Okwiri Oduor and Tope Folarin (whose attendance at the workshop means that two of his stories therefore feature in this anthology).

The writers were hosted at Chaminuka Lodge – a stunning game reserve 45 minutes' drive from Lusaka, set in 10,000 acres of land, teeming with wildlife, and housing – both in and around its main lodge – a thoughtfully curated collection of local and regional works of art. Thanks to the generosity of the owners, Mr and Mrs Andrew Sardanis, the 12 writers were given an extraordinary and inspiring space within which to compose their stories under the expert guidance of accomplished novelist Jamal Mahjoub and award-winning editor, book critic and former Man Booker Prize judge, Ellah Allfrey, who is also deputy chair of the Caine Prize.

The calibre and commitment of the participants to their craft has produced a pot pourri of intricate, masterful and imaginative storytelling in which an eclectic mix of themes and characters abound, from the weird and wonderful to the exquisite, ethereal and heart-breaking, with several doses of humour thrown in for good measure.

Some of the highlights of the workshop included two school visits, in which the writers split into groups, led workshops and spoke to the students about writing, reading and storytelling; an informal evening at Chaminuka Lodge, which provided a welcome opportunity to forge valuable links with members of PEN Zambia, local writers and artists and the National Arts Council, Zambia; and a public event at Foxdale Court, Roma, facilitated by Mulenga Kapwepwe, Chair of the National Arts Council, Zambia. We are grateful to the staff at Foxdale Court, Nicholas Kawinga and PEN Zambia, Mulenga Kapwepwe and staff at the National Arts Council of Zambia, and Gadsden Books for their help in making this an enjoyable evening.

The success of Zambian writer Namwali Serpell, who won

the Caine Prize in 2015, provided a tremendous boost both to the country's appetite for literature and to writers' willingness to share their own stories, and we were pleased to see an increase in the number of entries from Zambia to the competition this year – a trend which we hope will continue. In addition, the co-publishing arrangement with Sub-Saharan Publishers in Zambia, which has sold over 25,000 copies of Caine Prize anthologies in the last 18 months, remains instrumental in strengthening and supporting local and pan-African literary networks. The anthology is also available in Zimbabwe, Uganda, South Africa, Ghana, Nigeria and Kenya through our co-publishers, who receive a print-ready PDF free of charge. It can be read as an e-book supported by Kindle, iBooks and Kobo and, via a partnership with the literacy NGO Worldreader, some award-winning stories are available free to African readers through an app on their mobile phones.

The principal sponsors of the 2016 Prize were: the Oppenheimer Memorial Trust; the Booker Prize Foundation; the Miles Morland Foundation; Sigrid Rausing and Eric Abraham; John and Judy Niepold; Commonwealth Writers, an initiative of The Commonwealth Foundation; The British Council; The Imara Trust and The Wyfold Charitable Trust. We have also been generously supported by the Carnegie Corporation of New York, whose contribution ensured the success of this year's workshop. There were other generous private donations, and vital help in kind was given by: the Royal Over-Seas League; Bodley's Librarian; the Royal African Society; Marion Wallace of the British Library; Tricia Wombell, Co-ordinator of the Black Reading Group and Black Book News; and Brixton Library. We are immensely grateful for all this help, most of which has been given regularly over the past years and without which the Caine Prize would not be Africa's leading literary award.

Vimbai Shire
Acting Director
The Caine Prize for African Writing

The Caine Prize 2016
Shortlisted Stories

The Lifebloom Gift

Abdul Adan

Two days ago, I was fired from my TSA job at the airport. My boss convinced some offended fool to press sexual harassment charges against me. This was like the most preposterous thing. Everyone at work knows I am straight. I have nothing sexual whatsoever for men. I know it, my workmates know it, and the boss knows it. Even the offended fool knows it. I am just not the guy to like another guy sexually. Just before breaking the tragic news to me, my cold brute of a boss (Oh my, you should see the asshole! He has this bony, unlovable nose) took pains to explain my alleged offence. He said I had a tendency to *settle* when carrying out frisk searches.

I did use the word *settle* before, that much I concede. But it was nothing as creepy as he made it out to be. It was really just a break-room joke. A female workmate from the inner city had spilled her coffee and bent down to wipe it up. She had just removed her TSA uniform and placed it in the locker. She must have already clocked out or something. Anyway, I caught sight of her dangling breasts from the corner of my eye, and there he was! In my mind, Ted Lifebloom himself was kneeling to her right and trying to get his fat hands in there. But Ted was no longer a mother-loving child at this point. He was a giant of an adult and his hands wouldn't fit into the little space between her armpit and vest. So he lay below her, arms upwards, pulled her close into a kneeling position and made the loud wish of *settling* there forever. Now, *I* didn't do any of that, didn't go for the opening, nor did I *settle* between her bent torso and the floor. I only, harmlessly, said to my friendly supervisor that one could *settle* between her and the floor. You see, it was a comment one couldn't resist, given the circumstances. As for the 'tendency' my boss accuses me of, it was only one other occasion. Not enough to justify being called a 'tendency'.

Once in a while, a traveller comes along who feels like Ted Lifebloom. He or she doesn't have to be male or female, as the particular gift of Ted Lifebloom isn't a gender-based one. There are many women and men out there who have fleshy faces, soft chests (flat or full, it doesn't matter) and round necks with those sexy, fat rings. It might sound simple when put like that, but hear me out. The particular gift isn't really in the aforementioned features themselves. It's more like the features are *qualifiers* for the gift. One has to be touched by Ted or be a student of Ted's to be aware of the gift. A great number of people out there have no idea about their special place in the universe. Thousands or even millions of Lifebloomers.

That morning, a Turkish male came through the screening door at Lambert Airport. I knew immediately he stepped up for his search that he was a Lifebloomer. How did I know? Well, let's just say he had a fleshy face and a pebble of sweat on his earlobe. Being so generous, I decided right there and then, to, in the most subtle way, have him contemplate the Ted in his heart. Often, the fleshy-faced Lifebloomers (as opposed to those with hairy arms and pockets of fat under their abdomen), possess a mole behind their knees. To get them thinking, one had to locate the mole with the right thumb and press it. Fortunately, the traveller in this case was wearing shorts, which made things much easier. All I had to do was frisk him all the way down and pause at the back of his knee. Then I would momentarily *settle* on the mole. Don't get me wrong; I realize how creepy this sounds for those who don't understand. I was smart about it though. As soon as I got to the mole, I faced the challenge of devising a time-buying trick. I needed a good excuse for a 30-second press of my thumb at one spot on the back of his knee. Not an easy task, as anyone might guess. Here's what I did: I ran my hands on his body from the shoulders down, pausing routinely at the pockets, and, on arrival at the spot where I perceived the mole to be, feigned temporary dizziness. Leaning with my left hand on the ground, my face downwards, I went into a brief ecstasy, excited by the Lifeblooming agent hidden in the mole. Like all ignorant Lifebloomers, the man jerked his leg forward to shake off my grip, but I managed to hold on for a full 30 seconds. When he complained later, it was really useless. Everyone knew about my overly sensitive nose. His smelly shoes, as any wise person would assume, must have caused my dizziness on the spot. Still, I told my stupid boss (who kept a record of the event anyway) that I was nauseated by the traveller's perfume and was nearly unconscious for a few seconds – I needed that knee for support. I don't think he believed me then but who cares really? You can't fire a man for having an overly sensitive nose, much less for being a Lifebloomer.

My own journey of self-discovery started when I was working for a medical transportation agency some years ago. I drove a middle-aged woman from St Louis to the small town of Lonely Nest, Missouri. Her house was at the end of a long street, which featured uncountable Baptist churches, at least one Episcopalian church and a post office. I wouldn't have known there was an Episcopalian church if the old lady hadn't told me about it. I unloaded her stuff and helped her into her yard where I saw her fat son of about 30 outside, napping on the grass. A greyish Akita dog slept on his chest. On seeing us arrive, he sat up and asked, 'Mum, did someone help you with the stuff?' He could see me right there! Well, at least that was what I thought. His mum asked me to shake his hand, after which we spoke briefly. He seemed interested, but kept averting his gaze. But then, his mum disappeared into the house and the fat son, whom she introduced as Ted, gave me the kindest look ever. I thought I saw the universe in his eyes – the future and the past, and most of God's holy best. His mouth was small, his nose was fleshy, his cheeks were round, his hands were hairy, and his eyes, well, watery – if one may say so.

A few days later his mum had an appointment at Barnes Jewish Hospital in St Louis. I drove down to pick her up and, Ted, against her wishes, joined us. They both sat at the back. In the parking lot, his mum told me to watch him, which, in hindsight, was very selfish of her. She didn't want him going around stimulating other Lifebloomers from their unknowing stupor. Anyway, the next few minutes gave me a first-hand idea of why I had to watch Ted. His mum wasn't gone five minutes before Ted reached over and placed his hand on my shoulder and pretty much (as I came to learn later) *settled*. I am not sure how long his hand was there because I got carried into a greenish world I had only seen in dreams until then. Everything seemed as though I was on some yet-to-be-formulated drug. It was a thing of the heavens. Let me put it this way: I heard the song of birds and sneezes of horses, smelled the fur of dogs, felt a twitch in one of my nipples which, in turn, transformed into a brown lactating nipple... In short, I understood the meaning of love – almost. And this was just the shoulder! Suppose he got to my mole! Can you imagine that? I am now like the next thing after him among Lifebloomers. Ted not only had the gift to take you to that greenish world by a touch of his hand, but could transfer some of his gifts to you. To really use it, you have to be a bearer of at least one special mole and be willing to help other Lifebloomers discover themselves.

Not long after meeting Ted, I spotted an advert in a local scientific monthly. They were asking anthropology students at universities all over the state to send proposals for articles on animal and human expressions of love. A probably blond and flat-chested student from Mizzou had an article published about bonobos settling their quarrels by having gentle sex, which, really, was some superficial crap. So I thought, why not share the Lifebloom gift? I asked his mum if I could interview Ted about his life and she said yes. She didn't ask why. She knew I was either infected or had somehow discovered my Lifebloom status. Truth be told, I had no idea I was a Lifebloomer. I just knew Ted was a very special person. Nothing, however, could have prepared me for what was to come. The following is the case study I eventually sent to the magazine. I ask readers to politely disregard any references to abnormal conditions. Some of these are conclusions reached before my own awakening. I also ask the more generous readers to interpret the conditions as side effects of being the epicentre of the Lifebloom gift. It is not an easy responsibility. Trust me.

Blooming Ted: A Case Study
Introduction
Born in Lonely Nest, Missouri, in 1978, to white Episcopalian parents, Ted Lifebloom was 30 years old when I met him. His mother worked as a registered nurse throughout Ted's childhood. His father ran a Bible school at home in Lonely Nest. I came to learn about his special condition during a ride to St Louis when I drove his mother to a hospital appointment. While we waited for his mother in the parking lot, Ted placed his hand on my shoulder for what seemed like forever (although it was actually three minutes according to my watch) and informed me, without speaking, of his special abilities. He essentially sent me into a trance within seconds of contact with my shoulder, during which I learned something of the meaning of love. If only Ted's specialness was restricted to that! Ted is a sacrificial lamb of messianic proportions. The following information was gathered through a series of interviews with his parents, his former girlfriend and Ted himself.

Background

Ted lived with his mother and father until he was 20, after which his parents divorced and he remained with his mother. Between the ages of two and ten, while his mother worked as a nurse in St Louis, Ted saw her only on weekends. His childhood needs during this time were attended to by young females who came to his father's yard for their Bible lessons. His mother told me that, at one of his schools, a teacher said young Ted was too sentimental.

Whenever his mother came home on weekends, young Ted nearly always kept his hands in her blouse through the arm opening. On days that she wore blouses with loose sleeves, he was happier. He could get his hands in much easier than if the sleeves were tight and the collar was too far out of reach. He was once even said to have attempted a swift vertical reach through his mother's tight collar, during which he nearly choked her when his elbow got trapped between her chin and her neck. One evening, while his mother was away, a seven-year-old Ted had taken a pair of scissors and modified all of her tight blouses under both armpits, just so he could slide his hands in better and feel her breasts when she wore them. The manner of his touch, his mother said, was not exactly of a fondling nature. He would cup the breast in one of his palms and keep it there until his hands sweated against the breast. Sometimes he climbed into her bed while she slept and placed his hands on the narrow, smooth path between her breasts.

His father, whom I located in a retirement home in Mahomet, Illinois, admitted that he had been so fond of his son that he hadn't been able to resist cuddling him even as the boy approached pubescence.

Ted himself told me that to experience something, one had to touch it. He denied the existence of anything he couldn't touch, including air, the sun, the sky, the moon, and people he hadn't touched or at least brushed shoulders with. The untouched individual, he said, is a nonentity. To claim a place in Ted's gloriously green universe, the individual has to be touched.

Ted's former girlfriend, Elizabeth, who had since taken a job at a massage parlour in University City, Missouri, told me that Ted wasn't too different from her other lovers. 'He just touched a lot,' she said. In their love-making, she said Ted preferred the missionary position and, in positioning himself between her legs, he made such moves that I understood to be a mere settling on his part. She said she did not mind Ted's tendency to settle. Quite the contrary: she said it was the most attractive part of their six-year relationship and that, had he been more conventionally emotional, she would still have been with him. Apparently, Ted did not care much for the orgasm at the end. He simply relished every inch of the journey through her moist, corrugated innards, and stayed therein as long as he could, looking around abstractedly at the empty air in the room, and making such loud statements as: 'I wish you were as big as this whole space so I could swim your entirety.'

In the light of this, I should mention that Ted has never swum in anything. I also learnt from his mother that Ted suffers from bouts of temporary amnesia that can visit him every ten minutes. Once, during one of our interviews, Ted politely asked me to offer him my head so he could stroke it and reassure himself of my existence, to which I assented gladly. The bliss of his touch is, however, something that, unfortunately, much of the world out there will never experience. It defies every adjective. All I can think of now, in my generous bid to describe what it was like, are visions of smoothness (of any surface really), of special moles found on the bodies of aristocratic females of Kazakhstan, the dreadlocks of brotherly black men, the humble delicacy of certain unreachably shy females, the freckled faces of English tourists on African beaches, the moans of Asian porn stars.

Analysis

Young Ted was severely overprotected by his father. There's no doubt about that. In fact, his father was one of those extremely cuddly people with perpetually water-filled eyes. He did not so *much shake my hand as caress it when we met in Mahomet. He had a giggle about him that seemed to tickle anyone in his presence, after which he always brushed some wet residue from his eyes.*

Ted's mother was a tall, brown-haired woman, with shiny seductive eyes, the charm of which she had retained into middle age. Her breasts were youthful, and her feet were small and fidgety. When she hugged her friends, it was tight but brief, almost furtive. She seemed like she was in too much hurry for her age, and she had no business being busy really. Her eyes, unlike those of Ted's father, were clear and sharp ~ with darting glances. She laughed often and made a joke of nearly everything, much to Ted's displeasure. Her comments about Ted were made without any discernible emotion. It was as though she were a physician analysing a remote patient she hadn't even seen yet. I imagined the ten years she'd lived alone with Ted, after his father's move back to Mahomet, to be filled with uncountable days where Ted, too heavy to keep up with his mother, sat in the middle of the living room watching her slender figure walk from one corner of the house to another. I also imagine this period to contain such little scenes as her fat son pulling his perpetually hurrying mother by the end of her skirt in an attempt to settle on some soft part of her. Yet she seemed to care for Ted, tended to his needs, but, even in my presence, pulled back her hand from him to prevent him from, as she said jokingly, 'settling on it.'

Once, when Ted was 25, his uncle visited him and asked if he might consider finding a job (for Ted was pretty much slothful). Ted didn't really understand how one went about getting a job. He asked the uncle, for instance, to tell him more about jobs, including about their colour and texture, and especially their texture. When he was told one needed hard work to attain personal independence, the already overweight Ted stood up from his seat immediately and made two circular laps around the room, before coming back to sit down, saying amid gasps: 'This is it. Hard work itself.' No matter what was said to explain to him the idea of it, Ted's hard work never evolved beyond his indoor walks. Sometimes he bent down dejectedly and shook his head, like someone in mourning, lamenting his life. When asked why, he answered that it was what distressed people did, and unemployed people were supposed to be distressed.

Ted couldn't grasp any abstractions and simply saw everything as bits to be done and lived. He would shake his head or yell to express sadness or sorrow, and would walk about to respond to such phrases as 'work hard'. I surmised that Ted's excessively cuddly father, in combination with his loving but somewhat detached mother, confused him, turning him into a cloying wreck whenever he felt positively disposed towards another. His memory lapses are results of his mother's emotional and physical unavailability. Every time he'd reached out to her for comfort and, thereby, registered inside of himself her unquestionable loving presence, she had withdrawn suddenly, and sent his collective, cuddly feelings into dispersal, leading him to question if she had been there in the first place.

Once he had an attack of his memory lapses in my presence and had to ask me to offer him an arm, a leg, a neck, or a shoulder every ten minutes. On one of those occasions, so unsure of my existence was he that he felt my arm all the way to the elbow and further up to my armpit, settling us both into a greenish trance until his mother ran in to free us by shouting, as one would to a stubborn horse, 'snap out of it!' The second time it happened, she couldn't get any response to her verbal commands and had to hit him on the ankle with a baseball bat, fracturing it. I conclude that Ted suffers from an acute case of Sentimental Languor. (Reprinted with the permission of Klaus & Debbie's Science Magazine, St Louis.)

It should go without saying that, by the end of my case study, I had understood that Ted was love itself in human form. I knew also that Ted and I had a responsibility to help one more Lifebloomer at least. You see, Ted had already informed me that I was a genuine article from the Lifebloom factory that exists somewhere in the Alatau mountains and whose airborne agents make their way to a select few unborn foetuses. Both Ted and his mother agreed that Ted had at least six moles on the back of his body. The moles, said Ted, were all in special spots.

One evening, I mentioned the issue of moles to my sister, just in passing. I did not say what the moles were for. Just that some people have special ones, whereupon my saintly sister informed me of an elderly man residing in the nursing home she was working at, who had five moles on his back parts, and at least one of those, she said doubtfully, was behind the knee. Within a week, Ted and I set off for St Charles, to the nursing home where the potential Lifebloomer was residing. Ted had on a pair of khaki shorts, a white shirt, and a small grey coat he could barely wrap around his round belly. I drove the entire way to that nursing home in St Charles. I was going to park under the trees behind the parking lot (in case they had a CCTV) but Ted said we should park at a gas station a mile away and walk to the nursing home so he could feel the Lifebloomer's energy in gradual bits.

'This is it,' said Ted, a few minutes into the walk.

'What do you sense, Darlingness?' I asked. I often called him things like 'sweetness', 'darlingness' or 'sweet moles'. It is all love, really. They mean nothing, trust me. I don't ever even make fun of him.

'This is it,' repeated Ted. 'This is the man who could inherit my place. We are approaching a possible second epicentre here.'

Three days later, under the directions of Ted, we returned to the nursing home armed with four clothes pegs. The idea was that we would hold four of the moles by the pegs, while Ted *settled* on the fifth mole. So into the nursing home we walked, all smiles, pausing to greet and shake hands with some of the old ladies in the lounge. We were always civil like that, really. Our session with the special Lifebloomer (who so far had refused to speak to anyone who wasn't his family) was to take approximately three minutes. With quick steps, Ted and I, one after another, made our noble presence known to him. He was seeing us for the first time so you can imagine how *unsettled* he got. He was probably unstable too. You need not be sane to lead the Lifebloom world.

Ted was quick to take the old man's alarm bell away from him lest he called anyone. I grabbed his little wrinkly hands and told him to stay mute or face the Lifebloom wrath. That was it. We pulled down his pyjamas and set the pegs in the right order. The old fool kept squirming and convulsing so much that I had to hold him down by his back as Ted tended to each mole. Well, Ted pretty much *settled* with each press of the peg, causing much overstimulation to the poor man. But what option did we have? If he had stayed still I would have handled the pegs while Ted tended to the special fifth mole. When the pegs were in place Ted descended on the mole behind the knee with much care. Really, all he did, given the special circumstance, was suck on it to see if it would change colour. For sometimes, said Ted, extraordinary Lifebloom agents make themselves known by changing their colour. Once we were done, we climbed through the window, leaving the pegs in place. I climbed back in, seconds later, just before he got out of his Lifebloom trance, and wrote our unregistered cell number on his arm with the instructions, 'Call us tomorrow at 4pm and we will tell you all about it.'

The next day Ted and I sat in one of the bars in the Delmar Loop of St Louis and waited for the ignorant Lifebloomer's call. The hour passed and no call came. Ted kept going back and forth between the bathroom and the tables shaking the hands of perfect strangers as we waited. By sundown, it was time for Ted to express his grief about the failure of our project. I had the responsibility of leading him away from crowds so he could bend and shake his head, yell and kick pavements as necessary. Sometimes I felt so sorry for poor Ted that I had him sit down and stroked his chest, carefully staying clear of the Lifebloom agents that populated his body. Finally, he was quiet and did not say a word until halfway through the ride back to Lonely Nest, when he asked that I pull over so he could pee. He walked down through the shrubs, down the slope from the road, and, without looking back, disappeared into the darkness. It was the last I saw of Ted Lifebloom. If I had known he was going to disappear I would have pulled by the roadside much earlier, just so we could excite each other's moles and have a final swim in the green world of love, of wisdom and ecstasy. Lord, how it hurt to see him vanish without warning! I drove back to St Louis and, after a week of immersion, or rather, *settle*ment, among the comfiest of pillows, applied for a job at the dreaded TSA, where I hoped to carry out my Lifebloom duty by assessing potential Lifebloomers. And now, thanks to my brutish boss, there goes the job and any hope of locating an inheritor to Ted.

If, in my trial for sexual harassment, the soft-faced Magistrate of St Louis asks me to simplify for the court some of the grand visions of the Lifebloom ecstasy, I will give a list of images that include giant snakes slithering on bare backs of sunbathers, the kisses of toothless elderly Kazakh couples, the penetrative mouths of hyenas as they disembowel fleeing prey, the longing eyes of Akita dogs, the sweaty waists of African female dancers, the heaving chests of death-row inmates on the execution gurney, the tight jaws of some vindictive men.

Abdul Adan was born in Somalia, grew up in Kenya and lives in the United States. His work has appeared in African magazines *Kwani?*, *Jungle Jim, Gambit, Okike, Storytime, SCARF* and elsewhere. He was a participant in the 2014 Caine Prize workshop in Zimbabwe,and is a founding member of the Jalada collective. 'The Lifebloom Gift' was first published in *The Gonjon Pin and Other Stories: The Caine Prize for African Writing 2014* (New Internationalist, United Kingdom, 2014).

What it Means When a Man Falls from the Sky

Lesley Nneka Arimah

It means 24-hour news coverage. It means politicians doing damage control; activists egging on protests. It means Francisco Furcal's granddaughter at a press conference defending her family legacy.

'My grandfather's formula is sound. Math is constant and absolute. Any problems that arise are the fault of those who miscalculate it.'

Bad move, lady. This could only put everyone on the defensive, trotting out their transcripts and test results and every other thing that proved their genius. Nneoma tried to think of where she'd put her own documents after the move, but that led to thinking of where she'd moved from, which led to thinking of whom she'd left behind.

Best not to venture there. Best instead to concentrate on the shaky footage captured by a security camera. The motion-activated device had caught the last 50 feet of the man's fall, the windmill panic of flailing arms, the spread of his body on the ground. The newscast then jumped to the Mathematicians who had discovered the equation for flight. They were being ambushed at parties, while picking up their children in their sleek black cars, on their vacations, giving a glimpse of luxury that was foreign to the majority of the viewing public, who must have enjoyed the embarrassed faces and defensive outbursts from well-fed mouths that knew nothing of rations.

By blaming the Mathematicians instead of the Formula, Martina Furcal and the Center created a maelstrom around these supposedly infallible scientists and protected her family's legacy. And their money. Maybe not such a bad move after all.

Nneoma flipped through the channels, listening closely. If the rumor that Furcal's Formula was beginning to unravel around the edges gained any traction, it would eventually trickle down to the 2,400 Mathematicians like her who worked the globe and made their living calculating and subtracting emotions, drawing them from living bodies like poison from a wound.

She was one of the 57 registered Mathematicians who specialized in calculating grief, down from the 59 of last year. Alvin Claspell, the Australian, had committed suicide after, if the stories were to be believed, going mad and trying to eat himself. This work wasn't for everyone. And of course Kioni Mutahi had simply disappeared, leaving New Kenya with only one grief worker.

There were six grief workers in the Biafra-Britannia Alliance, where Nneoma now lived – the largest concentration of grief workers in any province to serve the largest concentration of the grieving. Well, the largest concentration that could pay.

It was the same footage over and over. Nneoma offed the unit. The brouhaha would last only as long as the flight guys took to wise up and blame the fallen man for miscalculating. 'Cover your ass,' as the North American saying went, though there wasn't much of that continent left to speak it.

A message dinged on the phone console and Nneoma hurried to press it, eager, then embarrassed at her eagerness, then further embarrassed when it wasn't even Kioni, just her assistant reminding her of the lecture she was to give at the school. She deleted it – of course she remembered – and became annoyed. She thought, again, of getting rid of the young woman. But sometimes you needed an assistant, such as when your girlfriend ends your relationship with the same polite coolness that she initiated it, leaving you to pack and relocate three years' worth of shit in one week. Assistants came in handy then. But that was eight weeks ago and Nneoma was over it. Really, she was.

She gathered her papers and rang the car, which pulled up to the glass doors almost immediately. Amadi was timely like that, always had been, even when she was a child. Her mother used to say that she could call Amadi on her way down the stairs and open the door to find him waiting. Mama was gone now and her father, who'd become undone, never left the house. Amadi had run Father's errands until Nneoma moved back from New Kenya, when her father had gifted him to her, like a basket of fine cheese. She'd accepted the driver as what she knew he was, a peace offering. And though it would never be the same between them, she called her father every other Sunday.

She directed Amadi to go to the store first. They drove through the wide streets of Enugu and passed a playground full of sweaty egg-white children. It wasn't that Nneoma had a problem with the Britons per se, but some of her father had rubbed off on her. At his harshest, Father would call them refugees rather than allies and he'd long been unwelcome in polite company.

'They come here with no country of their own and try to take over everything and don't contribute anything,' he'd often said.

That wasn't entirely true.

When the floods started swallowing the British Isles, they'd reached out to Biafra, a plea for help that was answered. Terms were drawn, equitable exchanges of services contracted. But while one hand reached out for help, the other wielded a knife. Once here, the Britons had insisted on their own lands and their own separate government. A compromise, aided by the British threat to deploy biological weapons, resulted in the Biafra-Britannia Alliance. Shared lands, shared governments, shared grievances. Her father had only been a boy when it happened, but held bitterly to the idea of Biafran independence, an independence his parents had died for in the late 2030s. He wasn't alone, but most people knew to keep their disagreements to themselves, especially if their daughter was a Mathematician, a profession that came with its own set of troubles. And better a mutually beneficial, if unwanted, alliance than what the French had done in Senegal, the Americans in Mexico.

As Amadi drove, he kept the rearview mirror partially trained on her, looking for an opening to start a chat that would no doubt lead to him saying that maybe they could swing by her father's place later, just for a moment, just to say hello. Nneoma avoided eye contact. She couldn't see her father, not for a quick hello, not today, not ever.

They pulled up to Shoprite and Nneoma hopped out. Her stomach grumbled and she loaded more fruit in her basket than she could eat in a week and cut the bread queue to the chagrin of the waiting customers. The man at the counter recognized her and handed over the usual selection of rolls and the crusty baguette she would eat with a twinge of guilt. The French didn't get money directly, but she still couldn't stop feeling as if she funded the idea of them. Ignoring the people staring at her, wondering who she might be (a diplomat? a Minister's girlfriend?), she walked the edges of the store, looping towards the checkout lane.

Then she felt him.

Nneoma slowed and picked up a small box of detergent, feigning interest in the instructions to track him from the corner of her eye. He was well dressed, but not overly so. He looked at her confused, not sure why he was so drawn to her. Nneoma could feel the sadness rolling off him and she knew if she focused she'd be able to see his grief, clear as a splinter. She would see the source of it, its architecture, and the way it anchored to him. And she would be able to remove it.

It started when she was 14, in math class. She'd always

been good at it, but had no designs on being a Mathematician. No one did. It wasn't a profession you chose or aspired to; you could either do it or you couldn't. That day, the teacher had showed them a long string of Furcal's Formula, purchased from the Center like a strain of a virus. To most of the other students, it was an impenetrable series of numbers and symbols, but to Nneoma it was as simple as the alphabet. Seeing the Formula unlocked something in her and from then on she could see a person's sadness as plainly as the clothes he wore.

The Center paid for the rest of her schooling, paid off the little debt her family had and bought them a new house. They trained her to hone her talents and go beyond merely seeing a person's grief till she knew how to remove it as well. She'd been doing it for so long she could exorcise the deepest of traumas for even the most resistant of patients. Then her mother died.

The man in the store stood there looking at her and Nneoma used his confusion to walk away. The grieving were often drawn to her, an inadvertent magnetic thing. It made her sheltered life blessed and necessary. The Center was very understanding and helped contracted Mathematicians screen their clients. No one was ever forced to do anything they didn't want to. Nneoma worked almost exclusively with parents who'd lost a child, wealthy couples who'd thought death couldn't touch them, till it did. When the Center partnered with governments to work with their distressed populations, the job was voluntary and most Mathematicians donated a few hours a week. Unlike Kioni, who worked with those people full time, and unlike Nneoma, who didn't work with them at all. *Mother Kioni*, Nneoma had called her, first with affection, then with increasing malice when it all turned ugly. The man in the tidy suit and good shoes was along the lines of her preferred clientele and he could very well become a client of hers in the future, but not today, not like this.

At checkout, the boy who scanned and bagged her

groceries had a name tag that read 'Martin,' which may or may not have been his name. The Britons preferred their service workers with names they could pronounce, and most companies obliged them. The tattoo on his wrist indicated his citizenship – an original Biafran – and his class, third. No doubt he lived outside of the city and was tracked the minute he crossed the electronic threshold till he finished his shift and left. He was luckier than most.

At the car, she checked her personal phone, the number only her father, her assistant and Kioni knew. Still no message. They hadn't spoken since she'd moved out. She had to know Nneoma worried, in spite of how they'd left things. None of their mutual New Kenyan contacts knew where to find her and Kioni's phone went unanswered. Maybe this was what it took for Kioni to exorcise her.

On the way to the school, Nneoma finished off two apples and a roll and flipped through her notes. She had done many such presentations, which were less about presenting and more about identifying potential Mathematicians, who had a way of feeling each other out. She ran a finger along the Formula, still mesmerized by it after all this time. She'd brought 57 lines of it, though she would only need a few to test the students.

When things began to fall apart, the world cracked open by earthquakes and long dormant volcanoes stretched, yawned and bellowed, the churches (mosques, temples) fell, not just the physical buildings shaken to dust by tremors, but the institutions as well. Into the vacuum stepped Francisco Furcal, a Chilean Mathematician who discovered a formula that explained the universe. It, like the universe, was infinite and the idea that the Formula had no end and, perhaps, by extension, humanity had no end, was exactly what the world had needed.

Over decades, people began to experiment with this infinite formula, and in the process discovered equations that coincided with the anatomy of the human body, making work like hers possible. A computer at the Center ran the Formula 24/7, testing its infiniteness. There were thousands and thousands of lines. People used to be able to tour the South African branch and watch the endless symbols race across a screen ticker-style. Then the Center closed to the public, and the rumors started that Furcal's Formula was wrong, not infinite, that the logic of it faltered millions and millions of permutations down the line, past anything a human could calculate in her lifetime.

They were just that, rumors, but then a man fell from the sky.

As they neared the school, they could see a few protesters with gleaming electronic placards. The angry red of angry men. Amadi slowed.

'Madam?'

'Keep going, there are only ten.'

But the number could triple by the time she was ready to leave. How did they always know where she'd be?

The car was waved through the school's outer gate, then the inner gate where Amadi's ID was checked, then double checked. When the guard decided that Amadi wasn't credentialled enough to wait within the inner gate, Nneoma stepped in. Her driver, her rules. The guard conceded as she'd known he would and Amadi parked the car under a covered spot out of the sun. Nneoma was greeted by Nkem Ozechi, the headmaster, a small, neat woman whose hands reminded her of Kioni's. She had a smug air about her and walked with a gait that was entirely too pleased with itself. She spoke to Nneoma as though they'd known each other for years. On a different day, Nneoma might have been charmed, interested, but she just wanted the session to be over with so she could go home.

The class was filled with bored faces, most around 13 or 14 (had she ever looked so young?) with few caring or understanding what she did, too untouched by tragedy to understand her necessity. But schools like these, which gathered the best and brightest several nations had to offer (according to Nkem Ozechi), paid the Center handsomely to have people like her speak and it was the easiest money she earned.

'How many of you can look at someone and know that they are sad?'

The whole class raised their hands.

'How many of you can tell someone is sad even if they are not crying?'

Most hands stayed up.

'How many of you can look at a person who is sad, know why they are sad and fix it?'

All hands lowered. She had their attention now as she explained what she did.

The talk lasted 15 minutes before she brought it to a close.

'Some Mathematicians remove pain, some of us deal in negative emotions, but we all fix the equation of a person. The bravest' – she winked – 'have tried their head at using the Formula to make the human body defy gravity, for physical endeavours, like flight.'

The class giggled, the fallen man fresh in their minds.

'Furcal's Formula means that one day the smartest people can access the very fabric of the universe.'

They applauded politely.

The headmaster stepped from the corner to moderate questions. The first were predictable and stupid. 'Can you make people fall in love?' No. 'Can you make someone become invisible?' No. Nkem Ozechi might have been embarrassed to know that their questions were no different from the children in the lower schools. Then (again predictably) someone posed a non-question.

'What you are doing is wrong.' From a reed-thin boy with large teeth. Despite his thinness there was a softness to him, a pampered look.

Nneoma put her hand up to stop Nkem Ozechi from interrupting. She could handle this. 'Explain.'

'Well, my dad says what you people do is wrong, that you shouldn't be stopping a person from feeling natural hardships. That's what it means to be human.'

Someone in the back started to clap until Nneoma again raised her hand for silence. She studied the boy and noted on his wrist his father's occupation (lawyer), his class (first). She'd argued down many a person like his father, people who'd lived easy lives, who'd had moderate but manageable difficulties then dared to compare their meagre hardship with unfathomable woes.

'Your father and those people protesting outside have no concept of what real pain is. As far as I'm concerned their feelings on this matter are invalid. I would never ask a person who hasn't tasted a dish whether it needs more salt.'

The boy sat with his arms crossed, pouting. She hadn't changed his mind, you never could with people like that, but she'd shut him up.

In the quiet that followed another hand was raised. *Not her*, Nneoma thought, *not her*. She'd been trying to ignore the girl since she walked into the classroom. She didn't need to look at her wrist to know that the girl was Senegalese, and had been affected by the Elimination. It was etched all over her, this sorrow.

'So you can make it go away?' They could have been the only two people in the room.

'Yes, I can.' And, to kill the dawning hope, 'But it is a highly regulated and very expensive process. Most of my clients are heavily subsidized by their governments, but even then...' And in case any hope remained, 'You have to be a citizen.'

The girl lowered her eyes to her lap, fighting tears. As though to mock her, she was flanked by a map on the wall, the entire globe splayed out as it had been 70 years ago and as it was now. Most of what had been North America was covered in water and a sea had replaced Europe. Russia was a soaked grave. The only continents unclaimed in whole or in part by the sea were Australia and what was now the

United Countries but had once been Africa. The Elimination began after a moment of relative peace, after the French had won the trust of their hosts. The Senegalese newspapers that issued warnings were dismissed as conspiracy rags, rabble-rousers inventing trouble. But then the camps, the raids, and the mysterious illness that wiped out millions. Then the cabinet members murdered in their beds. And the girl had survived it. To be here, at a school like this on one of the rare scholarships they offered to displaced children, the girl must have lived through the unthinkable. The weight of her mourning was too much and Nneoma left the room, followed by Nkem Ozechi who clicked hurriedly behind her.

'Maybe some of them will be Mathematicians, like you.'

Nneoma needed to gather herself. She saw the sign for the ladies' room and stepped inside, swinging the door in Nkem Ozechi's face. None of those children would ever be Mathematicians; the room was as bare of genius as a pool of fish.

She checked the stalls to make sure she was alone and bent forward to take deep breaths. She rarely worked with refugees, *true* refugees, for this reason. The complexity of their suffering always took something from her. The only time she'd felt anything as strongly was after her mother had passed and her father was in full lament, listing to the side of ruin. How could Nneoma tell him that she couldn't even look at him without being broken by it? He would never understand. The day she'd tried to work on him, to eat her father's grief, she finally understood why it was forbidden to work on close family members. Their grief was your own and you could never get out of your head long enough to calculate it. The attempt had ended with them both sobbing, holding each other in comfort and worry, till her father had gotten so angry at the futility of it, the uselessness of her talents this one particular moment and had said words he could not take back.

The bathroom door creaked open. Nneoma knew who it

was. The girl couldn't help but to seek her out. They stared at each other a while, the girl uncertain, till Nneoma held out her arms and the girl walked into them. Nneoma saw the sadness in her eyes and began to plot the results of it on an axis. At one point the girl's mother shredded by gunfire. Her brother taken in the night by a gang of thugs. Her father falling to the synthesized virus that attacked all the melanin in his skin till his body was an open sore. And other smaller hurts, hunger so deep she'd swallowed fistfuls of mud. Hiding from the men who'd turned on her after her father died. Sneaking into her old neighborhood to see the crisp new houses filled with the more fortunate of the French evacuees, those who hadn't been left behind to drown, and their children chased her away with rocks like she was a dog. Nneoma looked at every last suffering, traced the edges, weighed the mass. And then she took it.

No one had really been able to explain what happened then, why one person could take another person's grief. Mathematical theories abounded based on how humans were, in the plainest sense, a bulk of atoms held together by positives and negatives, an equation all their own, a type of cellular math. A theologian might call it a miracle, a kiss of grace from God's own mouth. Philosophers opined that it was actually the patient who gave up their sadness. But in that room it simply meant that a girl had an unbearable burden and then she did not.

***

The ride back home was silent, Amadi sensing her disquiet and resisting the casual detour he'd make past the junction that led to her father's house whenever they ventured to this side of town. At home, Nneoma went straight to bed, taking two of the pills that would let her sleep for 12 hours. After that she would be as close to normal as she could be. The girl's memories would lessen in rawness, becoming like a story she'd read in a book once. The girl would feel the same way. When Nneoma fell asleep, it was a deep, black, dreamless thing with no light.

The next morning, she turned on the unit to see much of the same coverage as the day before except now the fallen man's widow had jumped into the fray, calling for a full audit of the Center's records and of Furcal's Formula. Nneoma snorted. It was the sort of thing that sounded right enough to win public support, but the truth was that the only experts who knew enough to audit anything all worked for the Center and it would take them decades to pore over it. More likely this was a ploy for a payoff, which the woman would get. The Furcals could afford it.

Nneoma told herself she wouldn't check her messages again for at least another hour and prepared for her daily run. A quick peek revealed that there wasn't anything waiting anyway. She keyed the code into the gate to lock it behind her, stretched, and launched.

The run cleared the last vestiges of yesterday's ghosts. She would call Claudine today to see how serious this whole falling thing was. There'd only be so much the PR rep could legally say, but dinner and a few drinks might loosen her tongue. Nneoma lengthened her stride the last mile home, taking care to ease into it. The last time she'd burst into a sprint, she pulled a muscle and the pain eater assigned to her was a grim man with a non-existent bedside manner. She'd felt his disapproval as he worked on her. No doubt he thought his talents wasted in her cosy sector and tolerated this rotation till he could get back to the camps. Nneoma disliked Mathematicians like him and they disliked ones like her. It was a miracle she and Kioni had lasted as long as they did.

As she cleared the corner around her compound, she saw a small crowd gathered at her gate. *Protesters?* she wondered in shock before she registered the familiar faces of her neighbors. When she neared, a man she recognized but could not name caught her by the shoulders.

'We called medical right away. She was banging on your gate and screaming. She is your friend, no? I've seen her with you before.' He looked very sorry and suddenly Nneoma didn't want to know who was there to see her and why.

It was just a beggar. The woman wore no shoes and her toes were wounds. How on earth had she been able to bypass city security? Nneoma scrambled back when the woman reached out for her but was arrested by her fingers, delicate and spindly, like insect legs.

Those hands had once stroked her body. She had once kissed those palms and drawn those fingers into her mouth. She would recognize them anywhere.

'Kioni?'

'Nneoma we have to go, we have to go now.' She was frantic and kept looking behind her.

Every bare inch of her skin was scratched or bitten or cut in some way. Her dreadlocks, usually in a neat coif, were half missing, her scalp raw and puckered like someone had yanked them out. The smell that rolled from her was all sewage.

'Oh my god, Kioni, oh my god.'

Kioni grabbed her wrists and wouldn't surrender them. 'We have to go!'

Nneoma tried to talk around the horrified pit in her stomach. 'Who did this to you? Where do we have to go?'

Kioni shook her head and sank to her knees. Nneoma tried to free one of her hands and, when she couldn't, pressed and held the metal insert under her palm that would alert security at the Center. They would know what to do.

From her current angle, Nneoma could see more of the damage on the other woman, more scratches, more bites on her arms concentrated below the elbow. And then something nagged and nagged at her till she remembered the Australian and the stories of him trying to eat himself.

'Kioni, who did this?' Nneoma repeated, though her

suspicion was beginning to clot into certainty and she feared the answer.

Kioni continued shaking her head and pressed her lips together like a child refusing to confess a lie.

Their fight had started when Nneoma had done the unthinkable, violating every boundary of their relationship (and a handful of Center rules) and asked Kioni to work on her father. Kioni, who volunteered herself to the displaced Senegalese and Algerians and Burkinabes and even the evacuees, anyone in dire need of a grief worker, was the last person she should have asked for such a thing. Nneoma had called her sanctimonious and Kioni had called her a spoiled rich girl who thought her pain was more important than it actually was. And then Kioni had asked her to leave.

Now she needed to get Kioni to the Center and get her help. Whatever was happening had to be fixed. She remembered again the Australian who had killed himself.

'They just come and they come and they come.'

Nneoma crouched down to hear Kioni better. Most of her neighbors had moved beyond hearing distance, chased away by the smell. 'Who comes?' she asked, trying to keep Kioni with her. Aid must be on its way.

'All of them, can't you see?'

She began to see what was happening to her former girlfriend.

How many people had Kioni worked with over the last decade, five thousand? Ten? Ten thousand traumas in her psyche, squeezing past each other, vying for the attention of their host. What would happen if you couldn't forget, if every emotion from every person whose grief you'd eaten came back up? It could happen if something went wrong with the Formula millions and millions of permutations down the line. A thousand falling men landing on you.

Nneoma tried to retreat, to close her eyes and unsee, but she couldn't. Instinct took over and she raced to calculate it all. The breadth of it was so vast, *too* vast. It was just her and

Kioni together, their burden excessive, even for two.

The last clear thought she would ever have was of her father, how crimson his burden had been when she'd tried to shoulder it, and how very pale it all seemed now.

Lesley Nneka Arimah is a Nigerian writer living in Minneapolis. Her work has appeared in *The New Yorker, Harper's* and other publications. When she isn't spreading peace and joy on Twitter, Arimah is at work on a collection of short stories (*What it Means When a Man Falls from the Sky*) forthcoming in 2017 from Riverhead Books. There are rumors about a novel. 'What it Means When a Man Falls from the Sky' was first published in *Catapult* (Catapult, USA, 2015).

Genesis

Tope Folarin

She told me I could serve her in heaven.

She accompanied me to school each day. School was about a mile away, and a few hundred feet into my trek, just as my family's apartment building drifted out of view behind me, she would appear at my side.

I don't remember how she looked. Memory often summons a generic figure in her place: an elderly white woman with frizzled grey hair, slightly bent over, a smile featuring an assortment of gaps and silver linings. I do remember her touch however – it felt cool and papery, disarmingly comfortable on the hottest days of fall. She would often pat my head as we walked together, and a penetrating silence would cancel the morning sounds around us. I felt comfortable, protected somehow, in her presence. She never walked all the way to school with me, but her parting words were always the same:

'Remember, if you are a good boy here on earth, you can serve me in heaven.'

I was five years old. Her words sounded magical to me. Vast and alluring. I didn't know her, I barely knew her name, but the offer she held out to me each morning seemed far too generous to dismiss lightly. In class I would think about what servitude in heaven would be like. I imagined myself carrying buckets of water for her on streets of gold, rubbing her feet as angels sang praises in the background. I imagined that I'd have my own heavenly shack. I'd have time to do my own personal heavenly things as well.

How else would I get to heaven?

One day I told my father about her offer. We were talking about heaven, a favorite subject of his, and I mentioned that I already had a place there. 'I've already found someone to serve,' I said.

'What do you mean?'

Dad smiled warmly at me. I felt his love. I repeated myself: 'Daddy, I'm going to heaven.'

'And how are you going to get there?'

I told him about the old lady, my heavenly shack, the streets of gold. My father stared at me a moment, grief and sadness surging briefly to the surface of his face. And then anger. He leaned forward, stared into my eyes.

'Listen to me now. The only person you will serve in heaven is God. You will serve no one else.'

2

My father has told me many times that he settled in Utah because he didn't want to be where anyone else was. His cousins and siblings had left Nigeria for Athens, London, Rome, New York City and Houston. My father wanted to be an American, but he also craved isolation, so he decided he would travel to the one place in America that he knew nothing about.

He left Nigeria in 1979, after a school in Utah, Davis State University, offered him a place in its mechanical engineering program. His bride, my mother, accompanied him. They arrived in a country that bore little resemblance to the country they expected. Dad, a devout fan of television shows like *Gunsmoke* and *Bonanza*, was disappointed when he discovered that cowboy hats were no longer in style, and he sadly stowed his first American purchase – a brown ten-gallon hat – in his suitcase, and under his bed. Mom arrived in America expecting peace and love – she had fallen for the music of The Beatles and Bob Dylan as a high-school student in Lagos while listening to the records that her businessman father brought back from his trips abroad. Though she had imagined a country where love conquered all, where black people and white people had finally managed to surmount their differences, Mom and Dad arrived, instead, in a place where there were no other black people for miles around, a place dominated by a religion they'd never heard of before.

But this was America. And they were in love. They moved into a small apartment in Ogden, Utah, and began a family. I came first, in 1981, and my brother followed in 1983. Dad attended his classes during the day while Mom took care of us at home. Occasionally she explored the city while pushing my brother and me along in a double stroller. Soon enough we were all walking hand in hand.

At night my parents held each other close and spoke their dreams into existence. They would have more children. My father would start a business. They would become wealthy. They would send their children to the best schools. They would have many grandchildren. They would build their own version of paradise on a little slip of desert in a country that itself was a dream, a place that seemed impossible until they stepped off the plane, shielding the sun from their eyes, and saw for themselves the expanse of land that my father had idly pointed to on a fading map many years before.

3

As I look back now, especially with the knowledge of what will come after, the rest of my life set in unflattering relief, I realize that my first five years were the most ordinary of my childhood. We moved around frequently, but I can only remember joy.

One of my favorite memories from this era: for some reason I'm chasing my brother around our tiny apartment with a red crayon. When I catch him I pin him against the wall and color each of his teeth red as he screams. My mother shrieks when she sees him; she thinks he's bleeding because of the red wax that's shining from his teeth. She laughs when

I tell her that the blood isn't real, and then we all laugh and I allow my brother to color my teeth as well. Then we color Mom's teeth – she prefers lime green.

Life flowed easily until we moved to Bountiful. We settled there because my father had found a job at an auto repair shop in neighboring Layton, and Bountiful was one of the few places close by with any affordable housing. My father couldn't find a job as a mechanical engineer anywhere in northern Utah, but he knew a bit about cars, and he figured he would work as a mechanic until something better came along.

My mother's illness began to reveal itself to us shortly after we moved into our two-bedroom apartment, a tiny place near the centre of town with pale yellow walls and bristly carpet. Mom's voice, once quiet and reassuring, grew loud and fearsome. Her hugs, once warm and comforting, became cold and rigid. She stopped cooking for us – sometimes my brother and I didn't eat until my father returned from work in the evening. She began to spend more time in her room, away from us.

One morning my brother and I scrambled to our parents' room because we heard Dad crying. I didn't think such a thing was possible. We saw Mom standing over Dad, her eyes boiling with rage. My father was naked. His clothes, now nothing more than torn rags, were arrayed haphazardly around the room. He was bleeding from a wound on his thigh, and his face was wreathed in a constellation of sweat and tears. My brother and I reached over to him but Mom cursed at us:

GET THE FUCK OUT OF HERE!

I was terrified. I looked at Dad. His bottom lip was shaking. His teeth were red. 'Yes, go!' he said. 'What are you waiting for? Go now!'

We obliged. We hugged each other in the corner of our room. Moments later, Dad began to scream.

Over the course of the next few days my brother and I

witnessed this scene many times, my father cowering on the floor, my mother standing imperiously over him. He took her punishment whenever she descended into one of her moods, and afterwards he would tell us that Mom wasn't feeling like herself, but that everything would soon be OK. We tried our best to believe him.

Before long we realized the truth. After Dad left for work each morning my mother would lock herself in their room. She rarely interacted with us, but occasionally she would open the door and ask us to come inside. She would ask us to stand in the corner of the room, near the dresser. She would point to various places in the room: her closet, Dad's desk, the empty space near her full-length mirror. She would ask us if we saw it.

'See what, Mommy?'

'Don't you see that? What is wrong with you?'

My brother and I would look at each other. Was this a game?

'Mommy, I don't see anything. Can we go now?'

'No! Not until you tell me what it is doing there. Tell me why it won't leave!'

Sometimes my brother and I lied. We made up stories about what we saw and my mother would nod sagely. Sometimes she disagreed with us and told us to look again. We were always confused. We felt anxious. This could have been fun, but the wild look in my mother's eyes was unnerving.

She was seeing something we would never see, some figment of her afflicted mind had gained substance, was haunting her.

Sometimes she told us that we had to leave before they came to get us. 'Something about this place isn't right,' she'd say. 'Not right at all.'

Then she'd pull up her covers, switch on the radio, and mutter herself to sleep.

4

I started school on September 7, 1987, a few weeks before I

turned six. I was excited because I'd spent many mornings watching the kids of my neighborhood trip past my bedroom window with books under their arms and bags on their backs, like they were departing for another world. I dimly sensed that at school I could become something more than a brother or son, that each day I went I would come back carrying knowledge that was mine alone.

My family walked with me to school that first day, and I remember the principal extending her hand when I met her. I shyly extended mine as well, and as we shook hands she said, 'We are very happy you're here!'

It was in her eyes. The way she looked at me. Like I was something scary and unknown. That's how I knew I was different. On the playground all my classmates asked if they could touch my hair. I said OK. Then Simon rubbed my skin and ran away crying to the playground attendant.

'It won't come off!' he wailed. 'Why won't it come off?'

I was too tired after school to ask my father any questions, too excited about everything I had just experienced, but the next day, after another kid rubbed my arm until it was raw and bruised, I asked my father why my hair was so kinky, and why I couldn't wash the brown off my skin. He shook his head and frowned. He began talking about the importance of pride, the meaning of self-respect, but I didn't fully understand what he was saying.

As he spoke, I thought about the old lady I'd met on my way to school.

That morning, Dad had hugged me at the door of our apartment and told me that I'd have to walk to school by myself because he had to work and Mom wasn't feeling well. I said OK, but I was afraid because school seemed so far away.

As I walked to school, tentatively, nervously, she suddenly appeared, like I'd dreamed her into existence.

She told me her name was Mrs Hansen, and she asked me what I was doing. I told her I was walking to school. She smiled.

'I've never seen a little black boy around here before,' she said 'Where are you from?'

'I'm from here,' I said. She laughed and placed a hand on my shoulder.

She spoke as we walked, and I enjoyed hearing her voice, the gentle rise and fall of it, because it somehow seemed familiar to me. She asked me questions about Dad and Mom and my brother. She said that she'd always wanted to go to Africa, but she'd never had the chance.

When we were about a block from school she looked into my eyes and patted my head.

'I enjoyed speaking with you. You're a wonderful little boy.' She blinked slowly and nodded. 'Keep it up. Maybe one day you'll get to serve me in heaven. If you do, I promise you'll get everything you've ever wanted.'

The happiness I felt as I turned and ran to school, the sheer joy, is something I've been searching for ever since.

5

I woke up that morning to my mother rubbing my hair. Mom was smiling down at me when I opened my eyes. She looked beautiful. She was dressed in her favorite outfit: a finely embroidered purple blouse covered by a flowing wrapper, a matching headdress hovering atop her cascading braids. She asked me to wake up my brother and after hugging us she asked us to get dressed.

'Where are we going, Mommy?' I asked as I pulled on my pants.

'On an adventure!' she said, smiling widely. 'Now hurry so we won't be late.'

My brother and I moved quickly in the crisp darkness. We rushed into the living room when we were done, and Mom evaluated us in a single glance.

'Go get your backpacks and pack some clothes as well.'

'Where are we going?'

'I told you, on an adventure!'

'What about Daddy?'

Mom turned and glanced at the wall.

'He's coming later, after work.'

'How about school?' I asked. I'd only been in kindergarten for a month.

Mom gave me a half smile. 'Don't worry! Just get ready.'

We ran back to our bedroom and packed our bags with assorted socks, underwear, shirts, and pants. After a few minutes we returned to the living room.

'All done!' we yelled in unison.

She laughed.

'You guys were quick! OK, now wait, someone is coming to pick us up.'

We sat. My brother and I tried to blow smoke rings with the frosty air. Mom disappeared into her bedroom and when she returned she was dragging a rolling suitcase behind her. In her right hand she was clutching a few records. She had replaced her headdress with a large, brown cowboy hat. I'd never seen her so happy in my life.

Someone rapped on the door a few minutes later, and Mom nodded at us.

'Go ahead!' she exclaimed. 'This is part of the adventure!'

My brother and I raced to the door, but I got there first. There was a woman standing there. She had short red hair, and her freckles were so densely packed that I wondered how each one survived without space, without room to grow.

'How are you?' she asked. 'You are so cute! Are you ready to go?'

Mom joined us at the door.

'Yes, we are ready. Let us go before it is too late. We have so much to do today.'

We piled into the lady's car. I can't remember what kind of car it was, just that it was small and that my mother insisted that I sit in the front. The freckled lady turned the ignition and revved the engine while my mother held my brother close. The lady turned to me and asked if I was cold. I shook my head, but we sat in the dark until I felt the heat on my shoes and face. Then she put the car into gear and we drove off.

We passed the local grocery store, Smith's, and I suddenly realized that we weren't going on an adventure.

'Mommy, where is this woman taking us?'

'I already told you! Now be quiet and enjoy the ride.'

'Mommy, I don't believe you. Where are we going? Where's Daddy?'

Mom ignored me. The lady patted me on the head and turned on the radio. Stevie Wonder was singing something but I don't know what it was.

6

I don't remember what happened after I realized that we weren't actually going on an adventure. My mind skips, like a ruined compact disc, to a small room with bare walls at the YWCA in Salt Lake City. I start the day with a tutor who showers me with praise; she brings books for me to read every day, and she tells me I'm the smartest kid she's ever known. Most of her books are about African American leaders, but I don't know what an African American is yet. They all look black to me. We read about George Washington Carver, Booker T Washington, and WEB DuBois. She also tells me about Martin Luther King. I learn that he starts college when he's 15, that he attends a black school in Atlanta called Morehouse, and that he has a doctorate by the time he's 26. I don't hear much else because I'm still thinking about the black school in Atlanta. Where is Atlanta? And how is such a thing possible in America? Only black people, only people like me in a school? It seems an impossibility, but then I decide that the school, the city itself must be a relic of the past. My tutor smiles at me, her black hair shining. In her hands, the book looks brand new, like no one's ever opened it before. She turns the page. I don't know what's real and what's fake any more.

After my tutoring sessions I join my brother in the nursery. We play together until Joy stops by to pick us up. Joy has long blonde hair and a jagged, ruined face. She is beautiful.

She takes us to the common room and my brother sits on her lap. We spend the afternoon watching TV shows like *The People's Court* and *The Judge.* Joy rubs my head constantly, and bends down to kiss my forehead during the commercials. I think she does this because she knows how much I miss my father. I haven't seen him since Mom took us away. She must know that I feel so alone without him, that I would give anything just to hear his voice.

Sometimes her friends join us. I only remember them in caricature. One is fat and one is skinny. Like a pair of mismatched twins they bounce around the room and my memory, orbiting around our small impromptu family. By the time Joy walks us to our room my brother has fallen asleep, and I'm too tired to be scared of Mom.

The fear returns when we arrive at our door.

7

Sometimes Mom is better. I know she is taking her medicine now, and although she is never happy, she remembers herself.

This memory will never leave me. My brother and I walk into our small apartment in the shelter and look for Mom. I glance at our spotless kitchen on the left, and our spare living room on the right. A dusty table sits in the middle of the room. Mom steps out of the bedroom; she is small and thin, and has large, wide-set eyes. Her nose is as small as a button. She turns on the radio, finds an oldies station, and begins to hum. Sometimes The Mamas and the Papas come on, sometimes The Rolling Stones, sometimes The Beach Boys, sometimes Simon and Garfunkel, sometimes Dylan, but always, inevitably, The Beatles. My Mom smiles whenever she hears Paul singing. It doesn't seem odd to me then, a Nigerian woman with a Beatles obsession; the only thing I care about is that The Beatles bring her joy. I often wish the disembodied voices would skip everything else and just play The Beatles, only The Beatles, all evening, so Mom will feel better.

Mom stops cooking Nigerian food when we get to the shelter. She will only prepare frozen food, but my brother and I don't care. We're always happy when we see her busying herself in our tiny kitchen, opening the box of frozen fried chicken, the delicious rip of aluminium foil, placing the foil and chicken into the oven. Soon the savoury fumes tunnel into our nostrils. She dumps a dollop of store-bought crab salad onto our plates, sometimes some fried rice from the local Chinese restaurant if she has extra money, and the fried chicken. Before we eat, Mom switches off the radio, and if it's summer, the window is open, the breeze warming our backs.

To my mother, silence is love.

So we, in turn, learn to love silence. If our mother looks away as we walk in the door she is signalling her unending devotion to us. If she ignores us when we ask her a question she's actually telling us that we're smart enough to figure things out ourselves. If we call for her and she refuses to respond, we know she is hugging us all the same.

To my mother, awareness is anger.

If we feel her eyes on us while we're doing something, we know to stop before she becomes angry. But sometimes we're too late. Her voice erupts in hot waves from her throat, foaming in spittle at the edges of her lips. Her voice rises to the ceiling and hangs there, hovering above everything, and her sweat drips from her forehead and we stare ahead, trying to show her our love with our silence. Sometimes she gets it, she receives it, and her anger dissipates above us and her sweat cools and sinks into her face, and then she smiles and everything becomes still.

Usually, though, she doesn't get it. She takes our silence personally, she forgets her lifelong lesson to us, and she yells until she's exhausted herself. Then she sits against the wall and cries herself to sleep. My brother and I carry blankets from our side of the room and cover her with them, and we burrow in on each side of her. This, too, is love.

8

I dreamed constantly at the shelter. Dreaming was the same to me, no matter the time of day, whether my eyes were opened or closed. I could maintain a dream through the day if I woke myself up, so I tried to rise as early as possible each morning in order to preserve my connection to the other side.

I dreamed as I rubbed my eyes and went to the bathroom. I dreamed as I brushed my teeth and took a shower. I dreamed as I woke my mother and brother, as we started our day together.

I saw my father in the mirror as I brushed my teeth. He looked just like me, with his wide nose, his proud forehead. I nodded solemnly at him, and he nodded back. Instead of sitting on the floor with our food I saw that we were actually sitting on a brand new couch, and my father's favorite Sunny Ade record was playing, and our silence was laughter. When Mom pinched me up and down my back her hands became warm and supple. She embraced me through the punishment. Her slaps were a burst of hot water on my face. My tears were the drops trailing down my face after the water had hit the floor. Each slap made me clean. Her eyes seemed angry because they were so red. I reached forward with my magic eraser and erased all the red until her eyes were white again. When I was finished her anger was finished.

I soared, and I swam, and I dunked basketballs. No one ever told me that I was supposed to differentiate what I saw during the night from what I saw during the day, that I should privilege one over the other, so everything converged. I grew to believe that pain was temporary, that I was only a few steps from learning how to fly. I knew I would grow wings. It was only a matter of time.

9

My brother and I didn't see our father for three months. After we arrived at the shelter Mom told us that our father would be coming to live with us soon. A few weeks into our stay, though, she told us that he didn't want to live with us any more, so we probably wouldn't see him ever again. We didn't believe her. We knew too much about our father's love for us to believe that he had simply abandoned us.

One day, finally, the white lady with the freckles returned and told us we would be seeing Dad soon. She told us we would only be able to see him on weekends, because that's what the judge had said. Who is the judge? we wondered. Don't worry, she replied, just know that you will be safe. We will protect you.

I had no idea what she was talking about. I had never felt unsafe with my father. I was upset that we didn't have a chance to speak with the judge. I wanted to go on TV and speak with Judge Wapner – I knew that if I had a few minutes with him I could convince him that our family needed to be together again.

We met Dad in the common area of the shelter. He was crying.

'How are you doing?' he asked us. 'How have you been? Have they been taking care of you?'

We were upset with him.

'Why didn't you come for us before? Why did you leave us here? Where were you?' we asked him.

Dad extended his hands helplessly, like he didn't know what to say.

'I don't know. I am here now.'

My brother gave him a big hug, and I couldn't resist either. Dad held both of our hands and I turned around to see Mom stewing at us from the corner of the room. Dad told her he'd have us back by Sunday. Mom turned and walked away.

Our apartment felt strange though it looked exactly the

same. Dad had even left our toys on the ground where we'd discarded them the morning we were taken to the shelter. For a moment we just stood there, looking at each other. Then Dad flipped on the TV and asked us to sit on his lap.

That Saturday Hulk Hogan looked into our living room and told us to eat our vitamins, say our prayers, and listen to our parents. He was so big. Then we saw him wrestle. He was fighting a large, fearsome opponent, and he was winning, but then another wrestler jumped into the ring and punched the referee. He punched Hulk. Hulk was down on the ground, grimacing in pain, and the mysterious wrestler disappeared. Hulk's opponent hit him repeatedly on the head, and then he pinned him. We were silent, my brother, Dad and I, as Hulk lay on the mat, bleeding, on the verge of losing the match. But then he reached his hand to the sky and began to shake it. He shook his hand until the power from the sky seemed to course through his fingers into his arms and into his body. He shook on the ground like a new force was inside him, and he rose slowly from the canvas. He kept shaking even as his opponent beat him on the face and the chest, and then he made a great fist of both of his hands and slammed it down on his opponent's back. His opponent collapsed, and a few moments later the newly revived referee raised Hulk's arm in victory. We cheered and hugged each other. After my father tucked us in that night I spent hours with my hand raised to the ceiling, waiting for the mysterious power to enter my body.

The next day we sat and talked, but in the evening Dad told us we would have to go back to the shelter. We begged him to let us stay for just a few hours more, but he said it wasn't possible. We bundled into the car and he drove us back. We saw Mom as we were walking in, and she took our hands without saying anything to Dad. We heard him talking behind us.

'Theresa, what are you doing?'
Silence.

'Why are you trying to take my kids away? Why are you breaking up our family?'

Silence.

10

I don't remember talking much with my brother during this period. I'm sure we spoke often, but the words we exchanged are forever lost to me. I spent most of my time looking out for him. I shielded him whenever Mom reached for us in anger, and I talked to him under my breath through the long silences. I was glad that my mother took her anger out on me. I actually felt like a big boy when she raised my arm and pinched me down my side and back, gathering my skin between her nails and pressing as hard as she could each time. The welts were hot and red. Sometimes I counted them and wondered how many should have been for him.

After a while, though, I noticed that my mother stopped reaching for my brother altogether. She always lunged for me, even if she was angry with him.

And then she stopped being angry with my brother.

When she beat me she would sometimes call me by my father's name. I didn't know how to respond, and when I tried to tell her that I wasn't my father she beat me harder.

'Stop denying yourself,' she would say between slaps.

'Stop trying to be something you aren't,' she would say while pinching me.

I never told anyone what my mother was doing to me. I believed that my silence was a part of my maturity. If I told anyone, I would be admitting that I wasn't an adult. I don't know if my tutors ever suspected, but they were nicer to me as time passed; I received more hugs and kisses than any other kid in the shelter.

One night, after pinching me all over my back, Mom asked me if I loved her. I gave her a big hug and told my brother to join us. We sat there on the floor hugging for a long while, and then Mom told us that it was almost time for her to leave.

'Where are you going?' we asked her.

'I am too sick for this world,' she said. 'I won't be here for much longer.'

'Will you take me with you?' my brother asked expectantly.

She shook her head slowly. 'No. I wish I could, but no.'

11

About a week before it happened, Mom came into the living room and saw me sitting on the floor. I was exhausted. It was dark outside, and the window was open. My brother was sleeping on a mat on the other side of the room. Mom smiled as she approached me. A little of the moonlight touched her face.

I began to shiver because I thought she was going to hit me again. When she sat next to me I sneezed in fear. She raised her hand and I bowed my head, waiting for the hard sting of her hand against my face. Instead she rubbed my cheek, and I began to cry. I was so relieved.

'What is wrong with you?' Mom asked. I didn't respond. She held my hand. 'I just want you to know, I don't hate you,' she whispered. 'I hate your father.'

I didn't say a word.

'I hate him for bringing me here, and I hate him for giving me hope.'

I nodded.

'But you're too much like him,' she said. 'And that is why you and I can never be friends.'

I looked up at her.

'One day you will understand,' she said. 'Everything that I have done will make sense. You will see.'

I nodded again. Mom kissed my cheek. Then she got up and left.

12

Mom began to take her pills more frequently, soon every

hour, and then every few minutes. One evening, while she was preparing our fried chicken, she dropped the package of aluminium foil on the floor, whirled around, and opened the cabinet next to the fridge. She pulled a new bottle of pills from inside, flipped the top, and shoved everything down her throat, cotton balls and all. I remember her choking on the cotton balls, and falling to her hands and knees to retrieve the pills she had spit up. She crawled on the floor, saliva dripping from her mouth, slurping the yellow and red pills from the wood floor like an anteater. My brother and I watched her until she was done. When she had slurped down the last pill she leaned her body against the wall and smiled at us.

'That was fun,' she said.

Then she started nodding off. My brother ran over to her and began tapping, then shaking her, so she would stay awake. The oven started smoking, big noxious fumes, and soon we were all coughing, except for Mom. I ran out of the room and looked for Joy.

Dad picked us up the following morning. When we arrived at our apartment he didn't ask us any questions, he just told us to change our clothes. My brother and I became scared.

'Where are we going?'

'Don't worry, just hurry up.'

I started to cry. My brother ran off to our bedroom. We were still traumatized by what we had seen the night before, the strangers bending over Mom, Joy whisking us away and telling us Mom was fine even though we had seen her lying still, cotton balls scattered around her. Dad called my brother back to the living room and smiled at us.

'Come on now! Get ready! I promise we'll have fun!'

My brother and I changed and followed Dad to the car. We drove for a few minutes and then we stopped in front of my old school, the school I had attended for just a few weeks before Mom took us away. The school I hadn't seen in almost a year.

'You will be going back there soon,' my father said, pointing. 'Prepare yourself now. I expect both of you to be the best students in the school. There will be no excuses.'

We sat staring at the brick building. I read the sign in the parking lot, next to the flagpole. It said: Happy Thanksgiving! School resumes November 28th.

Dad then drove us to the mall. He bought cinnamon rolls for us and we sat on a bench near a department store. We saw all the moms and dads bustling from store to store with massive bags beneath their arms, some carrying, others dragging their children behind them. We saw a fake star affixed to a fake tree, and fake snow that was spread all over the fake presents below. I knew better than to ask Dad about our own Christmas presents. We munched on our rolls.

Dad drove us back to the shelter the following week. Mom smiled weakly when she saw us.

'My sons. I have missed you.'

She hugged each of us, and she held me longer than usual.

'I am very sorry. I love you, my child.'

She held our hands and we walked slowly back to our room.

'I have a very special surprise for both of you. Close your eyes.'

I felt her pushing something warm into my hands. I looked down and saw a plate with two pieces of oven-ready fried chicken, some green beans, Chinese rice, and a Santa Claus cookie on the side. He had an M&M nose and a beard of frosting.

We ate in silence.

13

The courtroom was much bigger than I thought it would be. I couldn't imagine how they fit everything inside the TV. Everyone was quiet as my brother and I walked in. It was the first time I remember wearing a suit.

How did we get here? I cannot remember. There are too

many pages of memory missing.

The judge was an old white man, but he wasn't Judge Wapner, or the judge from the other show we used to watch with Joy. He smiled at my brother and me.

'Don't be scared or nervous. We are all here because we want the best for you,' he said.

Something happened after this, I'm not sure what. And then the judge slowly swings his head – a massive, bearded pendulum – back in our direction.

'This could go on forever,' he says. 'But I think you guys know who you want to be with. I can't promise that I will do as you ask me, but I will weigh your words very carefully.'

My brother looks at me and I feel my face burning.

I look down at my shoes, and then I look up at the judge, his head shifting almost imperceptibly from left to right and back again, like it's keeping time.

'I want to stay with my father.'

'Are you sure?'

'Yes, I'm sure.'

'And you?'

We both look at my brother and he nods.

14

Did we see our Mom again after the trial? I don't know. Sometimes when I close my eyes and travel back to that bewildering time I see her shaking her head at me, shooting me hateful glances as we pack our things from her room and leave the shelter for the last time. Usually, though, she isn't there. Not even her ghost greets me, not even a blast of cold air. She disappears from the narrative. She evaporates. My brother and I move back to our apartment in Bountiful and move on with our lives.

I am both ashamed and not ashamed to say that I did not miss her initially. I just wanted to fly away, to leave all my sadness behind.

15

My mother lives in Nigeria now, and I know almost nothing about her life. Who she is, what she does, what she hopes to be. I haven't seen her since she left. I don't know if I'll ever see her again.

There are so many questions I would like to ask her.

When I think of her, now, I think of the old white lady who used to accompany me to school each day. This was before my mother took my brother and me to the shelter, before she lost herself in the haze of her illness. Mrs Hansen lived in a small house down the street from our apartment, and she would appear at my side as I walked to school. She would tell me a bit about her life, her struggles, her pain, and then she would tell me about the afterlife, about all the wonderful things that would happen to her after she passed away. When I told my father that I wanted to serve her in heaven, he wrung his hands and shook his head. He told me I would serve no one but God, and then he called my mother and asked her to walk me to school the following day. 'It'll be good for you to leave the house for a bit,' he said to her.

As Mom, my brother, and I walked together Mrs Hansen materialized beside us, and she told my mother that she, too, could serve her in heaven. Years later I learned that Mrs Hansen was referencing an old notion of the Mormon church, that black people, sons and daughters of Cain, could only get to heaven as servants.

Mom stopped and touched her face. She smiled warmly and told her that we would all be together in heaven as equals, all our earthly worries behind us forever, and wasn't that such a wonderful thing? Mrs Hansen nodded, and then she smiled like something joyous and satisfying had just occurred to her. She slowly tottered away, and I never saw her again.

I remember Mom smiling triumphantly as we walked the rest of the way to school, her face lovely and calm. She seemed perfect to me then.

Tope Folarin won the Caine Prize for African Writing in 2013, and in 2014 he was named on the *Africa39* list of the most promising African writers under 39. In addition, his work has been published in various anthologies and journals. He lives in Washington DC. 'Genesis' was first published in *Callaloo* (Johns Hopkins University Press, USA, 2014).

At Your Requiem

Bongani Kona

Where does it begin, the story of how you came to lie here in your dark blue suit?

Everyone thought we were twins. Your mother dressed us in matching clothes. The only difference is mine were red and yours were blue. We had the same broad shoulders and we looked alike; down to our jaw lines and dark brown eyes. 'No, we're just cousins,' you'd have to explain. Once, you said to Miss Saunders, the Sunday school teacher at Heathfield Christian Church, 'He's not my twin. Christopher's mother is dead. Aunt Julia is *my* mother.'

I'm at your requiem, and your rebuttal – 'Aunt Julia is *my* mother' – burns through my mind. The story of what happened between us – you, Aunt Julia and me – at the house on St Patrick's Road, stuck to everything in our lives like shattered glass. Now that you're dead, I'm the only one left with all these unspeakable things. Broken bits of the past, jagged pieces biting into me.

I rewind time to conjure you back to life.

The paramedics open the doors of the ambulance and wheel you out on a stretcher, your body covered in a white sheet. They walk you back to the jacaranda tree where we found you; your feet a metre off the ground. They leave your body dangling in the restless wind and drive out of New Haven Drug & Alcohol Rehabilitation Centre. Tears dry from our eyes as we file back to our beds and our sobs and screams suck back into our bodies.

Your vertebra snaps back into position and life returns,

flooding back into your arteries. You open your eyes and reach for the knot around your neck and untie it. You climb down and make your way to the blue house. You enter through the kitchen and place the nylon rope where you found it in the first place, in the garage, next to the pile of old magazines.

The hours pass and the purple, ochre and orange hues of daybreak darken into night. I loosen the grip of my arm around your neck. And the sound of my careless words – 'You've always been a weak son-of-a-bitch, a mommy's boy, Abraham! I don't fucking care if you go and kill yourself' – fade, like a fog scorched by the heat of the sun.

And there you stand, whole, restored.

I'm sitting at the Methodist Church in Green Market Square with your sponsor, Dirk, and the rest of the folks from New Haven. You'd been clean for 13 months in the picture they have of you up there. It's the one of you standing at the pier in Kalk Bay. The sky is clear and blue and seagulls fly overhead. That was four years ago.

Our faces still looked similar except for the scar above my left eye. Do you remember how that happened? We were seven that year and Miss Saunders had given me a prize, a set of watercolours and crayons, for reciting the beatitudes correctly. I still remember saying the words. 'Blessed are the pure of heart for they shall see God.'

At the end of the service Aunt Julia walked around with me, my hand nestled in hers, like a small bird. 'Look at what this clever son of mine did! Show them your prize, Christopher,' she said as we threaded through the congregation. You followed behind us, silent, a mistreated dog being yanked on a leash.

We drove back to the house on St Patrick's with me riding shotgun in the front of Aunt Julia's Mercedes. 'Abraham,' she said looking back, 'you should be more like Christopher instead of watching those silly cartoons the whole day.' You said nothing. Aunt Julia rubbed her hand on my thigh and let it linger, until its warmth started to burn. When we got home she kissed me on the lips before we went out back to play.

You picked up a sharp jagged stone from the ground and turned to me and said, 'I have an idea. Let's play a game we've never played before.'

'What kind of game?' I asked.

'You go stand over there.' You pointed to the mango tree overlooking the vegetable garden. It was early summer and the garden shone a bright green. 'I'll throw the stone like they do in American football. You catch it and then throw it back?'

There was something in the tone of your voice that I couldn't quite register.

'Stupid game,' I said, but you threw the stone anyway.

I remember vignettes of what happened after you give me the instructions. The jagged stone zigzagging towards me at a terrifying speed. Blood everywhere: on my face, on my hands, on my clothes. I let out a scream and Aunt Julia comes running like a rhinoceros, her heavy feet pounding the dry grass. I hear shouting, sobs, before everything goes blank.

I came back from Vincent Pallotti hospital a day or two later, with nine stitches and a bandage strapped over my head. We slept in the same room then, our beds almost nudging, because you were scared of the dark. Sometimes I think that's all you ever wanted – someone to watch over you.

That evening, at around midnight, Aunt Julia came into our room.

'Christopher,' she said, 'come and sleep in mommy's bed.' The glare of the bulb stung my eyes but I could still make out Aunt Julia. The braided hair which ran down the length of her shoulders; her almond brown skin and her thin face, features sharply defined like those of a wooden chess queen.

'But ma –'

'Quiet, Abraham!' she said.

'– I want to come too.'

'I don't want to hear a sound from you.'

I suppose that's when it all began. Something inside you broke that night. And maybe I lost something too.

***

'Days like this remind me of what a terrible thing addiction is,' Dirk says in his sing-song preacher's voice. The church is half empty and none of our family is here.

When Aunt Julia passed we sold the house on St Patrick's and split the money. Nobody would have anything to do with us after that. Uncles we hadn't seen in years called to tell us we were selfish bastards; a pair of rich kids who looked down on everyone in the family just because we'd gone to white schools. 'You caused her heart attack!' 'If it wasn't for you…' We didn't listen to a word they said. We wanted to bury the past and everything that came with it.

One night Aunt Julia was naked when I got under the duvet. It was winter. I remember the percussion of raindrops splashing against the tiled roof. She held me close, tight, my head pinned against her breasts. I pushed her away, or tried to, but she held firm. She unbuttoned my pyjamas. I lay in there, limp, my eyes wide open. I felt her bony fingers, cold against my chest, circling lines around my ribcage. 'My beautiful boy,' she whispered, as she kissed my belly button. 'You're my little husband. Who's my little husband? You're my little husband.'

I think I cried, but I'm not sure.

'Don't you love me, Christopher?' she said. A hot steady stream of tears started from my eyes. 'Oh, I'm not good enough for you. Is that it, you don't think I'm pretty?'

Years later, another winter, when you and I were having one of those spiteful fights of ours, you asked me, 'How do you think I feel knowing that my mother loved you more than me?'

'I got by on the programme by repeating the serenity prayer,' Dirk says, his eyes panning across the room. 'God grant me the serenity to accept the things I can't change and the courage to change the things I can and the wisdom to know the difference. I've been clean nine years and I can't tell you how many times I've said that prayer. Most of the time it works but there are days like this when it has no meaning.'

* * *

That summer, Aunt Julia kept summoning me to her room even after the scar above my eye had healed. Even now I can't find the words to truly speak of what happened and my memories are corroded with shame. But I recall how you retreated into yourself. You became quiet and sullen.

Do you remember when we were at St George's Grammar and you started crying in class? Ms Davies had to sit with you in the staff room until you dried your eyes and calmed down. She'd asked you to read your composition in front of the whole class because she liked it. She was fond of you too, I guess, but not the way Aunt Julia liked me.

'Class, shh, shh, quiet please,' Ms Davies said. She was heavyset, bespectacled, with short ash-blonde curls. 'For your homework I asked you to write about your family. Our Abraham has written the most wonderful story and I've asked him to share it with us this morning.'

Someone at the back – maybe it was me, I forget – muttered something and the rest of the class laughed. You must have been nervous. The way your legs shook, trembled, as you walked to the front.

'My family lives in a big house in Rosebank. There are three us: my mother, my father and me. My cousin Christopher lives with us because his mother died.'

'You liar!' I pushed back my chair, stood up. 'Your father went to start a new family. He doesn't want you, Abraham.' I hurled the words across the room: 'Your father doesn't want you!'

I remember the heavy silence which fell over the class.

Even Ms Davies didn't know what to do. She looked at me and blinked. You tried to say something but the words remained folded under your tongue.

You never forgave me for that, did you? You found every excuse not to speak to me. I'd usurped your mother's love and you resented me for it. No, I think the word is hate. You hated me for it.

We fought with each other, day and night almost, like the terriers from number 15 across the road from us. I'd run to Aunt Julia, every time, because she always took my side. She would come charging down the stairs and before you could say a word she would stop you with her words. 'Why do you always have to be a problem?' Once she slapped you across the face. 'What's wrong with you?' she'd yell. 'I send you to expensive schools! Buy you nice clothes! What's the use? Tell me, what's the use of spending so much money on someone like you? You're just like your father.'

The beating and the screaming grew worse. I remember Aunt Julia in a frenzy – your father this, your father that – and then she would sink into a state of remorse. As if someone else, not her, had done what she'd done.

Even in his absence your father was every bit a part of our lives. Whatever happened between them in the past seeped into the present, and as we grew older you became a reminder of the man she hated, and maybe she loved too; loved and hated in equal measure. The tall, dark, childhood sweetheart who wrote her love letters, pages long. The same man who once cracked three of her ribs, and had affairs with two of her close friends.

'The first time I met Abraham...' Bandile says, his voice cracking. It strikes me that I've never seen him without his hat. He's hardly 30 but he's almost bald. He starts over. 'The first time I met Abraham he said living has never been easy. Like most of us who've been using for a long time, he was fragile. He had those eyes of someone who'd lost something. But he was kind. He once told me that when his mother passed on and there was no-one to water the garden, it hurt him to see it die. Pained him physically. So he nurtured it, watered the flowers and vegetables until everything sprung back to life. "Maybe that's all we need," he said, "a little looking after."'

Bandile's eyes dart this way and that, as he says this, until he fixes them on me. I squint and look away. Outside, the traders on the cobblestoned streets go about their business like it's any other day.

What else? We rarely spoke about what happened between us – between you, Aunt Julia and me – at the old house on St Patrick's. Your mother had turned us against each other by the time she died. We had finished school then, and were taking our first steps towards manhood, when her heart stopped.

We made a silent pact to stay out of each other's way after we got rid of the house. That didn't take much doing. You were off on your own, scoring and getting high, picking up odd jobs in sleepy towns up the West Coast. I stayed behind in Cape Town and tried to make something of my life. I got started on a business major but I used to get so drunk I'd lose track of the days. I wouldn't show up on campus for weeks on end. When I think back to that time I have this picture in my head, of me walking down Long Street at 4am or some crazy hour, melancholy in the amber glow of the street lights, making promises to get sober.

Do you remember when you'd been clean for six months and you came back to find me? I'd been on a bender, drinking for three days straight, and it was the first time in our adult lives that I'd seen your eyes so clear. We talked.

'I *wanted* your mother to love me,' I told you. I never understood what it did to me. That's why I drank. A part of me thinks I wanted to make myself ugly. You sought comfort in drugs. You said you liked how it made you feel. It was the only time you never felt ugly and unwanted.

'I can never love anyone, Abraham,' I said. 'That's why I'm

like this.' I lit a cigarette and watched the blue flame envelop the tiny flat.

'Don't you get it, it wasn't your fault,' you said. 'She was sick. She was my mom. All that stuff that happened with her and my dad... It wasn't your fault.'

I threw a punch at you, staggered, and fell to the floor. You held me like you used to when we were kids.

'You can't go around hating yourself and everybody else.'

'Of all the people in the world why did it have to be me?'

'Stop feeling fucking sorry for yourself, Christopher. Get up and do something with your life. How do you think I feel? All those nights I watched you get up and go to her room?'

'What can a junkie teach me?' I said, pushing away from your embrace. 'Huh? You come in here acting like Jesus, all Hallelujah and forgiveness and everything, and dragging up the past. All I know is the bitch is dead. No more schools with fucking Latin mottos, no more talk about how beautiful I am. No more of that shit. I know that she was your mother but I'm fucking glad she's dead.'

You got your things and left.

For years I didn't see you, until we ran into each other at New Haven.

***

'Christopher and I were born two months apart and everyone thought we were twins. We always wore matching outfits when we were younger. The only difference is mine were red and his were blue,' I say. This is my goodbye.

I see the sadness of the faces looking back at me. But I can't tell them everything. Maybe the truth isn't always such a good thing. Maybe some things are better left unsaid. Look what happened when I told you the truth about how Aunt Julia died.

I was jealous of what you had when I came to New Haven. You had found peace of mind with all these folks around you. It's like back when we were kids after my mom died. I wanted your mother's attention. I wanted her to love me more than you.

I told you I'd gone to see her at the house on St Patrick's. 'I want money, Aunt Julia,' I demanded.

We were sitting in the kitchen. A glimmer of sunshine crept through the windows.

'You always want something, don't you, you're no good, like your father...' I wondered if she thought she was talking to you, Abraham. Mid-sentence, she slumped in her chair. She couldn't breathe. I knew she was sick, maybe dying, but I just sat there. I didn't call an ambulance. I watched her gasp. She clutched her chest with her hands, those same hands that always felt so cold against my bare skin. Our eyes met and I looked at her and I watched as she died.

'She was my mother, Christopher, you selfish fuck,' you said before you punched me in the face. I hit you back and you collapsed onto the wooden floor. I spat on you. 'You were a real mommy's boy, Abraham. I don't fucking care. Go! Go kill yourself.'

'She was my mother, Christopher, don't you get that?' you said. 'She was my mother.'

That was the last time I ever spoke to you.

'We had a difficult childhood, Abraham and I, and we weren't always on the best of terms,' I say, my voice splintering. 'But through all of it, I guess he was my brother. He is my brother.'

***

Some wounds cut too deep to heal, Abraham. That promise, *that God will raise us to such a height that we may glimpse the men we aspire to be, and his grace, like the heat of the sun, will burn away the men we have become*, was all child's play.

I'm sitting by the jacaranda tree where the story of your life ends. I can't rewind time and bring you back. What happened between us – between you, Aunt Julia and me – at the house on St Patrick's Road, burned through our lives like mountain fire in a high wind. There's nothing left. Everything is ravaged.

Bongani Kona is a freelance writer and contributing editor of *Chimurenga*. His writing has appeared in *Mail & Guardian, Rolling Stone* (South Africa), *Sunday Times* and other publications and websites. He is also enrolled as a Masters student in the Creative Writing department at the University of Cape Town. 'At Your Requiem' was first published in *Incredible Journey: Stories That Move You* (Burnet Media, South Africa, 2015).

Memories We Lost

Lidudumalingani

There was never a forewarning that this thing was coming. It came out of nowhere, as ghosts do, and it would disappear as it had come. Every time it left, I stretched my arms out in all directions, mumbled two short prayers, one to God and another to the ancestors, and then waited on my terrified sister to embrace me. The embraces, I remember, were always tight and long, as if she hoped the moment would last forever.

Every time this thing took her, she returned altered, unrecognizable, as if two people were trapped inside her, both fighting to get out, but not before tearing each other into pieces. The first thing that this thing took from her, from us, was speech, and then it took our memories. She began speaking in a language that was unfamiliar, her words trembling as if trying to relay unthinkable revelations from the gods. The memories faded one after the other until our past was a blur.

Some of the memories that have remained with me are of her screaming and running away from home. I remember when she ran out to the fields in the middle of the night, screaming, first waking my mother and me and then abducting the entire village from their sleep. Men and boys emerged from their houses carrying their knobkerries as if out to hunt an animal. Women and children stayed behind, frightened children clutching their mothers' nightgowns. The men and boys, disorientated and peeved, shuffled in the dark and split into small groups as instructed by a man who at the absence of a clear plan crowned himself a leader. Those with torches flicked them on and pushed back the darkness. Some took candles; they squeezed their bodies close and wrapped blankets around themselves in an attempt to block the wind, but all their matches extinguished before they could light a single candle.

Those without torches or candles walked on even though the next step in such darkness was possibly a plunge down a cliff. This was unlikely, it should be said, as most of them were born in the village, grew up there, got married there, had used that very same field as their toilet for all their lives, and had in overlapping periods only left the village when they went to work for the white man in large cities. They had a blueprint of the village in their minds; its walking paths, its indentations, its rivers, its mountains, its holes where ghosts lived were imprinted in their blood.

Hours later, the first small group of men and boys, and then another and another, emerged from the darkness. They did not find her. They had looked everywhere, at least they had claimed. They were worried about not finding my sister or annoyed at being woken in the middle of the night – I could not tell. Morphed into defeated men, their faces drooped to the floor, and their bodies slouched as if they had carried a heavy load. Each group was not aware of the other groups' whereabouts. They did not even know if the other groups still existed or if the night had swallowed them. They had last seen them when they wished them luck when they split up. They had heard them yell my sister's name, in the dark, before going silent.

She did not scream.

She did not cry.

She did not scream.

She did not cry.

She did not respond to the calls.

Each group chanted with great terror. With each group that emerged, I hoped that it would chant something else, but nothing changed; the chant was, as if it had been rehearsed for a long time, repeated the same each time, tearing my heart apart.

She did not scream.

She did not cry.

She did not scream.

She did not cry.

She did not respond to our screams.

The chant went on until all groups had returned.

Mother, a woman of tall build and wide hips, only returned home when the sun was way up in the sky the next day, carrying my sister on her back.

She would scream in intervals as if to taunt me, my mother said.

I remember another time my sister banged her head against the wall until she bled. She and I were racing around the rondavel to see who would return first to our starting point. I think we were 12 and 15 then. She had begun to grow breasts, and she was telling me how sensitive they were. She had brushed her fingers over them and a sensation she had never felt before had pulsed through her body. She did not know what was going on or what had caused her body to tingle apart from that touch. I remember trying to interject that she was becoming a woman, she was becoming sexual – not that I knew anything myself.

She dismissed me teasingly, in the gentle manner that she dismissed things, leaving one not convinced whether she was in agreement or not. You know nothing about breasts, she told me after examining my chest. I told her that I was a late bloomer. The lie came out of me as naturally as truth comes to others. I had made my mother, and anyone else who knew, promise that she must never know the truth about how my chest had no breasts. She teased me for a long time that day and days after. It was nothing malicious, it was in the manner that a sibling tells another sibling that they have a big head but get upset when someone else says the words.

Then it arrived. I did not see it approaching. I had always hoped that I would so that I could stop it. At the time I was convinced that if one observed more carefully one could see it coming, with horns, spikes and an oversized head – that's how I imagined it looked. I don't know if she ever saw it coming but I hope not. The horror of seeing a monster coming for you and not being able to run even though one is not in a dream would have been unbearable for her.

I was telling her how once I fooled the boys in my class that I had grown breasts. It was a Friday. I stuffed pantyhose into my shirt, to look like breasts, and wore my mother's bra. The stupid boys never stopped to wonder at the improbability of the situation. How is it possible that my breasts had grown in one day?

So the boys stared at me the whole day, convinced that I had suddenly bloomed in the night, I said to her.

I stared out into the landscape that began in my mother's garden and stretched far beyond sight. The sun was setting behind the forest and dust was floating everywhere. Where the dust was dense, one could see it sway this way and that way as if in the middle of a dance. A sophisticated dance, the kind that, I imagined, happened in other worlds, very far from the village. The village was settling into repose. The cold summer air had begun to torment the villagers' bare legs and arms. Everything was in silhouette, including the horses that trotted across the veld, the cattle that lowered their heads to graze, and the water that flowed down the cliff. The mountains, ancient but nevertheless still standing, were casting giant shadows over the landscape. The shadows stretched so far from the mountain that they began to exist as if they were solid entities on their own.

In the middle of a story I was telling her, she gently rocked back and forth then began hitting the back of her head against the wall. For a short time I thought she was providing rhythm for my anecdote. It was only when she began to scream, in an attempt to churn this thing out of her, that I became alarmed. By then she had smashed her head and left blood on the wall. She had transformed into someone else. She was not here. I tried to grab her or whatever was there. I tried to make her stop. I held her hands, bound them behind her back, laid my body against hers, but she pushed me away easily with a strength that came to her only when this thing tore her apart. Had it not been a mud wall, an old one at that, she would have cracked her skull open. Instead, she cracked the wall with her head.

The bloodstain remained visible on the wall long after my mother scraped it off; long after she had applied three layers of mud and new water paint. The stains stayed long after the sangoma came and cleansed the spot where my sister had bludgeoned her head. I began to smell the bloodstains in my dreams, in my clothes, in everything. The smell of blood lingered after many sunsets had come; even after the rain had come.

The other time that I remember this thing entering my sister was when she threw hot porridge on me. This thing arrived in her and abducted her while she hovered over a hot porridge pot. In the middle of a joke she never finished, she flung the pot across the room. It only just missed my face but my chest was not that fortunate. I don't remember opening the bottom half of the door of the rondavel but I found myself standing outside, naked, having pulled my dress off. The pain was unbearable. Hours later, when she gained consciousness, she was shocked and devastated about what had happened to me. I told her I had poured hot water on myself by mistake. She would never forgive herself.

Though it had been tough in other months, it was in November that things got worse. This thing, this thing that took over her followed her to school and she had to drop out. It arrived while she was in class. She was so strong, so out of control, that she flung a desk across the room and smashed a window. When I arrived in her class, everyone was standing around watching. She had broken a chair against the wall too, and she was screaming words I did not understand. I stood at a short distance from her. All she had to do was look into my eyes. Please look into my eyes, I begged. Her eyes had turned red and her entire body was shaking. When she did look at me, after scanning the bewildered faces of the crowd, she stopped screaming. She knew me. I stared right into her eyes and I could see this thing leave; I could see my sister returning.

After that incident I went truant from school. Every morning I threw up. I convinced my mother that I was sick. She asked a boy who went to the same school to tell my class teacher that I had come down with an illness.

I want to be in the same class with you, I said to my sister, so I am going to wait until you are fine so we can go to school together.

They will never allow that. Mother, the teachers, the principal.

Yes they will. It is not like I want to study a grade higher. I want to study with you in the same class.

She and I spent that week doing sketches. With a pencil she could sketch me onto the paper such that it appeared as if I was alive on the page, another me, more happy, less torn, existing elsewhere.

She begged and begged me to go to school and promised me that she would be fine and that every day when I came back she would have new sketches for me.

We spent our days talking, one ear listening out for my mother's footsteps. We would know she was coming by the sound of the door closing when she walked out of the main house, then her shadow would come first through the door of our house.

My mother took my sister to more sangomas and more churches and gave her more bottles of medication. She became unresponsive. She only nodded and shook her head at irrelevant moments – there was nothing else. It turned out later, when I went back to school, that my week of absence had gone unreported. This bothered neither my class teacher nor me. Over the years my sister had missed so much school that I had caught up with her and was, in fact, two grades above her.

A few weeks after I had returned to school, the teacher told us about schizophrenia and I knew then that this is what my sister had and that all the medication she had been taking would never help her. Instead, it was destroying her. The teacher told us that there is no cure for this thing but I knew that my sister deserved to feel something, anything.

The first thing my sister and I got rid of was her arsenal of medication. This is going to be our secret, I said. On our long walks, away from our mother, we dug holes and buried the roots she had to chew. The way to get rid of the medication drink, I demonstrated to her, was to pour it into the mug and take an empty sip, then when no-one was looking throw it out the back window that had grass growing below it. The window also opened to a large landscape where the cattle grazed. When mother asks if I have given you your medication you must nod, I told her.

I came back from school the following Monday afternoon and she took me to our house and poured her medication, took an empty sip, and threw it out the window with a smile. It was our game.

She began to recognize herself. She and I began to communicate again. We invented our own language because she had stopped talking. We simply gestured to each other and then over time we inserted a few words here and there.

We began to love each other again. I remember the day we connected again. We were in the same room we had always sat in, staring, as we always did, into the landscape, over the mountains, at the horizon, into the sun, until our eyes could not take us any further. It was a day of looking out, smiling, laughing, crying, holding hands.

We sat there and watched the day go by. We didn't even attempt to say a word. I realized then that she and I needed no words.

In the afternoon that day it began to rain. I dragged her out of the house. We jumped in the rain, begging it to pour on us so we could be tall, big, strong, bold. In that moment, my sister returned; she smiled, laughed. That day we began to form new childhood memories, filling the void left by the one that had been wiped out.

We lay on the wet ground, stretched out our arms and legs, rain falling on our faces, and felt free. But my mother had seen us laugh and jump and thought that this thing was going to come again.

The following day the entire village gathered outside our house for yet another ritual meant to cure my sister. She had been through all these rituals and church sermons and nothing had changed. Each time sangomas and pastors promised that she would be healed within days. There was once, at least according to the elders, a glimpse of these sangomas healing. The tobacco, meat and matches that had been put in the rondavel for the ancestors to take at night, in one of the many rituals, were not there by morning, leading them to believe that the ancestors had healed her. It was not long after that this thing came again, proving that the tobacco, meat and matches had simply been stolen by thieves.

The day of the ritual, I remember how the clouds moved across the sky in a hurry, and how thick fog hung on to the grass, the mountains, the riverbanks and forests as if to announce death. It hung so low that people appeared to be floating with their legs cut off below their knees. The women's chatter and songs reached us long before the crowd was visible. It appeared as if the fog had swallowed them and that the women would never come into sight; all the same, they did. They ululated and chanted songs as they approached our home.

Men came in silence, arms folded behind their backs, carrying sticks.

A few minutes after the women arrived, smoke escaped the fireplace into the sky, dancing with the moving clouds as if the sky was their dance floor. The children ran around and kicked soccer balls that had been made by stuffing papers into plastic bags. Everyone moved in a chaotic choreography. That way went an obese woman balancing a bucket of water on her head; this way went a child with a tablecloth; that way went a dog with a bone; this way went chickens; that way stood women gossiping about my sister. From our house, I could see the chaos amplifying as more people arrived.

I looked at my sister and found her face, as it had become in earlier months, emotionless. In the past few days she had given me hope that she had returned. Now tears rolled down our cheeks. I knew then that she still felt something, that the last few days of holding hands, laughing and jumping in the rain were not a dream.

The fog began to clear and everything came into focus. The mountains, landscape, river and the other villages were there, unmoved.

An old man who had been smoking his pipe behind the kraal emptied it and stuffed it in his pockets. The ritual began. Knives were drawn and the goat was first stabbed in the stomach to summon our ancestors from their enclaves, and then it was meat.

After some time, an old aunt came for us, calling for us to come out of the house. We hugged tightly, my sister and I, wiped each other's tears. It was only after we had heard her footsteps approaching our house that we walked out, holding hands, fingers tightly entwined. The only way to have torn me away from her would have been to cut us apart.

The villagers shouted insults at the 'thing', as it remained unknown to them. For what felt like an entire lifetime, while my sister and I sat at a corner in the kraal, our heads bowed, the elders kept referring to this thing as the devil's work and demons. None of them knew my sister; none of them cared. The sun was up now, thick shadows gathering around the house. Even though there was no wind, the windmill by the fields made a creaking sound.

My mother was torn and defeated and questioned why God gave this thing to my sister – and my father. Secrets stay buried for so long but one day they rise to open like seeds breaking free from the earth. Nobody had ever mentioned that my father had this thing. That he had left one day on his horse, to see distant relatives, and had never come back. To only be seen in the way the deceased are seen after their death, in dreams and hallucinations.

He had been seen in some village at least twice, my mother told me. The person who had seen him yelled and waved but he never bothered to look. They were not sure if it was my father but they were convinced that it had to be. He was never buried, though it is now 20 years later. There was nothing to bury. I have no memory of my father. There was always hope that he would return from somewhere; nobody knew where, nobody cared, as long as he returned.

The night of the ritual, my sister and I slept lying the same way, instead of in different directions. I woke up and she was holding me, squeezing me, and she had sunk her teeth in the pillow so she would not cry. She jerked for a few minutes and then fell asleep in my arms.

In the morning, I went to milk the goat. I saw two human shadows hovering above the kraal. At first, though it was unusual, I thought nothing of it even as they mumbled something to each other. In the shadows that leaped inside the kraal, with the smell of manure, I saw that it was my mother and an uncle who had come to stay with us for the ritual. It was as if their heads were bound together into one, creating a giant head, a ghost even. I had meant to get up but when I heard them mention my sister, I put the jug of milk down and crouched, leaning on the goat so it did not move.

My mother and Smellyfoot, the man who had moved in with my mother, were making plans to take my sister away.

The medication and the rituals did not work, my mother said. The way she saw it, my sister needed to go see Nkunzi. This thing is going to come back, she said.

Nkunzi was a sangoma from a remote village in which houses were lined miles apart from one another; he was famous for 'baking' people like my sister, claiming to cure them. It is said that whenever there was a car approaching his village, people would shout for Nkunzi to come out. Your demons are here, they would say.

Smellyfoot, a name that my sister had given him, agreed with my mother. We were not his kids; why would he care? And that was it, they decided: the next day my sister would be taken to Nkunzi to be baked. This is what they did with people who heard voices or demons, as they called them; they baked them until the demons left them. What was even more terrible than the baking was that people had come to be convinced of it.

I had heard of how Nkunzi baked people. He would make a fire from cow dung and wood, and once the fire burned red he would tie the demon-possessed person onto a section of zinc roofing then place it on the fire. He claimed to be baking the demons and that the person would recover from the burns a week later. I had not heard of anyone who had died but I had not heard of anyone who had lived either.

I could not allow this to happen to my sister.

After sunset I got my things and we left together. The twilight was approaching. I couldn't think where to go. We wandered first onto the main road; then I spotted many eyes staring at us so I changed direction and sank into the valley. My sister held tightly on to my hand. I did not tell her anything she did not need to know. We were going to see an aunt who had suddenly fallen ill. We have to see her before the sun rises tomorrow, I told her.

There was no aunt who was ill.

We walked in the valley, on the banks of the river, then up a wet mound and over a fence that had once stood but was now lying broken on the ground. We came to a bridge with a tar road and because we were both scared of water we crossed the bridge and walked on the road alongside the river.

We hardly noticed that it had become night; suddenly a giant moon had sneaked above us and stars had weaved patterns only gods understood. Mountains and landscape were now mere shapes, giant and indistinct, leaving us, tiny as we were then, the only things present in the world.

We walked by the river and then abandoned it, walked up a mountain and down the other side into a village. I was not sure whether it was Philani or another village. I had only ever been there once before and that visit was not even physical. My mother had mentioned it in one of her stories before she moved us into the new house – before a week later replacing our father, and us, with the Smellyfoot.

Once we descended the mountain and found ourselves in a strange village we would knock on the first house that had its light on and sleep there. That had been the initial plan, but it was flawed. Everyone in the villages knew everyone. I was convinced that whomever we asked for a place to sleep, even if we were to lie and give them false names, tell them that we were heading to the next village but something had delayed us, they would have recognized us, either because we have my grandfather's ears or my mother's nose or that they had seen us when we were toddlers, even stroked our buttocks. It had always been said that my sister had my grandfather's forehead. The plan was too risky.

We are close, I told my sister. Close to where, I had no idea. All the same, we were going forward, and it felt like we had reached where we were going, which was nowhere in particular. All that mattered was that we were now far from home.

We had no idea where we were going to sleep, what we were going to eat or how we were going to live, but returning home was not an option. Maybe when my mother dies, I said, maybe then we can return.

We crossed Philani village – I was still not sure which village it was – with dogs barking at us, or at something else, perhaps a pole that had always stood there. In no time at all we reached another village. My sister stopped asking me why we were leaving home. She squeezed my hand every now and then and I hers.

Many times, I contemplated telling my sister why we were running away from home but I could not. I did not know where to begin. There was and still is no perfect place to begin; the real story would destroy her.

My mother preferred her numb. I preferred a sister. A laughing sister, a talking sister, and a sister who looked into my eyes and cried and laughed. Imagine the reflections that suddenly appear when one stares into water and beats it. That is what happens to my sister. I want to tell her she has a mental disorder that makes it impossible for her to tell fiction from reality.

We could not see any lights. People had long gone to sleep. We had no idea where we were but we knew that we had reached another village. The moon had disappeared and the stars were now only dots in the sky. Morning was close, I thought, and I told my sister who nodded and smiled.

We had no idea what time it was but it had been a long time since we left home, and our feet hurt. We decided to sleep under a tree, to wake once the sun was up and walk again, to somewhere.

Lidudumalingani is a writer, filmmaker and photographer. He was born in the Eastern Cape province of South Africa, in a village called Zikhovane. Lidudumalingani has published short stories, non-fiction and criticism in various publications. His films have been screened at various film festivals. 'Memories We Lost' was first published in *Incredible Journey: Stories That Move You* (Burnet Media, South Africa, 2015).

The Caine Prize
African Writers' Workshop Stories 2016

His Middle Name Was Not Jesus

NoViolet Bulawayo

He was bringing them drinks – a Castle for him, a Zambezi for her – when he walked into it. Things had been fine when he left with their order, but now they had morphed into animals, all bared fangs, vicious, bloodthirsty. He didn't understand their language but he knew it from their boiling voices, from the heat on their faces, how they singed each other with their eyes.

He hesitated by the entrance, deciding what to do. Turn on his heel and go back? Wait for the storm to pass? Proceed to the table like nothing was happening? He caught the man's eye and gave a relieved nod, looked to him for a sign. The man continued speaking like spitting, without acknowledging him; he might as well not have been there. Hot blood roared in his head; if there was anything, a-n-y-t-h-i-n-g he hated most in the world, it was for someone to look right at him and still ignore him. And not just any someone too, a midget at that – the man was such a shrimp that even the wife could pee on him squatting.

He was standing like that, deciding what to do, when Francis, the manager, came down the hallway pushing a trolley, which left him no choice but to thrust himself quickly into the room. No need to give the man the opportunity to show he was manager, which he was always dying to do. He balanced the tray and moved with careful steps, the way you approach a rabid dog. The woman looked at him like she had never seen him before. It stung. He had done things for her. The midget too. Just that morning he had rescued the woman from a terrible downpour by stopping for her in the jeep and driving her the rest of the way to her cottage; once there, he had escorted her to the door under an umbrella. And now this treatment? This treatment, really? Mnccc.

He opened and served the sweaty bottles without smiling, without trying to meet their eyes; if they were going to be like that then, fine, he could be like that too – his middle name was not Jesus and he did not have to be nice. The thought gave him some satisfaction and he begun to hum, softly, but still loud enough for them to hear. He was encouraged now by the sudden drop in their voices; no doubt they didn't expect him to behave as he was doing. They were probably even talking about him too, this he could tell from the shift in their voices. If someone is talking about you, you just know it, even if you don't understand the language. It's a feeling.

'Tivuschutyzoberdustryongstiotchachadct' it sounded like the man said.

'Vzhustubinzhuclar' the woman said, whatever it meant. He had, until that point, thought her an effortlessly gorgeous woman. Whenever he saw her – at mealtimes, in the library where she liked to sit and read, at the verandah upstairs, or just roaming around the lodge, her beauty never failed to surprise him, as if he were encountering it for the first time. He revelled in it, like it was meant for him alone. It was this beauty that motivated him to go out of his way with his niceness, to do things for her. Now though, come to think of it, she wasn't even that beautiful. No. Not with those perpetually startled eyes, not with that long forehead. Besides, she had no ass. And the midget – the midget was not even worth talking about.

It pleased him to find that he was not even bothered by their talking about him. They didn't count, not any more. He took his time picking the tray before strolling off, making it a point not to say, 'Enjoy your drinks,' which he was supposed to. Enjoy your drinks. Why on earth did one have to tell an adult to enjoy his drink, his food – things that went into his own stomach? Mnccc. Nonsense.

He was nearing the kitchen when he heard a scream behind him. A few doors down, Musa, the chef, bobbed her head out of the kitchen and said, 'What?' with her long arms. He shook his head: I don't know. The scream was short-lived, though, and it was all quiet again. Musa shrugged, ducked back into the kitchen. Should he go back and check on them? But why, really, why? In life there were people who deserved to be checked on, but not these two. He sat the tray on an end table and headed back. It was not to check on them; it was in case Francis later got wind of it, whatever it was – he did not want to be interrogated on where he'd been, why he hadn't responded.

He found them huddled under the table. It had not struck him, until that moment when he saw them like that, a mess of tangled limbs, like silly kids really, how young they were. They could not have been out of their twenties. Which meant he was older than them, at least by a few years. Which counted for something. Which said they had no business treating him the way they did. Which made him want to pluck them from under the table and slap them like he would his young siblings if they needed it.

The woman pointed to the bat that was dancing in circles. He had already spotted Casper; a small frantic thing flying around the room. He was used to him coming out at the wrong moments and scaring some of the lodgers. Just yesterday, he had been called by a group of writers for the same reason. Casper had settled by the time he got there and he had not had to do anything, which was a waste of his time. The writers, all of them adults, big men included, had carried on without shame.

'It's a Bat,' the woman said.

'I know,' Mukuka said. He thrust his hands in his pockets and filled the doorway. His reflection looked back at him from the opposite window and he was pleased with what he saw. He took pride in his appearance and it showed. His white shirt was always spotless and wrinkle-free no matter the time of day, face clean-shaven, hair cropped close to his forehead, shoes polished. Even Francis, who had something to say about everything at Zambezi Lodge, never had anything bad to say about his appearance.

'Can it be removed?' the midget said. He was not spitting now, no. Subdued is what he was. He reminded Mukuka of a poor son-in-law negotiating an overwhelming bride price.

'You mean the bat?' Mukuka said. And Casper, as if he were hearing the conversation, as if he knew what was in Mukuka's head, danced and danced.

'Ihm,' Mukuka looked pensive, scratched his head. 'I have to find someone from the animal department or something. I'm not really trained to remove bats,' he said. The man bit his lower lip. A look of frustration crossed the woman's face. It all pleased Mukuka.

'Or, you can leave the room and go somewhere, maybe the bar,' he said, his voice satisfied. The woman looked at Casper, who continued round and round and round.

'I don't know, what if I'm walking to the door and it gets me on the neck? I heard they bite and they can have rabies. Or even worse, Ebola,' the woman said. Mukuka took his hands out of his pockets and frowned. The midget said something sharp in his language. The woman looked very shocked, and then began to cry. It came out all at once, the rush of tears, the sobbing, and Mukuka was taken off-guard by the emotion of it, the strangeness of it. He was no longer sure if she was crying because of the bat, or for something else. His instincts told him it was something else. He stepped into the room and walked toward them. By now, Casper had tucked himself behind a beam.

'Please don't cry, madam, the bat is gone. It's gone, see?' Mukuka said. His voice was something between coaxing and desperation. She covered her face with her hands and sobbed and sobbed, her upper body convulsing. Mukuka was not used to this, and he had not been told, when he was hired just a couple of months ago, what to do in such a situation. He looked at the husband to say something, do something, but the man pursed his thin lips and crawled out from under the table, grabbed his leather bag from the floor and stormed off.

'Where are you going, you midget you?' Mukuka said, but this was spoken quietly, inside his head. He wondered if he should go and find someone – Francis, no, not Francis. A woman. Musa or one of the girls maybe, to come and see about this. Maybe they would know what to do. He stood there thinking about it while she sobbed and sobbed. Then it occurred to him that, no, he didn't need to involve anyone after all. Not because this was a private matter, but because he had never really been alone with her like this. Her beauty had returned now, and she looked even lovelier crying. He felt an urge to crawl under the table, hold her to his chest and wrap his strong arms around her, but he just pulled up a chair and sat there facing her, his arms folded.

'Madam, how about a game drive, maybe before sunset, or even tomorrow?' Mukuka's tone was cajoling. It was a bit later, after the sobbing and heaving had stopped. He startled himself; he had not intended to say it out loud. It was just a thought; to get her out of her mood he figured maybe going out would do her good. The problem was there weren't that many options around Zambezi. There was the lake, and yes, it was beautiful, but being in the water made him anxious and dizzy. He also didn't know how to swim and what if something happened to the boat and he found himself in the water? There was also the wine tasting but he didn't think she drank, he had never seen her drink. And besides, he was terrible with pronunciation, it made him feel like an idiot having those unsayable wine names crowded in his mouth. What would have been great was a movie in town, something simple and nice and romantic, but the game park was located way out of the city. Mnccc. It would just have to be the game drive.

She looked at him as if she were hearing him from afar. Her face was peaceful and it had a kind of freshness to it, like she had in fact needed the cry.

'Yes, sure, I think I'd like that. And thank you for staying, that was sweet of you,' she said. He heard things in her voice – warmth, relief, tenderness. And something he couldn't quite name but he still liked the sound of it. She started to crawl out from under the table and he turned his head away, looked out the window at the pool, so she could have some dignity. The pool, just like the whole lodge, was deserted owing to the Easter holiday. When he looked at her again she had adjusted her scarf and put on her hat and glasses and looked cheerful; you wouldn't know, looking at her, what had just happened.

***

They went out in the safari car first thing in the morning: him sitting at the front with Moses, the driver; she in the back, sandwiched between her husband and Gloria, the guide. He had not counted on the midget coming and so was disappointed to see him emerge from the breakfast room, all dressed up in khakis to match her, and lugging a big camera. The madness from yesterday seemed gone from the midget's face and he looked happy – too happy in fact, Mukuka thought. This he had not planned for. Had he known the midget would involve himself he would not have suggested a game drive at all, he would have thought of something else. And, to add on to things, it was a woman in charge of the tour. What would it make him look like, sitting in the front like a loaf of bread, not even driving? Mnccc.

Francis appeared at the door of the main reception and made a salute. They all waved to him and the car pulled off.

'Fucking idiot. What's he saluting us for when our pay is

three weeks late? Give us our pay, motherfucker,' Moses said between his teeth. Because Mukuka was still new to Zambezi Lodge, and therefore still learning people, he busied himself with his watch and pretended he had not heard Moses, even if he agreed with him, even if he would have liked to add that the man was also not smart and didn't deserve his managing job. But better to keep your mouth shut with these kinds of things. And besides, there was something about Moses he didn't trust. He couldn't put a finger on it yet but it was there.

The car stopped at the main entrance and the tall guard held out a booklet for Moses to sign. Mukuka gave the man a brief nod before they pulled off.

'Man, I almost hit a giraffe. Just this Monday. Praise God I missed it,' Moses said. Nervous excitement laced his voice.

'Really,' Mukuka said. It was not a question.

'Oh yes-yes. There were two of them, grazing there just behind the anthill near the big baobab – that one. So I only saw the first, which I avoided fine-fine. Now the second, the second came out of nowhere. I just saw it land on my right is all I know. I mean I didn't even see it jump, it's like the thing just flew.'

'Ha,' Mukuka said.

'Exactly. I can't even imagine – do you know how much just one of those things costs?' Moses said. His voice had fattened now, and it said that yes, indeed, it could not even imagine, said that each of those things cost an enormous amount of money.

'Ihm,' Mukuka said. He was thinking of the day before, how she had called him sweet. Not nice, no, sweet. But what kind of sweet, exactly, had she meant? The sweet of honey? Of sugar? Candy or juicy mango? S-w-e-e-t.

They took a left where the main road curved, and the car crawled along the big fence north of Zambezi. Tall grass framed either side of the vehicle, and Mukuka was glad she was not seated in the path of stray grasses and branches – there were places where the road ran narrow and sometimes people got scratched. A footpath ran along the fence, and about 300 metres down it branched off to the left toward Sonondo settlement where Mukuka, Moses, Gloria and the other Zambezi workers lived. It was a shortcut, but Mukuka avoided it, preferring to stay on the main road even though it took him about twice as long to get to Sonondo.

What Mukuka knew was this: beyond the fence were cheetahs, lynxes, lions and hyenas, each kind of animal separated in its own enclosure. Yes, this was a game reserve and everything, but as far as Mukuka was concerned these were wild animals. A-n-i-m-a-l-s. One day some idiot would surely forget to lock the gate to one of the enclosures, or a poacher would cut the fence, or one of the beasts would just somehow discover how to climb out. It might seem very unlikely, but it would happen, he knew, because these things happened; it was only a matter of time. And when it did, he did not intend to be found on the footpath, taking a shortcut to Sonondo. No, that wouldn't be him. He fished a spotless handkerchief from his pocket and wiped his forehead. It was only morning but the sun was killing already, and he perspired easily.

They stopped at the second enclosure, where the two cheetahs lay in the shade. He could hardly see for the thick bush; all that was visible of the beasts was the head of one, and just a hint of the second – the rest of the animals' bodies were submerged in the grass. But this didn't disappoint Mukuka; he was in fact glad because it meant they didn't have to waste much time with the dangerous animals. In the back, the three were on their feet already, pointing and admiring. He imagined what her face looked like, her green eyes, the delicate dent in her chin.

'They are brother and sister,' he heard Gloria say.

'Interesting. How old are they?' the husband said.

'Do they have names?' she said. Her voice was full of awe.

'They are Simba and Dorothy. And I think he is three and she is about a year younger. Their parents came from

Livingstone, Dorothy was born here. She almost died when she was a couple of months old, though – we think some tourists accidentally fed her poisonous treats,' Gloria said.

They stood like that, watching the cheetahs they couldn't quite see clearly. After a while the midget said, 'Well, they're not moving.' It was one of those obvious observations that didn't even need to be said.

'Yes, they're resting. They don't really run around a lot because there isn't much space in there,' Gloria said.

'If they're not moving maybe we should go. See other things,' the midget said. There was a slight twinge of impatience in his voice. It annoyed Mukuka even if he himself was ready to go. It was he who had suggested the tour, so what was the midget calling the shots for?

He imagined the cheetahs getting up from their lazing, somehow making it through the fence through a hole that magically appeared, grabbing the midget, and carrying him back to their enclosure for an afternoon snack, the magic hole closing behind them. He knew it was an awful thought but he liked it – liked it so much that he had to suppress a satisfied laugh. Gloria slapped the roof of the car to say they should get moving. Moses started the engine and they snaked along once more.

There was no sight of the lion, the lynx, or the hyena in their respective enclosures, and so the car kept on. They turned left at the end of the fence and ploughed through the grass, headed toward the thick bush. It was hot in the car, but there was something comforting about the smell of earth and leaves, something thrilling about how the long grass raced toward the windshield as if it would crack it open, before the car's tyres devoured it.

'It's a pity the other animals weren't there, I really wanted to see the lion,' she said. There was a hint of disappointment in her voice. Mukuka was surprised by how her sadness got to him, how it made him feel sorry for being glad, earlier, that there hadn't been animals at the fence. It was not a wonderful feeling, and he regretted that there was nothing he could do about the situation.

'I know. We'll try again on our way back,' Gloria said. 'They're probably just at a separate part of their enclosures. Sometimes it's hit and miss with them, depends on timing, but don't worry, there are other animals to see.' Her voice was sympathetic and, for the first time, Mukuka was glad she was there with them, soothing her.

'It's sad we can't text them to get ready for us, we are coming, no?' the midget said. He laughed at his own joke, and would have laughed by himself had not Gloria joined out of politeness. Mukuka had never heard the midget laugh before, and was amazed by the power of the sound. He turned around, perhaps to convince himself that a midget could really laugh like a big man, and yes, sure enough, Mukuka saw that it was the midget indeed, laughing the laugh. But what pleased him was the fact that she was not laughing with him; her face was turned to the side, carefully scanning the landscape.

They found the zebra waiting by the human-made lake like the animals had heard the group was coming and needed a ride to somewhere important. She gasped from the backseat and leaned her head out of the car. Mukuka wanted to tell her to be careful, not to reach out that far. Because you never know.

'Oh, my God, look! They're beautiful!' she yelled. He would not have thought to use the word 'beautiful' for the animals, especially it being a word that he associated with her. He looked at their poised bodies, at the sharp contrast of their black-and-white stripes, and understood what she meant. The zebra were quite pleasing to look at.

He remembered that his grandmother, MaNyathi, had told him how, once upon a time, back when animals could talk, a man had married a woman who he thought to be the most beautiful in the village, until he woke up one day in the middle of the night to see her turn into a zebra and gallop off into the woods. The astounded man stayed up to see what would happen.

Hours later, just before dawn, the animal woman returned, changed back into a human being, and crawled into bed beside the husband she thought was sleeping. In the morning she woke up as usual and went on with the womanly business of fetching water, cleaning the home, preparing meals and tending the fields as if nothing was amiss. The stunned husband presented the matter to the village court, and it was promptly decided, after three repeated occasions of the woman turning into a zebra and bolting off into the dark, that she had to be killed. But, luckily for her, a young woman she had befriended could not bear the thought of her being slaughtered, especially as she was not harming anyone. She tipped the animal woman off and, on the morning she was supposed to be killed, she turned into a zebra in front of the whole village and galloped away, never to be seen again.

Now the safari car skirted the edge of the herd and the zebras bolted and made off in whips of colour. She continued making noises of appreciation. The midget took pictures and Gloria narrated. Mukuka wished it had just been the two of them in the car; he would have shared the animal-woman story with her and she would have enjoyed it. He watched the fleeing animals and wondered if they were female, wondered how it was that, even as they were scattering, they maintained formation, speeding off in neat rows. After a while of Moses chasing the skittish herd unsuccessfully, they drove off, away from the lake.

They had just passed the big baobab when they saw the pairs of ostriches. The birds, six of them, walked right in the centre of the road like kings. Dani had told him once that the males had the black and white feathers and the females the grey and brown. It seemed all reversed to him, all wrong somehow – the grey-brown was unremarkable to look at, while the black and white was bold and stood out quite grandly against the bare necks. It's the females that needed that brilliance, that needed to be attractive, Mukuka thought. When the car caught up with the ostriches, they broke into a trot. It always amazed Mukuka to see those bulky bodies, those long necks in motion, and he knew it filled her with wonder too because he heard her say, 'wow.' He turned around. Their eyes met and she smiled a smile that filled the cabin. Perspiration laced his brow. He reached for the handkerchief in his pocket.

'Could I please have some water?' she said. She was looking at the midget, who busied himself with the camera. Mukuka quickly reached between his feet and fished a bottle from the half-open cartoon. It was warm. He cussed softly to himself; why didn't this bigheaded Moses think to use his dense head and stock cold water ahead of a tour, especially if he didn't need to pay for it himself? And what if she rejected the warm water? What would they do, where would they find cold water in this bush? He passed it to her between the tiny window that separated the cabin and she held on a bit longer than necessary. Sweat dripped like a blob of honey down her jaw. He imagined wiping it off with a forefinger and licking it.

'You know those things can go up to 60 kilometres per hour?' Moses said. Mukuka wiped perspiration off his forehead. He was scolding himself for letting go of the bottle just a bit too soon. He shouldn't have done that; what he should have done was follow her lead and keep holding on, who knows what that moment wanted to become? Her fingers had felt cool brushing against his, even if briefly. But how was it possible to feel that cool in this heat? He thought of them now, the fingers, long and slender, on his forehead. He thought of sweetness too. He slid into his thoughts like they were a cool pool, got submerged so deep that the fingers and sweetness became real to him, realer than the climb of the car up an incline, the heat, the blue of the sky, the red earth.

***

'Me, I think this Julie is very nice.' Mukuka heard the voice as if in a dream; it jolted him. He looked at the green around him and didn't know where he was. Then he saw Moses. Then he glanced over his shoulder and saw them in the back. Her head was tilted up to the rain of finches overhead, dark bangs of hair on her forehead. He remembered where he was. He also remembered what he had been thinking. The memory pleased him. He smiled without meaning to.

'But tell me, boss. Who is it, surely?' Moses said. The car swerved to avoid a hare.

'What?' Mukuka said. His voice was just a little bit unsteady, like he'd been caught at something, and he was disappointed in his failure to keep it even.

'I mean I've never seen your teeth before until a moment ago,' Moses said. His voice was playful and nosy. Mukuka didn't like the sound of it, didn't trust it. Tree branches scratched the roof of the car. He sucked his teeth and tasted honey. They were passing the pond now, which meant they were headed back to Zambezi, and he was deeply disappointed by how soon it seemed, how the drive had felt so short. Had they really circled the whole park? What about the monkeys? The buffalo, the eland, the impala, the waterbuck? The tsessebe, the secretary bird, the porcupine, the giraffe, the warthog, the hammer cop, all these animals to see? Or had they actually seen all these things, and he'd been there but not there, lost in his thoughts? He wanted to ask Moses if they had indeed done the whole tour, but he didn't want to embarrass himself.

'Must be someone special,' Moses pressed on.

'What are you talking about, man?' Mukuka said. His voice had recovered, but now he wanted the conversation to end. It made him uncomfortable, especially with everyone in the car.

'Well, I'm just saying. It's like all of a sudden you left your body and went somewhere else. So, how about you just tell it, who's the girl?' Moses said.

'No, no, it's not like that at all,' Mukuka said, dismissively. He made to take a sly glance into the rearview mirror, hoping to catch her. The mirror was missing; some unthinking idiot must have removed it. Mnccc.

'Anyway, whatever has horns cannot be hidden in a sack. Check with Julia when we get to the lodge, she wanted to know when the dancers are coming. I told her you were taking a nap, seeing how gone you were.' Moses said. He manoeuvred the car through a small swamp and muddy water splashed all over.

'Julia?' Mukuka said.

'I mean the madam, at the back,' Moses said. He tilted his head a bit to indicate back.

'Julia, her name is Julia?' Mukuka said. He had said it loudly, and he regretted raising his voice. He glanced over his shoulder and all three of them were turned around, looking at the distance behind them.

'Yes, it is. I call her Julie. There's your grandfather,' Moses said, pointing. The car stopped. To the right of them, across the small human-made lake, was an elephant. It loomed above the grass and its trunk reached into the trees. The elephant was Mukuka's totem animal, and seeing it always gave him a thrill, stirred a deep pride in his blood. Now he stared at it and saw nothing but a small hill.

Julie. J-u-l-i-a. He didn't know that was her name; she hadn't told it to him and so he just called her madam. He hated Moses for knowing a name he himself was supposed to know but didn't, and saying it with such familiarity too, like it was his own grandmother's name. He wondered where exactly, and how, Moses had heard the name. If he had overhead it or if she had told him herself. The way her mouth had opened, how the tongue had licked the roof of the mouth when she said the –li part. The texture of the voice.

All three of them had by now climbed down from the back and were moving toward the hill. She and the midget were talking in their language, but they were not spitting. As if knowing it was the centre of attention, the hill raised its trunk toward the sky and trumpeted. She laughed and threw her arm around the midget. He gave the camera to Gloria and they struck a pose, the hill in the background. It trumpeted and trumpeted and trumpeted until Mukuka felt sick from the sound, until he thought he'd drown it. He looked down and swallowed bitter bile, felt it sear his insides.

***

It was around nine o'clock when they got back to Zambezi, and just over an hour after setting off. Moses turned the car around and parked in front of the reception. Doors opened behind them, and Mukuka heard her say, 'Thank you so much, this was just so very wonderful.' Her voice was enthused in a way that told him how her face was lit, how she was smiling. He knew she was expecting for him to turn around with his usual smile and usual small talk – glad you liked it madam, yes, it was great madam, you think so madam? – but he kept his shoulders stiffened and eyes trained ahead at the group of Asians boarding the blue minibus, perhaps headed for a city tour. If she thought he was her titisi, she would find out that he wasn't. He was Mukuka and he wasn't at Zambezi Lodge to please her. Mncccc. Mncccccccccccc.

'Hey hey hey boss, are you all right?' Moses said. Mukuka nodded, surprised by the question. What did this Moses mean, are you all right? Did he not look all right? Had he just said, mnccc, out loud? Sweat covered his forehead, trickled down the sides of his face. It made his shirt, the tailored shirt that people said went well with his complexion, that accentuated his chest, that he wore specifically for her after everything that happened yesterday, stick to his back. It was not a shirt he wore often; he would have to wash it first thing when he got back to Sonondo. He yawned a yawn that was not there.

'Ah, just tired my man. You know those writers partied late

last night, I hardly slept,' Mukuka said. Moses roared with laughter. Mukuka laughed along, but his was an uncertain, nervous laugh; he didn't know why Moses was laughing, which meant, therefore, that he didn't know why he himself was laughing. It felt like having earth in your mouth; it was not a good feeling.

'True that, we're all tired, boss,' Moses said. It was correct that Mukuka and a small group of workers had stayed up late tending to the partying writers. It had not been until three in the morning that he had finally climbed into bed, but it was not true that he was tired from it. He had in fact enjoyed himself and had been slightly disappointed to see the party break up when it did.

'I hear you. Tell you what, I'm off to Sonondo to pick up the cooks if you need a ride,' Moses said.

'Sure, great, thanks man,' Mukuka said.

'Fine-fine. Just wait here a minute. I want to know when I'm getting paid, I'm tired of this shit,' Moses said. He cut the ignition and jumped out of the car. By the time the door slammed he was already jogging toward Francis's office.

Mukuka shifted seats without getting out of the vehicle. Once he settled behind the wheel he reached for the steering and held on for a brief moment before releasing the brake and turning the ignition. The car slowly inched forward. His hands shook. At the gate the new guard waved from his shade. He waved back. He could see Moses from the side mirror now – he was running, his long arms flailing wildly. He couldn't hear him, but he knew he was shouting and telling him to stop. He didn't. The car picked up speed, made a right at the fence, and he was on the dusty main road. It stretched like a red belt in front of him. Tall, tall grass grew on both sides of the road, and it was green as far as he could see. He barrelled on.

He passed villas on the right, the round brick enclosure where they kept the elephant overnight, the lone petrol pump next to it. He passed the caretakers' houses, passed the small church that he'd never set foot in, passed the children's playing field with the lone see-saw, passed the sign that led to the dairy farm. Then he was done with houses and it was green again. His hands had long ceased shaking and he felt in charge behind the wheel. He had not known until then how much he needed the speed, needed the red dusty road racing to meet him, needed the warm wind rushing in through the windows. It felt like flying.

He thought of the first time he'd seen her. How she must have read his name from his nametag because she greeted him with his name pronounced so perfectly, like she'd said it all her life. He thought of that day when he'd saved her from the rain. Of answering her questions about the wild fruits they sometimes served for breakfast. Of giving her the emerald necklace that his sister made. Of teaching her how to say hello in his language, of waiting for her to finish crying under the table just yesterday. He thought of all these things until there was a ringing in his head, until he could see her face as clearly as if she were sitting right there by his side. Which would have been something, her sitting right there by his side while he was driving like this, flying like this. Just the two of them and nobody else. Not the midget, not Gloria, not that talkative idiot, Moses. But she was not there seated by his side, and he did not want her there anyway, sitting with him, not now that he knew the kind of person she was.

'You think. If you think you can just play with people,' he said to her face. He was shouting above the engine noise, and his voice filled his ears.

'Playing with people's heads like that, wasting people's time,' he said. The car's wheels mauled the road. He clutched the steering tighter, licked sweat off his upper lip.

'When all along you know what you're doing. Mnccc. Not even pretty to begin with, just who do you think you are?' he said. He gassed the car harder and flew and flew. He knew now that the biggest mistake he had made was being extra nice to her. Yes, being kind. For instance, he shouldn't have checked in on her yesterday, shouldn't have even stayed with her all that time she was under that table, bawling like a spoilt, silly child; he should have just abandoned her like she deserved, mnccc. Mnccccccccccccc.

He could see the cloud of dust boiling toward him, but at first he was so deeply engrossed in her face, in what he was saying to her, that he didn't really register what it was. He barrelled toward it. It was only when the enormous white head appeared, the horn honking wildly that Mukuka's stomach lurched and a sudden terror seized him. He immediately swung to the right of the narrow road and gradually applied the brakes, struggling to keep control of the belting car. He wasn't sure he was going to make it, and this thought terrified him all over again. His mind stampeded.

Long after the two cars zipped past each other, he pulled over, cut the engine, and gingerly stepped out. The air was so hot it shocked him, the smell of dust so strong he could taste it in his mouth. The ground felt unsteady beneath his feet and he stood still, but because he still felt dizzy he had to sit down. Heat seeped through his thin trousers and seared his skin. He listened to it spread and spread until he could feel it in his bones, until his blood warmed up, until his insides began to melt, until the urge to cry seized him.

NoViolet Bulawayo is the author of the novel *We Need New Names*. She won the Caine Prize for African Writing in 2011. She grew up in Zimbabwe, and currently lives in Oakland, California.

Koba Umwine – Peel It Yourself

Chilufya Chilangwa

Mumbi climbed out of bed and sat at the dresser, looking at herself in the mirror. The cuts on her lip and left cheek were still bleeding. She grabbed a tissue from the box on the table and gently dabbed her wounds. She could see her husband's back, reflected in the mirror, as he sat hunched over at the edge of the bed and ran his hands over his clean-shaven head. She turned her eyes back to herself. Her mother was going to be disappointed.

With unsteady hands she mixed her foundation and concealer in her palm, then realized that she had forgotten to ice her wounds. She took the ice cubes from the bar fridge and grabbed the hand towel from the bathroom. No one needed to know what had happened today. She held the ice against her cheek and with the other hand she combed her fingers through her untamed curls. Then licked her thumb and wiped the smudged eyeliner under her eyes. She swallowed hard and fought the tears back. If she cried it would make a mess of things again. She switched the ice from her cheek to her lip. With the other hand she dusted her dress. There was nothing on her dress. She straightened her back. She blinked tears away.

She wished she could turn back the clock and undo the affair. Having an affair was normal around her people. She knew her father had them. Their pastor at church had them.

Their neighbour whose husband travelled a lot had them. She never really knew why, until no one wanted to listen to her when she started having wedding jitters. Her maid of honour, Selina, her childhood friend, didn't hear her. Selina heard her mention something about the stress of choosing the bridesmaid dresses. Selina's response, a hug. Selina then promised she would sit the girls down and she was sure they would compromise. She tried to bring it up with her mother. Several times. Like that time when she finally caught her mother alone in the wedding hall. She was waiting for the florist.

'Mum?'

'Yes, darling.'

'What was it like when you were getting married?'

'What do you mean, my love?'

'I mean, were you nervous... anxious maybe?'

'Oh God yes! I was terrified!'

'But how did you know that Dad was the right one for you?'

'I always knew your father was the one. I knew because...' her mother's thoughts were interrupted by the florist's entrance. 'What's this?!?'

'Your flowers, madam.'

'No they are not! I ordered lavenders!' her mother raged. She threw her arms up and began to cry. 'Why, why? My daughter's wedding is ruined.' Was her mother really crying? Yes. She was. Mumbi stepped back and watched. The wedding planner sprinted in. He calmly convinced her mother that it was a beautiful accident to have luscious plum flowers and not lavender.

She had then thought about talking to her father. When she did, she realized it was a big mistake. He was not objective. He was more concerned about how he was going to introduce his future son-in-law – a son of 'the help' – to his elite friends.

She switched the towel from her lip to her cheek again and flinched. It stung. Why did she do it? What a stupid question. She knew exactly why she did it. The stress of the wedding was too much. The first time she had sex with her lover, it was three weeks before the wedding. It was in her parents' house, in the guest bathroom. That had always been her favourite secret hiding place for everything.

She removed the towel and looked at the swelling on her face and was glad to see that there was some improvement. She went back into the bedroom and sat at the dressing table. She caught her husband's reflection in the mirror. He was still sitting in the same spot as before. She was afraid to think of what was going through his mind... no, his heart. He started crying quietly and got up without saying a word. As he left the honeymoon suite she called out to him:

'Where are you going?'

He didn't answer.

Where was he going? Had he left her? In a panic, she rummaged through her handbag for her phone and was taken aback when a sudden 'hello' came from the other line after just two rings. She had hoped it would ring longer. She hadn't rehearsed or structured her thoughts properly yet. When she finally found her voice, it was the little voice that she hadn't heard in a long time.

'Mummy? I think Temwani has left me.'

'What are you talking about? Did you have an argument?'

'Yes.'

'What happened?'

'Oh Mummy, it's all my fault!' she cried.

'What happened?'

'I was with Richard. I have been with Richard for the past few weeks.'

'What?'

'But I went to tell him it was over! The night before the wedding I went to see him. I told him it was over. He didn't want to hear of it. Next thing I knew, Richard called me this morning and said he was here. In Zanzibar. He had taken the next flight after ours and is here, in the same hotel! So I went to see him and tell him that I was serious about us being over. He still didn't want to listen. He got upset and next thing I knew…'

The image flashed. His jagged gold ring had torn into her left cheek. She flew and caught her lip on the corner of the table.

'He hit me,' she finally said.

'What!' Her mother was astounded.

'Don't worry, Mummy. I got away.'

'Oh my God.'

'I'm fine. I have iced it down and it's better now.'

'I am so sorry, my child. I am so sorry.' Her mother's voice broke.

'I really do love Temwani, Mummy. I really do. Please tell me how to get him back.'

Her mother was still astounded.

'Mummy?'

'Yes, yes… I am still here.'

'Please tell me what to do.'

'Uh… um… give me a moment, my love. Give me a moment.' The mother held the receiver away from her face. She took a deep breath. She exhaled. Her head swooned. She had to sit down. She shut the door. Pulled up a chair and sat down. 'Okay. I am here. Why Richard? I don't understand.'

'I don't know. I got scared. The girls were gossiping about me choosing to marry Temwani. Dad doesn't like him either. It is hard, Mummy.'

She remembered how her friends excluded him from conversations. When they included him, it was to mock him.

'Of course it's hard to please everyone, my child.'

'I started having doubts about marrying him. I didn't know who to talk to. Things were moving fast. All the aunties and grannies were so excited. I didn't want to disappoint anyone.'

'Why didn't you come to me?'

'I did! Then I realized how much time and money you and Dad had spent on the wedding. It wouldn't have been fair.'

A sharp pain struck her mother in her chest.

'I am so sorry. But why Richard?'

'I don't know. He was there. He listened. Then it just happened.'

'Okay... Okay. I understand.'

There was a moment of silence. Her mother had to be careful of what she would say next. 'You have to get your love priority in order.'

'What do you mean?'

'Stop listening to other people. They can't tell you who to love. They will mess you up. Your grandfather always used to say to me, *Icupo kapapa ka pa mulomo. Koba umwine.* For a very long time, I didn't understand what it meant. I only understood it when your father started to have an affair. Too many people began to interfere. They wanted to fix my marriage for me. Even though they were doing it out of love, it wasn't theirs to fix. Marriage is like a small dry skin on the lip that needs to be peeled off. Ultimately, it is better peeled off by the person concerned. Another person would peel the small skin the wrong way, and in the process make it worse.'

Mumbi listened. She regretted taking her mother for granted over the years. Her mother wasn't disappointed in her.

***

He knew her angry footsteps. What did he do now? She threw the door of his study open and went and stood over his desk with folded arms. Her slender frame overpowered him.

'What the hell have you done? Are you trying to kill our daughter?'

'What are you talking about?'

'Your daughter has just called me. She was in tears about her marriage. I don't know what you are playing about here. I know you instigated everything.'

'You are already accusing me of something I don't know about. Slow down and tell me exactly what happened.'

She took a deep breath and relayed her conversation with her daughter to him.

'You hired that boy to interfere in their marriage, didn't you?'

'Oh my God. Is she okay?'

'Don't avoid the question. Did you or did you not hire Richard?'

He stood up from his desk. The realization of his uncalculated risk dawned on him.

'You did, didn't you?'

'Leave me alone. I need to think.' He waved her away and started pacing.

'Answer me! Did you, or did you not do it?'

'Honestly, do you *really* want our daughter to marry a son of "the help"?'

'Weren't you listening to me? It was Richard who beat our daughter. Not Temwani.'

'Agh, I don't believe you.'

'Our daughter is not the first girl Richard has beaten, you know. That's why I believe her. I want you to put an end to this now! Make sure that boy doesn't ever come near our daughter again.'

He sat back down at his desk. He put his head in his hands.

'Are you listening to me?'

'Ya, ya. Okay.' He didn't look at her.

'I know you want the best for her, but why Richard?'

'I didn't know he was crazy. I just thought... He comes from the right family, you know? It would have been good for us. Easy to manage, you know? She deserves someone who can take care of her financially.' He stood up. 'Yaba.'

'Yes. Exactly. Yaba.'

'She had never come to me to talk about boys before. When she came to me about Temwani, I got excited. I told her how I felt. So I spoke to Richard's father.'

'In the middle of wedding preparations?'

'You should have seen her. She was so sad. Confused. I

wanted to fix it for her. Cancelling the wedding at the last minute would have been worth it. Richard's father was okay with it.'

'Of course Richard's father would have been okay with it. That boy is wild. They think marriage will settle him down.'

'Call his father and tell him to tell his son to stop harassing our daughter. Otherwise we will press charges.'

'Ya, ya. You are right. I will call him now.'

***

The day was coming to an end. People weaved around Temwani on the sidewalk. It was the cacophony of hooting minibuses and bustling call boys that made him realize that he had walked too far from his hotel. Although he didn't know where he was, the familiar sounds reminded him of his home town, Kitwe. He had been walking aimlessly. Now he took long strides as if he knew exactly where he was going. The fat, red, bold, luminous words 'The Place' over the entrance of a bar got his attention and, without hesitation, he went straight in and sat on a stool at the bar.

'Ah! My first customer. What can I get for you?' the middle-aged barmaid said with a melodious tone.

'I don't know. What do you recommend? Actually... I uh... I don't drink...' He felt uncertain. 'I mean, I want to drink, but this is my first time to have a drink... Can you recommend something?'

'Oooh, a virgin to the bottle, I see!' She gave him a wide smile. 'I know just the drink for you. Aunty Rosie will take good care of you this evening.'

She poured him a drink in a shot glass, and nodded at him. Hesitantly, he reached for the small glass and put his lips to it to take the first sip.

'Uh-uh.' She shook her head. 'One quick shot, my child.'

He looked at her with uncertainty, but then he decided to trust her. He sat up straight in his chair and quickly tossed his drink back. Instantly he felt the back of his throat and chest burn. He coughed and banged his fist on his chest.

She laughed.

'You see. Aunty Rosie knows.' She refilled his glass. 'So what girl drove you to have your first drink?'

He frowned at her question.

'This one you drink slowly, okay?'

He nodded obediently and sipped his drink. It was only then that he noticed that under a light in the corner of the bar was a pianist playing a sombre blues tune he had never heard before. It reminded him of the tune he heard on the radio when they drove home from her parents' house after their first meeting about their wedding preparations. It had been a quiet ride. She had looked out her window the whole way. When he had asked her if she was okay, she had given a rapid nod and smile. 'Mhm,' she had said. Then she had looked straight back out the window again. She had also had the same looming sadness throughout the wedding preparations.

Then their honeymoon. She said she was going out to get something from the shops. She came back with bruises on her face.

Three weeks! How? How could he have missed the signs?

He tossed back his drink. Rosie refilled his glass.

Nothing was clear any more. He traced his thoughts back to where he wanted to be and hoped it would change the scenario of where they were today. He thought about their nothing days when they would sit on her large balcony cuddling each other and sipping tea while watching the sunset. Each time they would do that, he envisioned that they would have their own house with their lifetime of nothing days. He wanted it to be like the way it was when they met at the beginning of the mango season. Now the sweet smell of the mango season was going to give him a sour taste and painful tightness in his belly.

He looked into his drink. It danced before him and he tried to steady it with his eyes.

'Tell me,' he began, 'what makes a man want to hit a woman? I don't understand that.' Rosie looked at him with bottle in hand. He then realized he had spoken aloud.

'You know, I was married once,' Rosie said. 'He's the one who left me this bar. He was a good man. He took care of me and my children. That was the most important thing.' He shifted slightly in his seat with uneasiness and cleared his throat. He put some money on the bar. Gave Rosie a broken smile.

'Thank you,' he said.

***

Mumbi took a shower and slipped on a floral printed dress that Temwani liked. She sat on the side of the bed facing the door of the room and waited for him. She remembered the night she finally decided he had been the right choice for her. It was a couple of days before the wedding. She was sitting on the balcony of her apartment. She was conflicted. She heard him come in. He sat down next to her.

'Look at what I got for you.' He pulled out of his pocket two medium-sized mangos.

'Where did you get those? It's not even mango season yet.'

'My colleague just got back from a trip to India where it is still mango season.' She had laughed at the absurdity of him carrying two mangos in his pocket.

Where could he be? She got up to look out the window, but there wasn't much for her to see from the fifth floor. It was dark now. The sporadic dotted lamp posts barely lit the sidewalk. She walked over to the mirror to check her make-up. It was still flawless. She remembered the expression her mother had used earlier – *Koba umwine. Peel it yourself, my child. Anyone else would make it worse.* Her mother's words ran through her head. She didn't talk to her like a child any more. She talked to her like a woman.

Where was he? She got up again, glanced at her watch and

looked out the window. She went back and sat waiting for him. As the night wore on, she became tired and, just when she decided to lie down, Temwani walked in. She quickly sat up. They stared at each other for a moment. He sat down next to her and suddenly became weary from the long day.

'I am so sorry,' she said brokenly.

'I know.' There was another long wave of silence. He untied his shoes. 'I am tired.' He got up and started getting ready for bed.

That night, he feigned sleeping and thought about why she chose Richard. He turned over to watch her sleep and he wondered whether Richard was a better lover than him. He looked at her bruises and realized that he didn't do enough to protect her. He had failed her as a husband.

Unexpectedly, she opened her eyes and she caught him watching her sleep. They stared at each other. For a long moment they reflected each other's brokenness. He caressed her cheek with the back of his hand and gently ran his finger over the cut on her lip. She wrapped her arm around him. He responded. He pulled her in and hugged her tightly. Although the pain of what she had done was still there, he still loved her. He continued to nestle her in his arms until they both drifted into a long, restful, deep sleep.

Chilufya Chilangwa grew up in Amman, Jordan, where her father worked for the United Nations. She studied English Literature at Albright College in the US then moved to Johannesburg, South Africa, where she worked in the film and video industry for two and half years, before returning home to Zambia. After ten years working there as an independent editor, writer and communications consultant in the development sector, she shifted to providing investment services for international companies wanting to come to Zambia, and staff training for local business houses. She has been a contributing writer for various business publications and newspapers, has self-published a novel, *Remember the African Skies,* and currently supports independent Zambian writers as an editor.

The Goat

Tope Folarin

Our father lifts his axe into the air and brings it down heavily onto the goat's neck. A lush curtain of blood gushes down from the wound, muscles and tendons peeking out before tumbling into the grass. As the blood rushes out, our father snaps one of its legs. And then the other.

The goat convulses on its side in the middle of our backyard. It is bleating in muffled terror through a gag that our father placed around its mouth just a few minutes ago. The gag is so tight that it has stretched the goat's mouth into an evil caricature of a smile. A smile now refuted by a bleeding frown a few inches below.

Our uncle is laughing and jumping but we are horrified. We can't help it – we begin to cry, softly. Our father tells us to shut up. He wipes his face quickly, but not quickly enough. We have already seen his tears. 'What did I tell you before?' he screams. 'This is supposed to be a moment of joy!'

Yes, he told us this before, as we were planning how we would capture it. He told us that its life had been created for this purpose. He told us that God doesn't have to provide us with any justifications for His commandments, that our only responsibility is to follow His will. We screamed and cried and refused to help him, we told him we would never do what he had asked us to do, but in the end we obeyed him, because he is our father and he is a man of God. Yet now we know that we have made a terrible mistake. We have done something evil. It seems as if our father realizes this as well – his eyes are red and brimming. He rubs them and turns away from us.

The goat won't stop dying. It tries to wheeze the last notes of its life through its gag, but it is choking on the long tongues of blood that are violently ejaculated from its second mouth with each ragged breath. The tongues lap at our feet.

After a few minutes death finally comes. A shuddering last breath and it's over.

We stand silent for a bit, trying to remind ourselves what our father said when he woke us up this morning. That by doing this we are proving our faith and our commitment to God. That everything would be easier if we just thought of him as a goat. Dad drops his axe and glares at us. Trance broken, we pull on our gloves and aprons and collect the blades and buckets from the stoop.

Our hands will not stop shaking. We start with blades on its skin, cutting away the hair, so slowly, so carefully. Our father makes a long vertical cut from the second mouth to the anus. Something stinks, something is putrid and rotting, and then the steaming innards slide out. We bend and dump the gunk into our buckets. We go to work on the stuff in the buckets, cleaning everything; our father told us this morning that nothing can be thrown away, or none of this will work. Our father and our uncle continue working on the animal, methodically breaking it down. Our mother watches us from the window – she is saying something, no, she is screaming something but we cannot hear a single word because the window is closed.

***

My brothers say I eat too much.

Mom shakes her head as she places another pancake on my plate. 'That is the last one. OK? You've already had five.' She tugs at my ear. 'All this food you are eating, I don't know where it is going.'

'Five is definitely not enough for him,' says Dele.

'Yeah, he's like a monster or something,' says Seun.

They are twins, so they are always saying the same thing, always agreeing with each other, always double-teaming me and everyone else. In other words, they are annoying as hell.

Mom chuckles. 'And so? Both of you should mind your business. No one is talking to you. Let him eat. That is what makes him happy.'

Yes, I love to eat – anything. I am the family garbage disposal, a walking trashcan, and I'm still the skinniest kid in school, probably the skinniest kid in the city.

Just a few months ago, on the stern advice of my doctor, I went on a 3,000-calorie diet over the summer before trying out for the basketball team. Dr Kolson checked my reflexes, my blood pressure, placed his cool hands on my back, asked me to cough, and did a double-take when I told him my plans for the following school year.

'Well, son,' he said, pulling his glasses down his nose. 'You're going to have to gain some weight.'

Mom supported the idea, and Dad quietly acquiesced, so they bought me several boxes of power bars, and – on Dr Kolson's strict orders – I gorged myself on six meals a day all summer long. I'd never been happier. At the end of the summer, I stepped on a scale and, of course, a net loss of three pounds.

I polish off my pancake in about three seconds and join Mom at the stove. 'Please,' I say. I give her my best smile. The one she cannot resist. 'Just one more. I promise.' This is our Saturday morning ritual. After my fifth pancake I come and see her at the stove, and she'll make another one, and I'll devour it, and then another, and then another. Usually I eat ten pancakes. Sometimes more.

Mom's wearing one of her flowing fluorescent wrappers, and she looks over at Dad as she tucks in an unravelling edge. Dad turns a page in his Bible. The sun is streaming in from the kitchen window onto the table and his tired face. He hasn't said a word to me, to anyone this morning. A stack of pancakes sits uneaten next to his arm.

'That is all for now,' she says. 'Lunch is coming soon. Try to be patient.' She turns away from me.

For a moment all I feel is anger washing through me, for a moment I am actually full, this anger is so satisfying, but then my stomach begins to growl, loudly, insistently. I place my plate in the sink, go up to my bedroom and close the door.

***

'Can I come in?' the voice says. It's Mom.

'Yes, Ma.'

Mom opens the door and surveys my room. My *Star Trek: The Next Generation* poster on the wall, my slim bookshelf filled with my favourite fantasy novels, my unmade bed on the floor. I am sitting next to the bookshelf, bouncing a tennis ball off the wall.

'Can I come sit next to you?'

'Yes, Ma.'

Mom strides over and sits. She leans against me, and I can smell her hair. It smells earthy and brown, and I realize that I haven't smelled her hair in years. Now a rush of memories – my small arms around her hot neck; she's leaning close and rubbing her nose against mine; she's tickling my neck after whispering in my ear.

'I am sorry about earlier,' she says. 'I know you are still hungry. I am already preparing lunch.'

'It's OK.'

'That is actually the reason I came to see you.' She takes the ball from my hand. She tosses it into the air, catches it, tosses it again. Then she places it on the floor. She clears her throat.

'I know this will be difficult, but you need to find a way to eat less.'

'Ma?'

'You need to eat less food.'

'Why?'

Mom pauses.

'I can't tell you why. But trust me that it is for your own good.'

She stands and walks over to my bed. She sits. She looks down for a moment, and when she looks up her eyes are red, tears beading at the corners. 'Please, my son,' she says. 'Try to find the strength to eat less. Especially around your father. If you get too hungry, you can tell me and I will try to find something for you. But it is important that from today you find a way to be satisfied with what I feed you.' She leans towards me and grabs my hand. 'This is very, very important. Can you promise me that you will at least try? Can you try for your mother?'

She seems frantic now. I am bewildered. But I cannot stand to see my mother upset.

'Yes, Ma. I will try.'

'Yes, my son. Just do it for me. Just for a little bit. I love you so much.'

She hugs me and her shoulders are shaking and I rub her back like she once rubbed mine, in those days before I could walk or talk.

In those days before I consciously made promises I know I can never keep.

***

My father is a prophet.

God speaks to him all the time. God told him that Mr Parker, our mailman, had cancer. One day my father told Mr Parker to go see his doctor about his colon, and a few days later Mr Parker returned with his wife, and she would not stop hugging my father, she would not stop crying, she would not stop thanking my father for saving his life.

God told him that the Challenger would fall from the sky. I will never forget that morning, my entire family gathered around the television, the Challenger rising so beautifully into the air, my heart soaring with it, and then my father saying it is going to explode, it is going to explode, and I look back at my father with horror on my face, then back at the screen, praying that he's wrong, and then that beautiful white blip detonates and dissolves, a trail of fire in the sky, and I can't stand to look any longer, instead I look at my father, with hatred now, because something tells me he willed this into existence.

God told him that my uncle would be born retarded. My father has told us many times how he told his own mother that God was going to punish her because she refused to find another husband after her first husband – my grandfather – died. Because she abandoned my father and woke up in a new man's bed every morning. When she discovered she was pregnant she remained home, and her mother came by each day and fussed over her, did anything she asked, and her sisters hugged her close and read stories to her growing stomach. For the most part my father ignored her – the few times he spoke to her he told her she would be having a boy, and that the boy's brain would never function properly. She cursed at my father, told him to leave her alone, and then her waters broke and her family rushed her to the hospital and she returned home with a beautiful boy whose eyes were too far apart, whose mouth was locked in a permanent smile.

My father is not a prophet. God did not tell him that each of his businesses – including his computer business, his shoe business, his grocery store, his electronics store, his furniture store, his Nigerian clothes import-export business, his Nigerian news magazine – would fail.

God did not tell him that Mandela would leave prison one day. Whenever we heard about South Africa on the news, heard about how the world was applying pressure to the government of South Africa to release Mandela, my father would say it will never happen, it will never happen, Mandela will die in prison. He said this on the day we saw Mandela

Leabharlanna Fhine Gall

walk out of prison, looking older than we ever could have imagined; even as Mandela raised his fist in the air my father said it will never happen. To this day my father believes that Mandela died in the Seventies, that the man who left prison that day was an imposter.

God did not tell him that his mother would die. I'm not sure if my father ever believed she would die. One day he heard she was sick and he purchased a gold cross and prayed over it for three days. He sent the cross to her by express mail, and the following week his sister called and told him she had passed away. My father shook his head and hung up the phone and continued watching TV as if nothing had happened.

God did not tell my father that he would struggle so much in America. My father still can't believe that we are so poor. He still believes that our lives aren't real, that any day now he will wake up in a mansion with a squadron of luxury cars outside, hundreds of gold bars piled neatly under his bed.

If you ask my father about these things he will tell you that God has never lied. Someone will step forward and say that Mandela died in prison. His mother will poke out of her grave and visit us in America. My father will be wealthier than anyone who has ever lived.

***

Dad's sitting at the table when I get to the kitchen, almost like he's been waiting for me.

'I guess it's time for your nightly cookie,' he says.

Before I can deny it, or offer an excuse, Dad shakes his head. 'Don't worry, it's fine,' he says. 'Go get a couple, and get one for me as well.'

I wonder how long he's known. For the past year I've been sneaking cookies out of the kitchen every night, around midnight or so. I started doing this after I turned 16. Around then I noticed that my constant, gnawing hunger had only grown worse. It no longer mattered how much I ate during dinner; at midnight I'd wake up to my growling stomach, and I'd spend the rest of the night staring at the ceiling, waiting for the sun to rise so I could eat again. After a few days of this I decided that I'd steal a cookie or two out of the pantry at night, after everyone was asleep. I decided to do this even though my father once told me that my hunger is a burden I will have to bear for the rest of my life. That I would prove my worthiness to God if I learned how to control it. 'God gives each of us a weakness so that we have a chance to draw closer to Him,' he told me. I must have been nine or ten. 'Your weakness is your hunger. If you can learn to overcome it, you will be proving to God that your devotion to him is more important than your greatest temptation. And He will reward you greatly.'

For many years afterwards I repeated these words to myself at night, like it was my mantra, like it was a prayer, as my stomach knotted up and consumed itself. For a while these words were enough. But then I turned 16 and my hunger was threatening to become the most important part of me. I decided to do something about it. Just one or two cookies each night. Consumed quietly in the comfort of my bed.

Even after what Mom told me a few days ago I cannot stop. I cannot.

Now I go to the cupboard and pull three chocolate-chip cookies from the package on the top shelf. I pass one to Dad and sit across from him. He shoves it into his mouth. 'Come on, eat up,' he says.

I wonder if this is a test. Maybe he wants to see if I'll actually eat the cookies in front of him. If I will sin in his presence. I sit silently while he munches. When he finishes he asks me to pass him another one. 'And finish that one in your hand,' he says. 'I promise I won't bite you.'

I slip the cookie into my mouth and eat it. It doesn't taste as good as it does when I'm by myself. After I've finished it I wait for that surge of relief to pulse through me but it never comes.

My father rises and walks to the window.

'God has never led me astray,' he says. 'Never. Not once. Even when I think he's wrong. Even when I doubt His power and wisdom, He proves me wrong. But this thing that God has asked me to do now – it is too much.'

He's facing the window, so I can't tell if he's serious or not.

'Dad, I don't think I heard you.'

'Yes you did.'

God asking too much? I don't know what to say. This cannot be my father. My father who prays at least ten times a day. My father who insists that we attend church four times a week. My father who once banned us from watching anything but Christian television for a year. My father who instantly decided to marry my mother after she recited the first chapter of Psalms from memory during their first date. My father who fasts for days at a time, sometimes weeks, because, he says, God told him to.

I've never seen my father this unsure of himself before.

What has God asked him to do?

My father remains where he is. I don't say a word.

I shrug. 'Well, you've always told me to trust God, no matter what.'

Dad turns from the window and smiles at me. Then he returns to the table.

'Did I ever tell you that you were a miracle baby?' he says.

'No.'

'Ah. I guess I was waiting until you were a man. I might as well tell you now.'

He closes his eyes. 'When your mother was about five months pregnant we went to the hospital for a routine check-up. The moment the doctor placed the stethoscope on her stomach I could tell that something was wrong. The doctor turned on some machines and attached some wires to your mother and called some other doctors in. She didn't answer any of our questions. About half an hour later she told us that your heart had stopped beating.'

My father pauses. He licks a finger and presses it to the table. When he lifts it I can see that a few crumbs are attached. He slips the finger into his mouth and continues.

'Before your mother became pregnant with you she'd had five miscarriages. She had never carried a child for more than three months. When you got to four months I knew that you were meant to live. That you were our blessing. So when the doctor told me that your heart had stopped beating I smiled at her and told her that I respected her opinion, but that I answered to a higher power. Then I grabbed your mother's hand and we went to the car and I began to drive. We drove for about an hour, and then the car broke down. Your mother asked me where we were going. I ignored her. I got out of the car and fixed it and started driving again. Your mother started screaming at me, telling me that she wanted to go back home, that she needed some time to mourn. I told her that no one would be mourning anything. I continued to drive. By the time the car broke down again she had fallen asleep. I fixed the car once more and continued driving. Four hours later we arrived at the church where I was saved. I woke up your mother and we walked out of the car, and I knocked on the door until the pastor opened it. When he saw my face he knew what was happening.'

My father is smiling now, and I feel like something is expanding inside me.

'I thought the prayer would take hours and hours, but my pastor just laid his hands on her stomach and prayed for only a few minutes. And then he looked at me and said it was done. And though I have often doubted God's ability to do the impossible, at that moment I knew that you had been healed.' My father shakes his head. 'The pastor told me that you were the key to the success of this family. That you would serve a special purpose in our lives. And I believed him. I knew you would.'

My father rises, wipes his face with the back of his hand.

'So whatever happens, always remember that you are here

for a reason. Your purpose was preordained.' My father leans forward and kisses my forehead, something he's never done before. Then he walks up the stairs.

After a few moments I shut off the light and go to my room and slip under the covers.

My stomach is silent. I feel full, so so full.

***

Before last week I'd never heard Mom and Dad scream at each other. Before last week, whenever they were upset with each other, they'd exchange a look and disappear into their room for an hour or so, and when they emerged they'd smile at each other and the rest of us with their entire bodies. Last week, though, Mom said something to Dad, or maybe Dad said something to Mom, and they stomped off to their room and slammed the door and screamed at each other in Yoruba for almost two hours. After they finished they left their room separately, first Dad, then Mom. They ignored each other for the rest of the day.

This happened again the next day. And the next.

Now all they do is fight. Anywhere. Everywhere. They slam plates and slam doors and slam each other with their words. Dele says they are arguing about God. Seun says they are arguing about life and death. I'm not sure what they're arguing about – my Yoruba is OK, I guess, but for some reason Dele and Seun have always understood Yoruba better than me, even though they are younger, even though we were all born in the States. All I know for sure is that Mom is feeding me less and less. Last Saturday she prepared only four pancakes for me. There are no more cookies in the cupboard. Mom says I can't snack between meals any more.

I've never been this hungry in my life.

Two nights ago Mom came into my room and sat on my bed. I know it was her because I opened my eyes just a little when she walked in. She stroked my hair and kept stroking it. She said a prayer over me – I could not hear her words. Then she whispered something in my ear, like she used to when I was little. She said I will always be with you.

***

Dad says: 'Go. Chase them.'

My brothers and I stand, dumb, glancing at one another, and Dad says 'Go on.'

Uncle is laughing and clapping his hands. Dad's expression does not change. I don't think I've ever seen him so serious before.

'This is what my brothers and I did when we were your age. Your grandfather made us earn our food. All of you have been too spoiled by America. You can just go to the store and buy bread. You can just go to a machine and buy candy. That is why you don't value your food. It is not your fault. There is just too much here.'

And when he says 'here' he lifts his hands, indicating – I guess – the sky, the grass, the farm, the sun, the goats. Uncle nods solemnly, as if he's just heard someone deliver an acceptance speech for the Nobel, even though we've all heard this speech about a million times. About once every three or four months Dad drives us to some random farm somewhere, and he gives the same speech before asking us to milk some cows or feed some hens or pluck a few fat red apples from a tree. We've never had to chase any animals, though. Dele and Seun immediately assume a runner's stance but I don't move. I have my maturity to defend after all; I'm too old to be chasing a bunch of dirty-ass goats. I stare at the ground, but I know that Dad is losing patience, charm exhausted, giving me his better-do-it-or-I-will-embarrass-you-in-public look. Which, considering where we are, is kind of ironic. My father isn't into irony. I lean forward and place my hands on the ground, like Carl Lewis.

'More like it,' Dad says. 'So here are the rules: This isn't just about the chasing. The first to catch a goat and tackle it to the ground wins.'

'Wins what?' I ask, petulantly.

Dad says, mysteriously: 'You'll see.'

He lifts his head slightly: 'ON YOUR MARKS!'

I sense my brothers at the edges of my peripheral vision, just far enough out so that I can't really see them, but I can feel them lurking, waiting for an opportunity to burst onto my field of sight.

'GET SET!'

The goats start rustling; maybe they notice the tension in our legs.

'GO!!!'

The goats immediately scatter; we chase them for five solid minutes, probably looking quite goatish ourselves, while Dad and Uncle yell directions at us. The goats are quick, cutting from one direction to another in an instant, kicking the air with their hind legs when they sense that we are close.

Dad says USE YOUR BRAINS, NOT YOUR LEGS! and I examine my surroundings for the first time. There's a large chain-link fence bordering the field, and the goats – only three of them – are basically running from one end to the other, and sometimes through us as if we're in the way. I focus on the goat directly in front of me. It has mottled black-and-grey fur, and is shooting shit pellets at me with every step. I stop to catch my breath and Dad says NO STOPPING so I jog while trying to formulate a plan. I figure if I can somehow chase the goat into the fence, angle it in a certain direction, I can pounce just as it's about to turn. I experiment with this approach, I run hard at the goat and try to force it towards the fence, but the goat catches on to my plan after a few seconds, and now it will only run parallel to the fence. Dad yells NICE TRY, SON.

Another plan. I slow down, almost to a walk, and try to lull the goat into thinking I'm tired. The damn goat figures out what I'm doing before I can start sprinting again, though, and runs even faster.

GETTING TIRED? Dad asks, and Uncle begins to laugh once more.

I drop all the intellectual pretence and began running full-throttle at the goat in front of me. The goat looks back and for the first time I see fear in its eyes. I keep running, imagining the ground as a massive trampoline, trying to leap forward with each step. I gain on the goat and keep going and keep going. Just as I'm about to jump on the goat and tackle it to the ground, I look back and notice that Dad is chasing me. I laugh, enjoying the surprise, executing sharp cuts in the dirt, turning suddenly to the left when Dad tries to cut me off, threatening him constantly with my high back kick. I look back again and see my father breathing hard, wheezing, and I laugh louder, run faster, I'm gaining strength, the goats are my friends now. I feel the wind resisting my face and arms, but the running is glorious. I hear someone grunt and look back again; Uncle's chasing me too, I laugh harder while evading, dodging, cutting, wondering why is he using his arms like that? So awkward, so ungainly, almost as if he's never run before, for the two seconds I see him running he has already pushed himself to the edge of exhaustion.

I dodge again. Uncle and Dad try to work together, they try to trap me in a corner, and when they're about to jump I bolt between them, galloping triumphantly away, sticking my tongue out at them, I run, run, run. Dad and Uncle finally stop, they're grabbing their knees and panting at the ground, and I stop too, pointing and laughing, jumping up and down with excitement, and someone kicks me hard in the small of my back. The air is evacuating my lungs as I collapse, and someone punches me in the ribs and slams my head into the ground. I feel my arms and legs being tied together and I hear Seun yelling I GOT HIM! I GOT HIM! Dad says GOOD JOB, SON, I'M PROUD OF YOU and lifts me into the air. Someone punches me hard in my kidney. What is happening? Why are they doing this? I'm terrified, I don't know if this is a game. What did I do wrong and why are they hurting me? Fists coming at me from every direction, someone spitting on my face, stabbing me with sharp metal. I GOT HIM, I GOT HIM, says Seun and I feel myself being lowered, hands violating every part of my body, and they swing me one, two, three times and throw me into the trunk of the station wagon.

***

Dad ignores me as I lie bleeding on the grass. Everything hurts. I want to apologize for whatever it is that I did wrong, to promise that I'll never sin again, but there is a gag in my mouth. I start to scream but my father ignores me. Seun and Dele are standing far away from me. They look terrified. Almost as terrified as me. Where is Mom? I try to scream her name. My father looks up at the sky. He keeps saying the same thing: ARE YOU SURE? ARE YOU SURE? ARE YOU SURE? ARE YOU SURE? ARE YOU SURE? Then he looks off to the side, wildly, like he is expecting someone to show up. No one does. My father is crying, his shoulders are heaving, he lifts his axe into the air and I close my eyes.

Tope Folarin won the Caine Prize for African Writing in 2013, and in 2014 he was named on the *Africa39* list of the most promising African writers under 39. In addition, his work has been published in various anthologies and journals. He lives in Washington DC.

Walking

Elnathan John

1

I have never been able to run. Even in secondary school, when I joined the boys to play football, there was always some relief when the ball went out for a throw-in or goal kick, so that I could catch my breath. I notice now how the older men clinging onto health and vitality, jogging furiously on the same route I follow, regard my walking with a level of contempt. It has grown on me now, and the urgency of becoming less obese has diminished any consequence these stares may have had. Most days, I listen to Adele. I know. A grown man, walking to heartbreak songs. Adele puts a spring in my step and gives me a rhythm that seems to imbue the whole exercise with some meaning deeper than merely reducing the fat along my waistline and thighs and stomach and neck. Something transcendental almost.

Especially when I start out very early, I have learned to look down for mounds of faeces deposited under the cover of darkness by people living in temporary shacks and uncompleted buildings – and maybe even by police on night duty. The first time, I stepped right into one and had to cut short my morning walk, cursing under my breath all the way home.

2

The first time I see her, she is wearing a flimsy, stretched-out t-shirt with the inscription 'Papa Adieu 1949-2014'. The rest of the text is in a different, lighter colour – faded from washing. The t-shirt is skewed to the right, partly because of the sweat making it stick to the left part of her torso and partly because a bit of the t-shirt is stuck under the right strap of her bra. She is half running, half walking and I am wondering if her breasts jumping up and down with each step aren't making her uncomfortable. There is an earnestness in her eyes and her creased forehead and her pursed lips that make me think she is preparing for something momentous. She must want to get into a wedding dress, or get her man back from the wild, sticky arms of a fit, sexy woman, or from many women. Or god forbid, from another man. Not that I think there is hope once her husband has gone that way. Her eyes are fixed on the ground and, even though we pass each other twice, she does not raise her head. I giggle to myself when I realize I sucked in my belly when I got close.

3

There are things you cannot observe about a city unless you walk, things that will not manifest to anyone moving too quickly. Like all the manholes without covers that have become rubbish dumps. Like the boarded-up windows in one of the rooms of an uncompleted three-storey building. Like the anthills that seem freshly made every morning. Like the roots of trees that grow into fat horizontal veins and push up all the interlocking tiles on the sidewalks. Like the used condoms under trees in dark corners. Like the smashed-up side windows of cars which broke down at night and had to be left by the roadside until morning because it was too late to reach a mechanic.

4

Very early, there is a silver Mercedes on a quiet street – one of the few streets the other walkers and runners have not yet invaded. I am looking to see if the side windows are smashed – if the car stereo is missing or not. Then I see the hands, intertwined – one dark, one fair. I feel the muscles on my neck and face tighten and my teeth begin to grind.

> *I pick up a big stick and aim at their interlocked hands,*
> *hitting so hard that when they disengage, their flesh is all*
> *mashed up. So mashed up that neither of them can tell which*
> *bits of red falling flesh are theirs; so that the hands with*
> *which they prepare for their perversity are permanently put*
> *out of use.*

When their eyes meet mine, they stop. I walk away quickly.

5

I am about to replay Adele's 'Set Fire To The Rain' because
my mind strayed and I caught only the end of the song. I like
it loud and ignore the phone warning that setting the volume
higher is unsafe for my ears.

'Psst, Psst,' a small woman calls from behind a short back
fence with razor wire.

I look at her with the corner of my eye and see that she has
dropped something over the fence. I do not turn. I hope she
thinks that the earphones in my ear mean I cannot hear her.
I do not want to help her. I do not know why I do not want to
help her. She will have to go round the very long street to get
it. Perhaps someone will have taken it by the time she gets
here, whatever it is. A few houses away, I start to feel bad,
then quickly kill the thought and focus on the lyrics of the
song. I have just loaded phone credit. I debate in my head
whether to throw the recharge card on the floor or tuck it
in my pocket. Then I tell myself – more like another voice
inside me really – that if everyone flung out trash, the city
would be unbearable to live in. And I put the spent voucher
in my back pocket.

6

The woman who wears the Papa Adieu t-shirts – I realize
now she has more than one – is trying to fit into a wedding
dress. I am sure of it. She looks dehydrated today. Or maybe
she has lost weight from some extreme dieting. Like fat Lara,

my last girlfriend in polytechnic, who was determined to become slim before she left school for National Youth Service Corps, and started eating only carrots and water. One day she passed out and ended up in hospital for two weeks where she became depressed and ended up gaining ten kilos. *You have big bones,* her father would say. *You will always be fat. Accept it.* She never accepted it.

These days when people who knew Lara in university meet her, they comment on how thin she is. Not slim. Thin. And they all say to her, *You looked much finer when you were fat.* I wish now that I had lied to her when she asked the last time she called, *Do I look sick? One woman said that I look sick.*

I wish I hadn't said yes.

Today Papa Adieu woman looks up. She does not nod or smile or anything but her eyes cast a glance of recognition, of acknowledgement. I want to tell her that she looks like a scarecrow with huge breasts. She looked better with the flesh on, like fat Lara. I want to tell her she is also starting to look like a shrivelled potato and whatever diet she is on, she needs to be drinking more water and eating more fruit. But then, I also wish that my body was like hers – that in just two weeks of whatever she has been doing in addition to jogging, I could lose that much weight.

7

When skinny Myrlène says I am fat, half-complaining, but still rubbing my tummy and playing with the fat around my neck like those who complain about DSTV being the worst TV service but never fail to renew their subscriptions, I want to light a fire under her arm. Mostly, I want to say to her, you drink too much. Because that is not very different from what she is saying to me. I eat. She drinks. I get fat. She gets fucked up. I can burn this fat away. She cannot wish away all the relationships she has lost because she got too drunk and went home with someone else. She cannot get back the car she totalled last June. Okay, she *can* get a new one, but she cannot get *that* one back, the one she said she had a sentimental attachment to, because she got it off her mother who told her that, for a brief moment, in the months before her father's death, he had driven in that car.

The crash would've killed her if the airbags of her Highlander hadn't held her skinny frame in the seat. But I don't say any of that to her. Because, as free as her mouth is, she cannot handle tough words. She has been that way since my mother first introduced her as my cousin ten years ago. My uncle had had a baby with a Haitian woman he met in France when his company sent him on a six-month training course. He had disappeared but she tracked him down when she turned 21 and decided she wanted to live in Nigeria.

If you ask me my biggest motivation for walking, it will be a tie between shutting Myrlène up and wanting to be able to see my penis when I sit on the toilet seat.

8

Growing up, I did not know that it was possible to actively dislike one's sibling. I spent most of my childhood not hating Tersoo, because I thought that somehow, even if I wanted to, I could not. I couldn't *not* arrange to beat up Kenechukwu who bullied him for being like a girl, even though I probably thought worse of it than anyone did and glowered at each flailing of his arm, and each time he burst into tears. I couldn't *not* say yes when they asked if he was my brother each time he got in trouble, but I felt it in my chest that I did not want him to be my brother.

And now I spend my days choosing, even though I do not have to, making up for all the times I did not know I could. I *can* say hello to a stranger walking past me. Or not reply when they say hello to me.

I have chosen not to say hello to Papa Adieu woman, even if our now-familiar eyes meet.

9

I am getting bored with my route. I begin my walk two streets
away, east of my regular path. It is a street I have driven by
before but never walked on. It is quiet and the sidewalks are
dark even in daytime because of the huge umbrella trees that
hang low. There is a woman who has made a home on one
of the concrete slabs with what looks like a dozen flattened
cartons. It has just rained and everything around her looks
damp except the bold red wig she is wearing which I think
she took off when it was raining. The wig looks worn out as I
come closer but has a history of once having been classy. She
is staring across the road. When I reach within a few metres
of her, I increase my pace and look down until I pass her. I am
not sure why I do this. She does not turn or say anything and
I feel shame instantly descend upon me. When I interrogate
myself, I think I was afraid she might say something, or beg
for money, or lunge at me in rage or deranged excitement.

10

There is a bearded man who always sits by the Bahama grass
before the bridge closest to my house. If I pass by between 8
and 8.30, he is there, pulling on his wiry beards and looking
at nothing in particular. Once I was early enough to catch
him emerging from beneath the bridge. I know his two pairs
of trousers. There is the baggy, faded gabardine which used
to be red that he wears only with the dirty red sneakers.
And there are the tighter, faded, olive-green jeans which he
only wears with the grass-green sneakers. He has one brown
bucket hat which he wears so that it almost covers his eyes. I
wonder if he is going bald. Sometimes I feel like saying hello
because technically he is a neighbour.

Today when I see him standing by the roadside in his green
gabardine, I wonder if they have ever met, these two homeless
people in posh Abuja. I wonder what she would say if he took
a liking to her, if she would consider it beneath her to desire
a man who has settled comfortably into homelessness, a

man who does not seem ambitious enough to want housing. Thinking of it again, the homeless woman looked to me like she was waiting for something. Her bags were always packed and her wig always kempt. She seemed to be at least working on a plan to leave this concrete slab. But the man – he had this settled look. Resignation. Contentment.

11

Myrlène sees me from a car across the road right in front of the traffic lights. She is waving and giggling. I cannot hear what she is saying but I am praying that the seconds move faster so the lights can turn green. I do not take the earphones out of my ear. I just wave back.

> *I am better than you, Myrlène. I may be fat. But I do not have a double chin. How does a skinny person manage to have a double chin?*

12

I have decided. I will say hello to Homeless Woman the next time I see her.

13

I try never to stop completely to rest. My muscles become weak when I do and it is hard to regain momentum. But the earthworms make me stop. The sun is out and hot, earlier than the past few days, and it seems the earthworms calculated wrongly as they tried to make it across from the left of the concrete sidewalk to the other muddy side. Dozens of them were caught halfway and most were already dead. Some were still writhing. Others were struggling to crawl over the dead ones to save themselves from the sun. I want to pick them all up and take them to the other side but stop myself when I think I could be upsetting the balance of things. Sometimes nature does this. Natural selection. And perhaps some bird will swoop down and have a feast. Or some stray chicken.

14

How many kilos have you lost? Myrlène asks, stifling a laugh when I run into her in the new Shoprite, which is exactly like all the other soulless Shoprites I have seen in Lagos and Accra and Lusaka. She is in the fruits section picking up tomatoes. In her trolley there is a Martini Bianco, a Jack Daniels, a Smirnoff Vodka and large green apples.

'As much as you have consumed in alcohol,' I say, pushing my trolley right past her.

She freezes.

As I pay for my items at the till I see her behind me, glowering at me with teary eyes.

I am petty. But then, she will never make fun of my weight again.

15

Just before I head out I stand naked in front of the mirror. I turn sideways to see if anything has changed around my tummy area. I inhale deeply, sucking in my belly, wishing it could be this way normally.

How many kilos have you lost? Myrlène says again.

I don't do shit like that, getting on scales, watching calories, all that pretentious nonsense. I just want to see and feel a difference. You know, like grab a fistful of tummy flesh and think, oh, it's gone down.

Myrlène then grabs a fistful of flesh just beneath my navel and says: oh, it's gone down.

16

The traffic police that sit by the junction closest to my house are here again today. I always feel their eyes when I walk past. Once, our eyes met and I felt accused of being privileged enough to undertake non-essential activities like just walking through the city with earphones on a Thursday morning. Today they do not notice me walking past. The smaller one, who looks like he was recovering from being malnourished, is helping the other one burst a pimple on his face. The one with the pimple has his head arched back, his eyes shut tight, wincing in pain. The one doing the bursting has his lips bunched as he squeezes the pimple between the nails of his thumbs. I think of Saheed, my secondary-school classmate who always offered to burst our pimples. I still don't understand how anyone can enjoy doing this.

17

It is not shame that makes me hate thinking about my brother. There are many things I feel but shame is not one of them. Sometimes I wonder if I would have felt the same way if people had not attacked and disfigured him in the village where he had been doing his one-year compulsory National Youth Service Corps after university; if he wasn't this silent, sick man sitting in chains with one bad leg and a million scars on his face. There are questions I want to ask him which I think of now as I begin my walk. How could he take such risks in a village he did not know? When did he sit down and decide that it was okay to touch and let himself be touched by boys? Why did he wake up from the coma after he was beaten by dozens of villagers who caught him with a local boy?

18

I pick up a small snail on my way. As kids we would always go into our small vegetable garden in the backyard and touch the slimy, shiny bodies, especially the eyes. We could never have enough of touching the snails' eyes and watching it retract sometimes partially and sometimes completely into the shell. I can't remember how many snails I smashed open to try to figure out which was male and which was female. They all looked the same on the inside.

I am a snail and Myrlène is an impetuous child poking her fingers in my eye. I am a snail that cannot get away from her too quickly. I can only retract to protect myself.

I throw the snail into the grass to prevent someone from stepping on it.

19

Papa Adieu Woman, who I have not seen for a few days, is jogging very fast toward me. She is wearing shorts for the first time and I notice she has very bad knock-knees. It must hurt, to have the knees brushing against each other while jogging.

I stretch out my feet and trip her and she falls, bouncing on her breasts as if they were balloons.

When she passes by, I inhale to smell her. She smells of lavender and sweat.

When is the wedding?

20

Homeless Man is not wearing a shirt. But he has his brown bucket hat on. He is twirling the wiry hair on his chest, looking lost like always. Will he take a shirt if I offer him one? Or will he feel insulted?

21

I told my friend Emma I walk every morning and she said, 'Oh we must walk together!' But she was drunk when she said it. I am not surprised that she hasn't called or responded to my messages about walking since she said it three weeks ago, even though she sends an email every Friday about *drinks*. I don't mind going out with her on Fridays except for the times when she gets drunk and tries to kiss me when we are dancing. We are good friends, but I don't like her *like that*. She always apologizes after. I always say it is okay.

I make up for not walking on Saturday mornings by walking twice the distance on Sundays.

22

Homeless Woman is rolling what looks like a rosary between her thumb and forefinger. It is milk-coloured and because most of it is lying in her lap I cannot see if it is a Muslim chasbi, a Catholic rosary or if she is just playing with beads. As I get closer and try to peep, she looks up and our eyes meet. I nod nervously to say hello.

'What is it?' she says angrily. 'You are always looking at me here when you pass.'

I have a confused look on my face and a pounding heart in my chest. Pretending to be confused is the least embarrassing way of dealing with this.

'Are you well? Why are you looking at me?'

She sounds very educated.

I want to apologize but I just walk away quickly.

23

Emma had an affair with her married gym instructor in Abuja. They often had sex in the sauna, she says, and he turned out to be doing the same with at least three other women at the gym. At first she said she thought it was sexy. She probably wouldn't have told me all of this if we hadn't been taking shots of tequila. After telling me the whole story, she got drunk and still tried to kiss me.

I'd rather walk and feel the breeze than be indoors with the smells and bodily fluids of strangers.

Sex in the sauna. That's just nasty.

Abuja gym instructors deserve a place in hell.

24

Homeless Woman has vanished. There is no trace of her. No flattened cartons. No food wrappings. No empty water bottles. Her concrete slab and everything around it has been swept clean. I feel a bit relieved because I was nervous about walking past her again. Then I feel pride when I think that perhaps she really is as ambitious as I imagined; that perhaps she has moved on and started living in a house. Perhaps it was a bad idea to connect the unambitious homeless man to the ambitious homeless woman.

A little ahead I see a man crouching in the grass burning wood and flattened cartons. When I walk closer I see him gathering old cigarette butts into a pile. He puts one old butt into the fire and attempts to smoke it. I walk past quickly, angry that this mad man may have made Homeless Woman pack up and leave. And when I finally see the beads she was rolling in her hand on the floor beside the man, I am angry that my theory of Homeless Woman moving on is shattered.

25

I have stopped seeing Papa Adieu Woman. Maybe she got married. Maybe she got too thin and died.

I still hope that Homeless Woman has found a home. She deserves it.

26

I grab a fistful of flesh around my abdomen.

It has gone down, I think.

Elnathan John is a novelist and satirist based in Abuja, Nigeria. He was born in Kaduna, North Central Nigeria, where he also trained to become a lawyer. After a few years, he quit legal practice to write full time in 2012. His work was shortlisted for the Caine Prize for African Writing in 2013 and again in 2015. His debut novel, *Born on a Tuesday*, is published by Cassava Republic Press in the UK and Nigeria, by Grove Atlantic in the US and by Galaade in France.

Shiko

Billy Kahora

When I drive into the Junction Mall in my old Toyota I cannot find parking for an hour. Range Rover Sports, Audis and Benzes are ushered into fake reserved spaces by the watchmen. Ngoja. Wait, they say. I come here with one of Ivy's chariots, the Prado especially, and I get parking in quick dakikas. Ivy and I have had an epic fight about chums, what's next after two years of us, and so I have to use my own ride. I double-park, sit in the car and the ngoma from Mercury upstairs sounds like it's coming from my own music tenje. I can see all the summer bunny mamas up there in the neon. I could just go there and try to hook up and forget about seeing my old classmates from Mappen. Ivy is too mad to come over tonight after our fight. I'm home alone – a rare opportunity. I weigh that against going back 15 years at the Whisky Bar especially given what happened with Desmond 'Dessie' Wambugu and Stephen 'Kwara' Mbatia – Dessie and Kwara, my best friends at Mappen.

A Chrysler as big as a battleship cruises in. Shit. The first I've ever seen outside of the movies. It floats past me to the parking spot that I've been chilling for. This midget in a white Kaunda suit and a deep purple cravat emerges. It's fucking Eliud Wamae. The Junction did not exist 15 years ago when we were at Mappen, which is actually not too far away. This could even have been one of those grand ideas he was always fantasizing about. That's why we started calling him the Fantasist. He's now as real as it gets. A player of maana. A tenderpreneur. Now, I am the one who can't get parking. I try and slip the watchie a 50 bob and he looks at me with bile. I give him 200 and he lets me slide into Disabled.

I enter the mall and move against all these chaguo la teeniez chicks, high with being out so late. When I catch their eye they sneer at me with madharau. I turn and I almost get caught in their slipstream to Mercury Bar.

Victor 'Colonel' Otieno – star rugby winger, Mappen First 15 '91 – is already at the Whisky Bar. We do an awkward handshake man-hug thing. 'Alan, man. Many years.' His loud laugh, I swear, is exactly the same.

'How many years, man.' His voice is uji slow. 'How many years.' Yeah, he used to repeat everything twice. But out on the wing of a rugby pitch, damn he was a bat. I used to see him at Impala and Quins when he was still playing after I was discontinued from Civil Engineering, UON. He has not put on a kg in these 15 years; his face is still stuck in a perpetual beam. Mercury is calling. I am furious at myself. I need a Glenfiddich.

I told Morris 'The Amerucan' Munyao that I would come if he would get the whiskies. The Amerucan's the only one who's kept in touch with all of us. Ever since I can remember, the Meru bastard always wanted to go to America. We used to laugh and call him the Amerucan till he went Wall Street after community college in bum-fuck South Carolina.

For this reunion the Colonel and the Fantasist have chosen one of the long tables with the thick couches with tall backs like thrones. I sit down like King Herod and make sure I can check out the Mall thoroughfare. The Fantasist says: 'You. You. You.' I want to punch him. 'You,' he says again. I am forced to grin. In school this midget was the greatest con artist ever. How many pennies did he leave school owing us? Something's changed with his jaw since then – it juts out, makes his face the newspaper mugshot that's always in the papers. He is always in and out of High Court. Huge land and city-council deals. Tenderpreneur number one.

I have shown this face to Ivy: 'See. I went to school with this man.'

'Fucking hell, babe. Even my father knows Wamae,' she says.

The Fantasist disappeared after Mappen. The rest of us remained babies. Those of us who stayed, waliowachwa, went to UON Nairobi campus mostly. Waliotuacha, those who left, went to the States and the UK. We are here to try and make our first major investment. I feel like a rabble in front of the Fantasist. By the end of Moi times the Fantasist was a millionaire. Lately the Government wants him for a 1,000-acre parcel in Lamu that's too close to the airport. The Gupta Shah murder case that he is linked to is still in court. Fucking robber baron.

I sip the Glen, 12 years, he has ordered for me and the nectar brings tears to my eyes. It floods into the sides of my stomach. The edges of my vision turn golden. Fuck, it's been a while since I've been on the good shit.

When Ivy and I come here we always sit at the bar and fight. A month ago we brought Catherine, her sister, and her friends here for her birthday. Ivy can't hold her Shiraz. Shit got messy. Ivy hates whisky. Ivy loathes whisky in me. And sure she brought up how I become an asshole on the nectar. I started holding forth about how whisky makes me want to be the man for her.

'This negro. Gets whisky dick every time we are out,' she said to the whole place. 'How is that for being the man for me when you can't get it up.'

I got cocky. 'Whisky forever. Whisky Bar for life. Ivy, my eternity,' I proclaimed.

'You know what,' she said quietly. 'Pay for your own fucking Glen.'

I had to back-pedal. I conceded that the place was actually called Wine Bar. All of Catherine's friends cracked up. Later, Ivy paid the attendant and we made up in the toilet. Catherine says that Ivy was not mental like this before the accident. Ivy was 14 when she got the limp. Catherine was 16.

As the Fantasist, the Colonel and I wait for the wazees, the chaguo la teeniez girls prance away in the Mall. Wiggle it. Just a little bit. I wanna see you wiggle it. Just a little bit. I sip at the nectar. I look at the Colonel and remember how badly he wanted to join the Air Force but then IT took off in Kenya and he went into that. I was the maths guy. Top 5 Kenya. Number 2 KCSE '91 Maths Paper 1. Then the drama of my life became small.

The wazees start to show up. They come around the corner, one by one, with that halting step of the soon-to-be 40 male. Every foot is placed with some emphasis, the insecure marker of a new prosperity. We came here through the emails from the Amerucan and Stephen Mbatia. Paul Kiprotich, Joel Mudavadi, Michael Kieni and James Mbithi roll up.

Some of us have seen each other in passing – others have kept up serious friendships over the years. The Amerucan never let anyone drift away – he always kept in touch even when he went to the States. Even with Dessie.

When everyone settles we wait for Bertiez. That's what everyone calls Stephen Mbatia nowadays. We used to call him Kwara. That's schoolboy shit for you. In our warped minds he looked like a girl when we were rabbles. He's the one who's thrown in the Ruwa land deal on email. And of course, Desmond 'Fisi' Wambugu. I think of him and I feel like a triple whisky. That shit he pulled on me during our final Mappen year. The Amerucan told me he's 50-50 for this meeting. I swear I'll order a bottle if he shows up. Maybe go medieval. Fuck that. I hear he became a cop. That animal would kill me.

We mull. Now that we are all here it is clear one and a half decades have done a serious number on us – especially those who stayed. We are all '72-'73 borns but at this table some could have at least a decade on others. I work with numbers at Heidelmann. Polls. Statistics. Market research. I take apart these soon-to-be 40 men by recreating the last 15 years. Ivy goes at me all the time about nyama choma, beers, bad life calls, bad marriages, car accidents, death of parents and aging. I can see the 20-year hustle etched in the faces of those who were left behind. Waliowachwa. They should all be wearing t-shirts that say 'I am a Moi-era survivor'. I can make out the dents – we look ten years older. But we are the ones who know how to get around the Ministry Of Lands, the Police and the City.

The Amerucan, Michael and Alex Nderitu are small leaguers. Mere culprits and victims of sub-prime loans, credit-card default and the internet bubble, and now they want to get into the game. They have foreign savings. Waliotuwacha. We natives are here to offer local investment advice. Native intelligence. In Vino. Veritas. In Whisky. I Trust. I look at them and I can see they are smirking at the dents on our faces.

Michael says to the Colonel we should start. Bertiez has sent a text to the Amerucan that he has been held up. Ten minutes. Michael doesn't like this. He is still a bully. Obese, light-skinned, he was the Mappen First XV's Number 8. He has shrunk. No, all of us have grown to his girth. His head has ballooned like he's on Toivo and split his hair into two, right down the middle. His hair, a thick black forest, clings to the sides and the back of his Mt Kenya dome. Michael was a real asshole back then – we had our problems but they were not as bad as what happened between Desmond 'Fisi' Wambugu and me.

Ten minutes. Ah, we get into the sorry state of Mappen. That's what we still call it even if it had already been renamed 15 years before we got there. The golf course we prized so much is gone, now a maize plantation. Someone reports that Meadows, the rugby pitch of all schoolboy rugby pitches, is overgrown and is used as a cattle paddock. There is a thick joviality, some abrupt silent phases, the Fantasist looks up every now and then and the drinks rounds come.

Those of us drinking whisky swirl, sniff and sip, let the golden liquid settle into our mouths, suffuse into our faces and frown across the table at those who are drinking beer and wine and even Jamieson. I am surprised that the Whisky

Bar actually serves Jamieson. Our faces loosen and age with every sip per minute. We sigh without realizing.

JM Mbithi used to be the class clown with his stutter. He reminds us of a string of our schoolboy idiocies in the stutter that used to kill us back then. We laugh from the liver at gang-fucking the Mappen teachers' maids. Stealing whole trays of food from the dining hall. Sneaking out to Riruta to drink Toivo. Somebody asks whether Dessie is still coming. He was always in the middle of all the shit. The golden edges in my vision disappear. We all remember Dessie in different ways.

I look at the bar and I imagine Ivy sitting there. Ivy is mad supu with her crazy beautiful eyes and the whisky is making me miss her. I wish she was here so these clowns could see her. How I got a woman ten years younger than me. That's how I roll. Maybe Ivy and I should get engaged. I muse at this till the Colonel speaks up. The man is smiling. Unbelievable, this permanent beam he carries with all the shit there is around.

'It's a bit late and some of us are going mbali,' he says in his calm way. Michael is seated next to him and nods. 'Can we agree on the basics? All of you have seen the emails. We all know why we are here.'

The Colonel looks at Michael and he takes over. The asshole stares hard at everyone. 'Guys, it's simple. As Bertiez said on email, we need ten million.' He looks up and down the table. 'If we are all in, it's about one metre each. The idea, as you know, is to buy these available plots in Ruwa. Develop high-rises. Of course, if anyone has any other business ideas we should also be still open to that.'

The Amerucan is now looking at me and he says: 'The other thing I want to say is that access is also important. Some of us have access to important info. Some of us are proper insiders. We are talking hard money. But we are also talking info.'

Michael notices the looks we give each other. 'Amerucan,' he says. 'We have to be careful. No free rides here. We've been talking shares: ten shares for ten of us. An equal number of shares for those who front up cash.' This asshole. Sisi tuliowachwa sit up at this.

The Amerucan steps in. 'Of course, equal shares for everyone. We leave this open to this original group. Like the email said, 50k to start with. To show commitment. Then we can sell shares at agreed-upon rates. But the info some of you gentlemen have over here is as good as cash.' He looks at JM too when he says this. I wonder whether he has the same deal as I have. Info for shares in the venture.

The Fantasist speaks up for the first time. We know we will never see him again after this first meeting. 'Let me tell you something for free before I take off,' he says. 'You might want to check out Siokimau. Kajiado. South Coast. I can send you contacts, details.' With this he puts up his hand and the waiter brings another round. 'Tafadhali, bring the bill,' he says. He stands up like a proper mheshimwa and we all fawn like rabbles. 'Gentlemen, you will have to excuse me.'

The Amerucan also stands up and walks him out. We mull. I wonder why I'm still here. The Amerucan told me that I could get in with the corporate investment files I have access to at Heidelmann.

When the Amerucan comes back he is sweating slightly. He reports that the Fantasist has made a pledge of one million – he will buy a full share of whatever idea we agree on. With that small bone that we've been thrown, the gauntlet is laid.

I quickly do the maths. For 15 years we will all pay 70k per year to get in on the deal. After loan repayments on the Toyota, that's like two thirds of my salary a month.

It is midnight. Fuck what they say that it is usually worst before dawn. Michael suggests one month for each of us to deposit 50k to show commitment. The one and half million shillings can be done in instalments. Yippee. Fucking yay.

I'm dying for Mercury. The chagua teeniez girls have become tipsy and they chase each other around the place. The returnees leave one by one. Michael. Paul Kiprotich.

The natives mill around. Then it is just the Amerucan and me. I don't think he's done more than three beers. Now that business is done his eyes are poppin' at the chagua teeniez.

'Do the thafus of this whole thing make sense?' he asks.

I nod.

'Does that mean you are in?' The whisky is clawing at my back. I hear contempt in his voice. This is a guy I tutored Math in O-levels. He got a B- because of me, for fuck's sake.

Fuck that. Fuck symbiosis.

'In how? I'm in how. You know how crazy my chums shit is.' I can't help the boo-hoo in my voice. I hold up my empty whisky glass and the Amerucan laughs but he signals the waiter.

There is a bowl in the middle of the long table. Everybody has left several business cards on the table apart from the Fantasist. I play around with the cards and I realize that almost everyone at the table was in Mappen's First XV '91. Paul Kiprotich second row. Joel Mudavadi fly-half. Fuck. And of course a few were part of that Fourth Form secret council that held Mappen in thrall seeking out what they branded tabia mbaya. Ati Homos. Ushoga.

The Amerucan and I finish up and we get up to go to Mercury.

The Amerucan smiles at a very tall individual who has just come in. I look closely. Lo. It's Kwara but he is Kwara no more. He is now over six feet, his voice has ballast sprinkled with kokoto. 'Hey, people,' he says.

'Mr Stephen Mbatia,' I say.

He looms over me. 'Bertiez. It's just Bertiez now.' All cool. He's changed the most of all of us. The girlish gawky Kwara is gone.

✳✳✳

We are in Mercury by the large windows looking out into Nairobi neon. Bertiez, the Amerucan and I are all legless.

There is a very high moon that tells of the coming of the early dawn. I keep on looking for signs of the indescribable, back at Mappen, in Bertiez's face. I wonder whether Dessie and he kept in touch.

But Bertiez's face is as empty as the parking lot. I can see my lone Toyota. We mumble at the three tall girls we've picked. They dance silently, their helpless faces smile and make us horny.

I pick the tallest girl and she follows me outside. In the parking my Toyota refuses to start. I look at her properly for the first time as I release the Toyota's choke. The girl is a silhouette against the window, the moon. The car remains silent. She bends out of sight and when she appears she is heading back to the mall. She holds her heels in one hand and runs like a gazelle. She is a fucking model. She is not ukimwi skinny. I wish I had borrowed Ivy's Benz, Audi or Land Rover. I sit in the music from Mercury and I think about the one million shillings. A Range Rover Sports and a Benz squat in the parking opposite me in the distance. The Amerucan and Bertiez. I will need a ride.

✳✳✳

I sleep most of Sunday. I wake up at 11am, put half my head into the guest-room toilet bowl and let it all come out till only the yellow stuff that is bitter is coming out in small stringy spurts. I sleep again to sweat out all the sour.

I find myself in a large field. A rugby field. I am on Meadows and it is a big game. I am on the blind wing. The other team is these half-gazelle half-model chicks. I recognize the girl with heels in her hand from the reunion night. She has the ball and she comes my way and tries to go around me and I chase and she giggles and throws come-hithers. She makes sure she does not quite get away from me. Whisky dreams.

✳✳✳

I head to the office in the morning. I work on the Sexualities Bill file all morning. When I open my email at the office at 2pm there is a flurry of emails from Morris titled 1M. He says that he spoke to Michael and if I get him the right info they can waive 0.5M.

Since the Amerucan came back from the States three years ago I have been feeding him information from the files of our select investment clients. We do research for at least the top five NSE companies. This stuff gives a shark like him clues as to where the money is leaning. Where the next huge investments will happen. Where the next mall will be built. Which highways will be improved. Where the Chinese will come in. It's good shit and he knows it. He does me in kind. Whisky. A few tens of Gs here and there. I am on 140 net a month over at Heidelmann. I can't keep Ivy and the nectar on that.

Lately, we've started getting a lot of work from the big Ford Foundation grantees, the Alternative Sexualities people. Haki Elimu. Urgent Action Fund. I get back on that.

On Tuesday evening Ivy calls me after I've just popped a Xanax. Her voice trips along the line, buoyant. 'Fucking hell, babe. We still together?'

'Your phone has been off,' I say.

'How was your Baba meeting?' she asks. Last Friday's fight is now in the ether. I think of that little gazelle at Mercury that got away. My balls ache.

'We need to talk,' I say.

'Fucking hell, babe' – Ivy's phone signature if there is one. 'Sure, babe.'

I do not push. I'll probably see her over the weekend. The Xanax is tipping me over. It is not the best time to bring up the 1M. We say ciao. The Xanax drops me. I dream again of gazelles playing rugby at Meadows.

***

I leave work at lunchtime on Friday and drive into town, go past Globe Cinema to Kariokor. I stop there and get some nyama. I eat while I drive. I go through Eastleigh, Majengo, Shauri Moyo, Kamkunji. I look at the sprawl, the dust, the joyous hint of violence everywhere, the cocky pedestrian refusal to move for cars on the road. I am going home. I get on Route 23. I went up this road all my life in mathrees and my Dad's Vokie. I am tempted to stop at the Baha Shopping Centre. Maybe my Dad is already there in the Mateso Bar. Mateso Bila Chuki. Suffering without bitterness. It's 2pm but I can't see Dad's Vokie. The place is already teeming with the 4x4s of local overlords who always come back home to show they made good. I look at these behemoths and feel the Toyota squeezing the shit out of me.

I go past Salem and I'm in Kimathi. I grew up here in these white-washed bungalows that are now the colour of brown sugar. The windows of each house are opaque with dust. The juala kiosks have spread like Kikuyu grass. Plastic bags are the new flowers of these Kimathi times. The roads are pitted and the Toyota almost breaks into two. I can't be mad – this is home. Every one of our neighbours has built a 15-foot wall and a black gate of reinforced steel. When I played here as a child with my late brother, the hedge fences were barely taller than us. That la vida shit ended with the Eighties.

When I was in First Year campus, Mum started complaining about headaches one night. She went to bed and did not wake up the next day. My brother broke bad and started hanging out in Salem. He was gunned down not too far from here in Majengo. Flying squad.

The streetlights we played under as kids, my late brother and I, lean and threaten to fall on the Toyota as I make my way to my Dad's house. I can still hear my Mum's voice when the lights still used to work, coming on in the night, us refusing to go in and playing on and on till even 10pm during the school holidays. Shit was safe.

I make my way down to the first row of houses overlooking

Mathare Valley proper. To think this estate was named after freedom fighter Dedan Kimathi. I have yet to bring Ivy to this zoo. I keep on telling her she will be eaten alive. Driving her big cars here. Please. She begs me to bring her every month or so and I tell her we have to go in my Toyota. Please, she says. Ivy is yet to believe that being jacked in Nairobi is real.

My father's old white Vokie is parked outside our house. The sound of its engine is so much part of my internal make-up that I can hear the song of Volkswagen. German engineering. I knock on the 20-foot black gate and I hear a shout. I knock again and I hear a door open. I peep through the thin space in the middle of the gate and I see Dad coming. He has become hairier at an age when most men go bald. He still has a head full of hair. He stopped buttoning the top half of his dirty white shirt a decade ago. I can smell last week's beer even this far off. He is sprinkled with dandruff. He carries his thick open notebook in one hand.

He shouts again before he opens the gate. His voice surprises me – the faint English accent from his time in Cambridge. This man used to be Professor Muigai, Maths Department, Chiromo Campus, University of Nairobi. National genius.

'Ni mimi,' I say. Kariuki. He opens the gate and does not move aside to let me enter but looks me over.

'Kariuki,' he says. 'Kariuki. How is the Applied Mathematician? The Statistician.' We both laugh. He quickly looks out into the street with the old fear in his eyes and then he steps aside and lets me in. He has a scar on his forehead from the last time some vijanas broke in and came for him. This happens every other month.

He lives with Wamaitha, our old housemaid, who is like my second mother. The best thing about the house is the perfect lawn and the bougainvillea fence that she tends every day. I look at the green carpet and know my father is not all gone. We go around the house. I want to lie there on the back lawn and go to sleep, to become a kijana again. Start all over. Bring back Mum. Bring back Kungu, my brother. Go to Alliance. Avoid Dessie and all the other bad shit. But I hoist myself up the high back wall on some crates and look out. Mathare Valley in all its glory. The hundreds and hundreds of paper-shack lives. The Nairobi River spine that feeds them. This is where we used to go hunting. Then I went to campus and came back to Animal Planet.

Shit, Ivy needs to see this. I climb down and look at my father and wonder how he sleeps with all this wildlife and just a wall in between.

'I am not moving,' he says. As we walk into the house he says, 'Tell me about Heidelmann.'

'Pure servitude and horror,' I say. 'Maisha at Heidelmann.'

'How is Were?' He is talking about his old professor friend who hooked me up after I was discontinued from Civil Engineering.

'I don't see the Prof that much any more. He is always in SA. They have this big deal coming up. He might be selling to some South Africans. Synovate, I think they are called. Steadmann might be going that way too.'

'Ah.' My father says. 'Were was always greedy. The millions KANU paid him for 2002, God knows.' My father thinks everyone is greedy. I don't get him. This is Kenya Inc. Kuna wananchi. Na wenyenchi. Kuna viatu, Kuna watu.

'What do they call you over there nowadays?' he asks.

'Monitoring and Evaluation Officer.'

He winces. 'You need to finish your MBA. Get into siasa poll numbers. Do the MBA and I'll talk to Were.'

We head into the house, the sitting room of my childhood, now a shrunken universe of all that was once probable in the Kenyan world but is now unlikely. Once large in the imagination of my childhood are the measly cheap leather sofas with vitambaas we were not allowed to sit on, my brother and I, till we were 16. As kids we watched TV from the floor. And only strictly on Saturdays between 6 and 8pm.

Old photos of Professor Muigai adorn the walls. Makerere.

Helsinki '68. Boston '72. Cairo '77. All the places that my father went through. My father knew Obama Senior. He knew President Kibaki. Ati Professor Saitoti. He boasts how he taught Professor Saitoti. How he set up the current systems at Treasury, Ministry of Finance. There is Mum in all her haloed beauty – she gave up med school for this man. After his work for Treasury we were finally going to be rich. All Mum asked for was to move away from Kimathi before it became Mathare. Then the headaches came that night a long time ago and she passed on. She is the only one I told about what happened at Mappen with Dessie.

I listen to my Father's complaints against the University even if it's now at least five years since they forced him out. I wonder whether the police took away his gun from him after he threatened matatu people in traffic for what he saw as disrespect. That's what the vijanas are always breaking into the house for.

I just come out and say it. 'Dad. I need a loan.'

He goes quiet and looks at me. 'I hope you are not thinking Treasury Bills.'

'I need one million.' He sighs, realizing I am serious.

'Let me get my coat. Let's go talk about this at Mateso.'

As I wait for him, I stand up and go to a corner where there is a small shrine placed on a cow-drum table that is testament to my mathematical achievements. There are all these framed Maths prizes. I do not recognize a small framed A4 page. Old Maths exercise-book page. I unhook the frame from the wall. I can tell my childish handwriting.

$$a\,x^2 + b\,x + c = 0$$

We head to Mateso. Suffering. Mateso Bila Chuki. Suffering Without Bitterness. We order White Caps and I tell him about the reunion, the new investment chama we want to start. As he listens he starts drawing a complex quadratic equation in his large squared notebook. When I finish he looks at me

– then he turns the notebook for me to look at. He points at all these equations and figures he has drawn up. 'From what you tell me there are several variables at hand. The first is the money you, actually I, put in. The second variable is the money you say you will make.'

I soar. There might be some hope. My dad raised my brother and me up by rewarding us any time we solved a Maths problem he put in front of us. I suspect I know where he's going with this. I might just get something from him. Maybe 500k. Mateso is now filling up. Kenya Inc is alive and well.

'I've been thinking about that thing you used to teach Kungu and me all the time. By some Greek. Tortoise and Hare in some race,' I say.

Kalulu Hare gives Bwana Tortoise a head start of 100 metres in a race. They both have a constant speed. After Hare runs 100 he will get to where Tortoise started. By then, Tortoise will have run at least 10 metres. Hare then runs the 10. Tortoise runs one metre. Hare reaches where Tortoise has been but he still has farther to go. Because Hare must reach where Tortoise has already been, he can never overtake the Tortoise.

That's how he used to tell it.

'Yes, the philosopher Zeno. At least you remember something I taught you. Forget him for now.' He points at the notebook. 'Look at this carefully. Let's consider the constants. You are the one and only constant.' He picks up his White Cap, looks into my eyes. He writes down a list of figures. 'This is all the money you owe me to date.' Fuck. Fuck. Fuck.

'This is what I can do,' he says. 'I will write you a cheque made out directly to the University of Nairobi. Finish your MBA then we can talk.'

I leave him there to his notebook. I am tired Hare. I am in a series of endless infinities that never catch up. He is Tortoise.

***

Sato is here. Ivy has a trip to Dubai on Monday. She is not sure whether we will get together tonight or kesho, Sunday. She says she has all this shit to do. Spruce herself up. Nails. Hair salon. Her OG father is driving her nuts again.

We are on the phone. I tell her we need to talk.

'Fucking hell, babe,' she says. 'Dubs is calling.' I repeat that we need to talk. 'Now?' she shouts.

'Just tell me now, babe,' she says. 'Alan, what's wrong?' There is a pause – some activity in the background – on her end. 'You are not fucking breaking up with me. Are you?'

I laugh and she's cool.

'Babe, I love you.' She sounds relieved. 'Just chill. I'll call you. The peeps in Dubs are on my ass.'

I get off the phone. I cannot go to Barclays for 1M. I am already paying a car-loan deni for the Toyota from two years ago. The Amerucan hooked me up with some guy who I bought the Toyota from in '04. I got played on the mileage. I owe 800k. I pay 80k every month. The thafus of my life are oppressive.

Ivy finally pitches up Sunday night – when I open the door, no hug. She just pushes me aside and immediately starts going on about how she needs 320k before she takes off to buy tyres for the Merc. Her dad won't give her the money.

'Erm babe, can you help me with my suitcase from downstairs?' She throws me the Audi keys. I go outside, open the boot of the car and haul her suitcase all the way.

'In here,' she says. I take it to the guestroom.

She looks over her dresses and panties to see what she needs for Dubai. I ask her whether we can talk for ten minutes. She looks at me, placing some of her clothes aside, and ignores me while she prepares for Dubai. After a while she says she feels like some Shiraz.

'Are you sure? Your flight is at 6am.' I want her sober for the 1M convo.

'What are you talking about? Are you being funny? So what if I'm leaving at 6am?' She sidles up to me and makes a playful grab at my crotch. I slap her hand away.

She sits on the bed. 'I can see you don't want to get me drunk. I know you won't miss me. You are so boring. Now I feel like a burger.'

I look at her bare shoulders and wonder where it all goes. She's as skinny as fuck.

'Can we order in?' I remain quiet. 'Do you have any cash?' I head back to the sitting room without saying anything.

She wanders in. 'What is it?' she asks.

I tell her about it all. The Amerucan. The Mappen reunion. Her silence gets me going.

I build into it. I take it to the bridge. I soar. I am an eagle. I am R Kelly. How I believe I can fly. I take it to PCEA church. This is my best presentation ever. My life depends on it. I finish. Fall back to the sofa.

'Is that it?' Her face is inscrutable.

'Yes. Will you lend me the cash?'

Ivy looks at me like I am a giraffe. Then she starts to laugh. The thing about Ivy's laugh is that it's the most infectious thing there is. Fuck. Fuck. Fuck.

'Who are these idiots?' she asks.

'Morris, you've met,' I say. 'We call him the Amerucan.'

'That baba friend of yours who is going on 62. Babe, seriously. Where did you meet these fuckwits?'

'School,' I say. 'Mappen.'

I start to sing. Clowns to the right of me. Jokers to the left. Here I am stuck in the middle with you. She does not crack a smile. I would like to just fuck right there and forget about the whole 1M thing. My two constants, my father and long-term girlfriend, have become unreliable variables.

She shakes her head and goes off to finish packing. We watch some TV, order dial-a-delivery and fall asleep on the sofa. At some point we wander off to bed staggering under the weight of sleep.

Ivy wakes me up at 5am. I have whisky dick and she is not impressed that it takes me 30 minutes to get it up. We mercy-fuck. It's horrible. We lie there and she sighs and goes off to shower. As she gets all dressed I struggle to stay awake.

Then I wake up and she is astride of me, screaming. 'Negro, you can't keep awake for like half an hour to keep me company before I leave. You won't see me for two weeks, remember.' Then, God, it's time for her to get into the taxi. She looks spectacular. This apparition is unbelievably mine. She looks at me and laughs with some shyness when she catches me watching her.

'Look, about what you asked for – I'll think about it. I'll try to find 300k tops. If this thing in Dubai goes through. Definitely. But if it does we should also talk about what next between us.'

She says this looking into the mirror. She purses her lips, adds some gloss. Then she turns to me. 'Fucking hell, babe. Give me a kiss.' I do that and she rubs a finger hard against my lips to rub off the gloss. I follow her to the door. She blocks me. She wrinkles her face. At times like this, she tears easily. 'You don't have to come out. It's cold.' I take her downstairs anyway.

She takes off and the world goes quiet. There is a police siren somewhere. Some cats yowl in early-morning ecstasy. At least she left the keys to the Audi. I am to email her, though, if I want to use it.

A few hours later when I wake up again, the Toyota refuses to start. The Audi just sits there. Fuck it. I cruise out in it. Inside its grand universe Monday morning Nairobi actually looks half-sane. Full of possibilities. Maybe I could sell the Toyota for 500k and get in on the game. Maybe Ivy will lend me one of her cars, any one of them, for three months till I recoup my investment.

I get to the office and go through emails. The Mappen Hall Company has been on email all weekend. Paul Kiprotich says that he's moving back to the States – Kenya is not working out for him. JM Mbithi says his father has cancer and he has to spend all the loose cash he has on his treatment. And just like that we are six men still standing. The Amerucan says that we will all need to put in 1.5M now.

***

Solar Gardens is famous for its 24-hour sexual professionals and the bjs they give in the garden after midnight. During the day it's an informal office for all of Nairobi's aspiring tenderpreneurs. They play pool all day and drink between 9 and 5pm and go home like the rest of us. And they hope against hope for all the deals in the Kenyan world. It is fitting that Solar Gardens used to be a Nairobi City Council town clerk's house until he went bankrupt. The new owner is said to be negotiating with developers. A block of apartments will soon be coming up here.

I am at Solar Gardens to meet the Amerucan. I have the kind of information in the brown envelope I am holding for the broke town clerk, for the lean and mean tenderpreneurs I see skulking around. I have what the Amerucan wants. I'm in the deal. The last email update showed that I now need 1.5M to get into the deal.

I walk around looking for the Amerucan but I can't see anyone sitting alone. I go to the bar and hang out there and wait for him.

Just then he calls.

'Alan, uko wapi.'

'I am here,' I say.

'The fuck where.' The Amerucan sounds drunk. Wow. 'We saw you pita us just now. We are outside.'

I head out and I make out three figures in a far corner waving at me.

I head there and I recognize the Amerucan and Bertiez, who are seated facing me. The other man has his back to me and turns. It's Desmond Wambugu. Fucking hell. I give the Amerucan a look. What the fuck. I should just give him the envelope and leave.

They all stand. We slap and dash. Dessie and I measure each other up.

'Alan Kariuki Muigai,' he growls. 'I can't believe you are still alive.'

'You look well, man,' I say. The Amerucan and Bertiez laugh at this. Wah, the man has dents. He looks like he's just come back from ten tours with GSU in North Frontier District. There is a whole bottle of Johnny Walker Black on the table. I place the envelope in front of the Amerucan. He takes in air, grabs the envelope and shakes it.

'You are the fucking man,' the Amerucan says. All these years and I have never seen him this drunk. He grabs at the Johnny Walker and pours me a hefty shot.

The Amerucan says: 'Michael and I will go through this and give you a shout. Also, because Kiprotich and JM have fallen out we need more jamaas. Otherwise everybody now needs to put in 2M. Dessie says he's in. That means we only need to do 1.6M if everybody else stays.' He lists, mostly for Dessie's benefit, all the ideas that have come through the Mappen Hall Company so far.

The Amerucan continues. 'Also, Dessie knows a lot of shit that will come in handy. He knows the ins and outs of places that we might need. He has people in CID.'

The last I'd heard was that Dessie went to Moi University out in Eldoret. He says he was posted as a teacher somewhere in Kajiado. I lap this shit up. This news is excellent. A fucking mwalimu. Then fuck that, he says, he managed to get into CID training. He did a few years as a corporal and then went into private security. Entertainment mostly. But he also does a lot of private bodyguard stuff. He looks at me and asks whether I need a bodyguard. He's heard I am rolling in an Audi. His eyes have a speculative look when he says this. I need a bodyguard, yes, from this motherfucker.

Apart from the dents, Dessie's face is held together in lumps like he also became a boxer at some point. His eyes are set deep and small in the big lump that is his forehead and the bottom half that is one huge mess. I can tell he's still super-fit though. I notice that his knuckles are all broken. If I met him at night I would be, like: 'this man is a killer'.

Malizeni. Malizeni. The Amerucan is threatening to get another bottle. I take it easy on the Johnny Black. All three have a head-start on me and things could get crazy. I am worried that the Amerucan will lose the envelope that is now my ticket.

Then someone's phone rings. Dessie picks up. He listens and laughs long and loud. Then he says to the person he's talking to, 'Are you here? Uka. Come.'

'Guys,' he says, smiling his fisi smile. 'I have some friends of mine who have done very well for themselves who want to join us. I hope you don't mind.'

He turns on his stool and we see two women standing a bit far away, looking around. Dessie waves at them. The two women approach very gingerly in their heels and very tight mini-dresses. Dessie looks at them and whistles. 'Stop the press.'

The women look like they've just woken up and rolled around in make-up to hide their dents. Shit is ridiculous. At least they are not professionals, though. The Amerucan shouts: 'This is the Dessie we know.' One of the women is tall and dark. The other is short, fat and very light. They greet us with some Kiuk contempt and introduce themselves. The tall one is Wambui Grace and her friend is Wangui Caro. Wambui says to Dessie in Kikuyu, looking at Wangui. 'Haiya, look at this one. Kwani, he started drinking in the morning.' Dessie looks at her with a baleful glance.

'You smell like you woke up with changaa,' Wambui says. Dessie reaches and grabs her neck in one fluid movement and brings her face close to his as if he's going to headbutt her. She almost topples on her heels but Dessie holds tight. He brings her forehead against his and slowly applies pressure.

'Pole,' she says like she's about to cry. 'Sorreee. Sorreeee.' He lets her go and she moves back as if she will take a swing at him. Her face is contorted in pain but there is a hot and bothered look too. He smiles slowly at her and she sits down.

'Wait till we are nyumbani,' she says.

Wangui sits next to me. The four of us look like those ugly couples on TV that fight about how much they love each other. Bertiez and the Amerucan disassociate themselves from our side of the table – they go deep into how much money there is in wheat farming.

Dessie orders a bottle of Spice Gold for Wambui and Wangui. The women also ask for one kilo of wet fry. Wambui and Dessie turn to each other. Wangui tells me that she and Wambui import mitumba. They have exhibitions all over the City Centre. They travel to Turkey every month, buy wholesale and sell retail all over East Africa. The wet fry comes and Wangui and Wambui go at it like wow. Even the Amerucan and Bertiez forget wheat and watch. The shit is efficient. Fuck I've got to go.

But after some whisky shots I am beyond leaving. I am in the bottle and the bottle is inside of me. When I look up, the Amerucan has fallen asleep on his stool. I stand up and go to him. Dessie puts up his hand and looks at me. 'What are you doing?'

The Amerucan drools in his sleep. 'Look at him. We need to get him home. I'll get him a taxi.' Dessie laughs and looks around the table. 'Haiya. Who went and made you prefect. Si you found us here. Let him sleep for half an hour. He'll wake up feeling better.'

Dessie's eyes have gone warthog mean from the Black. I feel my balls try and go back home. I remember those eyes from back when. There goes my escape plan. Bertiez floats away to somewhere safe. He has switched to White Cap Light. Smart man.

Wangui and Wambui stand with their hands to their side after destroying the fry. They have a slight sheen to their faces as they head off to the bathroom. Dessie watches them as they waddle away and looks at me. 'Sasa Chief. Unataka?'

You want?

'I'm good,' I say.

'Niambie. You want Wangui? I can organize. Wambui is mine.'

I look at Bertiez. He is smiling at some very distant spot in the night that only he can see. He is somewhere in between what happened with him at Mappen 15 years ago and now.

'Kwara?' Dessie turns and says. 'Kwara was just telling me he's married,' he says to me as if that is the most unbelievable thing. 'That makes Wangui yours.'

'Hey man,' I say. 'I am engaged.'

'I've heard.' Dessie laughs. 'You are going out with the daughter of some millionaire. Wangui also has a lot of cash.'

He laughs again and looks as if he will say something but then sips at the Black.

'Why are you here? Where is this intended of yours?'

'Majuu. Out of the country.'

'You trust her?'

I look at him and say jack. He throws back the whisky but his small warthog eyes are still on me. He pours and flashes some more Johnny Black. Turns to me. I brace myself.

'Ama, it's something else.'

'What?'

He laughs. 'Well, I've heard she's not 100 per cent. A kaguru. Pole man. That's why I thought you might want to test something that works.'

He nods as the women appear in the distance. 'Wangui is always good to go.' He grabs at his crotch. 'Wangui is a night runner in bed. I should know. She also just bought a house in Garden Estate.' He laughs again.

'Fifteen years ago you were very different.'

'We all were.'

Dessie holds out his hand, broken knuckles and all, spreads his fingers. And then shakes it like a wriggling snake. He laughs out loud and pours more whisky.

'What's wrong with me? Forgive me. Tuji-enjoy. I believe

you. You are engaged. We should celebrate. I was just trying to be nice about Wangui.'

Wangui and Wambui come back and they have splattered more war paint on their faces. Dessie's batteries are recharged – he grabs Wambui's naked thigh and squeezes hard, grinning at me. Wangui parks herself right beside me.

Dessie points at me. 'You women should know that these two guys used to be my best friends in High School. We are going into business together. Men only.' He turns to both women. 'What is mine also belongs to these gentlemen. We shared everything in school, especially with Bertiez over here.' Bertiez makes a sound like a child's balloon losing air very quickly.

'Alan and I had some problems. I put that down to being young, not knowing how the world works.' Wangui and Wambui laugh in appreciation at this circus. The Amerucan suddenly stirs and mutters in his sleep. He froths at the mouth and sleep-mutters. The fool stays asleep.

Wambui is now drunk. 'Haiya. Mashetani. Evil spirits,' she says, looking at the Amerucan's sleeping figure. Wangui laughs and puts her arm on my shoulder.

'Let sleeping dogs lie,' Dessie says to me. 'If you wake them up they will bite you.'

Dessie stands up and comes around to where I am sitting. He looks down at me and hauls me to my feet. 'Come, let's talk.' He leads me a few metres away. The table behind us has gone quiet.

'Hey, I hope there are no hard feelings,' he says. 'Because if there are, I would have to do something about it.'

The sky is a smothering blanket. Solar Gardens is a tipping boat and I am tottering in it.

'I need a favour. Kuja with us to Simmers. Wambui and I need to fuck. But she will bring drama if Wangui does not get one of you.' He turns and looks over at the table. 'We both know Bertiez can't manage. He's just not man enough. No dume.'

Bertiez is now talking to the two women. From where we are he seems to have deflated in his suit. We go back to the table. Dessie seems relaxed. I try and will myself just to get up and walk away. I stand up and head off. I find myself in the toilet. When I get back I flash what's left in my glass without sitting down. I pull out my wallet. I am not sure what I have in it.

Dessie says, 'Don't worry, we'll get it.' He looks at the two women: both of them are now drunk and they laugh. Wangui reaches into her bag and throws a wad of thousands next to the bill. Dessie pours himself another whisky and breathes in deeply. He turns to me. 'I just want to know one thing before you go back to your kaguru chick. Are you still a homo?'

The whisky portal shuts. I go as sober as a judge. There's a point where whisky gets where the immediate world and the senses lose touch. In that vacuum, lost and deep memories stream, whole portals in the brain are reopened. I look around Solar Gardens and I suddenly feel every part of me linked with all the hopeless peeps in here, their miseries and their dire knowledge. The last 15 years and what happened at Mappen seem like yesterday. I'd forgotten that word. Homo.

We all fall quiet. Dessie stares at me hard and long. I see all the craziness in the world in there. I am the coward of the county. I did not do anything back then when I saw him with Bertiez. Flagrante. And I will not do anything now.

'Don't worry,' Dessie says. 'I love you, man. But you know what. You are still a fucking shoga.'

He stands up and pulls back his coat and stretches. We all see the gun. It is small and is holstered underneath his armpit. He does not say kwaheri. I look at Bertiez and I suddenly see Kwara – tall, gawky and girlish. After Dessie and his women leave, we sit there in some kind of mutual relief and finish the bottle. We wait for the Amerucan to wake up. Bertiez asks me whether I have managed to put together the 1.5M. I feel like a rabble again. I look at Bertiez and his eyes are dry and empty.

A few years ago Mappen was in the papers. This was after it was renamed when a new headmaster took over. A rabble had been raped by some Third Formers. I remember what Dessie did to Bertiez and I want to cry.

✳ ✳ ✳

Mappen used to be King of Nairobi's National Schools. It did not have the dry swottiness of Bush. It was not as Catholic as Strath. It did not have the jock culture of Changes. It did not have the thuggery of Jamu. It did not have the ujinga of Patch. Highway and Eastleigh are not worth bringing up – they were oboho schools. And Mappen did not have the snobbery of Saints. It did not have the ugly uniforms of Starehe. With these advantages it set out to become a school between Strath and Changes.

My father wanted me to go to Alliance but I missed that by five points. I ended up at Mappen. Dessie, Kwara before he became Bertiez and I drifted together in Third Form because Dessie and I were Eastlands. Kwara wanted to toughen up and believed we were his best allies in this quest. By Fourth Form we were studying together, doing everything together. Then, Dessie made Mappen First XV flanker. He was not big but ferocious. He had to keep super-fit. That's when he convinced Kwara and me to get up at 5am to train together. Mappen had eight houses – four were far away. The other four were in an arc around the main school block.

The three of us were all in neighbouring houses on the road that wrapped itself around the main block. Every morning, Dessie would wake me first at my house. And then we would run off to the house that Kwara was in.

One morning at the beginning of the second term, Dessie came to my house-dorm and rapped at my window. I jumped out of bed and into my games kit and we set off to pick up Kwara. We reached his house-dorm and Dessie went to wake him up. As I waited, I decided to do a quick lap around the house. This was not more than 200 metres. I went off in the morning mist and when I came back to the entrance of the house dorm, Kwara and Dessie were not outside yet. I decided to go check on them through the yard of the Fourth Form dorm.

I reached the row of windows and I peered in. I could see that Kwara was still in bed under this white blanket he used to have. Dessie was nowhere to be seen. I was about to take off but something caught the corner of my eye. Just beneath the window I made out a form sitting against the wall. I could see that Kwara was still asleep. And then the white blanket started wriggling. I could see a hand under the white blanket. It rose and fell and rose and fell. I saw Kwara's form dancing with the movement of the hand. And then the white blanket shifted. I saw Kwara. There was a hand around his neck. As he squirmed, Dessie came from under the window into view. His other hand moved up and down. My hands pushed against the glass. There they both were, locked in a silent dance. I stepped back and Dessie's head turned. In the dark, his eyes gleamed.

I ran off into the night. I ran around the block and all the way to the main school gate. It was locked and I turned back. I ran around the main school block again and again and again.

There was this thing we used to call 'shiko' at Mappen. Shiko was a concept, a kind of measurement of success, a philosophy of survival in boarding-school life. But we also used it to mean a slyness, a deceptive streak and a cunning. A good cunning. The Hare vs Tortoise kind. If you dawdled, partied with others but ended up doing well in class at the end of term you were a shikoist. If you misled everyone as to what you were about you were a shikoist. Its practice was essential for success in schoolboy Kenya. It was the best apprenticeship for life thereafter. I used to be quite good at shiko. I used to be a shikoist. Then I started running. I started being taken shiko.

***

Ivy sends me emails that say that she's still chasing the same deal in Dubai. I am no longer getting emails from the Mappen House Company. Catherine, Ivy's sister, has been trying to call me for weeks. A few days ago, after I'd ignored her calls, she sent me a text asking when she could come and pick up the Audi.

I am going through my wallet one evening after another weekend with the Audi when I find a crumpled note inside. I open it and make out a number. The name, Shiku. I call the number and I recognize the voice. It's the gazelle. 'Sasa,' she says in a voice that is weightless and unmoored.

'Shiku,' I say. 'We met at Mercury. The Junction.'

I pick up her up on Friday in Kileleshwa where she shares a one-room bedsitter with a friend. When she sees the Audi she laughs and all is right in her world.

'Whose other car was thaaat?' she asks. We go to the other Mercury. ABC – the original Mercury. An hour into drinks, Shiku asks where I live. I say Parklands and she crinkles her nose. 'It's okaaay,' she says. Try time.

Mercury is happening. We bop at the Bar. The place is bega kwa bega full. Someone taps me on the shoulder. I turn and Catherine is standing there.

'Hey, player,' she says. The music is loud but I hear her clearly. She looks Shiku up and down and holds out her palm. I put the keys of the Audi in her hand. She looks at me and shakes her head and walks away. Shiku asks what's wrong. I can see the Audi out in the parking lot. It is beautiful. It is the only constant.

Billy Kahora lives and writes in Nairobi. His short fiction and creative non-fiction have appeared in *Chimurenga, McSweeney's, Granta Online, Internazionale, Vanity Fair* and *Kwani?* He has written a non-fiction novella titled *The True Story Of David Munyakei*. He was shortlisted for the Caine Prize for African Writing with 'Urban

Zoning' in 2012 and 'The Gorilla's Apprentice' in 2014. He wrote the screenplay for *Soul Boy* and co-wrote *Nairobi Half Life*. He is working on a novel titled *The Applications*. A short-story collection *The Cape Cod Bicycle War and Other Youthful Follies* will be released in late 2016. He is also Managing Editor of Kwani Trust and has edited seven issues of the *Kwani?* journal and other Kwani publications including *Nairobi 24* and *Kenya Burning*. He is also a Contributing Editor with the *Chimurenga Chronic*.

The Wandering Festival

Bwanga 'Benny Blow' Kapumpa

It was a three-day hike to the festival grounds. My *ng'anga* friend and I had to hop off our bus at the edge of a bumpy road that cut through a seemingly random location. In a sense, I was thankful for it because it meant the end of the awkward gawking from the other passengers that had ostracized us and chosen to sit on the other side of the bus. I couldn't blame them; they were scared shitless of my weirdly dressed companion and his adopted undead friend. But on the other hand, I would have rather sat on my foam-deficient raggedy bus seat with eyeballs and gazes rudely fondling my company and I (one of whom was muzzled) than trek through hours of nowhere-land flora.

The trek was a crash course in Living and Surviving in Obscure Forests. I learned which leaves did not leave your anus with a burning rash when used as toilet paper; which berries gave you a 22-hour erection; which tree sap you could use as disinfectant; which lizards tasted just like chicken and the location of a nearby stream I could bathe in. We would camp out in clearings we came across for two consecutive nights. Our undead *chitumbi* had to be tied to a tree lest he develop a taste for livers.

Our destination was an ancient holy ground I suspect had never been mapped. This really got my sweaty boxers in a bunch. Why couldn't it have been somewhere convenient? Surely a creepy lover of the occult must have owned a rusty-ass-goal-post stadium that he could let us use in exchange for magic dust or something.

Tonga legend has it that when lightning licked the earth, Tilo – the god of the blue sky – hurled Thunder Boulders and divinely appointed *ng'angas* would scour the land looking for these large heavenly stones. The stones would then be enshrined in small temples and used as mediums. Each temple was the charge of a *ng'anga* and acted as both a transmitter and receiver of spiritual alternating current from the great beyond. This particular area we were in had five of these shrines spread out into a perfect circle with a circumference the size of a grand arena.

I'd been told that there would be a human sacrifice at this thing, but being a living, breathing human myself, I wasn't looking forward to witnessing it. I still had to; I had a story to write. The Wandering Festival occurred every ten years and its host nation would hold it in an insanely remote area that was not only tedious to get to, but often times the journey to it would be life-threatening. Maybe it would get great reviews if it weren't always held on the fringes of nowhere. *Rolling Stone Paranormal* would rate it as, 'A damn ghoul time!', *GQ Afterlife* would say, 'It's the top festival of the other side', and *Phantom! Magazine* with its absurdity would advise the ultimate festivalgoer to commit suicide to fully appreciate it.

I was a writer that prided himself on delving into the world of the weird and wonderful. My blog got abysmal views but I'd still post in the hopes that I'd blip on somebody's radar. And as life would have it, *Rolling Stone Paranormal* wouldn't publish my work. *GQ Afterlife* wouldn't even respond to my emails. And *Phantom! Magazine* claimed my pieces were too tame. Paranormal events and mysticism didn't get the coverage I thought they deserved.

Cheerless websites run by criminally insane conspiracy theorists had made it their mission to shed light on the unusual, but they often did so with the grace of a three-legged gazelle. There were only a handful of credible magazines that wrote on the subject and breaking into any one of them was extremely difficult. Nonetheless I had dedicated every action

I took, every keystroke, to seeing myself in the editorial staff section of these publications. I mean, sure, being a freelance writer had its allure and adventure, but it didn't pay nearly as many bills as it would have in other parts of the world. I got decent cheques writing articles for wedding magazines and my sparse contributions to *Lonely Planet*. Sometimes I submitted to the occasional 'Illuminati Secrets Revealed Dot Com' and these gigs helped me meet some of my expenses. But my passion was rooted in covering paranormal *extracurricular* activity. Not to be confused with paranormal activity, paranormal extracurricular activity was what exorcised demons got up to so as to recover from the hangover caused by being torn from a body they had long inhabited.

But who actually read this content? Who read about the fancy soirées of blueblood phantoms? For one, I liked to imagine ghosts that appreciated any form of literature. I wasn't entirely sure how they went about getting their subscription to *Phantom!* but I assumed they enjoyed reading about the more social activities of the undead.

My true target audience was open-minded people. People who cared nothing about religion or race. People who were intrigued by the weird. Those who were not swayed by science's attempts to debunk the existence of something beyond the bridge of our noses. Thinkers that fervently searched for answers in African myths and folklore and believed their ancestors were not kooky witchdoctors and cult leaders but conduits of something we didn't fully understand. Individuals like myself, convinced of the reality of a spiritual realm only revealed by the tearing of the thin veil that existed between our world and the next. I wrote for curious minds. An article on this festival would surely etch me into those minds forever.

I met my *ng'anga* comrade when I was interviewing him for an investigative piece for my blog. I was inquiring into the truth of the claims of spiritual healers and herbalists and their ability to bring back lost lovers, increase wealth and all the other assertions propagated by their badly printed flyers. He turned out to be the real deal. And most times his abilities would be too much of the real deal. He once shared an anecdote about a woman that yearned for her lost lover to return. She had assumed that her lover's three-week disappearance was surely fuelled by infidelity and that he had run off with someone. It turned out the man had climbed into a large tanker of opaque beer that had veered off the road and he'd drowned inside its belly. My *ng'anga* informant said he resurrected the man through sophisticated sorcery. The *chitumbi* rose and staggered from the mortuary to his client's home, reeking of *Chibuku* and not in possession of his soul or mental faculties. He'd become a zombie and the *ng'anga*'s client had demanded a refund.

'She wanted her lost lover back, so I brought her lost lover back. I was pretty sure that would have held up in court and so she didn't pursue the matter,' he laughed. Today, he and the *chitumbi* are best buddies.

✳✳✳

I suspect the Wandering Festival derived its name from the nomadic tendencies of a number of the continent's civilizations. Every decade it is hosted in a different African country and is a celebration of our ancestral heritage through food, beverages and prayer. It is a reminder to the people that their deities and ancestors or deceased still exist. It is also a celebration of the bizarre. I'm told that at the last festival, a drunken reveller got his insides mauled by a bloodthirsty poltergeist band when he jumped on stage during a performance.

After I'd set up camp in the forest outside the stadium-sized clearing, I was to report to my *ng'anga*'s narrow temple to donate a pint of blood as admission into the festival.

'The blood…,' he said, 'the blood is what I will use to write the calligraphy on the Thunder Stones to summon the spirits.'

He could tell I was sceptical. 'You will not be the only one,' he said, in a poor attempt to calm me, 'all the other *ng'angas* are doing it.' When he saw that I was still hesitant, he moved on to our zombie friend. He then pulled out a ghost-white knife made from bone – human or animal I could not tell, but the intricacy of its detailed engravings intrigued me. He slit a vertical line worthy of a surgeon's envy at the base of the *chitumbi*'s palm and squeezed out a reddish-black sludge that was the coagulated blood of this ash-pale zombie. The sludge hit the bottom of a caramel calabash with a 'splat' that made my skin crawl. The *chitumbi* seemed not to feel a thing. He looked down at his wound, then at the *ng'anga*, back at his wound and then up at me.

The *ng'anga* turned to me with open arms and a face that seemed to say, 'See? That wasn't so bad! Now it's your turn.' I never donated blood. Needles made me squeamish. And this guy was about to slit my wrist with a Shogun-sharp bone-shank. But more than the size of the scar I'd get; more than the pain I'd feel and more than how much blood I would lose; I kept thinking about what he would use to sterilize his damn knife.

✳ ✳ ✳

I was violently yanked from a lucid dream I was having by a droning that seemed to hum from an eternal place. This strange noise reminded me of a *didgeridoo* – a musical instrument with a very peculiar sound. I'd passed out from the sight of my own blood earlier and was still a little woozy. I thought what was happening might have been a part of my lucid dream, but that escalating droning was too loud for any hallucination. The strange humming was coming from the nether regions of the *ng'angas'* throats and tuning into the frequency of the threads of our reality's fabric. It gradually reached a crescendo and at its peak was humming inside my skull, drowning out my thoughts and throwing them against chaotic winds. I was afraid. What had I got myself into?

I grasped at my swirling thoughts and emotions, only seeming to grab a tight hold of fear. I latched onto it for dear life. I suspected if I didn't, I'd surely go insane before the muscly bits of my brain festooned the tiny temple. I blocked my ears in a futile attempt to block out the sound within the core of my mind and staggered outside. The *chitumbi* groaned something primal and looked more bewildered than I was. And then, dead silence. The droning had ceased.

Before I could fully embrace my new-found appreciation for silence, another sound tore through the ether. It was as if a colossal cosmic being was angrily tearing the light textile of the sky and was drawing closer. The sun had already packed up shop and this cloudless evening sky began to sound like a domestic quarrel between two lightning bolts. Two humungous solid oak doors cometed through the sky toward our location and I scampered for safety. But where was safety? I didn't know where the wretched things would land and so I scrambled like a headless chicken. The doors hit the ground with a thunderous BOOM and floored me. I was in what looked like the centre of the clearing and the two god-size doors stood at a distance. I squinted a little and could see their intricate engravings. It was the most beautiful, terrifying thing I had ever seen.

***

The moon spilt its natural light onto the domineering wooden doors. They looked like they belonged at the entrance of a great *nephilim*'s castle. They were fashioned from the richest African Oakwood and were emblazoned with chestnut-coloured carvings of the most complicated detail. The carvings depicted scenes of song, dance and copious celebration. Masks whose symbols and patterns seemed to tell their own stories embossed this gate and evoked both fear and awe. It was extraordinary.

While I marvelled at this very large structure, the ground below me began to rumble. Pebbles and stones vibrated violently and the earth began to rise. The turbulent rumbling made it difficult for me to stand, but I managed to get to my feet and leapt off the rising rectangle beneath me. Terrified didn't begin to describe how I felt. I patted the back of my pants and smelt my fingers to see if I'd shat myself. Sand and dirt poured to the ground below and the chasm left by the rising platform gradually closed up. It ascended a few metres off the ground and then halted, staying suspended in mid-air. Four rectangular pillars with round hollows in their centres jutted upwards from each of the corners; African drums of various shapes and sizes sprouted up in the same manner and an array of band instruments materialized and hovered above what was now evidently a music stage. Bright orbs of psychedelic light floated around this grand stage in firefly patterns before they multiplied and shot off to other parts of the location, complementing the starlit sky.

The large carved doors let out a thunderous creaking as they opened outward. When the doors extended fully and opened the gateway, all manner of spirits, ectoplasm, ghouls, *tokoloshes,* buffalo-headed minotaurs, some human beings and a multitude of creatures I'd never seen before poured in like a flood of energy. The levees had broken. The Wandering Festival had finally begun.

✳✳✳

The festival had no banners, pull-ups or projectors screaming consumerist rhetoric at attendants. Not a single, 'Drink Brew Beer!' or 'Proudly sponsored by...' flyer assaulted fest-goers. Balls of slimy ectoplasm sat on long vertical staffs glowing softly, lighting a pathway or simply adding to the aesthetics on steroids that made the Wandering Festival. Streamers of *chitenge* cloth with artistic patterns hung from stretched hemp twine. Multi-coloured string beads rattled when separated to enter a tent. The loud chatter of relatives catching up with the deceased pierced through the night's air and drumming and chanting were a constant chorus. The smell of green vegetables and culinary adventures tickled the nose. Culture was woven into several straw mats lining the floors of food kiosks and would act as makeshift beds for people and creatures that could not hold their liquor. Stone carvings and sculptures had burrowed from below ground just as the stage had, and there were many fantastic floating lights that would implode like mini supernovas and then reappear again.

Occasionally a spectre would frolic by, probably hopped up on some afterlife *chamba* smoke, and phase right through a human body. I'm not entirely sure how many other human beings were present at this spectacle, but there were a few. Some freely associated and drank with the odd ghosts they had never met before and others were there both to mourn and to celebrate. I watched a family of four place wrapped gifts, food and expensive-looking fabric while performing a macabre combination of crying and dance before the resting place of a lost loved one. The deceased had appeared at the festival for one last goodbye and watching this scene play out completely moved me. I rattled my head to find the words to capture the moment in my article. Perhaps I could move my readers too.

I also witnessed my fair share of vertically challenged imps try to reach underneath the dresses of some women and wondered why these people would come here to be subjected to all this strangeness. Imps and *tokoloshes* were vile perverted creatures no one should have the displeasure of rubbing knees with. What drew them here? Was it the opportunity to reunite with a long-dead father?

Or perhaps they wished to gain favour with their ancestors and possibly amass wealth? People did the strangest things for money.

A small band of novice *sangomas* would tour the place and

also compete in astonishing sorcery showdowns. They were there for a two-day workshop for Beginners in the Occult. I immersed myself in the festival and jotted it all down furiously in my notepad. 'It was a smorgasbord of deeply rooted mysticism and tradition'. I wandered around wide eyed, barely wrapping my head around what was occurring before me when I tripped and bumped into someone I was not prepared to meet.

A thick, liquid-like smoke clothed and floated around this tall, black porcelain skeleton, forming a robe that cowled over its skull in a ghostly cloak. This thing looked like an elaborate installation; like a monk had got his skin and bones charred while staring into the distance. It spoke.

'I am the severer of ties between this life and what lies beyond. Through the ages, some have referred to me as the Grim Reaper, but my true name is Impundulu, the servant of death. But do not be alarmed! I am not here to collect your soul!'

Even though I was terrified at first, I was glad I'd bumped into Death. He became my unofficial guide to the Wandering Festival and recommended the most fascinating sights and sounds. When I asked about why he was out there having a good time and not performing his deathly duties, he said he was still at work.

'Death is everywhere,' he said nonchalantly and threw some brew to the back of his skinless mouth.

He'd been attending the festival since its inception and was there just to chill and hang out. He provided a wealth of knowledge for my article. He said, at every festival a deity from the host nation was celebrated along with the spirits of great people that had passed on. Impundulu showed me the various attractions and acts to look out for, using his extensive knowledge of everyone living and deceased. You'd be surprised how many musicians reinvented themselves in the afterlife and started thriving careers.

Our headlining act that night, for example, was the

legendary Paul Ngozi. Bright lights beamed from the stage when he got on and nubile ghosts screamed and jumped frantically. Ectoplasmic fireworks shot to the sky when he made his electric guitar wail and I absolutely loved the pyrotechnics. I was briefly distracted when their hot glowing slime landed on my shoulder but hardly noticed it because you didn't get to see a live posthumous performance from Paul Ngozi every day. Coachella's hologram performances had nothing on this.

He performed some of his old hits, including *Bauze* and *Vina Bwela Mo Chedwa*. The music would go off at intervals on his cue and the audience would sing along in acapella. '*Bauze! Bauze, Ngozi!*' they chanted in unison. '*Bauze! Ba mvesese lelo!*'

Impundulu didn't sing along. He said he didn't really like the posterboy of Zamrock. Paul Ngozi wasn't a very nice man (or ghost) in his opinion. Apparently he'd thrown a bitch-fit about his accommodation and had demanded that the plumbing be reworked so he could get pure ectoplasm for his shower.

One would never imagine sharing any common interests with Death. But it turned out that we both appreciated the athleticism and choreography of professional wrestling. The festival's music was out of this world, to say the least, and it also offered the curious mind a rainbow of other bizarre activities. Impundulu led us to a large mud hut whose walls were lined with various *Nyau* masks and where a fighting ring was dug out in its centre. The masks would detach from the walls and their bodies begin to mould themselves from clay as they leapt into the ring below in high-flying wrestling fashion. These beings threw down their clay bodies to the rhythm of the self-beating drums and clapping from the audience that surrounded them in a series of suplexes and violent grapples. The *Nyau* wrestlers danced from side to side and thudded the heels of their feet on the ring's floor. It was a musical Lucha Libre meets the motherland's WWE. There is nothing quite like the display of grown *Nyau* dancers flinging themselves to the ground.

The one time I saw my Grim Reaper guide express something close to excitement was just before the last performance of the night. Even though he had no facial muscles, lips or any flesh at all, I could tell he had a fan-girl expression on his skull when he frantically waved his hands and talked about the last act.

'You simply MUST see this!' he told me.

When she got onto the stage the lights dimmed. She had no ensemble with her, no over-elaborate band or ridiculous costume and not the slightest wink at the possibility of a memorable performance. However, the locks on her head were not of your average variety. They looked like they were made of water; like thin, flowing streams that had formed dreadlocks, parting at the top of her forehead and then flowing down her back and over her shoulders. She stood there staring into the crowd as if waiting for us to shut up. And then she opened her mouth to sing.

I felt the hairs on the back of my neck slowly rising as my mouth gaped. The clouds above us converged and it began to shower. The heavens were so moved they shed tears of joy. Time stood still and I felt my entirety being drawn in by this being. Her voice was angelic. She was a beautiful siren speaking directly to my soul. I had never been so aware of myself. My earliest memories came flooding back to me: the very first gasp of breath I ever took; the feeling of breaking my arm when I was younger; the sensation of my first ejaculation; the hurt of losing someone dear and the sharp sting of heartbreak. I knew that I was in love with her.

No backstage existed at this place because the platform was raised, but Impundulu pointed his bony finger in the direction I could find the enchanting songstress. I had to speak with her. She would probably have excellent quotes for my article. Why had she performed solo? What motivated her? Who were some of her influences? Her insight and thoughts were exactly what my article needed. This was what would catapult me into the elite of paranormal extracurricular activity! But of course that was a load of bull. I just wanted to – no – I just NEEDED to talk to her.

When I found her, she was staring into a small pond on the outskirts of the festival grounds.

'Hi,' I said.

'Hello,' she replied, smiling.

Her name was Mlengavuwa – 'Mlenga for short,' she said. Though the nimbus clouds had cleared right after she had got off the stage, when you came close to her, you could hear the distinct whisper of rainfall. Her hair was alive; a constant stream of liquid dreadlocks emanated from the top of her head and covered her bare breasts. I tried to maintain eye contact, but I'd occasionally glance at her chest when I thought it was safe. It was like looking through frosted glass. I could only see the sensual curve of her breasts and the vague shape of her dark areola. I felt teased and overwhelmed by it; my glances became more frequent. When she caught me she only smiled. Her face was a song in itself, a sweet melody you could see with your eyes. She was beautiful, and she smelt like the essence of rain. Petrichor, the geeks call it. It was now the scent of love.

I kept fumbling my words. Every question I asked sounded more stupid than the last. She giggled at my escalating foolery but I didn't feel the slightest sting of mockery – she seemed to like me too. Mlenga squatted and tugged at my pants leg in a gesture to get me to squat with her. She looked into the pond with deep intent, her aqua-hair swimming in itself and doing things to my emotions I never thought possible. She grabbed a frog from a lily pad and asked me to lick it.

'What?'

'Lick it.'

'What? Why?'

'Just trust me and lick the frog,' she said, her tone childlike and endearing.

So I licked the damn frog.

'If this thing turns into a prince and you run off with him, I don't know if I'll ever forgive myself.'

She laughed. That whisper of rainfall got slightly louder whenever she did. I'd never seen anything so magical. Not until the festival got trippy.

The frog secreted a psychoactive enzyme that took our adventure to new heights. Mlenga licked it as well, took my hand and led. We went from staring at the playful designs of bright-coloured beaded mats for hours to laughing hard at Impundulu's terrible tales of soul reaping. The music from the festival sounded incredible, I swear I could almost taste it. Though I strongly suspect that may have been the aftertaste of the frog's trippy juices. At some point during our adventure, Mlenga had to restrain me from trying to get onto the main stage. I laboured to get a long bamboo ladder to the stage platform so I could climb it and see what the view was like from there. I would have succeeded too if it wasn't for that immaculate creature. She brought out the worst in me and I loved it.

The sun was beginning to rear its head and the sky would soon transform into a Technicolour dream. A few people were strewn across the dusty ground, their heads probably splitting from drinking too much *katata*. Mlenga and I sat on the branch of a large tree and watched the colours of the sky gradually morph from black to a scene from an abstract painting with carefree streaks of orange.

I turned to look at Mlenga, her face even more beautiful in the creeping light. I looked into her big eyes and drowned in the pools of their spellbinding essence. She slowly faded and disappeared with the rising sun, along with the rest of the non-human festival attendees.

*** * ***

I mostly slept like a rock for half of that day but would

sometimes be woken up by my screaming body and overwhelming thoughts of Mlenga. I couldn't hold any internal conversation. She derailed any train of thought that didn't lead to her station. Why did I feel this way for someone I'd just met? I was convinced I was more than just infatuated. All I wanted to do was spend the rest of my days with her; to grow old and father cute babies with rivers for hair and have a home that smelled like rain. My last thought before I finally passed out was of us holding hands in the twilight of our lives. We would say nothing but share a singular thought of happiness. She would still whisper the song of the rain without even parting her lips.

I woke up from the same dream I had when I had reached this strange place. In it, the *ng'angas* stood in a circle around me, their eyes rolled into the back of their heads as they chanted something arcane. It was all very freakish, but I wasn't afraid. In fact, I'd never felt calmer. I had no interior turmoil about what I'd do for money nor did I feel the overbearing shadow of an impending deadline. And then it rained.

The *ng'angas'* droning rudely plucked me from my dream and thrust me into reality. Their incantations tuned into the frequency of the next realm and once more summoned the spirits as the sun tucked itself into the horizon. I had one thing on my mind. But before I could set foot on the festival holy grounds, my *ng'anga* friend needed to tell me all he knew about Mlengavuwa.

'She is a goddess,' he said.

'Yeah,' I agreed, 'Something real divine about her!'

'No,' he replied, 'I mean she is *really* a goddess. She's the daughter of Tilo, god of the sky,'

I couldn't believe it. I should have been less surprised by this information. She did have flowing water for hair and I'd seen many strange things at this festival, after all. But I never thought I'd ever hold hands and fall in love with a real-life goddess.

Her name meant 'rain maker' and her heavenly waters would bring bountiful crops and prosperity to the people. Her song was a message to them to say she would create a covenant and that covenant was to be bound at the festival.

'Tonight we will have her coming-of-age ceremony. You will definitely enjoy it,' he said to me, exposing a rotten-toothed grin.

I needed to see her again. My article be damned! Nothing else mattered more in that moment. *Rolling Stone Paranormal* could wait. *GQ Afterlife* didn't need another festival piece and *Phantom! Magazine* probably wouldn't appreciate something of this magnitude. Even with all its fascinating spectacles and believe-it-or-not activities, all I was concerned with was Mlenga.

Not even Shaka and the Impis – an outworld band whose frontman was the great war spirit that had once possessed Shaka Zulu – could fully arrest my attention. 'Rain maker,' I whispered to myself over the menacing booming that blared from the clay speakers.

The spirit's Impis furiously beat their war drums while the band's bass guitarist violently hugged his instrument and plucked at its strings. All I could hear was Mlenga's bewitching song.

When the war spirit took to the microphone, every single entity present listened except for me. His voice resonated throughout the festival grounds like the baritone lamentations of a large oil drum. The backing vocals were wild war cries and ululations as the dancers kicked their legs and stomped the hovering stage. *Rain maker.* All I heard was the polyamorous sound of her song, that perfect synergy of fright, melody and emotion.

I'd searched for her all evening and had grown weary of brushing shoulders with drunken people and phasing through inebriated spirits. My mind trained its eye on one thing. When it was time for her ceremony, something awakened my consciousness and I made my way to the floating stage.

A throne stood in the centre of the stage and nestling within it was the goddess I'd fallen in love with. The throne was covered with the same intricate engravings that emblazoned the festival gates. Some women danced around Mlenga and let out frantic ululations while others clapped and beat drums. The moonlight shone on their white streaks of body paint as their bodies gyrated and their *chitenges* tightly hugged their curves. Mlenga sat still with her head lowered and her hair in that constant flux. One of the women tossed herself to the ground in a melodramatic gesture and rolled around singing praises.

The stage began to descend slowly and made contact with the ground just before the chatter stopped. My *ng'anga* stepped forward with his undead lost lover carrying a calabash in tow. I locked eyes with Mlenga and was mesmerized again. The *ng'anga* called to his peers and they each appeared with their own wards holding calabashes. It all seemed strangely familiar. Déjà vu. And then Mlenga began to sing her song.

I was pulled toward the large platform, one foot moving in front of the other involuntarily. I was going to be with Mlenga. She stretched her hand out to me while she sang. I stretched mine out and held hers forever. She would lead as she had the previous night. But something within me suspected we would not be going on an adventure. We would not be licking narcotic frogs and marvelling at the psychedelic patterns of colourful mats. Impundulu's living cloak emerged from the ground and he materialized next to me. I'd never attended one, but this wasn't what I'd imagined a coming-of-age ceremony would be like. The *ng'angas* broke into a chorus of eerie chants. It was all coming to life. The dream I had had was playing out right before my eyes. What did this mean? Why had I been the only person drawn to this stage?

And then it all dawned on me. Looking around at the people I'd assumed were my friends, I felt a pang of betrayal. I turned to Impundulu.

'So you *are* actually here to collect my soul?'

He nodded once.

'I thought you just enjoyed hanging out with me.'

And then I turned to Mlenga. When I looked into her eyes, I was content with my fate. I wholeheartedly accepted what I realized was my predestined purpose. *I* was the human sacrifice. Black clouds had merged above the stage and the skies began to weep. My goddess had never looked more beautiful. As Impundulu swung his glinting scythe, I thought, *maybe I could write a great story about the afterlife.*

Bwanga 'Benny Blow' Kapumpa is a freelance writer, content manager and an avid storyteller. Qualified as a chartered accountant, he decided to pursue more creative aspirations and charted a path from blogger to copywriter. He currently writes for a number of Zambian magazines, blogs and online publications and writes a bi-weekly webcomic that's slowly gaining popularity in Lusaka. He would like to be a leader and knowledge sharer in Zambia's creative and digital media space, and is honing his craft as a writer of fiction.

In The Garden

FT Kola

My princess is playing in the garden. In a grove of cedar trees she is searching for her companion, an aristocratic girl chosen for her loveliness, for my princess must have nothing that is not fine in her presence. This girl, who is soft and smooth and sleek like a baby seal, whose brown body the ladies of the court adorn with turquoise and gold each morning, has buried herself in a feathery bed of cedar fronds for my princess to unearth, and my princess, leaning her brow gently against the trunk of a tree as if it were the chest of her father, closes her eyes and counts to ten.

At the edge of the grove stands a band of attendants. My princess will play for no longer than a half hour, but still, here stand the musicians with their lyres and oboes, filling the sultry air with music for my princess's pleasure; here stand bronzed boys like statues, holding censers of balsam and incense aloft, perfuming that same air; here stand handmaidens holding silver dishes of fragrant rosewater should she wish to cool her childish fingers; here stands the nurse, who watches my princess anxiously, whose dark nipples, two shadows beneath her linen shift, still smart from my princess's once-aggressive feeding; here stand two robust Syrians who, should she tire, will lift my princess into a palanquin stuffed with pillows of Chinese silk; here stands a venerable wizard of Memphis, foul-smelling from his magical ointments, who as a boy blinded himself with a burning stick and is now whispering urgent incantations against snakes and scorpions, for death by such creatures is more probable than nature would suggest, and, though my princess is the middle of a litter of six, still there are those who ask, what will she grow into?; here stand two noble and haughty Abyssinian ladies of the court, one of whom cradles a mewling lion cub with milky eyes that – when it suckles honey off my princess's thumb – sends her into fits of laughter, the other guarding a cedar chest lined with melted pearls and filled with amusements befitting my princess's royal divinity: a pale blue shard of shell from the egg that hatched Helen, tiny clay figurines representing every race under the empire and so lifelike that each took a year to fashion, a burnished pine cone (still fragrant) from the thyrsus of Dionysus, an albino crocodile hatchling (stiff and preserved, with Indian rubies for eyes), miniature plates and cups of beaten gold with which to hold play banquets; here stands the Scythian cook, a gift from the king of Mathura, famed for his temper, and his kitchen boys, whom he beats mercilessly, and who now submerge pitchers of milk in cool river water, who hold forth platters of pomegranate seeds like heaps of rubies and bunches of grapes translucent with sunlight, and who have spent hours decorating in intricate detail a hundred tiny cakes, each with a surprise inside (a toy, a silver ring, a fat fig) on the chance that my princess, who is indifferent to all food, is moved to eat. Here stand I.

We are assembled as we are every morning, but today my princess is in a state of disquiet. There is, as there has never been before, a restiveness in her. She is a great lover of games, of pranks, but today the hunt seems to leave her dissatisfied. She glances around at us, at her nurse, at the pink and blue and yellow villas that dot the palace grounds, as if she suspects us of disappearing when her back is turned and she wishes to catch us in the act. Rosewater, pomegranates, silk – none of it would soothe her. I know my princess's moods; I read them as effortlessly as I read the scrolls in the library. My princess is the tenth of the languages in which I am fluent, of the languages in which I have been reciting and writing poetry since I was a boy. The slackness of her limbs as she moves about the cedars, the wilful toss of her lank hair, the nervous twitch of the corner of her mouth – these are as clear to me as the marks I make on my own papyrus, in my own steady hand. I watch as she stops, lifts a knee, and leans forward to pluck off a sandal. Her nurse gathers her skirts in her hands and makes to move towards her, but my princess says, 'No!', a harsh word in Egyptian, a language that of all her family only she has learned to speak, since they hold in high esteem their Greek heritage and disdain most things native, apart from a ceremonial tidbit here and there. The nurse – who cannot read my princess as I do, even though my princess has never said a word to me, and so for me she is like the lost language of some forgotten tribe, I read her without the benefit of conversation – hovers, an anxious gadfly. My princess shakes a surplus of cedar feathers from her small gold sandal. Then she pulls it back on, slopes over to the cedar pile, and points at it, and when the pretty companion leaps up and we all applaud her cleverness, Cleopatra sighs.

I am one of the many scribes of the palace. Of all of the palace's unseen machinery – its cooks and guards and servants and pages and gardeners and keepers of the royal roses and keepers of the sacred crocodiles and handmaidens and stable boys and soldiers and laundry-maids – we are the least noticed, for we do nothing but watch and record. One scribe records the king's diet and his bowel movements, another the utterances of the royal astronomer, another the portentous dreams of the ladies of the court. I could have been the scribe of the graceful Berenice, three years older than Cleopatra and groomed for the throne, or I could have been the scribe of the younger, headstrong Arsinoe, who commands with a pointed finger. Instead I am the scribe of Cleopatra, her father's beloved, wedged between her sisters. There have been Cleopatras before her, hundreds of them, but only she is mine.

I have known my princess all the eight years (almost nine, it will be her birthday soon) of her life, from the time that her mother dropped her wailing onto a wooden plank carved with magical hieroglyphs, to now, where she stands alert, her body small and solitary against the great dark mass of cedar trees. Let me say, in the name of the truth to which I am devoted (for what am I but the most faithful chronicler of *all* of my princess, her delights and pleasures, the contours of her mind, what she conceals, and what she allows to be seen?), that my princess has not yet achieved what the common people would call loveliness. If she were not divine, if she did not wear the white silk ribbon of a descendant of Alexander upon her brow, if her father were not king, she would not, perhaps, be chosen as her own companion. But pretty girls are as transient as the multitudes of apple blossoms that bloom from green branches for a single, spring day, and by nightfall are browned and bruised on the ground.

Her handmaidens tell me that at night my princess howls with pain, as the hollows behind her knees and the crooks of her elbows ache with growing pains, that she will not sleep unless, as if she were a teething infant again, they rub an ointment of fly dirt and poppy juice on her gums, and I believe it, because my princess grows day by day not into loveliness but into clumsiness. She is a series of sharp angles that will not accede to her will: in the mornings when her nurse brushes her hair she accidentally elbows the old woman in the stomach, and when she runs down the walkways of the palace, which are cool in the shadows of Corinthian columns and lofty palms, she inevitably trips and falls, so that her already embittered legs are further bruised and her nurse must seat her on the edge of her bath each evening and pluck the pebbles and grit out of her poor, scarred knees. She bites her cuticles, my princess does, she carves tiny cruciforms with a torn fingernail into the mosquito bites on her arms – I have seen flecks of blood on the white linen of her play-dress – she picks at the corners of her mouth until the skin bleeds, and when it does, as she sits with her tutor and practises her Greek vocabulary (*abdominous, whelp, hircine*) she worries at the sores with her unconscious tongue. Of late, she blushes, as if someone has dipped a brush into coloured ink and touched it to her cheeks. A blush of shame, I believe, at her body's constant betrayal.

I am to keep a record of her days: here did Cleopatra, daughter of Auletes, appear in a procession at the palace at Memphis and pay honour to the gods, her sisters by her side; here was Cleopatra presented with a dress of fine-spun gold by the society of silk merchants; here was Cleopatra presented to the visiting King of Mauretania, who praised her pretty manners. These facts give the shape but not the colour of my princess's days. And I am a poet, not a keeper of kitchen accounts. Great rivers of scrolls we scribes produce, to be poured into the thousands of cubbyholes of the library of Alexandria, and there they collect dust, for the library contains every text in the world, more than can ever be read even by the scholars that toil there constantly, and to their burden we daily add more. The dutiful diary I file alongside the rest, so that in time it will serve to cross the eyes of some future scholar with boredom. The real work I keep for myself. My secret pleasure: the reams of papyrus that I fill each night alone in my scribe's chamber, with every detail of my princess's day, accounts of her shifting moods as one might record the changing weather. What I do not see I gather, for I am trusted all about the palace, and what I do not gather I imagine.

This morning Cleopatra awoke at dawn. The city of Alexandria was turning from ivory to rose, the sun touching sweetly the columns of the great white marble palace, the limestone sphinxes that line the avenues, and the pearly domes of the Greek temples, bathing in vermilion the wide expanse of the desert and the crumbling tombs of the kings. Cleopatra lay in her bed in billows of lambswool and panther skin, her eyes lifted to the sky above her balcony, where birds of prey swooped and dove, and beneath which Alexandria turned aureate, roseate, alive. Rising, she let out a cry of horror. A viscous substance, for a moment utterly mysterious, was stuck to her thigh.

Then the realization. She had gone to sleep with her favourite pet, a white mouse who would scurry in panicked bursts over her childish arms and tremble in her cupped hands, and some time in the night she must have crushed him, because there in the chaos of her sheets was now only the approximation of a mouse, a bloodied piece of fur, pathetic and small. Cleopatra wept. Three times. First, with the shock of disgust, like any healthy young girl. Then, with a tender, biting remorse, for she loved her pet, loved him as she does all things that love her and bring her pleasure. But what of the third time? I see her there, in her white bed, as a small thing lost in drifts of sand, weeping, and I imagine that at some point as she wept the second time, her grief slowly began to clear, like mist dissolved by sunlight, and there emerged the world around her. The cloying scent of roses and lilies from the bower above her bed, the soft brush of panther fur against her childish ankles, the buzz and rattle of a dying beetle in some corner of her chamber, the rising heat from the city beyond the balcony, and beyond that the great untamed world, and above it all, the pleasing resonance of her own sobs, echoing off the marble columns and rising in high, pure notes to the ceiling. And so the third time must have been an experiment: above the pulpy body of the now-forgotten mouse Cleopatra would have twisted and turned her girlish body and practised varieties of despair, modes of sorrowful repose: now she was Achilles, wild with grief over the slain body of Patroclus; now Demeter, lying in anguish in a field of poppies. Oh, how she wept! What good are tears if they are not beautiful? How much more lovely is one's grief, when it is known to be seen?

Her nurse, fetched by an anxious handmaiden, pushed her way into the girl's chamber, and I – who had been waiting outside the door with the rest of her faithful retinue – followed. As with kings, no door is closed to a eunuch, especially one still a limp, docile boy, with the pallor of a scholar. So I saw what they did: the wretched figure of my princess kneeling on her soft bed, her head bent to her chest, and her hands fixed as claws in her hair, as if she would tear it out. As they rushed to save my princess from her despair, I saw what they did not. There, between her knees, was a mirror. A small, still pond, in which an ungainly girl might admire the comeliness of her own tears.

This morning, as every morning, her nurse led her out of her chamber, scented and aglow from a bath of precious oils, satiated on milk and honeycomb. Then it was time for her lessons. Before playtime in the garden, she had lessons for three stifling hours. Her tutor's room is small and exhibits the most irritating kind of false modesty – he has a simple cot that one cannot help but notice when walking into the room, but that upon closer examination reveals itself to be of the finest ebony. He is Roman, the type who stumbles through Alexandria speaking only Latin and Greek, believing the common languages beneath him, and as a result being cheated every day in the marketplace. He is short with the servants, annoyed at the smallest of crimes (the wine too sweet, the drapes open when he wished them closed), and so they fear him. He is a large man, ox-like, with hair like a sheaf of wheat atop his big round skull. His teeth are rotten. He is famous amongst Alexandria's many scholars for his poetry, which he is ready to recite and hold forth about at a moment's notice, without even an invitation or the excuse of drunkenness, and which I have always thought pointlessly ponderous, much like his body. He takes up so much space, hunching broad-shouldered through doorways, and yet he never seems concerned by it, never considers how he may be crowding the rest of us. His eyes unsettle me the most: eyes like two grey pebbles protruding, watching everything, interested. When he considers Cleopatra's answers to his questions (Who are Aphrodite's parents? Is it better to be the lover or the beloved? Why do the Romans believe that the Egyptian seasons and the Nile run backwards?) he lifts his gaze to the ceiling, rolls his big wet eyes, and pushes the septum of his nose upwards with a thick forefinger.

Cleopatra is nothing if not talkative, particularly during her lessons, which she attends to with fervent devotion. Like anyone she has occasion to speak to, from her nurse to the woman who braids pearls into her dark hair and asks if they're arranged to her liking, she interrogates her tutor on subjects beyond the remit of the occasion: his childhood, if he has nightmares, his favourite foods, the name of this fruit or that colour in the language he spoke at his mother's knee, why he has chosen to wear a blue robe today rather than the red one. He does not have the will, or perhaps the imagination, to answer; he sticks to the lesson plan. If her mind is a river, quick and lively, he is the great stone that sits in the middle of it, interrupting its flow and rebuffing its touch. He never notices me where I stand every morning in the corner of the room, a mute witness to the lesson, placed like an ornament between the nurse and the servant who carries a pitcher of watered wine. But I have seen him often. This morning, in those three stifling hours before playtime, I watched him as carefully as I did her. Just as the memory of the warm, febrile mouse against her thigh must still have been on her mind, he too held a mystery, for I had seen him the night before, in circumstances I had still not yet come to understand.

I have never been able to sleep, not since I left home. When I was a boy in Samaria my father had a vision that I should be a priest, and so he sent me away to Jerusalem, where, with six other boys to whom I could not speak, all of us having different languages, I was carved into perpetual virginity and trained, from dawn to dusk, in letters. When they could not make a priest out of me, I went to Tyre and found a job on a merchant ship, tallying goods. Then one night, like all young men of the empire, I found myself, inevitably, in Alexandria, alighting under the fierce eye of its great lighthouse, which winked at me slowly, as if to say, *I have been expecting you.*

Even for someone who will always be a boy, Alexandria has its pleasures. At night I walk its streets and, I confess, I imagine Cleopatra at my side. I talk to her, I show her what she will never learn from her tutor's questions about units of grain and the migratory patterns of the ibis. Leaning as she does against the parapet of her balcony in the day, she sees an Alexandria of sunlight: silk banners shining and rippling proudly in the breeze, streets shimmering, sphinxes and statues of the gods glowing nobly. But at night, my ghost princess, whose slight, small frame hovers at my right-hand side, sees the statues awash in moonlight, spectral and strange, and the palace shining like a distant, white tomb. In the inky gloom we move along the streets, two inkier shadows, and I say, Cleopatra, please observe: the smell of charred and burnt meat mingling with the scent of the sweet, rotten water pumped from the perfumeries along the river; the laughter and soft music drifting from the brothel windows, lit pink and green, behind whose gauzy curtains all men of the empire are rendered equal, the centurion and the slave aligned in their desire; the rancid stink of the tannery; the *hup, hup, hup* of the Nile as it laps its banks and the whimpers of lovers hidden in its rushes; the yelps and growls of feral dogs fighting over scraps in the alleyways; the stink of urine at every street corner; the soft chants of the eastern men in saffron robes behind the high walls of the monastery; the wailing of infants from the house of the woman who takes the babies of unwed girls to raise in exchange for weekly payments of grain and fruit and whose dirt floor is a graveyard; the beckoning and cajoling voices of the women whose work can only be done at certain enchanted hours, who for a small sum of money will perform spells or mix love potions for nervous brides; the nasal songs of snake charmers and the cheerful songs of street performers; and the agitated chatter of mongrel languages from low houses and gambling halls, for in Alexandria all the world is absorbed and blended together.

Last night, the last night that Cleopatra's little mouse would feel her adoring hands encompass him, before her indifferent thigh would kill him, I went to one of the brothels. Not all comfort is of the basest kind. In a brothel even the lowliest person can be seen, can be, for a moment, a master. I picked out a Judean girl with dopey, sleep-filled eyes, and let her lead me with clammy hands to her lamp-lit room. There we went through the usual routine of surprise and explanation. She reached an unenthusiastic hand under my robe; I pushed it away; she was willing enough to let me lay my head in her lap so that she could stroke my hair and engage in small talk. She feigned wonder when I told her I am a scribe and asked a few uninspired questions about life in the palace, all of which I declined to answer – I do not tell anything, I do not betray my princess. Just as we had settled into amiable silence, just as the girl had begun to emit a soft, whinnying snore, her hands still lost in my hair, we heard a cry, then a cacophony of shouting. We raced into the corridor, which was already filled with whores and their clients: a sudden assembly of various states of undress and rapidly deflating states of arousal. There, at the centre of the drama, was my princess's tutor. He was hurrying away from a naked older woman with an elaborate knot of hair above her head and hundreds of tiny scars down her back, who was alternately wailing and spitting curses at him, and reaching out long arms to grab him, her bangles jangling like alarm bells. He stumbled, tripping over his own thick legs, a stupid look of bovine panic on his face as he bent to gather the bunch of clothes he had dropped, undressed and surprisingly hairless, his little worm jiggling pathetically against his testicles, beneath the overhang of a disconcertingly smooth belly (how grateful was I, in that moment, to have been spared a lifetime of attending to such an absurd appendage), the whore bellowing to the women holding her back to let her go and kill him. I could not get the story out of anyone, and the Judean girl, clearly animated by the fact of someone else's incoherent tragedy, had forgotten me altogether, and so there was nothing else for me to do but walk home in the gloom, for once my imaginary princess not by my side, but rather, irritatingly, her tutor's face instead at the forefront of my mind.

This morning, as Cleopatra recited verses from Ovid and he corrected her Latin, I searched carefully for any detail of the night before in his passive face but, like stone, he gave away nothing, and so neither did I. Following the nurse and the servant meekly when the lesson was done, I took my place in the playtime assemblage. I kept his secret unwillingly – if it is one – as silently as I keep my own.

In the garden, which has now grown too hot to bear, playtime is finishing. The nurse is wiping away dirt from my princess's face and fingernails with a cloth doused in rosewater. The kitchen boys are being herded along to the hot ovens over which they must suffer, the untouched cakes in their hands. It is high noon, and Alexandria is at its most brilliant. In the marketplace the stalls will be shuttered against the relentless beating of the sun's brightness for an hour or two; the sacred cats that stalk the palace gardens and for whom the cook prepares special, costly dishes of delicate songbirds will declare a truce with the cobras and retreat to dusty beds beneath the rose bushes, where both dwell, to nap; in the library the scholars will sit down to plates of bread and chickpeas and let the words in their brains subside to a dull roar; in the brothels the whores and musicians will just now be getting to sleep, curling up in shaded rooms, their bodies and instruments for a moment at rest. It is time too for Cleopatra to retreat to her cool, cavernous chamber, eat a dish of cucumber and radishes soaked in cold vinegar, and rest on a bench of marble until the sun has been driven into a more forgiving afternoon sky.

But something is not right. The world, which should be

melting into soundlessness, is suddenly filled with crackling noise: there, over the balcony that edges the palace garden, something is happening on the broad avenue and steps that lead up to the ivory monolith of the palace. The shouts of a crowd, an evolving spectacle, the air crackling with some terrible possibility. Etiquette dissolves. Cleopatra's retinue, all of us in the garden, we are all led by the swelling clamour: the Syrians first who, alert to any risk to the princess, rush over to the parapet. The kitchen boys, too, hesitate, paused mid-march, and then one breaks away to see the commotion and the Scythian cook is suddenly powerless to command them: the others follow. The handmaidens cower together, the Abyssinian ladies hold fast the princess's treasures and try, in a panic, to command the palanquin to take them into the safety of the palace. The musicians, eager to show that they are less impressed by drama, exchange curious but measured banter, and slowly drift over to see what gives. The wizard of Memphis attempts to direct us, threatens to curse us if we do not listen, but his voice is lost in the surging noise, which has now become so loud that into the garden are vomited servants and scribes and astronomers and chambermaids and builders, all of whom rush to line along the parapet, pushing each other aside. The nurse alone stands beneath a cedar tree, my princess's pretty girl companion clutching her around the waist. My princess is nowhere to be seen.

I walk to the parapet, shove an oboist aside, and look down to the palace steps. The crowd is in its hundreds now, and I recognize, in flashes of crimson and emerald and gold, the city's whores, who have assembled en masse, along with a distinctive smattering of white and blue – the robed priests – and a dingy lot of market sellers and street boys who, seeing such a strange stream of the profane and the divine flowing along the avenue, would have been unable to resist joining it. A woman in red is halfway up the steps, a priest's hand on her wrist as he pulls her along, urging her towards the palace, and at first I think she has done something wrong, because she stands still, resists him, but then I realize she is pausing to pull something out from the folds of her robes – something small and orange, which the priest takes, lifts into the air above his head, to the roar of the crowd. The breeze carries up to us the oniony tang of sweat from the bodies below, and I feel disgusted. The priest lays the orange thing reverently on the steps, and the whore falls to her knees and lets out an agonized wail. She is tall, and only now do I notice the elaborate knot upon her head – it is the woman from last night, the one who chased the tutor from her room.

Now, from stage right, a new action commences. The crowd surges forth like a wave from one side, kicking a man onto the steps, raining blows upon him. From here I make out his sheaf of wheat hair, his great mass, being rolled onto the steps like a stone. He is cowering in a ball, an arm over his face, as they kick him towards the orange thing. From all of the incoherent cries and shouts, one word rises, again and again, above the rest: cat. It becomes clear, now, what has happened. My princess's tutor killed the woman's cat. It must have happened last night, an accident I am sure, but now I understand it, that dumb panic on his face. In Alexandria, cats are sacred. The killing of a cat is met by death.

From up here, the crowd seems to move as one, like a great sluggish beast rolling and heaving, basking in sunlight. Those at the front have spotted something, and word of it travels through the crowd like a spine rippling. Someone is emerging from the palace. A figure, walking briskly, flanked by two men in white robes. The king! It is Auletes, Cleopatra's father, a soft little man who prefers to spend most of his day playing his flute, sitting in a tub of scented water, while handmaidens dance about him. I imagine that was what he was doing now, before he was disrupted. Cool water probably still clings to the nape of his neck, the pads of his fingers are likely pruned and wrinkled. He must be thinking of how quickly he can put this commotion to sleep and get back to his bath. He has never been one for statesmanship. He is hustling on short legs towards the crowd, his pate glinting gold in the sunlight. When he reaches the top of the steps, he raises his hands. He is speaking. We all lean over the parapet to listen – I wonder if it will hold or if we will all come crashing down. In this brief, subdued moment, I hear the distant cry of the nurse behind us, like an anxious seabird, calling yet for Cleopatra.

We can hear very little from here. Auletes moves his hands as if conducting music, I catch a few words in Greek, which only a few in the crowd will understand, they turn to each other confused: *this man* and *hasty* and *peaceful* and *stay* and *gods will judge* and *why* and at one point a loud *go home!* But it seems to have an effect. The timorous Auletes seems to have done something, the crowd is quieter, though not quite still – the people shuffle around, a sense of puzzlement hangs in the air, a mild current of chatter and debate. Every now and then there is an outraged comment, and a few people at the edges of the assembly drift off. But the woman is still on her knees, proffering her cat to the king, her head bowed in submission. He does not acknowledge her. Cleopatra's tutor is curled up like a fat grey snail at the bottom of the steps, where the crowd left him. *Go home!* Auletes shouts, again, a tremor in his voice, though also, I detect, a note of satisfaction. The crowd murmurs – they seem persuaded, if dissatisfied. The tutor moves his arm from his eyes, peeks at the king.

But now. The palace doors flash open, and something comes forth. A little streak of blue. I'd know that gait anywhere, that enthusiastic run that usually ends in a fall, but now she stops, and begins to walk deliberately towards her father, each step incredibly slow, as if she were in a trance, as if she were a bride taking measured steps towards her groom. The ribbon upon her brow shines white and dazzling – as if Helios, at the helm of the sun, has finally found the thing most worthy of his brilliant caress. My princess moves, unhurriedly. Somebody shoves me aside, a warm bulk at my elbow – Cleopatra's nurse. She murmurs the princess's name softly, sounding disappointed.

Cleopatra is now in front of her father. With those slow steps, she descends towards the woman, who has yet to lift her head, but, I think, or perhaps I imagine it, is trembling with anticipation. When she gets to the orange offering Cleopatra kneels before it. She is silent. The woman bends her face lower to the ground, touching her forehead to the marble steps. Cleopatra is still, and somehow all the fervour, all the emotion of the crowd seems to have become condensed in that small figure, that dot of blue against the blinding white steps. There is an expectant pause. Everyone is waiting and no one speaks. All eyes are on my princess, and I feel as if I have been joined by a host of people, as if the crowd looks with my eyes, as if, in my looking, every soul in Alexandria is behind me. There is no sound.

And then, a singular noise. Like a high note on a flute, it emerges, silvery in the air, gaining strength, until we realize it is the sound of weeping. Cleopatra is crying over the cat's body. Her sobs intensify in pitch, and the crowd begins to murmur, begins to swell once more. 'No!' – her one Egyptian word, rising high above the noise of the crowd, the purest sound. 'No, no, no!' Her voice sounds younger than it does in her tutor's room or in her chamber, the voice of a little girl in a nursery. Her small hands move along the orange body, as if feeling for something inside it, as if she might discover life hidden in that pitiable heap of fur. The woman presses her forehead hard against the marble steps in supplication. A man standing over the tutor brings his foot down on the soft part of his flank. A priest lifts two arms into the air, and issues a rallying cry. Up here on the parapet, people put their hands over their mouths, murmur to themselves. I glance at the nurse, looking for some reaction, but her face is uncomprehending: she does not yet understand. A noise that one might mistake for thunder is rising from below: the communal growl of the crowd, as they descend upon the tutor. He is rolling along the ground – now and then we see flashes of his hair or some tender part of his big body – until suddenly, as if all at once, there is not one whole piece of him left, or rather, parts of him are everywhere at once. A man lifts a sheaf of hair high into the air, another emerges with blood on his face and stumbles away. There is the raw smell of meat in the air, the smell of blood baking in the hot sun. The smell of a charnel house, of the skinned bodies of goats and sheep that hang grotesque from the butcheries at night.

I turn my eyes to the blue figure on the white steps, who bends over the orange cat, still lying intact on the palace steps. The crowd no longer have their eyes on her, their mistress, as they move before her, heaving and convulsing, a great beast. But she is unmoving, fixed in a position I have seen before, just this morning, like a statue, her hands frozen as claws at the side of her skull in a perfect attitude of anguish, as if she would tear her hair out – and I am quite sure, beneath that dark hair, she is smiling.

✳✳✳

I do what I have never done. I go to my scribe's room, which has no prospect and looks out upon the marshes, and which is in a part of the palace long forgotten, somewhere between the kitchen and the stables. I ignore my desk, and lie down instead on my cot, which is made of the plainest wood. The heat in my room is suffocating. I stare at the gloomy corners of the ceiling, watching a fly buzz halfheartedly, unaware of me. He is missing the great party on the steps of the palace, which is now emptied of people, and where the flies and the beetles now sit down to a banquet.

At first I do not know how to read what my princess has done. I had felt, as I watched her, the confusion I once felt as a child, in a room full of children just like me, who babbled in other tongues, who looked at me with dark eyes, who pointed and spoke to me and seemed to need to tell me something urgent, but whose sounds remained just that: incoherent sounds. But I lie on my bed and I think the mystery through, just as I would if in one of the library's many untouched texts I were to come across some obscure word in a language that I otherwise know well, in which I otherwise dwell comfortably. If I know the context, I can discover the meaning.

She wept to show that she wept – I understand the shape of her tears. I know that in that moment she felt torn between two possibilities: that of her father, the small sunlit figure behind her; and that of the rippling sea of humanity before her, the people who exist solely that she might one day rule over them, who yearned for something terrible, whose outrage will turn easily to lust. What she did was, I think, an act of something approaching love. The way one might allow a beloved dog that scents a hare to spring from your side and bring it down for the sheer joy of it; the way one might allow a favoured servant to sing as she makes the bed, disrupting the stillness of a morning. She granted them her favour. She let them unleash their fury in her name. She said, *I am one of you.* She said, *I love you.*

FT Kola was born in South Africa, grew up in Australia, and lived in London and New York thereafter. She is currently a fellow in fiction at the Michener Center for Writers at the University of Texas at Austin. She was shortlisted for the Caine Prize for African Writing in 2015 for her first-ever published story, 'A Party for the Colonel'. Her work has appeared in *One Story* and *The Guardian*.

'When Cleopatra was nine… a visiting official had accidentally killed a cat, an animal held sacred in Egypt. A furious mob assembled, with whom Auletes' representative attempted to reason. While this was a crime for an Egyptian, surely a foreigner merited a special exemption? He could not save the visitor from the bloodthirsty crowd.' From Stacey Schiff's *Cleopatra*

Duty

Timwa Lipenga

This time around, I will take two packets of brown sugar with me. Everyone says it's healthy. Rich, brown sugar, the kind that we finally decided to like. The kind that we didn't think was real sugar back in the days when I was a little girl, but which costs so much these days.

But wait, maybe I should take four packets. After all, I have always bought groceries in bulk, so my family would still have enough sugar left for the next two months. Maybe four packets would buy me some conversation with him. We could talk about the rising cost of sugar, the quality and even the quantity. We could talk about how we all used to heap brown sugar into our teacups, spoonful after spoonful, because it wasn't as sweet as the white type. We did this until Ma got so fed up with us and decided to take matters into her own hands. She would put sugar straight into the teapot in the kitchen, and the sugar-bowl was banned from the dining room. She, and she alone, knew just how much sugar was enough for everyone. She didn't even budge when Agogo came to visit. It was service with a smile, of course; Ma brought out the best mug, placed it on a silver tray, together with two scones she had baked herself. Nothing but the best for her mother-in-law, who smiled in appreciation when she saw the efforts Ma had gone to. Only Ma could make such wonderful scones, Agogo said, but where was the sugar?

Ma, still smiling, told her that it was much better to have sugar in the teapot these days; it saved everyone the trouble of having to put sugar in their teacups. I think Agogo started saying it was no trouble at all, really, she didn't mind putting sugar in her own cup…but Ma kept pouring the tea, with that steely smile on her face.

Ma would have known just how many packets of sugar I need to take today, or if I even need to take any at all. Or if I even need to visit.

I visit him once every month. I usually go on a Sunday afternoon. In the early days, I couldn't stand the crowd, and I would schedule my visits for the middle of the week, when there would be fewer people milling around, especially in the evening. But I soon realized that the din of voices is reassuring. With everyone raising their voices, struggling to make themselves heard, I can tell myself that it is the noise that makes it difficult for us to talk. Yes, I tell myself this. Sometimes I even yell it to myself.

It will take me one hour to drive from Blantyre to Zomba, where he is. If I take a minibus, it will take me longer, but it will cost me less. Am I willing to sit and wait, believing the minibus is full, only to have the fake travellers – the seat warmers – trickle out grinning as the real travellers get in? Plus am I ready to face those eyes in the minibus? I always feel as if everyone in there has their eyes on me. When I turn to catch them at it, the eyes are averted, but I imagine them; cold, relentless slivers of curiosity down my back. Sometimes I even shiver just from the thought of it. I am convinced everyone knows my story, our story. There was that day on the bus, when a two-year-old boy threw a tantrum because he wanted a lollipop. When his mother said, *Shhhh*, I thought she was about to whisper, *Shhhhe's the one, she's the one, she's the one.*

Should I take the car instead? Should I just grit my teeth and pay for fuel, all for the sake of a smooth journey?

This trip is costly, no matter what choice I make. I quickly take six packets of sugar from the pantry, throw them into a plastic bag, and make my way towards the car.

***

Six months ago, driving to Zomba was an exercise in manoeuvring around potholes; I would drive with my whole body, winding, weaving, braking, negotiating the corners. After the drive I would come home with a dull pain in my back from all the bending and twisting.

They have now fixed the road; it's tarmac all the way. But I can't help it; I'm still winding and weaving, clenching the wheel, remembering the potholes. By the time I return home I will have the dull ache again; I just know I will.

A minibus overtakes me; maybe my journey would have been faster by bus after all.

Father taught me to drive when I was 16. He had taught Chimwemwe, my brother, two years earlier. By the time we went to driving school, we already knew all there was to know about driving, although we tried to hide it. As Father pointed out at the time, no driving instructor likes a know-it-all. It was better to act like we didn't know anything; to give the instructor the pleasure of thinking he was teaching us something new. I don't know if we ever fooled our instructor.

I drive past Nyungwe, the trading area along the road. Ma used to buy vegetables here for the restaurant she ran with Father. We would come as a family, taking turns to drive. The place looks deserted now. There are some young girls along the road, trying to sell fresh cabbage. Their young faces look wilted with anxiety; no-one is willing to pull over just to buy cabbage.

You would think there would be more to sell; people celebrated a good harvest this year. There was plenty of maize, and we were actually able to have a small garden at the orphanage where I work. The children loved it, and when my colleague Sandra and I went to work, they would welcome us with hot maize. I could never bring myself to tell them I had already eaten maize with my family at home; it was easier just to eat with them.

The minibus which overtook me about 20 minutes earlier has stopped by the roadside. Burst tyre? Or has the driver run out of fuel? As I draw closer, I see two police officers close to the minibus. *I have done nothing wrong, I have done nothing wrong*, I tell myself, clenching the steering wheel even more tightly.

One of the officers notices me slowing down. He smiles and waves me on. Is that an innocent smile? A complicit smile? Or a simple, friendly smile?

I have really got to stop doing this to myself. He is only a traffic officer. But these days I don't know if I believe in all the sub-categories. When it comes to the police, an officer-is-an-officer-is-an-officer, even if he's on the gate at Zomba Prison, or the man who writes your name in the old, tattered visitors' book, the one who makes sure the visiting queue is disciplined, the one who makes you taste the bread, *nsima* or rice you have brought, just in case you want to poison the inmates. An officer is still an officer, even the one who guides you into those dingy, crowded rooms, points to a grimy bench which you are too nervous to wipe with the tissue in your handbag in case you give the wrong impression, the one who yells 'Time Up' after one hour of non-conversation. The sight of a police officer, no matter where, is always a reminder of what I have done, and what I am doing. Yes, I know it's about what he did, but these days I feel all fingers, including my own, point to me.

* * *

My brother is the one who often gets told to pull over by the police. Father always said Chimwemwe drives too fast. If you are in a rush to get to wherever you are going, then maybe you should just start off a day earlier, he would say.

But Father drove quickly, too, the day Ma fainted. I was home from college for the weekend. One minute she was slicing vegetables at the kitchen counter, the next she was on the floor. We all bundled into our twin-cab, and rushed to Queen Elizabeth Central Hospital.

We didn't even know she had malaria, that she had had it for over a week. For Ma, those aches and pains had simply meant stress after a long day's work; first at the restaurant, and then at home. It was stress that would disappear after a soothing cup of tea. And so she nurtured the disease, and we all helped her to nurture it, because we simply didn't know. We should have caught the signs earlier. It didn't matter how fast Father drove, it was too late.

Afterwards, we didn't drive around as much as we had before. Father put all his energy into the restaurant, and even opened another one at the city centre. He also continued helping the poorer families in our neighbourhood. He had always done this even when Ma was alive; I think that's how he got the nickname Dr Dispenser. I've lost count of the many students that he paid fees for, the school uniforms that he bought. Once in a while, he and I would drive down to the neighbouring Goliyo township with clothes and large food containers, which we would distribute to the children. The girls would fight over the dresses I had brought. In the end, Father and I chose a leader from the group. She must have been 16, although the etched lines around her unsmiling face gave her the look of someone older. I learned a lot from that girl; she knew how to be firm, how to refuse to give out the dresses until everyone had calmed down. I can't remember her name.

By the time I graduated, I knew just what kind of job I wanted to do. I had trained as a social worker in college, and when I saw the vacancy at the orphanage, I knew that job was meant for me. I don't think I gave the panellists much of a choice, between reeling off my classroom knowledge and my experiences at Goliyo. I remember how Chimwemwe, who had studied Accounting, used to tease me, calling me Little Miss Dispenser.

But Chimwemwe himself hasn't gone far from the fold; after graduating as an accountant, he joined the family business. To him, the restaurant is The Business.

Is this what Ma would have wanted for us all?

***

I check the dashboard. It's two o'clock. I'll be arriving around 2.45. I am not late; I would not be late even if I tried. Lockdown is at six, so yes, I will have plenty of time.

Two months ago, I took two loaves of bread. I walked through the dark prison corridor, and sat on the grimy spot on the bench on my side of the waiting room; it's divided into two by steel bars, and the prisoners wait on the other side of the bar. He was already there when I arrived. I greeted him. He nodded.

I took out the bread.

'It's great bread! From Wonder Bakery!' I yelled as the others yelled at the inmates they had come to see.

He proffered both hands. I struggled to squeeze in the bread through the bars. I winced as my hand brushed against the metallic bars. Surely he could have called the warden, who was standing close by on his side of the room, to come and help? I flinched at the thought of his hand touching mine; I all but dropped the loaves into his hands before quickly withdrawing my hand.

He turned to the warden, motioned to him. The warden, used to these visits by now, came forward. I saw the bread I had brought, the bread I hadn't even bought for my own family, I saw that bread given to the warden, who could not hide his greedy glee. He walked away with the bread he had just been given.

It was just the two of us now. He looked at me with expressionless eyes, then got up, leaving me staring.

Last month, I brought sweet potatoes. He ate them quickly, without a word, and then pushed his chair back again. Again I was left staring at his back.

That has been the pattern so far. There are days when he acknowledges my presence, sometimes with a nod, days when he will eat what I have brought. But on the days when he can overcome his need for food beyond what the prison offers, he makes those grand gestures and gives what I have painstakingly chosen to the warden or the other inmates.

***

Don't do it, Chimwemwe said. *Don't.*

Don't do it, Sandra said. She was with me when the girl and her sister came to the orphanage.

Don't do it, my husband said.

Don't do it, my father said.

Don't do it, Agogo knelt on her arthritic knees and wrapped her gnarled hands around mine. *Please.*

I thought of my daughter Leah, the echo of her laughter around our house. She is 12. She is in boarding school, and I thought of how she is growing up to be an independent, spirited girl.

I thought of Alina, the girl who came to the orphanage with her sister. Together they looked like bent bamboo stalks. They were wearing beautiful dresses that were held together with safety pins. The girls reminded me of Leah playing dress-up.

Alina and her sister were begging for a home at the orphanage. For them, home was not safe any more, not since he had chosen them. It was not safe, not since he had started bringing them clothes and food. I looked at the girls, at those trapped, anxious eyes, and I knew. I knew.

Don't do it, the girls' mother said, averting her eyes.

Don't do it. Don't.

***

You are not allowed to drive beyond the gate, not unless you work for Zomba Prison. I get out of the car, open the passenger door at the back and pick up the six packets of sugar. I walk towards the man at the gate. His eyes widen at the sight of the packets.

'Sugar is quite difficult to find these days, isn't it? Would you believe I spent a good part of yesterday trying to look for it, and only came home with one measly packet? So expensive, too!'

I nod and move on.

My next stop is the little room close to the gate. Today there is a woman there, with the same old, tattered visitors' book. I write down my name and begin the uphill journey. The queue slowly winds its way up, supervised by the 'discipline man', who carries a gun, just in case we decide to cause a riot. The plastic bag feels heavy in my hands. I've opted to cradle it; these bags are flimsy, and I wouldn't want the packets of sugar to split and spill, not on this dusty road.

The line crawls on. Today, I will talk to him. If he walks away, I will yell. *You know why I had to do it, don't you*?

I thought I would feel free after I did it. But I didn't. When I was alone, memory would seize me none too gently and hurl me towards childhood. And then Agogo had the stroke, and even though no-one said it, I felt as if they were saying, 'This wouldn't have happened if you had kept your mouth shut.'

Chimwemwe makes his own visits; it is the kind of thing we cannot do together. I don't know what they talk about. I know Chimwemwe paid a huge sum to keep the story out of the press. We act as if it never happened.

But we know people talk about it. One day, Leah, back from boarding school, asked me, 'Mum, why is Grandfather in prison?'

And I mumbled something about a business deal gone wrong. She will find out one day, but I'm not ready to take away the innocence of a 12-year-old.

Maybe one day she will ask, 'Mum, they say you sent him there. Is that true?'

Until that day comes, I will say nothing about it, and continue standing in these queues, burdened by packets, and staring at my feet, which have gone all dusty from the slippers I always wear here. The slippers are my attempt to blend in. So is the brown headscarf, tied at the back of my head. The other day, I saw a young woman standing in the queue in a tight-fitting red dress, and I wondered how she had dared to bring colour into this drab place. I usually wear a long grey dress or a black one.

I look at the woman in front of me; she is in a *chitenje* outfit, and in deep conversation with the man in front of her.

'I'm visiting my husband... arrested four weeks ago... they say he bought a stolen phone... but really, how was he to know?'

'...my brother... part of a gang, but he was the driver... he didn't do the actual stealing...'

The stories go back and forth in the queue; stories of claims to innocence, of being in the wrong place at the wrong time, of sheer hard luck. For as long as I don't have a similar story to share, I might as well be wearing a red dress.

I worry about all eyes on me when I'm in public places. When I'm at home, though, no-one looks me in the eye. Not even my husband, who carefully averts his eyes from me with this apologetic look on his face. He talks to me as if I were a patient; choosing his words carefully.

Last week, I went to our childhood home. Chimwemwe was there; we talked about the restaurants and the renovations he is planning to make.

'Business has really picked up, not like it was after...' and he fell silent and picked up the paper.

'After?' I probed.

He shrugged.

'You know,' and he made a point of flipping through the paper.

Sandra is one of the few who will meet my eye, but it is always with such pity that I turn away. Leah, who doesn't know, still looks at me the way she used to in the past; curious, ready to tell a story, or to hear one. I often catch myself staring at Leah; would I know if something happened to her? Would she tell me?

Alina and her sister, who are now at the orphanage, do not avert their eyes from me. They talk about the maize garden, about classes, about the new friends they have made. They have such weary, weary eyes. I wonder if they judge me.

I do a head-count of the queue. There are ten more people to go. I pass the man who checks the food. He tells me to proceed. I move on.

Seven more people to go, then I'll be ushered in by the final policeman.

Eight months. It's been eight months, and he has eight more years to go.

Conversation flies around me, over my head, behind me, in front of me.

'The porridge they have... quite lumpy... doesn't have any sugar...'

We really need to talk today.

We need to talk, Father. You've got to understand why I did this.

'And if they get any tea at all, well, that's a lucky day for them...'

We need to talk, Father. Tell me why you did this.

'...wouldn't want to spend a night...'

Did Ma know? When did it all begin? Why?

Does it matter why? How could you?

'...there's... a man... imagine... young girls...'

Father, did you see the look on that girl's face? The-girl-whose-home-wasn't-safe-any-more–Alina-who-wanted-to-stay-at-the-orphanage-the-girl-and-her-sister-with-the-oversized-clothes-the-girl-the-girl-who-could-be-Leah's-age-the-girl-who-asked-me-to-help-her-the-girl-with-the-wilted-face-selling-fresh-cabbage-the-girl-who-helped-us-share-out-the-clothes-the-girl-Father-we-need-to-talk.

I step back, shivering.

'Oh, Madam, please watch what you're doing. You've stepped on my foot.'

I look behind. There's a young girl gingerly rubbing at her foot.

We need to talk. Do we need to talk?

I step away from the queue. People stare.

'Is something wrong, sister?' the woman in the *chitenje* asks.

I shake my head and begin the descent towards the gate. Past the man who checks the food.

'Why did she come all the way here then?'

'Hmm, some of these people...'

'That's...'

I don't know how that sentence ends. It could be 'That's the woman I was talking about.' It could be 'That's his daughter.'

I move past the 'discipline man' who cocks his gun, just in case, then lowers it, disappointed.

I reach the little room by the gate, sign my name in the 'Out' column of the old, tattered visitors' book. I move towards the man at the gate and hesitate, clutching at the plastic bag in my arms.

I walk on, out of the gate, with the sugar.

Timwa Lipenga teaches French at the University of Malawi, Chancellor College. She worked as a journalist for a daily newspaper in Malawi (*The Nation*) before joining the university as a lecturer. She enjoys reading and writing.

77 Steps

Kafula Mwila

There it stood, stalwart! St Mark's Cathedral looked back at him. It was as if it had been waiting for this day. Waiting for him! It towered over him, daring him, intimidating. Yet he was not afraid. He was angry, very angry. He was ready to hit back. The grey building had brightly coloured narrow windows, which made the building come alive. Without them, the cathedral would have just been another ugly structure in an affluent neighbourhood. He swept his eyes all the way to the roof. It did not appear as attractive as before. The huge cross right at the top of the building looked like it was about to ascend into the clouds. 'Golgotha,' he thought, and winced.

The infrastructure was built out of grey stone, roughly cut. The stones were neatly piled on top of each other. Because they were unpolished, the Cathedral blended in with its colourful surroundings: the neatly cut green grass, rose bushes and bright flowers. The front wall had deliberately been erected slightly taller than the rest of the walls. This made the entire building look as though it were leaning back slightly, but in an elegant fashion. It gave the Cathedral a sassy look. In between the front and the back, several walls spanned outward, like pages. They appeared as though they were constructed independent of each other but narrow windows joined them, connecting the back and front. The back of the building did not have as much beauty as the front. The huge oak doors in the middle of the front wall lent the Cathedral a bold appearance. The narrow, pentagon-shaped windows in the front wall formed a beautiful pattern.

The roof, which comprised three arches, was green. Mabvuto had admired the Cathedral as a child. He had even thought about becoming an architect. Today, as he stood facing it, that desire had been replaced with bitterness.

Mabvuto's mouth tightened. He clenched his teeth. His feelings towards the building went beyond the huge oak doors. They penetrated the thick walls to what was carefully hidden inside. He held the building responsible for causing him so much pain. His mother had called him 'Mabvuto', meaning 'troubles', and he had lived true to the reputation of his name. He had driven past St Mark's every morning on his way to work. Each time, its huge oak doors were shut. They were resolute.

'We'll never let him out,' they seemed to say. 'Come and get him yourself.'

Today, he had stopped over at the Cathedral. He had arrived in the morning. After parking his car, he had walked as if in a hurry, only to stop in front of the building. He had made up his mind. His eyes fell on the steps. He knew exactly how many steps led to the top.

'Seventy-seven', he muttered.

Every week, during his childhood, Mabvuto went to Sunday school, together with all the other children, while his mother attended Mass with the other parents. It was during that time that he learned about forgiveness. One Sunday, the teacher asked them to count the steps. The children had ascended all the way to the top while holding each other's hands.

'Seventy-seven,' they'd chorused to the teacher, who was waiting for them at the bottom. Then they'd run back down.

'Why not 50?' Mabvuto was always the inquisitive one. 'Then it would've been easier to climb up.'

'Well,' the teacher replied, '77 is a special number.'

'Special? What do you mean special?'

'Who remembers what we learned last time?'

Hands shot up.

'Forgiveness!' shouted one of them.

There was a thunderous 'yes' from the small group of enthusiasts.

'The Bible teaches us to forgive others 77 times.' The announcement was received with another chorused, 'Ooooooh!'

'You mean if my friend keeps stealing my pencil, I should forgive him so many times?' Mabvuto had asked, wide-eyed.

Now that lesson was haunting him – in fact it had haunted him nearly all his life.

As his eyes travelled up and down the steps, he was exasperated. He lifted his right foot and started climbing. It was the tensest moment of his life. Slowly, rage was rising like a soft breeze that caresses gently on the cheek. He knew what would happen if he allowed it to become stronger. So he breathed again and again and started counting the steps to occupy his mind.

'One, two, three… 10, 11… 14'. He was 14 years old when he overheard teachers talking about his mother. How she had died suddenly. He had tried in vain to get his grandmother to tell him the truth. That day she was seated at the back of the house pounding groundnuts. She had not looked up. She was afraid of looking into his eyes. So he had momentarily dismissed it. He would bring up the subject another day.

'15, 16, 17, 18,' he was not in a hurry. He looked up and this time his eyes fell on the narrow windows again. The multi-coloured window panes shimmered in the midmorning sun; there were blues, greens and yellows but the scarlet ones shone brightest.

'Scarlet' and Isaiah 1:18 flashed in his mind. *'Though your sins are like scarlet, they shall be as white as snow.'* How could he forget the worst punishment he had ever had in secondary school? He was made to write that one scripture a thousand times, for forgetting to memorize it for the next lesson.

At the end of that school day, he had practically run home, barged into the small kitchen where his grandmother was seated. He had run past her and gone straight into the shower. She had followed him. Standing outside the bathroom door, she had listened to how he muttered. Later, when she had placed a bowl of rice and beans in front of him, she watched as he shoved food into his mouth.

'You don't need to carry around this burden.'

'Then why don't we talk about it, Grandma, why?'

Tears formed in the old woman's eyes.

'You won't understand.' She raised both her arms.

'One day I'll be old enough to understand, old enough to do something about it.'

As he went up the stairs, memories of his grandmother played in his mind like a movie he had watched over and over. She had preached love and forgiveness until her last breath. That is what Mabvuto had failed to understand. Indeed, the capabilities of one human cannot be compared with the failures of another. His grandmother had held on to the truth, just as much as the Cathedral had hidden it behind those huge oak doors. She had been a wise woman but, as far as he was concerned, she was weak. 'Too weak,' Mabvuto whispered. No matter what she had told him, he was not going to get off his path. Nothing could deter him from the choices he had made. It was a silent vow he had made to himself, to the memory of his mother. His grandmother's questions irritated him. She knew the answer. She knew why he was so upset, why he sulked most of the time, why his speech was imbued with frustration. When she asked him he gave her that look, the kind that tore at her spine. His grandmother also knew that that was a question he would never answer. She died when he was 18 years old.

Mabvuto was now 33 years old. He was a very successful lawyer. He had earned himself accolades and his peers admired him. Despite his admirable physique, a toned body, his chest ached from the heavy load he had been carrying. It was something he had borne from the day his mother died. He was ten then. He would cry himself to sleep. Some days he went without eating. Then there were days when he would demand that his grandmother took him to her grave. He would kneel on the tombstone and just stare. Tears would flow freely. With time his grandmother had grown weary and stopped taking him. She had continued to grieve in her own way. Then his sense of loss had turned into anger. He had chosen to hold on to it. It was the fuel that energized him. It was the strength that sustained him. It woke him up every morning with the determination to go on, to fight. It had woken him up at the crack of dawn this day when he had made up his mind to act. He had put on a pair of blue jeans and thrown over a white sleeveless shirt. He had not bothered about socks but had slipped into a pair of dark brown moccasins.

'18, 19, 20... 30.' His shoulders were getting heavier. It was getting hotter. Droplets of sweat were forming on his forehead. He looked back down the cathedral steps. He had come a long way. He still remembered how his grandmother had told him that he needed to conquer the demon of rage that controlled him. It was then that he had switched interests from becoming an architect to wanting to be a lawyer. He had walked into the office of the Counselling and Guidance teacher in secondary school. Sitting opposite Mr Mwale, Mabvuto had informed him about his decision.

'You've always wanted to be an architect?' Mr Mwale was surprised.

The three arches no longer appealed to him but he did not say anything.

When his teacher realized that he was not going to answer, he continued. 'So you want me to move you from the Design and Technology class?'

Mabvuto nodded.

'Religious Studies it is then,' Mr Mwale said.

'31, 32, 33.' It had finally come, the moment he had been waiting for. He had spent his 33rd birthday in his study reading and getting ready for this day. The guilt of his grandmother had been passed on to him after she died. He imagined that if she had been brave enough, this day would not have come.

'34…' The Sun had shifted. The cross on the roof of the cathedral now cast a shadow onto the steps. This provided temporary shelter from the blazing solar rays. His right hand rested on the thick wooden rail from time to time. He took out a handkerchief, started by wiping off the stickiness from between his fingers and then patted his face lightly. The white piece of cotton became wet immediately. He kept it in his hands, holding on to one corner. He was getting closer. His grip on the hanky tightened. He had learned to control himself over time but there were days he had exploded. He had taken it out on his friends a few times at the bar and occasionally anyone who provoked him had felt that wrath physically.

'There was no need for that fight,' his girlfriend had told him one day. He had taken her out to a movie. Well, she had insisted on watching 'Angels and Demons'. By the end of the movie he was worked up. Walking out of the cinema, someone bumped into him.

'You must apologize,' Mabvuto insisted.

'Come on, man, it wasn't intentional.'

The guy didn't see it coming when Mabvuto gave him a blow to the face. It was a terrible fight that landed both men at the police station. Of course, Mabvuto was able to get himself out of the tight spot. His relationship with the girl, though, did not last.

'She didn't understand me,' he had told his close friend.

'Yeah, neither do I,' his friend had replied. 'No girl will ever understand you, it seems.'

No one understood Mabvuto except for Jairos, who had been famously known as 'the fool'. That was back in the shanty where Mabvuto grew up. Jairos had known Mabvuto from the time he was born. He had gone to the same high school as Mabvuto's mother. The two had separated when she went to study to become a teacher and he to become a doctor. When they met again, years later, Mabvuto's mother was a secondary-school teacher. Jairos had failed lamentably. It was not clear where he lived but he was found every day at the local market, where he did odd jobs. Mabvuto had forgotten about him. At least he did not want anything that reminded him of his childhood after he moved out of his grandmother's house. But Jairos had reappeared from nowhere, pleading for employment. The least Mabvuto could do was to offer him a job as a gardener.

Jairos watched from afar as Mabvuto climbed up the cathedral steps. Briefly taking his eyes off him, Jairos opened the Bible he had brought with him and took out a photo. Mabvuto's mother was beautiful, 'just like a queen', he thought and smiled. He looked back at Mabvuto, whose shoulders were hanging, and that made Jairos pity him.

'This day has been a long time coming,' thought Jairos.

'39!' Mabvuto exclaimed. He felt sore all over his back. It was as if someone had been whipping him, whipping all his life. He rubbed his shoulders and the back of his neck but that did not help. He kept moving up and when he was about to say '70' he was interrupted.

'Excuse me.'

Mabvuto stopped and turned back to face the intruder.

'I'm looking for the church office.' It was a handsome boy. Not very tall, dark complexion and neatly cut hair.

Mabvuto needed to clear his throat and calm down before he could speak. 'You'd have to go round that way,' he pointed.

'Ah,' the youngster said cheerfully. He made to leave but stopped and faced Mabvuto again.

'Are you a member here?' he asked.

Mabvuto hesitated and shook his head.

'Oh, I'm new in town and I'm looking for somewhere to celebrate Mass this coming Sunday.'

He extended his hand. Mabvuto took it.

'This place is close to home. So yah.'

The young man nodded, turned and headed back down

the steps. He descended with so much ease. Mabvuto's gaze followed him to the bottom of the stairs, until he turned and disappeared. It was at about that age that he had stopped coming for mass. He had announced it to his grandmother who had remained quiet. She had equally not asked him for a reason.

'I believe you know why – you do know, right?' he repeated. She understood perfectly what he meant but she was not going to 'open Pandora's Box'.

His grandmother's quietness frustrated him. He understood that she was hurt. He had stumbled upon her crying in her room several times. He did not understand why she kept silent.

Turning to face the church again, Mabvuto dragged himself up the steps slowly. Calvary crossed his mind.

'77.' He had finally reached the top and his ankles hurt.

He looked at the large brass door knobs. They were polished. His face reflected back at him, distorted. Even though they were not clear, he saw the questions that his eyes asked him.

He hesitated and then reached for the door. It creaked. The church was empty and the sound of the doors echoed. He dipped his fingers in the holy water that was in the grotto to his right. He made the sign of the cross: first touching his forehead then down to the middle of the chest, to the left and then right. He bowed. When he lifted his head, his eyes were looking straight at the Crucifix. The body of Jesus Christ hung on a wooden cross. His head, with a crown of thorns tilted to one side. Whoever had carved it had made the scars on Jesus' body very visible. Mabvuto's 'wounds' however, had not dried. Instead, they had festered and a boiling fluid of hate oozed.

'Hey!' It was the young man again. He was in the company of an elderly man. 'This is the caretaker of the cathedral,' the young man announced.

'I can see you found your way.' Mabvuto temporarily

moved his gaze from the Crucifix.

The young man nodded. 'Taking a tour,' he said.

Mabvuto nodded and then after a brief silence said, 'I'm here to see the Priest.'

The caretaker disappeared, leaving him with the young man.

'It's a marvel, isn't it?' the young man said, pointing to the Crucifix. 'No man has ever laid down his life for that of others,' he added.

Mabvuto moved his eyes back to the Crucifix and nodded.

The young man looked at Mabvuto. 'I was an altar boy in my previous church,' the young man announced with pride.

Mabvuto said nothing but remembered that his mother had wanted him to be an altar boy.

The caretaker came back and announced, 'Father Mulaisho is waiting for you.'

Mabvuto muttered a 'thank you'.

'That's the greatest act of forgiveness,' the young man declared as he pointed to the Crucifix again. Then he and the caretaker continued on their tour.

'What is forgiveness?' Mabvuto asked himself.

Facing the Crucifix, he went down on one knee and made the sign of the cross again; this time in preparation for confession. He needed to pray first but his mind was blank. He opened his mouth a few times but no words came forth. After several attempts, he gave up and made his way to the confession box. It was the only place where everything would finally make sense. He reached for the door. This time droplets of sweat ran down his back. His hands were slippery.

Once inside, he was briefly disoriented because there wasn't enough light. Mabvuto knelt on the crimson cushion that was placed on the floor. There was a white screen that separated confessor and confessee.

'In the name of the Father and the Son and the Holy Spirit,' a deep, soft voice came from the other side of the screen. Mabvuto had not forgotten that voice. The man on the other side used to come to his grandmother's house every month soon after his mother died. Then the man had suddenly stopped.

'You know that man who has been bringing us food and money?' his grandmother had asked one day.

Mabvuto had nodded.

'Well, I have asked him to stop coming.'

At first Mabvuto had been quite inquisitive about this man, about the visits. He had wanted to know everything; why he came, why he brought them food. Why he bought Mabvuto clothes every so often. He was much younger then and there was so much he did not know. But with time, he had given up. He had not asked his grandmother for an explanation. The months that followed were difficult for them. His grandmother set up a stall in front of their small house to sell vegetables but that was not enough. When he was not in school Mabvuto joined other boys like him at the market. The small errands brought in a small income, even though his grandmother did not approve.

Back in the confession box, Mabvuto was now sweating profusely. The sweat ran down his brow. He looked for his handkerchief but couldn't find it. He gave up and used the back of his hand and part of his shirt to wipe his forehead.

'Bless me, Father, for I have sinned,' Mabvuto said after a few minutes.

'How long has it been since your last confession?'

Mabvuto took a deep breath and released it slowly. This was his first confession. The closest he had got to it was the little prank he had played on his friend in primary school. This was soon after the lesson on forgiveness. For how else was he going to count up to 77?

'But I'm not the one who took your pencil this time,' his friend had protested.

'You did,' Mabvuto was adamant.

'I didn't take your pencil, Mav,' his friend had replied, teary-eyed.

'And you do it all the time.'

'Okay, I'm sorry.'

'That's not enough.'

'What?'

'I want you to kneel and say "sorry" ten times, then I'll forgive you.'

'He doesn't need to do that,' one of the other boys who were looking on protested.

'Then I'll go tell,' Mabvuto put it clearly. They all knew his mother. She taught in the secondary school.

There was movement on the other side of the confession box. The noise brought the confessor back to the present time. 'This is my first confession,' Mabvuto said reluctantly.

On the other side of the confessional, the priest made some movements, a chair squeaked. Then he straightened his garments. Something was bothering the 'man of the cloth'. He couldn't 'put his finger on it'. Was it the dream? She had come to the church just like she used to every Saturday together with other women from the community. They cleaned the church. She had on that smile that had first allured him. The one that had made him want to kiss her again and again. He could have touched her; run his hands over her soft skin. It was almost real; her perfume, her soft laughter.

'And I have not been able to forgive,' the confessor had finished off.

'Forgive?' Father Mulaisho butted in. He had not been paying attention.

'It has been like a burden,' Mabvuto said hesitantly.

'Burden,' Father Mulaisho thought. He looked at his hands. He too had been carrying a burden. Then he said, 'The yoke you carry can only be made light if it is shared.'

Mabvuto remained silent for a while. Why had he waited so long to find out the truth?

Then he finally said, 'When I was young, I would cry myself to sleep but with time...' He fell silent again.

'Go on,' Father Mulaisho could hear the anguish in the confessor's voice.

'Argh!' Mabvuto's frustration disturbed his speech.

'I'm listening…' Father Mulaisho said.

Mabvuto took in a deep breath. 'Does God forgive all manner of sin?'

'God's mercy has no limits,' Father Mulaisho continued to speak. His voice was shaky.

'What if the sin is old – decades old?'

There was a rustling sound as Father Mulaisho rearranged his garments again. He had loved her. She had possessed him and dragged him into her soul and he lived there. When the women would finish with the cleaning, Father Mulaisho drove them home. She was usually the last one to be dropped off. Then they would drive to a small house he had rented outside town.

'That doesn't matter,' Father Mulaisho said, after clearing his throat.

'Are there people who are exempted?'

'What do you mean?' Father Mulaisho's worry could be traced in his voice. He looked at his knuckles. His hands were shaking. He was older now and his rage was under control.

'I mean, are there people who can get away with sin? Those who do not need to get punished?'

'By that do you have any particular kind of sin in mind?'

Mabvuto steadied his hands. 'Like murderers.' He spoke a little louder.

There was a long silence on the other side of the screen.

'No, son,' Father Mulaisho began, 'all have sinned and fall short of his glory.' He took a deep breath. He recalled her big, beautiful eyes, imploring him to let her go. That used to upset him a lot and he would hit her. 'I will leave you,' she would threaten. 'I want to start a family, a real family.'

'Does the "all" include a priest?' Mabvuto asked. The question took Father Mulaisho by surprise.

There was a loud sound of a latch being pulled back. Then the screen was forcefully pushed to one side. The two men in the confessional were now facing each other.

'Tell me more,' the priest demanded. He stood up and turned on the light. It was bright. Mabvuto covered his face briefly and then put his hands down. His shirt was soaked in sweat. His entire body shook.

'More?' Mabvuto asked, as if surprised.

Father Mulaisho moved closer to the confessor and stared into his face and saw her. The priest pulled back sharply.

'What are you doing here?' Father Mulaisho stuttered.

Mabvuto hesitated and said, 'I just want to find out something.' He sighed. He looked at the shocked priest. 'I want to know the truth. I want this pain to go away.'

'The truth?' Father Mulaisho asked. 'You wouldn't understand the truth.'

'Make me understand.' Mabvuto tried hard to control himself.

'Understand' – that is what she had wanted him to do. 'You must let me go,' she had told him. 'Or I will tell everybody about us, about your son.'

Father Mulaisho sighed. He could not say anything. He tried but failed.

Mabvuto rose from the cushion.

'Have you forgiven yourself, Father?'

Father Mulaisho remained seated. He looked at the agony on his son's face. He shared in that agony. He looked down at his feet. Then his eyes travelled to his hands. They were wrinkled and there were dark circles around the knuckles. Their last fight had spiralled out of control. 'She had asked for it?' He sighed. No, he had lost control. Then there was a body. The body was supposed to be hidden. No, he had to get rid of it. When he had gone to dump it in the bush that was very near the shanty compound, he had thought he was alone. But someone had watched him as he took out the limp body from his car. The bush was mostly unused except for during the rainy season, when people from the compound grew maize or pumpkins or sweet potatoes.

'Just tell me, why did you do it?'

Mabvuto moved away from the priest and stood near the door. Then he looked back at him. The priest was old now, his hair was grey. Mabvuto felt sorry for him. He opened the door and looked back once more. He was not going to get an answer – he knew that his father would not answer him.

He walked out. He ran into the young man again. There was a bright smile on his face. 'This is a great place to celebrate Mass,' he announced.

Mabvuto nodded. He turned and made his way out of the building. He looked down from the top of the steps and sighed deeply. He felt it roll off his shoulders. He could see it fall off, the ugly, dirty bag of bitterness. There it went down the 77 steps. He breathed again. He made his way down slowly. Tears flowed freely. They went down his cheeks, over his clean-shaven chin, over the white collar of his shirt and some of them trickled onto his chest. The wetness felt good. Nothing mattered any more.

He walked to the parking area and sat in his car for a moment then started the engine. He breathed again and again; relief, finally. He remembered the look on the priest's face. Had the past two decades been a life sentence? Whatever had happened to the priest in the past years, Mabvuto was glad he had confronted him.

He made his way to the cemetery. He had put new tombstones on the two graves. After placing flowers on his grandmother's, he walked over to his mother's. He stood there and read over and over.

'Margaret Mwai Daka,
Born: 10 October 1958
Died: 29 March 1983
Loving mother.'

Kafula Mwila lives and works in Zambia, where she was born and raised. She taught English Literature in secondary school for 22 years before becoming a developmental worker focusing on the promotion of child rights. Her creative work includes two novels, *Deflowered* and *Shorn Lambs of the City*, published in 2009 and 2012 respectively. Her most recent collection of short stories *Desolate Altars* can be read online at www.kafulamwila.com. She currently lives in Lusaka and works as a novelist, poet, educator, historian, playwright and child-rights activist.

Space II

Masande Ntshanga

Yesterday, Lona showed me a picture of her daughter, the second one, before she told me she couldn't get wet for her boyfriend. We'd gone straight up without starting out at the bar with Lukhanyo, the bar-back, next to the slots, and I wanted to tell her that I didn't ask, but she pressed my fingers against the side of her thigh, and before I could answer, the two of us got drowned by a siren wailing down from Claim Street. They're shooting at more kids on that campus in Parktown, she said, before turning over to sleep, and while I sat next to her, I traced the small scab on her elbow with my front finger, picking at it a little, before she opened her legs and I waited for the siren to fade before we could start.

***

I go there once a week, now, and we always work it out the same way. Lona's new – a few months on the job – and they keep her on the top floor with the premiums – that's 22-year-olds from Mozambique and Swaziland, Bots and Zam – where she splits the blinds and tells me to undo my belt and drop my shoes next to the bin with the used rubbers and wipes. Lona tells me to turn off the light, too, and I do as she says, most times, but sometimes I'll ask her if she wants me there and she'll turn around, the covers hitching up against the crook of her waist, and a bruise brushing up from the small of her back up to her neck. I don't even know you, I imagine her thinking, during those times, and I'll start to feel a fever touching me at the base of my neck, but other times she won't turn and I'll feel her dry hands pulling on the loose skin between my legs – a way of bringing me back, I tell myself.

***

Once a week, after shedding half a grand on Lona at the club, I'll get in touch with my father on the line. I'm edgy, my ex used to say, and I'd tell her how Pa used to get me that way since I was young. He'd heave me up on his shoulders in our hallway, eBhisho, until my stomach would churn, the acid catching at the back of my throat from fear. I figure it's the only reason we still get on – I act like he's still got his old size and Pa believes he could push his palms through a wall. He likes to make claims, my father, harkening us back to things past and things shared, he apportions us blame, and places me here and himself there, before marking the events that led to his collapse. I'll let him, most times, but sometimes I'll ask him how things were before Ma, just to set him off, and we'll go through the Seventies – his bachelor years in the hotel lobbies of Umthatha – with me acting like I can't hear how deep he's sunk into his nip, or that I wouldn't find him scattered the same way the following day. Do you remember when we found her in the garage after the 'rover crashed? It was '02, back in the old house, and we had just the mattresses at the back behind the Nissan.

I don't, I tell him.

You don't?

I don't.

It isn't unusual for us to fall silent over the line. Pa's my last living relation, and we used to have him set up in a home in Port Alfred after his collapse, where it was the house policy for long-distance clients to keep up with calls. I used to try and negotiate them off it.

He's not really sick.

He isn't?

It's grief.

There'd be silence on the line. We prefer to preserve a contented atmosphere.

Is that realistic?

He's your father.

I know he's my father, I'd sigh.

Eventually, when I lost my first job at the ISP in Victory Park, we had to cut Pa's insurance down and move him out to a small two-room close enough to a lake.

Clean air, he told me, meant he didn't have to keep up with old friends.

Fair enough, I said, but I knew by then the calls were a habit for him.

*** *** ***

On weekdays, I do the admin support for a campus network in town, where we're set up as an FET, a squat block with its windows lined opposite the soccer pitch at Ellis Park. It isn't hard. We split the duties down the middle, myself and Colin, and take turns on the maintenance jobs, before we do our rounds at the computer labs with the first-years. Most of the time, we manage to tell ourselves that being here is fine. We even have a sign. This department has not yet been outsourced, but you may want to refer to management for confirmation.

*** *** ***

We'd met at some party, Thembi and I, the housewarming of a distant acquaintance, this French-Canadian post-grad we'd both later discard without much thought. There were American students at the digs, pink and sweaty from excursions into the neighbouring townships, drawling give-me-fives in the living room and dressed in the robes of ancient pillages, spilling pink potato-chip crumbs on the wooden floors under the high ceilings, and I guess celebrating Halloween there. I found Thembi in the kitchen, replacing a hidden bottle of Jameson in a cabinet below the basin; she was slender, with a fatigue vest and faded jeans.

You always steal from your hosts? I said.

Only the wealthy ones, she told me.

Well, you're in luck, then, I said, and pointed at my chest.

I don't know. You don't look like this word I just used.

I'm in disguise.

I watched her get on the cluttered counter, nursing the drink in both hands.

You from outreach?

No.

Well, here, she said, tossing me a t-shirt with a solar logo on it. It was hers, I thought.

Thanks.

Is that the move, though, these days?

What is?

Looking for kegs to crash at community outreach.

No, I know the guy, I said, and hooked a thumb over my shoulder.

Right, she said. James. Of course you do.

I grinned to show that I'd been caught.

Then I reached behind her, got a glass and rinsed it; after Thembi poured us both a shot and stirred the ice in with her finger, I told her I'd seen her before.

***

On the way to work today we passed a taxi overturned in a ditch next to Empire Road. It was caused by a cellphone, our driver said, and some of us took photos of it as he drove past. I leaned my head back against the window after the wreckage had receded, and watched the road as we came to a stop at the following intersection, near Constitution Hill, where a line of men and women in red berets were holding up placards, chanting a protest song, and blocking our line of traffic from gaining passage through the crossing. From the cracked backseat, I remembered how this morning, on street lights across the city, the headlines from the dailies had reported the EFF's call to return the ownership of the stock exchange to its workers. The march had started in Newtown and was set to end in Sandton, and up front our driver drew down his window and hooted, whistling in support as he banged out a rhythm from the side of his door. The men and women laughed and began to separate in turn, and when I looked back again, they seemed to have grown into an even bigger mass. I closed my eyes, then, and remembered how my father had once tried to explain the stock exchange to me; in those days, Pa had been an economics lecturer at a Technikon in East London, and we'd both been sitting on the living-room floor with a stack of his grading when the stocks had come up on TV.

He called me, yesterday.

It's about your mother, he said. Call me back.

I deleted the message and called Lona, but there was no answer. I called Pa back, but there was no answer there, too. Then I reached into my pants, but felt limp in my palm.

I texted Lona.

Nothing is as beautiful as the hood between your legs, I said.

Then I thought about it.

Not even you, I told her.

It took me over an hour to fall asleep, later, and I woke up to a please call me from her number. I'd never got a response from Lona, before, or anyone I'd ever met at the clubs.

***

I walk into work late and find Colin with his legs crossed over our counter, watching the TV we took from one of the staff common rooms for indefinite repairs.

How are things on the outsource front? I ask him.

He uncrosses his legs. No labour brokers at the gate, sir.

Hear, hear, I tell him.

Then I walk into our kitchen, rinse out a mug and scoop out Ricoffy and Cremora. I make it sweet and, waiting for it to cool down, open Lona's message and call her back. The phone rings once before the call is declined, but I wait and get a text message from her a moment later. Meet me at the McDonald's down from the club, she says.

I write to her that I will.

Then I sit down next to Colin and point at the TV.

He shrugs. I left it on anything but the news.

I look at the screen again, a beach scene blurred behind a veil of static, and think of how much Thembi used to like to travel towards the end. We'd part over the course of her different destinations but, before then, I remember how she told me she lost a phone in Zimbabwe once, close to the border, and how she couldn't drink the tap water in Thailand, and how in Zambia, she'd taken so badly to a course of Malanil, that she couldn't pet the cheetahs for all the time she spent over the sink in a lodge in Lusaka. The art was something to see, though, she'd added to me over the phone.

I stretch my arms now, and finish the coffee.

Who's got lab, today? I ask Colin.

You're on, he says, before leaning forward to turn off the TV.

I leave the IT room and make my way down the lino in the corridor.

You should see our students. Twice as many of them arrive for registration towards the end of Feb, and by the time we start on our second semester, they've been culled down in half: most of it from fees; the other cases from grades. It's tempting to think of them as survivors, on certain days, braving the corridors of Ellis Park in Chuck Taylors and tank tops, but most of the time, I can't help but think of them as pushing towards something rumoured. I stop at Mrs Mokoena's office, and knock twice on the chipped door; I can hear her talking on the line before she pauses to invite me in.

Dumela, mme, le kae? I say at the door.

I'm fine, she says, and, as usual, I watch her hand wave me towards the key cabinet, where I find the double set we use for the labs.

On my way out, again, I hear her calling for me.

Placing a palm over the receiver, Mrs Mokoena looks at me and smiles. Tell me, she says. Isn't it enough to be late once a day? You've had those students waiting for ten minutes in the corridor next to Mr Dukisa's class. You know he doesn't like to be disturbed.

I scratch my head. I thought they'd changed the schedule.

You thought they'd changed the schedule, she says. Just go, will you.

I go and find half of them on the floor in the next block, leaning against the wall of the computer lab, their backpacks set between their legs, and their faces fixed on their phones. I tell them to get up.

If you start getting here any earlier, I say, I'll be out of a job.

They laugh and, as they do that, I open the door to set them up for their tutorial class. It's one of the introduction sets from Mr Longela – they start a new chapter of Matlab the following month – and they get through the 45-minute exercise in half an hour. We spend the rest of the time watching the clock.

Teacher, did you hear two students were hospitalized from Parktown?

Wits?

Yes. Not even rubber bullets. They're shooting to kill us, now.

I nod, thinking of Lona, again, and open a browser and direct it to Google. Ever since the start of the protests, Lona's filled her head with the plight of the students, and I've even come close to telling her of how I grew up in Bhisho during the year of the massacre, and how I came to lose my mother to another version of this.

My head hurts. It says here they torched a bus, I tell them.

Yes, they did. The students need to be heard, now. This is a matter of free education and ending financial segregation. We cannot back down from colonial administrators.

This comes from Philani, an engineering student in a black track top, the zip left undone to reveal a yellow SASCO shirt. The ribbing on the sides of his sweater looks bright in the light, almost bleached, and his hair is shaved close to his skull and trimmed.

I nod at him and get up from my desk.

Right, I say. It's time to pack up and log off.

Then I take another look at their scores.

You all did well, today, I say, but they can't hear me over the sound of their packing; after they've cleared out, I lock up and get back to Mrs Mokoena before finding Colin asleep. I look at the TV and it's back on, again, full of static, and set on the news.

***

I get in touch with Pa after work. He lets the phone ring once before he picks it up, sounding out of breath, and I brace myself outside a spaza shop in Kew. Inside my line of view, the Joburg traffic is turned up, jammed at the crossing near Wynberg.

You took your time, he says.

I tried you last night; what's wrong with your breathing?

Nothing.

You sound like you're losing air.

I was out gardening.

You were out gardening?

I listen to him laugh for a while. Yes. Madala does the garden in the yard next door and I asked him over and then I gave him a hand. I gave him two hands.

It's past six, I start to say, but decide against it. You told me I should call you back.

We need to talk.

I heard that much.

I'm thinking of a trip.

I cup my brow in my palm and choose each word. Where to?

To my son, he says. The City of Gold.

I breathe for a while. Fine. Let me arrange you a ticket.

I've already bought a Greyhound, he says. I arrive tomorrow.

I see.

Then Pa takes a moment to clear his throat. How are you?

I'm fine, I tell him. I have to go.

✳✳✳

I take a taxi to Bree, before I connect to Hillbrow at the rank, and then I ride until the bus stop on Edith Cavell, and walk up Pretoria Street, where I find the McDonald's at the corner of Claim. I look inside and find Lona sitting at a table towards the back, nursing a fountain soda and a copy of *The Star*. I use my hand to clear the crumbs from the seat in front of her.

You South Africans used to be lucky, she says, but look at this, now.

I look and see students standing in front of riot police in Soshanguve some time last week; and place a palm over her fingers, feeling surprised when she doesn't flinch.

I sigh. They were promised even more than we were, I tell her.

It's easy to see that.

That's what we all say. Do you want to eat before we go upstairs?

I can eat, she says, but can you?

No one knows me here, I tell her, but even if they did.

Then what?

Then nothing.

I come back with a tray holding a pair of cheeseburgers and two cartons of fries. Placing them on the table, I refill Lona's fountain Coke from mine.

You look good in the light, I tell her.

Well, you don't; what happened to your tooth?

I smile. It got knocked against a beer bottle. You've never seen it before?

Of course I've seen it before. Does no one ever play with you?

I laugh at that. Not that I can remember, I say.

Later, I take my hand and push it between her cheeks like I used to with Thembi and she pushes it away; we carry on, twisting over each other as the dawn blushes her cracked window a pink shade, and we go at it twice before I get up to drop the plastic in the bin next to her door. I get back in the covers with her as the morning traffic begins to hum and, closing my eyes, I think of how the two of us could be trapped inside the hull of a giant machine, but Lona's body feels warm against my own, and I decide to listen to her breathe.

I need your help, she says, and, still lying in bed, I don't say anything back. Lowering the covers, Lona lifts her arm and shows me the bruise on its underside. I got this in the car accident, she says, but I didn't tell you how it happened.

How did it happen?

I was drinking in Mbabane.

I listen for more.

My parents are in Joburg this weekend, she says, and I want to see my daughter.

Then I think about what Lona tells me next for a while.

I'll do it, I tell her.

***

I arrive at Park Station on time, but Pa's bus is delayed, having broken down on the national road outside Kokstad. I go back to the parking lot, absorb the morning sun, and rest my head over my forearms. Then I get up to find him again, which I do, next to the escalators.

I help him with his suitcase.

These roads, he says. This country won't run out of ways to kill us.

I laugh to set the two of us at ease. You're safe, at least, I say.

That's why you go with Greyhound, he tells me.

That's why you go with Greyhound, I echo him.

Out in the parking lot, I take out my cellphone and call for a taxi; after the Uber arrives, I help pack Pa's baggage into the boot. My father takes the back seat and I sit up front, on the passenger side, so I can direct the driver towards the shortest route. Then we drive out onto Rissik and merge into Victoria towards Parktown.

I'll start us off at the mall for something to eat, I say.

I hope it's affordable. I know you people like to spend.

We join Oxford and head out towards Rosebank before Pa tells me he doesn't understand why I don't have a car. You're definitely smart enough for it.

I shrug. I'm working on affording the instalments, I tell him.

Do you remember when you scored 139 for that IQ test?

I thought it meant my life would be different, I tell him, but I don't really like computers. Then I wait for him to say something, but Pa only leans back in his seat.

We drive past Killarney, going through Riviera, and when we come to a stop at an intersection with an armless man holding up a sign with his chin, I look out of the window and where we are reminds me of an old colleague I used to have.

Chantel used to wear shaded glasses; she had a sharp chin and always shared her pack of Rothmans with the rest of us on the team. We were colleagues at MWEB, the second-largest internet service provider in the country, and our offices were stationed in Victory Park, between Randburg and Parkhurst. Even though we'd been hired as customer-service reps – most of us were latched onto tech support through inbound calls – our duties were extended to include sales that summer in order to facilitate the roll-out of the country's first uncapped ADSL service. It was during this time that Chantel and I were teamed together and scheduled on the same route close to town.

We'd park our van at the start of each block, check the log for the houses that needed tech support, and we'd cover those first before we knocked on the doors of the rest, asking if they were interested in upgrading to the company's latest broadband package.

We'd get through them quick, most times. Chantel and I had both done well at A+ in college, and she had a way with the people who came from these neighbourhoods, too – Illovo, Parktown North, Riviera – that made them open their doors long enough for us to sell.

We had a lot of downtime as a result. We'd park the van under a tree, share cigarettes and listen to the countdown on Y. Chantel thought she'd be rich from what we'd gone to school for, and I used to tell her that I thought she was thinking of a different time.

It went on like this for most of the summer that year until one day, after I'd gone down on Chantel inside the van, we serviced the router of a client in Illovo who waited for us to drive off before she called our offices in Victory Park, lodging a complaint with client services that she'd picked up the smell of marijuana.

The two of us were called in, having already decided that I would shoulder it for the sake of her son and, after my dismissal, Chantel gave me a contact number linked to her sister, who worked for a mobile clinic initiative in town, where they were looking to install a network for stock taking and keeping records for their returning patients.

I joined Chantel's sister Catherine the following week, and on my first day on the job we took the clinic out to the corner of Commissioner and Polly, the first stop in a series of brothels that were getting HIV treatment in preparation for the World Cup. In the bus, during her break, I told Catherine about the first man I'd seen suffer from the illness it led to. I was a child in Bhisho, I told her, and I'd seen the father of a friend of mine fade in a shed at the back of a tavern in '92. We headed up to Royal Park, after that, starting off at the Hillbrow Inn, before we parked outside The Summit, which was how I started going to the club, years before I would come across the Lona I know now, whom I'd find late one Wednesday evening, dancing on the floor without a top on under a blue strobe.

✳✳✳

Our driver banks into Tyrwhitt Avenue and comes to a stop before the boom gates that lead into the parking bays at Rosebank Mall. I get out and help Pa with his suitcase. Then we walk past the Woolies store and settle ourselves under a sunshade at Café Europa, next to the craft market with its curios, and opposite the Mimmos Eatalian, where two businessmen sit in front of a chicken finger platter, taking sips from draughts of craft beer.

You don't like computers, Pa says. I always told your mother she was spoiling you with those videogames, but she broke her back for them. Now you don't like computers.

That's different.

I know it's different, he says. You were clever. You needed the stimulation.

I order an espresso from the waiter; Pa asks for a tea and gets honey to sweeten it. We sip on the drinks when they arrive, and I look out towards the lawn with the artificial grass.

You made time for me, he says.

I take a sip from the espresso. Then the two of us watch as two girls walk past the café, dressed in high-waisted jeans and black, printed tank tops.

You used to have a girlfriend, he says.

I blow on the coffee before I finish it. Then I leave both hands in the sunlight.

Ma never liked her, I tell him.

Your mother always wanted happiness for people. It wasn't realistic.

We spent some time apart, me and Ma. Thembi was someone who understood that.

Did she?

We both didn't understand our parents, I tell him, and in the end, when she said the two of us were too similar in our unhappiness, it was hard for me to disagree.

I look at him and Pa traces his finger along the rim of an ashtray set on the table.

I could never talk to my father either, he says. I suspect it could be this country.

I lean back on my seat as a black jeep approaches the rear end of the mall, close to the FNB ATMs, and I hear 'Face Down' by White Lung coming out from its speakers.

I've moved from Port Alfred, he says.

I look up.

It's true. I've gone home to eDutywa.

You have?

The old plot was abandoned and growing weeds, he tells me, and I used my retirement on it. I feel it's the best decision I've made in the last ten years.

Pa looks at me then, and smiles. I'll be herding goats like my father, now, he says, and that makes the two of us laugh. We cause the table to rock until our waiter arrives to take our orders, and after lunch, when the taxi arrives and we pack Pa's suitcase inside the boot, he tells me changing our focus doesn't have to mean we're forgetting. Then my father pauses again, and before he closes the backseat door, he tells me he doesn't think it's possible to.

***

I install him in my flat in Kew, take his suitcase to my bedroom, and sit him down on the couch in front of the second half of a soccer game.

No, I want to read, Pa tells me, and I turn off the TV.

Then I walk to the kitchen and fill up a glass with ice before he calls me back to the living room. I close the tap and, when I walk to him, I find Pa holding up an old photo of himself: he has an afro in the picture, and his moustache is thick and glistening.

This is what I looked like when I met your mother, he says.

I nod and take a sip from the water.

I was working as a sales rep, back then, before going back to school.

I know, I tell him.

Your mother was a beauty, Pa says, and packs the photo away.

I take a seat next to him and turn the TV back on, pressing the volume down to mute the match. You never stayed with us at the house on Rharhabe Road, I say. It was her, Nana and myself. I remember meeting you for the first time. That doesn't seem right as a memory.

It was a different time. We were living in an occupied country.

There were things you could've protected me from.

Pa sighs. It broke families, this place, and you could say it still does.

We watch the flickering green of the soccer pitch, the ball leaping between players.

Well, I'm glad you came back, I tell him.

I'm glad, too, he says. You, your mother and I had a good ten years before her health problems started. You know, I had no idea, and sometimes, I think even she forgot.

The only thing I remember about that year is trying to fail Afrikaans and seeing a dying man at Ma Thano's, I tell him. I remember Ma working, too. I remember how she'd been promoted at her job and how she wanted to get me to a better school.

Pa smiles before he lets his face drop again. It's what made it all so surprising, he says. That she would do what she did on top of everything else.

I tell him that I know.

There was something remarkable in her, he says. Then he turns to look at me and tells me he's certain it's something I have, too.

I smile enough to make him turn back, and then I switch off the TV.

Later, after he tells me he's tired, I set Pa up in the bedroom and take my laptop back to the lounge. There, I open my browser and look at my history tab: Roxy Reynolds, Ms Goddess, Harley Dean, Cassidy Clay, Jasmine Jae, Teanna Trump, Shazia Sahari, Sabrina Taylor, Maya Hills, Jazmine Cashmere, Valentina Nappi, Franceska Jaimes, Noemilk, Mya G, Leah Jaye, Sahara Knight, Marquetta Jewel, Loona Luxx, Ashlyn Brooke, Sophia Knight, Diamond Legacy, Penelope Cum, Giselle Mona, Lela Star, Sara Jay, Susana Caliente.

The list goes on, and I remember how I couldn't stop touching myself the morning we got up to bury my mother. It had started in a moment of inattention, I guessed, a disbelief that reached towards the force of habit – aiming to fend off the morning's facts – but the act solidified into a respite that felt like putting her death on hold. I couldn't tell whether or not it was the act or the anticipation – the rush of blood that changed the feeling of nausea into light-headedness – but after a while, the only thing that gave more relief than arousal or coming was sharing them with someone else.

Ma had died 15 years after sustaining a bullet wound at the Bhisho massacre in '92, when 80,000 protesters, led by the ANC and aiming to dissolve the Bantustan, had been gunned down by the Ciskei Defence Force, killing 28 and injuring over 200.

I hadn't known about it on the day it happened; Ma was gone for a fortnight, that month, and my grandmother, Nana, and I got help from our neighbour, Sis' Khethiwe, before my father arrived with his bags a week after Ma's return. We moved towns after that, but Ma never told us that the wound had given her complications that would last her the rest of her life, and even ten years later, when she crashed the Land Rover – complaining of a momentary loss of consciousness – my father and I, who'd found her sitting alone on a mattress inside the garage next to the Nissan, had been none the wiser.

***

I rummage for my passport in the cabinet below the TV. Then I sit down at the coffee table and write a note for Pa, which I take back to my room and tape onto the door for him to find. I watch him on the bed; he's fallen asleep sitting upright against the wall, the book he was reading – *The Lost World* by Arthur Conan Doyle – split in half and sliding down to his thighs. I place it on the bedside with a bookmark. Then I close the door and make it out of the apartment to the parking lot, where the air feels warm and moist on my skin.

I call a taxi to Hillbrow, and on the way there the driver asks me how life's been treating me in the city. I turn the question back on him and look out of the window again, watching as the orange lights glow against the darkened skyline below the Vodacom tower.

It's about money, big man, he says, and I grunt to show agreement.

I'm saving up for my own car, he tells me. These white people have everything, you see, and all we can do is work, no?

I nod, and we go silent for a while before the cab drops me off at the corner of Van der Merwe. I take out a hundred for the doorman and see Lukhanyo, the bar-back, next to the entrance after I've been patted down. I walk over to him.

Long time, he says, and I nod.

I ask him if he's still working the slots.

No, mfowethu, I gave that up. You can't make money that way.

The bass thumps against the walls around us, and the blue and pink strobe lights cut thick beams against the dark. Lukhanyo lifts his forefinger and rubs it under his nostrils.

I shake my head, saying no, and ask him if that's what he's doing, now.

Ja, I sell a little here and there, but nothing to the girls.

I nod. You have to be careful.

You know me, he says, and I tell him that I do.

Then I point a finger towards the ceiling.

I haven't seen her come down today, boss, but she should be up there.

We shake hands and I walk towards the lift, where two girls eye me from inside the elevator car, and I smile back without taking on their offer. The two of them walk past me, into the club, and I make my way up to Lona on the top floor. When I knock, she tells me it's open and that I should lock the door behind me. I find her sitting up in bed, smoking a Dunhill Light and scrolling through her phone.

Yesterday, when Lona told me her parents' conditions for letting her see her daughter, I didn't think much of the hour of pretence it would take from me.

Now I sit on the edge of the bed, take out my passport, and flip through the pages in front of her, asking if her parents will believe her fiancé's papers.

Lona laughs, and later, when I can feel her sweat cooling down on my skin, she asks me if I don't ever want to see the other girls, downstairs, or even the dancing.

I tell her not more than anyone else.

Maybe that means something, then, from what you've told me about yourself.

I think about what she means by that for a long time.

Then I tell her that maybe it does.

Masande Ntshanga won the inaugural PEN International New Voices Award in 2013, and was shortlisted for the Caine Prize in 2015. He was born in 1986 in East London, South Africa, and graduated with degrees in Film and Media and in English Studies from the University of Cape Town, where he became a Creative Writing Fellow, completing his Masters in Creative Writing under the Mellon Mays Foundation. He received a Fulbright Award, an NRF Freestanding Masters scholarship, a Civitella Ranieri Fellowship and a Bundanon Trust Award. His work has appeared in *The White Review*, *Chimurenga*, *VICE* and *n + 1*. He has also written for *Rolling Stone* magazine.

The Daily Assortment of Astonishing Things

Okwiri Oduor

It was Dudu who made his mama leave. He would not eat his leek soup and he would not take his afternoon nap and he would not wear his gumboots when it rained. He would not swallow the cod-liver oil and he would not say bless you when a person sneezed and he would not stop drawing porcupines on the sitting-room wall. His mama threw her hands in the air. She said, My god, I am not the type of mama who can take all this mud. So she packed up her things and left.

Dudu was already grown then – his feet could almost touch the floor when he sat at the dining table, and he could chew on a slice of lemon without scrunching his face, and he could squeeze a cockroach until its gut burst and the creamy phlegm inside it slathered all over his palm. Dudu did not really need a mama.

He stood on the veranda and watched his mama go – duffel bag slung over her shoulder, scarf tied on her head, sweat dribbling down her temples. He held his breath in a tight ball inside his chest, afraid that she would stop walking, afraid that she would turn back and say, No-no-no I am the type of mama who can take all this mud.

His mama was not a great mama. Her name was Mayoni. Her breath always smelt of camphor. She wore rumpled nylon dresses and drank bitter coffee with no sugar in it. Sometimes she chewed her fingernails and spat the shreds out on the table. Every morning, she bought a loaf of bread from Al-Fatah Petty Cash Vouchers and Flashlights, and the bread always tasted of rosewater. On Sundays, she dabbed Ear De Toilet in the inside of her wrist and made the whole house smell of mothballs.

The worst thing about his mama, though, was her split gaze. When she looked at you, one eye nestled on the bridge of your nose and the other eye strayed, scratching at the drapes behind you. The first eye, the one which nestled on the bridge of your nose, was a regular eye. The eye which fleeted about of its own volition was a sheep's eye.

One day, Dudu cut off his eyelashes with paper scissors. He had heard on *The Daily Assortment of Astonishing Things* that a person could not walk in a straight line if all their lashes were gone. He wanted to see if this was true. His mama found him on the kitchen floor, the scissors held near his brow.

His mama said, See this boy, just see this boy! She pried her sheep's eye out of its socket, rolled it about in her palm, and then hurled it at Dudu. She said, Is this what you are trying to do now, are you trying to take your eye out? You think it is *fan-tas-tic* not to have an eye?

The sheep's eye missed Dudu's face. It bounced against a cabinet door and rolled beneath the refrigerator. Dudu crouched low to get it, not because he liked to be kind and to do things for his mama, but because he wanted to pop the sheep's eye. He had always wondered if the sheep's eye would tremble between his fingers just like a boiled egg.

The sheep's eye was hard as flint and would not pop. His mama held it beneath the tap, then she dried it on a tea towel and slid it back inside her face. She took Dudu's scissors and waddled away. When her back was turned, Dudu tugged at the silverware drawer. He rummaged about for a paring knife, found one, and finished cutting off his lashes. It was true – a person could not walk in a straight line if all their lashes were gone.

Dudu's legs ached. He shifted his weight from one foot to

another. A lizard crawled onto the veranda, its beady eyes glistening, watching him. He said to the lizard, What are you looking at, Stupid? The lizard did not turn away, so he hurled a rock at it. The lizard darted into the lemongrass bushes.

Dudu looked out onto the footpath. He watched his mama pause, watched her turn back and regard the house. He and his mama stared at each other. Dudu whispered beneath his breath, Please-please-please don't come back. His mama placed her duffel bag on the ground. She dabbed at her sweaty temples with the corner of her rumpled nylon dress. Then she straightened, crossed her arms beneath her breasts and gazed at Dudu. He knew that she wanted him to run after her, to say, Mama please I was only playing please-please I am not full of mud at all!

But Dudu was not the type of boy to do such a thing. His mama shook her head sorrowfully, picked up her duffel bag and disappeared round the bend. Dudu let out the breath he had been holding. He said to himself, Dudu, you made your mama go!

He pulled off his shirt, waved it about in the air and then tossed it across the yard. He did three back flips. Then he danced ndombolo, his waist twisting round and round.

Dudu ate all the peanut butter in the jar. He plucked his mama's aloes and broke them down the shaft. He chewed on baobab seeds and spat the mangled shreds into the pots of lentil soup simmering on strangers' verandas.

He set traps for hornbills. He swam in the bog and hoped to catch bilharzia. He pulled the sheet out of his mama's bed and made a hammock in the mango trees. He rolled down grit hills. He plundered fruit from the church orchard. He stole a chicken from the neighbour's backyard, stepped on its wings to immobilize it, and then bashed its head with a stone.

He said to himself, Dudu, what else do you want to do? He said to himself, I want to stay out all night. The air was frosty, but he was not the type of boy to bother himself with cardigans or jackets. Bare-chested, he walked out into the street, singing *Kuna Mtu Shambani*. The bitter air nibbled at him. He plucked tufts of grass, stuck them with saliva onto himself, and pretended that he wore a fur coat.

He said to himself, Dudu, I wish I had a kitten.

He once heard on *The Daily Assortment of Astonishing Things* that if a kitten scratched you, you could get lockjaw and die. He wanted to see if this was true at all. If he had a kitten, he would name it Swi-Swi. He would carry Swi-Swi by the ears, swinging it back and forth to the marketplace. He would go to Josephat's stall and say, Scratch him, Swi-Swi, scratch him!

Josephat was the maize-roaster. He had the type of face that was just asking to be scratched – his forehead was cockled and his eyes were smudged and trickling. His nose was always slithering down his face like a caterpillar. Swi-Swi would scratch Josephat, then maybe Josephat would get lockjaw and die.

Dudu wondered where his mama was right now. Then he said to himself, Dudu, who cares where your mama is right now?

The sky was the colour of the old ash in his mama's hearth. It hung low, its lumps breaking over chimneys and eaves, over bloomers billowing on yellow balconies. In the trees, leaves huddled close, trembling, answering the call of the wind with tiny, breathless stutters.

Dudu kicked dustbins, frightening rats and mongooses, scattering slimy refuse across the pavement. He scaled lampposts and cupped the yellow light in his hands, and the light spilled in sticky strings between his fingers. He climbed onto the bonnets of parked cars, and he jumped up and down, and the cars groaned, their bonnets crumpling.

Then he clambered up a brick wall and crouched on his haunches and was very still. He said to himself, Dudu, this is what it must feel like to be a barn owl. The moon trickled from the sky and seeped onto his tongue. The moon did not taste of caramel the way a person might expect. It was bitter, like a glob of wax that someone had coaxed out of their earhole.

The salamanders crept out of their nests and the sky ripped on the church spire and hail pecked at him, cackling shrilly. Dudu curled up beneath an old Chevrolet. He listened to the low churring of nightjars, and to the moan of crickets in the bramble, and to the wind ululating through the sycamores. He said to himself, Dudu, is it not *fan-tas-tic* to be without a mama?

Dudu dug his fingers through the earth, searching for earth-worms. He once heard on *The Daily Assortment of Astonishing Things* that each worm was really just two different worms stuck together with glue. The earth was damp from the rain. It crumbled in his palm.

He plucked the wriggling worms and raised them to his face. He studied them, trying to make out the place where each ended and the other began, to make out the place where they were stuck together with glue. Then he tore the worms apart and watched as each shred scuttled away.

Nearby, a child sucked on a soggy banana. The child's name was Bakari. Its father owned Fare Thee Well Coffin Extravaganza in town.

You, Dudu said to the child.

The child squinted up at Dudu. Its eyes were tiny flecks of grit that the wind had blown onto its face.

Dudu said to the child, What happened to your nose?

The child raised its hand to its face. It said, Nothing happened to my nose.

Dudu said, Your nose is missing.

The child's forehead crinkled. Tears filled its tiny dull eyes. It said, I... I don't have a nose?

Dudu said, It must have fallen on the street somewhere.

The child broke into sobs, its whole body writhing. Dudu said to it, Maybe your nose got crushed by a milk cart.

The child began to wail. It threw its banana on the ground and ran off to find its mama. Dudu reached for the banana.

He wiped it against his poplin shorts, then he stuffed it inside his mouth.

The ground beneath Dudu's feet started to heave. He fell to his knees, put his ear to the gravel, and listened to the rumbling inside the earth. He said to himself, Dudu, that's the cargo train!

He took off through the creek and the bramble. Twigs and leaves and wet pebbles rose into the air behind him. The breeze was cold, it stung his nose and brought tears to his eyes. The world blurred – there were no trees, no birds, no grasshoppers, no moths, just Dudu running so fast that his feet did not touch the ground.

He ran to the edge of the cliff and stared at the rattling tracks below. He said to himself, Red lorry yellow lorry blue lorry, and by the time he finished saying that, the train had emerged. He said to himself, Jump, Dudu, jump, and now the ground ended and now the air began, and he soared through it like a flamingo. He said to himself, Let yourself down, Dudu, and he let himself down, landing on the hot roof of a coach.

Dudu's mama would never have let him do a thing like that. Mamas were not the type of people to let you just jump onto the roofs of trains or hang onto the backs of trailers or ride in strangers' pickup trucks. Dudu clicked his tongue to the roof of his mouth. He said to himself, Mamas are so full of mud!

The train slowed down as it neared a railway crossing. Dudu leapt off the roof of the coach. He landed on a pile of dead leaves. His arms itched from the bites of little bramble rodents and from the scratches of prickly pears. He tore at them until his fingernails were bloody. He watched the train stagger away, watched it burrow itself into the horizon. He said to himself, Dudu, this is the best day of your life.

He had learned to make spit bombs from the instructions given on *The Daily Assortment of Astonishing Things*. This is what you did: You got the tube of a biro pen, and then you chewed on a piece of paper and soaked it with your saliva, and then you spit the wet piece of paper into the biro pen tube and aimed it at a person's face, and then you launched the spit bomb by blowing hard into the biro pen tube.

Dudu climbed an avocado tree and sat on a high branch, his legs dangling beneath him. He chewed on a piece of newspaper that he had found outside the butcher's shop. He spat it into the biro pen tube and waited for someone to walk in the street beneath the avocado tree.

A woman in a tailored suit ambled by, her shiny pumps going kong-kong-kong on the pavement. Dudu launched a spit bomb at her. The woman slapped at her neck. She looked up into the sky and said, Those foolish seagulls are shitting on people again.

Father Anthony Munanira walked down the street. He was the priest from Our Lady of Lourdes. He clutched the corner of his cassock so it would not drag in the mud. Dudu launched a spit bomb at him. Father Anthony Munanira slapped at his forehead. He raised his Navarre Bible in the air and waved it at the seagulls. He said, You little nincompoops!

Dudu launched another spit bomb. It hit a woman on the temple. The woman took a rock and threw it at the seagulls, yelling, You nasty piece of shit. The seagulls squawked away, their cawing shrill and wounded. Dudu laughed until his sides ached.

He tucked the biro pen tube behind his ear and gazed out into the town. The sun was high in the sky. It baked the dicky-birds coursing through the air, and the dicky-birds crumpled down and smouldered in brown pools of water.

One moment the sky was empty, and then the next, a rogue whirlwind tore away suckling babies and spinning bicycles and radios still screeching Christmas carols. These things bobbed up high and were pinned like stars and like moons and like the half-hearted desires of people too lazy to fall down to their knees to pray.

The town was a dripping pomegranate, and then it was a drum with a throbbing goatskin resonator, and then it was a swarm of flies contorting itself into the shapes of milk bottles and trout and bougainvillea branches.

Then the muezzin chanted a call to prayer, his voice tremulous through his megaphone. Dudu's heart leapt into his throat. He said to himself, Dudu, *The Daily Assortment of Astonishing Things* is about to start!

He had never missed a show. Every afternoon, when the muezzin sang in the minaret, Dudu knew that it was time to take out a pitcher of tamarind juice and to drink it all in two gulps and to sit out on the veranda with his mama's transistor radio cradled in his lap.

Dudu clambered down the tree, chest heaving, palms slippery, throat parched and dry. The bark tore at his shorts and the poplin fabric ripped. The biro pen tube fell from behind his ear, but he did not stop to pick it up.

He ran across the street, past the marabou storks and the parked tuktuks and the vandalized lampposts. He ran past the cobbler's hovel and the milliner's shack and the mechanic's oil-stained lot. He ran past the man who hawked a cure for syphillis and a salve for knock-knees. He wished that another cargo train would crawl out of its lair, wished that he could jump onto the roof of one of its coaches and ride all the way home.

The muezzin stopped singing. Dudu's head throbbed. He gulped some air and it lodged itself inside his throat like a boulder. He doubled over, coughing. He spat onto the gravel. His saliva was pink. He poked at it with his index finger.

When he caught his breath again, he surged forward. His house emerged piecemeal from the trees – a window ledge, a brick chimney, a door plastered with posters that read, *Come And Fetch Your Anointing With Pastor Eusabius Wamunyolo.*

Dudu ran through ochre-coloured puddles. Mud crusted his calves and shins. Some of it sploshed onto his chin and forehead. Some of it splattered across the veranda. Dudu slipped on the mud and fell, landing on his backside. He said to the veranda, Stupid veranda! Then he rose to his feet, kicked the door and burst into the house.

He dragged a stool across the kitchen floor, climbed onto it and scanned the top of the refrigerator. The transistor radio was not in its usual place. He opened the cabinets and peered inside. He scrambled beneath the dining table. He tugged at the curtains. He opened drawers and spilled cutlery all over his muddy feet. He toppled the laundry basket. He threw clothes out of his mama's closet. He even went to the toilet and checked inside the cistern.

The transistor radio was gone. His mama had taken it with her when she left. Dudu sank to the ground. He buried his head in his hands. His shoulders jerked. His eyes welled with hot, angry tears – they dribbled down his chin and seeped into the slash of his navel. He said to himself, Dudu, this is the worst day of your life.

Later, he walked out to the yard and searched for the t-shirt he had flung there the day before. The wind had blown it to the barbed-wire fence. He plucked black-jack needles and ladybirds from its collar, and then he wiggled into it. The t-shirt was damp on his body. It had mud down its front.

A dog stood in the footpath. It was mangy and flea-ridden, with a ribcage like a pair of wings tucked into its sides. The dog's name was Je Huu Ni Ungwana. It belonged to the leper who begged on the street corner. The dog stared at Dudu through slimy, curdled eyes. Dudu scratched at a scab on his elbow. The dog turned its head away. Dudu said, Please-please-please don't go, but the dog scampered off.

Next door, Maimuna the neighbour-woman stood at the wash lines. She clamped plastic pegs between her teeth. She wrung towels and frocks. Water soaked her terrycloth gown and ran down her legs in little foamy rivulets.

Maimuna was 26 years old. Everyone called her an old maid, and Dudu could see why – she had clumps of white hair growing out of her scalp. Dudu was sure that Maimuna did not have much longer to live.

Maimuna nodded at Dudu. She said, How are you today, Dudu?

Dudu said, Fine-fine. He wanted to say to her, Mind your own business, but you could not be rude to a dying person.

Maimuna smiled at him. Good, she said.

She picked up her buckets and waddled towards her house. Dudu bounded to the barbed-wire fence. He said, Wait, Maimuna, do you have a radio?

Maimuna said, I do, Dudu, but I am listening to the cooking show. Today they are teaching us how to make marmalade out of tangerines. Maimuna pushed her door and disappeared inside it.

Dudu picked up a rock and hurled it at her orchids. He turned away and crossed the yard. In the street, a crowd gathered near a telephone booth. Dudu wiggled his way through people's legs. A man stood at the centre of the crowd. He wore a dark robe. A leather satchel hung from his shoulder. He dabbed at his face with a crumpled handkerchief. The man said, I greet you on this very auspicious red-letter day, my sisters and brothers.

The people said, We greet you too.

The man reached for a bottle of Fanta Cream which stood at his feet. His throat wiggled up and down as he swallowed. He wiped his mouth with the back of his hand. He said, Kivuva is the name that was imparted upon my being on the incredible occasion of my springing from the womb of the wench who bore me. I have been sauntering in the wilderness for 12 days and 12 nights, searching for this your gracious domicile which the good Lord saw wise to adorn on the landscape of our mighty country. I come here objurgating the power of he who was discombobulated by the luminescence. Can I get an Amen?

The crowd said, Amen.

Kivuva took a vial from his satchel and held it up in the

air. He said, You must be conferring inside yourself about the macrocosm that exists inside this glass vessel. This, my brothers and sisters, is seawater from Mombasa. My sisters and brothers, do not confound yourselves. Do not perverse yourselves. Do not flummox yourselves. This seawater from Mombasa bears the vastitude of your destiny inside it. If you were going to flounder, this seawater will say to you, Verily verily there shall be no floundering today. This seawater from Mombasa is ordained by He whose very luminescence sent me here today. Can I get an Amen?

The crowd said, Amen.

Dudu shifted from one foot to the next. He wondered if *The Daily Assortment of Astonishing Things* was over already.

Kivuva said, The doubters and the unbelievers are formulating the inquiry: Why seawater from Mombasa? Let me just tell you, my sisters and brothers. There was a fish in the sea, you hear? And this fish was caught, you hear? And when they caught it they turned it over, you hear? And it had words on its belly. The doubters and the unbelievers are formulating another inquiry. They are asking themselves, What did the words on the fish's belly say? Well, it said this: Surely, the Lord will save you from the fowler's snare and from the deadly pestilence. Can I have an Amen?

The crowd said, Amen.

Dudu scratched at a welt on his knee. He wondered if the fish with the Scripture on its belly had been a blue marlin. He once heard on *The Daily Assortment of Astonishing Things* that blue marlins had swords growing out of their noses. He wondered what happened to the fish after it was caught. He wondered if the fishermen laid it out on the sand and took out their penknives and split it in such a way that each fisherman received a word of scripture to cook inside their soup.

Dudu watched as people reached inside their camisoles and boxer shorts for hidden coins. They handed Kivuva their warm sweaty money, and he handed them vials of seawater from Mombasa. Dudu tugged at Kivuva's sleeve. He said, Do you have a radio?

Kivuva slung his satchel over his shoulder. He said, You if you just look at my face closely, do you see like my name could be Mr Radio-man?

Dudu said to himself, This man is so full of mud. He elbowed his way out of the crowd. The sun burnt the back of his neck. Hornets circled his face. He slapped at them and, when they dove at him, he ducked into Mutheu Must Go Café.

At one table, a man fondled his mug, swirling the tea inside it. The man's name was Born-Free Opondo. He lived in a tenement two streets from the café. His house was filled with cats and roosters and dusty bric-a-brac. One time, Born-Free Opondo rummaged through the papers stacked on his sitting-room sofa. Underneath them, he discovered a child whom the newspapers had reported missing for months. The child was dead when Born-Free Opondo found him.

At another table, a woman peeled a pear with a butter knife. Her name was Electine Zuzu. She always wore Savco jeans whose waistbands went up to her armpits. Electine Zuzu had the type of walk which was not a walk but a skulk. People said that it was because she had an STD. Dudu had heard on the *Daily Assortment of Astonishing Things* that STD meant Standard Three Dropout. He hoped to one day have an STD too.

Born-Free Opondo and Electine Zuzu looked up at Dudu. Born-Free Opondo slurped at his tea. Electine Zuzu wiped sugar off the PVC tabletop. She placed her pear down and rubbed her palms on her jeans.

Dudu said, Do any of you have a radio?

Born-Free Opondo snorted. He said, Even if I had one, why would I give it to you?

Electine Zuzu gathered the pear peels in a square of toilet paper. She said, Children of nowadays! Just see this one asking-asking for a radio. As if he even knows how many shillings a radio costs.

Dudu said to himself, These people are so full of mud. He turned away from the café. The hornets were gone. He strode into the yellow sunshine and leaned against a lamppost. A helicopter hovered low, its rotors whirring, casting shadows on the ground. A man urinated into a guava tree. A girl dropped her candy stick, bent down, retrieved it, and wiped the dirt against her frock. A child examined a locust that had got squashed beneath a stranger's boot. A porter waddled by, sacks of grain hoisted high on his shoulders.

Dudu wondered how the street could be so busy, how any of these people could bear to be away from the radio. *The Daily Assortment of Astonishing Things* had taught him everything he knew – how to suck the cuffs of his shirt, and how to wear rubber bands round his forehead, and how to make chocolate bars by mixing sugar, cocoa powder and Blue Band margarine. He had learned that a millipede was the baby of a spitting cobra; that queen cake crumbs turned into driver ants when left out in the sun to dry; that if you sucked ink from the nib of a fountain pen, then your blood would turn blue.

Dudu's throat clenched. He said to himself, Dudu, you cannot live without *The Daily Assortment of Astonishing Things*. He walked across the street, weaving between tuktuks whose agitated drivers would not stop hooting. He paused at the end of the street, staring at the smattering of tin-roofed stone houses over the escarpment.

The marketplace where his mama worked was at the edge of town. Dudu ran past women watering their black-eyed Susans and past men smoking in their yards. He ran past the Stagecoach bus that always teetered from side to side as it went down the road. He ran past housemaids lighting the wicks of kerosene stoves. He ran past the brew-house where raucous laughter seeped through the window shutters.

He slowed down when he saw Ali Brassiere by his heap of second-hand women's underwear. Ali Brassiere wore Betty Boop panties like a skullcap on his head. He wore a corset strapped round his wiry frame. The cups of the corset were filled with oranges. Ali Brassiere called out, Fifty cents! Fifty cents!

His mama's stall was next to Ali Brassiere's heap. Dudu wiped his hands on his shorts, leaving wet prints on the fabric. He was thirsty, so he sucked on his tongue until his mouth was filled with saliva, and he swallowed that in one gulp. He peered into the stall. His mama sat at the Singer sewing machine, head bent, forehead scrunched, lips pursed.

Beads of sweat fell from her brow and soaked into the gingham frock that she was hemming. She hummed as she worked, her throat wiggling, dragging inside it mallet-shaped and rock-shaped and marble-shaped songs. The songs got stuck in the crevices of her throat, clinking, clanging, knocking against the tiny bones in her neck.

Dudu looked about his mama's stall. Wooden soda crates were piled high in one corner, the glass bottles in them half-filled with yellow-brown liquid, straws bobbing up and down. In another corner was a metal box where his mama stored all the frocks that she sewed.

The transistor radio sat on the window ledge, its antenna pulled out so far that it grazed the ceiling. The man inside the radio said, Sammy Onyango... Sammy... Sammy... Sammy passes it to Peter Dawo... Peter takes off like the F-5 fighter jet... He is not playing any jokes, this Peter... You cannot catch this Peter, he goes one-two one-two and GOAAAAL! I am telling you, Gor Mahia has scored against AFC, and all the fans are stripping naked!

Dudu tugged at his earlobe. He said, Mama?

His mama's left hand turned the spinning wheel and her right hand fed cloth to the needle. Chk-chk-chk, the machine stammered.

Mama? Dudu repeated, this time louder.

His mama pulled the frock away. The spinning wheel of the sewing machine revolved on its own, unaware that his mama's hand was now working the shears over the seams.

His mama lifted the dress to the light, and the shears on the table trembled before resting on their side. His mama snipped at loose threads with her teeth.

Dudu said, Mama please I am not full of mud please-please come back home.

His mama looked up from the frock in her hands. Her good eye rested on Dudu's face. Her sheep's eye strayed out onto Ali Brassiere's tangled heap. She said, Are you sure you are not full of mud, Dudu?

Dudu looked from the transistor radio to his mama's damp face and then back to the transistor radio. He said, Yes I am sure mama please I am not full of mud at all.

His mama placed the frock in her lap and pulled at its zipper. She said, People who are full of mud are always the ones saying that they are not full of mud.

Dudu wiped his forehead with the back of his hand. He said, Mama please I swear I am not full of mud!

His mama chewed on the nail of her thumb. She gave Dudu a sidelong glance, her good eye tinkering about his face, trying to take it apart, trying to see the things hiding inside it. She said, How do I know you are not lying to me, Dudu?

Dudu shifted from one foot to the other. With his eyes on the transistor radio, he said, Mama, I come here ob juda gating the power of he whose disco ball floated by the luminous. Do not confound yourself, mama. Do not perverse yourself, mama. Do not flummox yourself, mama. Verily, verily I say to you mama, this your boy called Dudu is not full of mud!

His mama let out a long sigh. She said, I don't know what any of that means, Dudu, but it sure sounds like you are not full of mud any more.

I am not, mama!

You will eat your leek soup and take your afternoon nap and wear your gumboots when it rains?

Dudu crossed his fingers behind his back. He had heard on *The Daily Assortment of Astonishing Things* that that was the thing to do if you had to make promises that you did not really mean. Yes mama, he said.

And you will swallow the cod-liver oil and say bless you when a person sneezes and stop drawing porcupines on the sitting-room wall?

Yes mama.

Alright then, Dudu, his mama said. She folded the frock she had been sewing and put it away. She stuffed her pinking shears and thimble and spool into an old butterscotch cookies container. She took out a tub of Vaseline, scooped some onto her palm and spread it over her elbows. She slung her bag over her shoulder. She said, Let us go home now, Dudu.

Dudu reached for the transistor radio. He pushed the antenna back in. He tucked the radio tightly beneath his arm, stroking the speaker with his fingers. He decided that some day, after he had turned into a man, he would have two houses.

The first house would be his regular house, with a sofa and a wall-unit and a footstool and a bed. He would have a second house next door to the first, and this one would have a thousand transistor radios inside it. He would go there every afternoon and drink tamarind juice straight from the pitcher and switch on all the radios and then lie down on the terrazzo floor with his arms beneath his head and listen to *The Daily Assortment of Astonishing Things*.

Okwiri Oduor was born in Nairobi, Kenya. Her short story 'My Father's Head' won the 2014 Caine Prize for African Writing as well as Short Story Day Africa's *Feast, Famine and Potluck* story contest. She was a 2014 MacDowell Colony Fellow. She is currently at work on her debut novel and pursuing an MFA in Creative Writing at the Iowa Writers' Workshop.

Zo'ona

Namwali Serpell

One may as well begin with Mr Kurtz's messages to his assistant.

> Fwd: FW: Your credit card statement is available online
>
> ---
>
> George Antoine Kurtz
> to me
> 2 hours ago
>
> take care of it

Sanjay squinted at the screen of his phone, blurry with last night's fingerprints. Take care of what? Beneath the message, there was a small grey rectangle containing three white dots, an ellipsis. Sanjay thumbed it and the page opened downward, as if he had unfolded it.

> On Mar 26, 2016, at 4:12 AM, George Antoine Kurtz <gakurtz@companies.com> wrote:
>
> SJ--WTF?
>
> George Antoine Kurtz
> Director of The Company
> 100 Wall Street
> New York, NY
> gakurtz@companies.com

This electronic transmission (and any attached documents) contains information from The Company & Co, is for the sole use of the individual/individuals or entity/entities to whom it is addressed, and may be privileged or confidential. Any other dissemination or copying of this transmission by persons or entities other than the intended recipient is strictly prohibited. If you receive this message in error, please contact the sender immediately and delete the message (and any attached documents).

Sanjay turned onto his side, propping himself on an elbow to protect his morning wood. The message itself explained nothing. His eyes flitted over the sea of legal jargon below his boss's signature, seeking places to land, a pair of dragonflies hovering over the water. Lovers or hunters. Sanjay loved his boss. He did. It's true. He was seeking words of love in the muck, though he believed he was hunting for clues. Neither were forthcoming. Take care of it. WTF? Two messages, both sent late at night. There was another ellipsis below. Sanjay thumbed it.

---------- Forwarded message ----------
From: Clarissa Kurtz <clarissa.kurtz@email.com>
Date: Fri, Mar 25, 2016 at 10:57 AM
Subject: FW: Your credit card statement is available online
To: "George Antoine Kurtz" <gakurtz@companies.com>

I'm leaving you

---------- Forwarded message ----------
Date: Thu, 24 Mar 2016 15:14:25 -0500
From: no-reply@alerts.hunt.com
To: clarissa.kurtz@email.com
Subject: Your credit card statement is available online

Dear CLARISSA KURTZ:

We are writing to let you know the statement for your credit card account ending in 0589 is available online. To see your statement or download it, log on to www.hunt.com. You can also make a payment online or set up a reminder for when your payment is due.

Sincerely,
CardMember Services

E-mail intended for: CLARISSA KURTZ. For your card ending in: 0589. Please do not reply to this automatically generated e-mail. If you are concerned about the authenticity of this message or want to report a suspicious e-mail, please call the Customer Service Line.

Sanjay cursed. The girl lying next to him mumbled unbeautifully, an animal in sleep. He was sitting up now, the blood ebbing from his boner. He couldn't bear to turn to her. The dawn light in the hotel room was no brighter than the mood lighting at the bar last night. It was the same pale gold, broken into the same thin bars – here by the slats of the window shades, there by some contrivance of abstract design – and it would probably make her skin glow the same way. She had shimmered like heat in the air last night. But he had pierced that ethereal vision. Now she would be ragged and damp and material, the way wrung cloth can be. He couldn't bear to look.

Sanjay stood, erection completely gone now, thumb still flicking obscenely against the screen. No more ellipses, no more trails of dots to follow. Sanjay read the block of legalese below K's signature again, slowly this time. Its very presence in his inbox contravened its content. K had literally copied and disseminated this privileged and confidential information. But while an error was involved in his receipt of this message, Sanjay knew how to read K's tone; he would not be deleting it just yet. And neither would he be contacting its sender, who was probably on a flight halfway across the ocean by now.

Why had K forwarded this to him? True, Sanjay often made purchases for his boss that went beyond the personal, that were practically medical in their intimacy. But Sanjay couldn't think what credit-card purchase could have led to this – statement. There was no attachment, no link. If he tried to guess the password to the Kurtzes' shared account, the website would eventually shut him out, permission denied. What had Clarissa seen? She had never threatened to leave K before. There was ample reason, but she had always seemed indifferent, or abiding. Maybe she'd just been biding.

Sanjay dressed quickly, checking that his wallet was still in his back pocket. You never know with hook ups. A hollow nausea. The drinks, the girl? No. If he didn't fix this, he would be fired. He let the hotel door click shut behind him and reread the messages on his way to the elevator. What item on their shared bank statement...? K had been confused at first too. WTF, he'd said. Sanjay pressed the elevator button. WTF. It came to him. Fuuck. Of course. The elevator chimed and opened its mouth to eat him. Clarissa must have seen the flowers. Sanjay clicked off the phone that was warming his hand, or warmed by it.

Down the elevator plummeted. Take care of it. But how? And really, Clarissa? You're leaving your husband over fucking flowers? Sanjay sighed with exasperation, smelling his own bitter breath. The elevator doors chimed open and he moved into the murmur of people in the lobby. He knew railing against Clarissa was a distraction. He alone had made this error. He alone had typed the credit-card number into the website and he alone had clicked the button. Purchase. Something he'd done a million times for K. Only this time he'd used the wrong card. And he'd happened to buy a ridiculously pricey bunch of flowers. A Lovers Bouquet.

The gold handle on the glass door of the lobby was cold. Exit. A blurring wind – Sanjay's eyes smarted – and the murmur of people in the street grew tumultuous. He looked up. Framed by the edges of skyscrapers, the clouds above gloomed, brooding still over the city. It was going to rain soon. He looked down again, thumbprinted his phone on, checked Uber – surge pricing – and shook his head. He stepped forward and raised his hand.

In the back of the cab, balancing himself in the halt and swerve of morning traffic, ignoring Taxi TV shouting advertisements at him – Virgin, Apple, Alfa Romeo – Sanjay checked the markets, then thumbed through his other emails. Yes, no, no, yes, no, one item pending, one item pendulous. His mind was divided unto itself, into layers, scrims that floated over each other. The business day, the business at hand, this business with Clarissa, the busyness of the city beyond the windshield with its vinyl-record scratches, the cabbie's hedged jaw in the mirror, the *gulab jamun* song – heavy and sickly sweet – coming over the speakers, the sway of the flat pine tree dangling from the rearview, tapping against the serene and jolly Ganesh. Just above, the cabbie's eyes darted into the mirror.

Sanjay held his phone in front of his face like a woman with a compact mirror. He was in no mood for another blathering immigrant conversation, the parsing of similarities and differences in a shared brown condition. Yes, we are from the same place, Sanjay wanted to say. But it doesn't hold. We are in the same taxi, too – isn't that just as coincidental? No country fever for Sanjay. Once, he'd ridden a cab driven by a fellow countryman, judging by the name on the licence in the window. The cabbie had listened to music on his earphones the whole ride, singing along as if he were alone. The swell in Sanjay's chest was the closest to a patriotic feeling he'd ever had, and it depended entirely on the driver's insularity, his ownworldliness.

This driver was the right sort too. The car slowed smoothly

as it approached the curb. The cabbie pressed some buttons. The machine in the back spoke. Sanjay slid his credit card between its thin lips. The machine in the front tattled, then sneered out a white tongue of paper that the cabbie ripped from its teeth. Sanjay snatched the receipt and stepped out, closing the door with an efficient, impersonal slam. A blissfully wordless exchange.

According to his phone, the walk from the leather seat in the cab to the leather seat in his office was 133 steps – just enough time for Sanjay to make a plan. It was quiet in the office this time of the morning, everyone still at home or on their commute. Sanjay turned away from his window – shuttered, he did not enjoy a view of his own – and pulled out his wallet. He slid K's credit card out – not the usual one, but the one for the credit line K shared with his wife. Plucking the receiver of his desk phone – less traceable than his cell – Sanjay dialled the number on the back of the card.

Purr, purr. Purr, purr. The orchestral swell, then the placating voice.

Hello. Thank you for calling the Hunt Topaz Visa Customer Service line. Your call is very important to us. It is our privilege to serve you. Please listen to all of the following options, as the menu may have changed. To return to the main menu at any time, please press nine.

A rich, creamy silence.

To continue in English, press one now. Para español, oprima el numero – Thank you. If you are a customer, please press one now. If you are – Thank you. If you are calling about your credit car – I'm sorry, I don't recognize that instruction. If you are calling about your credit-card balance, please press one. If you are calling about a recent purchase, please – Thank you. Please enter the 16-digit number on the front of your credit card, followed by the pound sign. Thank you. Please enter the four-digit expiration date on the front of your card, followed – Thank you. Please enter the three-digit – Thank you. Please hold.

Tremulous trumpet, the scratchy squeak of music too loud for a phone receiver. A flute –

Thank you for holding. Your current balance on this account is – Please hold while I connect you to the next available customer-service representative. This call may be monitored or recorded for quality-assurance purposes. I'm sorry. All customer-service representatives are currently assisting other callers. Please stay on the line and one of our customer-service representatives will be with you as soon as possible.

The orchestral swell again, this time giving way to a steady metronome of classical music. On hold. The baroque familiarity of being. On. Hold. Sanjay waited in the lull, shuffling scrims of thought – the meeting at nine, whether he'd remembered to put in K's flight preferences, two reports to look over, the word *privilege* – as the seconds surged to the drag rhythm of Vivaldi's violins, it must be spring, no spring is when you hear the rain, arrows of notes scampering down, then tumbling, then thudding, and now sex began to thread its way between Sanjay's scrims, the promise of sex or its aftermath, the girl from last night, the filigree of damp hair at her temples as they sweated together, she had been a little too tall, her nipples triumphant as the peaks of waves, her canine tooth nipping her lip as she gasped, her eyelashes clotted with mascara –

Good afternoon. My name is Randy. How may I help you today?

Sanjay groaned internally. Randy? More like Rahul. Hi, my – I mean, I made a purchase, uh, by accident. I'd like to stop payment on that item.

Most certainly, sir. I can definitely help with that. I will just need to confirm your identity.

Sure. Sanjay ran his fingers along the edge of his desk. He'd pretended to be Kurtz before.

I will just need you to answer some security questions. What is your date of birth?

August 15, 1947.

Thank you, sir. What a happy coincidence –

Sanjay frowned. What coincidence?

– your mother's maiden name?

Sanjay looked up, casting about the perforated ceiling for the answer. Right, the Foundation.

It's Wilcox.

Please hold.

Sanjay groaned, externally this time. No music, just the empty vault of being. On. Hold. In the hold of a vessel. He spun his chair to face the window and used the credit card in his hand to tap the shades apart. The rain was pathetic here, scattered and thin like meagre applause. The grey clouds made him hungry though. Hungry for fried and sweet things. His mother's *pakora* and *chai*.

Thank you so very much, Mr Kurtz. How can I help you today?

Right, so like I said, I made a purchase? From Flower After Flower? Do you see it?

Mmmm. Yes, sir, I can see it. A... Lovers Bouquet, $241.98, purchased February the 29th?

Yeah. So I need you to stop that payment.

Yes, of course, thank you, sir. I am privileged to assist you. The echoey clicks of keys. I'm sorry, sir, that transaction has already been authorized and paid for, sir.

No, look. I basically need it gone. Can you cancel the payment?

I'm sorry, sir, Mr Kurtz. This month's statement has already been issued. But if you would like to contest the transaction and apply for a refund, I am happy to assist you.

This was a mistake. This purchase isn't mine.

Oh, sir, this is a fraudulent purchase? I will connect you immediately with our consumer fraud department to cancel your credit card. If you could please hold –

No! Sanjay's chest was tight as he rifled through his options. If the card got cancelled, Clarissa would lose her mind. But if the transaction got refunded, K could at least claim the purchase had been an error, a mix-up. A bouquet for Clarissa that just never got delivered.

No, it wasn't fraudulent, just my mistake. Look, could you – let's just contest the payment.

Absolutely sir, if you could please hold –

No! Don't put me on hold! He wanted no more of that dead-air time.

Yes, sir, thank you sir, I am happy for you to remain on the line while I contest this transaction. A long spell of keys clacketing, tiny horses galloping with tin shoes down a brick road. Mr Kurtz, sir, to contest this transaction, I will just need you to provide some information.

Sanjay sighed. Okay. What do you need?

I'll just need you to answer some security questions –

I just –   Sanjay gritted his teeth. Okay, go ahead.

What is your place of birth?

New York.

Are you certain, Mr Kurtz?

Sanjay paused. But of course he knew where his boss was born. He'd even been to K's old neighbourhood, on one of those nostalgia tours that strike the fancy of a rich man when he begins to resemble his father. Sanjay recalled flashes of leafy trees and brown walls, but his strongest memory was the weight of K's arm around his neck, strung along his shoulders like a bough a man might use to carry two pails of water. The weight of confidence. Of being taken into confidence.

Like I said. New York.

Ah, yes, of course. What great fortune to have been born in such a great city!

Uh, thanks… Randy.

What is the name of your favourite pet?

Oh, come on! Listen, could we just hurry this up?

Yes, of course, sir. My apologies, sir. What is the reason for this cancellation?

I bought the... bouquet by accident. I wanted to buy a –
look, can you just cancel it?

Yes, sir, of course, sir. Just one moment while I enter your
cancellation.

As the keys tapped peppily in the background, Randy
began to make small talk, the smallest talk, the talk of ants.
I myself feel grateful to have been born in Bangalore but the
circumstances – Sanjay's mind drifted back to the girl's body,
wandering from her shut eyes to her sprung nipples, the
sound of her breath in his ear, a panting that synced oddly
with Randy's laughter, keys still rattling in the background,
dice in a cup, the word confidential, the girl gripping his
balls, god she was a pro, maybe he should have said goodbye
this morning, Randy saying as you know, the girl licking his
ear, giggling about the hair there, where are you from, Randy
saying people like us –

Wait, what do you mean?

Oh, no, Mr Kurtz, I didn't mean anything. I was just saying
that –

What the hell, Randy, this your first day?

It's just that I can hear from your voice that you are from –

I told you – I'm from fucking New York! You know what?
Let me talk to your manager.

That won't be necessary, Mr Kurtz, I meant absolutely no
harm.

Your manager. Now.

Yes, sir. Thank you, sir. Please hold.

Sanjay breathed fury, spinning the credit card between his
fingers as Vivaldi cooed in his ear. Would he never be rid
of it? The unbanishable accent. Like a dog following him
around, moonily licking his knee. He went by Jay sometimes
but to no avail. You would have thought that his British
schooling would have fixed it. That England, that cold,
imperious spinster aunt of a country, would have scrubbed
it from his tongue with soap. But no, the minute he opened

his mouth – Where are you from? No, but really, where are you *from*? Sanjay grinned through his teeth at the pretty little white girls. Even K mocked him for it. But he loved his boss. It's true. He did. He could take the curry jokes, the patel-patel patter from K. But not from this other man, this 'Randy', this sham stranger-friend pretending to a solidarity from which Sanjay had deliberately severed himself, until his separateness was as thick as the hair on his head, as thick as his very skin.

Hello, is this Mr Kurtz? A mellifluous voice, accented, contralto.

Yes, said Sanjay.

My name is Charity Kalabula and I'm one of the Customer Service managers here at Hunt. How can I help you?

This guy – he just – Sanjay stuttered. What had Randy done exactly? Look, can you just help me cancel this transaction on my credit card? I just want to fix this and get on with my day.

Certainly, Mr Kurtz. I'll just need you to answer some security questions to verify your identity. What is the name of your favourite pet?

✳✳✳

Stately, plump Charity Kalabula stepped off the elevator, bearing a fake designer purse on which an L and a V lay crossed. She shoved her hip against the exit door of her office for the very last time, head held high. Her yellow raincoat, unzipped, flapped ungentle behind her on the wild evening wind. Even as she marched resolutely toward Liverpool Street station, Charity couldn't help but reveal how dismal she felt. It was her fate – to be see-through, feelings swarming in technicolour on her face. Children knew it, and dogs, who nuzzled her when she was sad, and cats, who insinuated themselves into her lap when she was happy. Men in the street, businessmen, postmen, binmen, they all read her hormonal levels as precisely as a pregnancy test. It was dreadful when she made her daily Skype home, her mother's frown on the screen as harsh as a badly lit mirror.

As the rain began to fall, Charity hurried toward the tube station, the knockoff bag knocking her hip. Her mind was divided unto itself, into spheres, marbles of thought that tapped against each other, drifting in and out of focus. Charity was thinking of the hole in the toe of her pantyhose, and the umbrella she had left hanging on the back of her office door, and the piece of rocket stuck in her teeth from lunch, and the job she had just lost. Or rather, the job she would lose. Bureaucratic protocol at the Hunt Bank Visa Services Customer Service Department moved at a glacial pace, as Charity well knew. They had taken so long to process her work permit that, though she had been working there as a manager for five months on a Working Holidaymaker Visa, her position was still pending, still precarious. And in this market, she was barely holding onto the ledge of employment. This stupid phone call with this supposed Mr Kurtz would pry her fingers off the edge, send her over it, and down she would fall, all the way back to Lusaka.

As she ploughed onward to the tube station, the thought of going back home sailed across the floor of Charity's mind, knocking all the other marbles out of the way. It was usually a clear and sturdy thought: the promise of strong tea and sour mango and greasy *chitumbua* bought from the side of the road, tastier for being an afterthought. But that was the promise of visiting home, not going home for good. Not losing her job, then her visa. Not returning in disgrace. Charity pulled her jacket hood over her plaits so they wouldn't fray in the damp. It would be raining in Lusaka too. At home, rain was a blessing, as rare and necessary as all of life's liquid emissions. Her mother would scoff at this. Don't you know about cholera? It's true, Charity. Water carries diseases like low voices in its murmur. Soon enough, these would be her worries: a runny tummy, a feverish headache. She felt that way now anyway, striding along the streets of London, soon to be sacked, profoundly hungover.

The drops on her eyelashes – rain or tears or both – pixellated the sign above Liverpool Street station. She tramped down the steps, wrangled her wallet from her bag, and kissed it to the machine's flat eye. The big glass teeth parted to let her through and shut behind her with a whir, swallowing her into the system. Charity entered the current of bodies streaming through the station, with its white tiles and black filth and silver fittings. London's labyrinthine loo. She slumped down some steps, slumped onto a train, slumped into a furry seat, slumped against the divider. What a parade of misery, what a parody! Maybe she was an open book to the world not because she wished to be read but because she wished to write herself. Once upon a time, Charity Kalabula got sacked.

His voice had been trembling when he put the call through. Calm down, Raghu. Charity rehearsed their conversation in her head, trying to recall the words that had sunk her. Calm down, she'd said. Tell me what happened. Yes. Okay. And then what did he say? This was her forte. Charity was a master of management, and though her mother said managerial work was beneath her talents, she saw no shame in it. It did take talent to sort and unsort and redistribute all the important feelings – of the representative, of the client, even of the account and of the market – feelings like notes on a piano, Charity's job to make them harmonize. These were the lessons of Mrs Phiri's course on Human Resources as Human Relations at Evelyn Hone back home.

Right, Raghu, you shouldn't have presumed. I know you've been trying to connect better with… yes, I saw the note on your last review. Right. But you went too far. Right. Don't worry, I'll take care of it. In the future, Raghu – she had raised her voice to pierce the clutter of his apologies and thank yous – *never* assume anything about a customer. But then the man on the line had been so angry. Not just customer angry or man angry. Implacable and bitter.

The train was losing passengers, the muggy air clearing as the seats did. A teenager plonked himself next to her anyway, knees spread as wide as a YouPornstar in the videos Charity often watched alone in her bed, in the quietest dark of night, pretending she just needed the orgasm to get to sleep. This boy's knee pressing into her thigh, this bone in her flesh – Charity's ears grew warm.

What had she done wrong? Right off, she had asked Mr Kurtz the security question that's supposed to trigger the simple joy of owning an animal. But he'd lost his mind, ranting and threatening and lobbing the name 'Randy' at her. She saw why Raghu had made his mistake, why he had presumed. Mr Kurtz couldn't answer questions about purchases on the account: Ivy League dues ($500.00 annually), an exclusive gym membership ($245.00 monthly), first-class plane tickets ($15,878.63 last month). The man did not match the profile, she felt this intuitively. A Mr Kurtz, born in New York, in 1947? No.

The train slid to a stop and the robot said its piece and Charity heaved herself off the train and out of the renovated Shepherd's Bush station, as vaulted and shiny as a spaceship. Westfield mall was a pale cliff in the distance, older buildings crowded up against it like henchmen. The new Virgin billboard flashed its letters individually through the dusk. Charity weaved around the circus of umbrellas on the pavement, doused by their clash as other people scurried to their jobs, their homes. That's all anyone wants. A job and a home and an umbrella. None of the above for Charity Kalabula. The trees in the Green gloomed darkly, their leaves snickering in the wind. Greggs had its doors open despite the rain, and it exhaled its smells at her: mouldy soap, fried coriander, an icy blue, a dozen sweetnesses. A man smoking a fag under the bakery's overhang barked an offer to suck her nipples, and then instructed her to smile. Because she was Charity Kalabula, she did.

What was it about her that made men so blithely aggressive? Even Albert, whose smile had seemed so kind when she'd swiped his profile pic right on her phone, who had been rounder and shorter in person, less intimidating and therefore more inviting. It turned out that even Albert, with the thick spectacles that kept his eyes at a safe distance, contained unfathomable depths of rage. At the pub last night, four Hennys in, he had pushed his spectacles up his nose, and, in his calm and gentle way, excoriated her. For neglecting him, disrespecting him, for only returning his calls when it was late or she was tipsy.

Charity suspected the real reason for his rage was that he had never made her come. He just always went the wrong way in bed, slow when speed was needed, soft when she needed a hardness to throw herself against, when she wanted to be left spent. Albert had sat there at the bar, calmly, gently calling her a whore, a cunt, a bitch. Charity had sat there beside him, sipping her Henny, nodding slowly, unable to wipe the smile from her face. When he had finally left, she'd stayed, swallowed down two more drinks, swiping right on her phone until the last call bell rang and the pub lights brightened. Cha, time to go home. God, she was hungover.

You do your job every day, you wire money home every month, you treat yourself once in a while, a tipple at the bar, a dance with a bloke who's chubbier or spottier than his profile pic, you rub your bum against his pelvis, then a giggly stumble home, a nightcap, and into bed with you. But then one night a man calls you a whore and you get blessed drunk to forget it and you show up at work the next day with a hangover so fierce that when another man calls the number on the back of a card, you say the wrong thing and you get yourself fired.

The thing is, you were just doing your job, how could you have known he'd call you racist of all things, you're good at this job, even if your mother is constantly harassing you about getting an official work permit, but look how it turned out in the end, and how awful it would have been to rise and rise, only to sink anyway.

The rain had stopped but all was damp and shuffly: the harried steps of wet shoes, frowzy pigeons pecking at the washed-up dreck, ads for Apple Watch dripping from the walls like melted candy. Charity should have known better than to hold a customer to account like that. Not because she was herself brown and an immigrant, well acquainted with the feeling of being mistaken for someone she was not, but because she had been professionally trained to know better. It had been with a dull sense of shock that she heard, and knew had been recorded for quality-assurance purposes, the words tumbling out of her mouth over the line. Mr Kurtz, you are not who you say you are. It was as if someone had spoken for her or through her, or as if she were already sitting with her gritted smile in the HR office, listening to the mp3 recording of the fateful call.

Charity opened her front door and let her bag fall to the carpet. It was quiet in the flat at this time of day, everyone still at work or on their commute. Standing in the mail on the welcome mat, muddying the envelopes, Charity leaned back against the door and closed her eyes, trying to fix the last words of the call. What had she said exactly? Sir, you cannot possibly be who you say you are. And the man, who could not possibly be a Mr Kurtz, had said: Let me speak to your manager.

The next morning, still in her pyjamas, Charity pried open her old laptop like the jaw of a stubborn animal. She had used a photograph for the background: Charity and her sisters in front of a chaos of colour, the bright petals and rich leaves of her mother's garden. Her sisters had all stayed home. Charity had been the sole satellite, the far-flung child, a bottomless bank for the whole bloody family. She let her eyes drown in the green on the screen – there's no green like home green. Maybe her mother would say, Come home, Charity. We miss you anyway, just come. Not likely. Maybe Charity would fly home first, pretend it was for a visit, confide in her mother there. She imagined them sitting on the veranda, dipping shortbread biscuits in hot tea, saying *ach!* when a biscuit crumbled or drowned, laughing at the dissolution of the best-laid plans. Charity would wait until their laughter sighed down. She would wait and then she would say, *BaMayi,* I lost my job.

Charity clicked on the blue icon with its little white worm. A window bloomed with an airy sound – a questioning sound, like the sceptical hmmm?s of gossiping women – that ended with a pop. The list of contacts tumbled down the screen. The only green bubble with a white check mark was next to her mother's icon, a blurry, shrunken image of her face. Charity clicked it. Cartoon beeps for the dial tones, always the same no matter the number – an up-and-down ditty – then the purr-purr of the ringing. In Charity's personal hell, if anyone ever bothered to design one, these Skype sounds would be a special torment. The call cut abruptly – a drop of water down a drain, coins snatched from your hand – and redialled automatically. Charity watched impatiently as the red phone icon pulsed. If it would only connect. Two more tries. Finally, the two-tone bubble burst. A scraping wind, a hiccupping robot, her mother's voice. Hallooo?

BaMayi, can you hear me?

Can you see – oh there you are! Hallo, Chacha! Can you see me?

Charity leaned forward, straining to build a face out of the blurry blocks. The screen, with great effort, spat out a patch of clarity in the general clutter: her mother's smile. Mrs Kalabula had a beautiful mouth, large and clean edged, almost architectural. Her lips opened and closed, out of sync with the words sputtering through the computer's speakers. It was like watching a dubbed movie.

BaMayi, where are you? Are you at the market?

– this connection is horrible, can we ring again? These Skypings are – oh, me? I'm at Showgrounds, can you-ya-you-you s-s-s-see miss-miss-mistah – the glitch resolved and hurried the next words like she'd been put on fastforward – Mwanza-he-says-when-are-you-coming-HA-llo?

The screen veered. There were flashes of blue and white and pink – the sky and the walls of the garden centre at Showgrounds – as she angled her computer screen. Mr Mwanza's face came into view, cocked at an angle, surprisingly clear.

Muli bwanji, BaCharity! Muza bwela liti?

He had used the honorific even though she had always felt like a daughter to him. By funding her mother's business, which employed him, Charity had become a benefactor to this man whose legs she used to hug whenever she was afraid, as if he were a tree in a flood. She waved back at him and said that she would be coming back home soon. He stared blankly at her and she stared back, waiting for the connection to catch up. They blinked at each other across the delay. How handsome he was! She never knew if her love for Zambian faces was about beauty, or in her blood, or sheer homesickness. She often found herself seeking Zambian contours and skin tones in the profile pics on Tinder here in London. And whenever she went home, it made her practically bisexual, even omnisexual, pangs in her chest whether the face were male or female, young or old. A broad and patriotic lust.

The screen scrambled and unscrambled and her mother's face appeared, in full now, but haloed at the edges. Charity nodded compulsively as her mother rattled on about the plants she was buying for the new business. Mrs Kalabula concluded with a note of uncharacteristic optimism.

It's almost flourishing! Anyway there's a demand. How about you, Chacha, any new friends?

This was Mrs Kalabula's way of asking Charity whether she had found love since their call yesterday. As Charity launched into a series of defensive excuses, she realized that this business with the flowers would make it even harder to tell her mother that she'd lost her job. During the terse meeting in the HR office, Charity's superior, an Irish woman with a smile like barbed wire, had told her that she would receive severance after her two weeks' notice. But there was no longer a position for Charity at the company; her behaviour with Mr Kurtz, however proper her intentions, had been libellous and discriminatory. Charity hadn't argued. She'd sat there, silent, furious, smiling helplessly. She knew she was dispensable and costly. Just another foreigner without a work permit.

Her mother's face had frozen on screen, her mouth unhappily agape. Charity stared into it: the rude front tooth, the flash of a gold filling, the beached mollusc of her tongue. The speakers still whinged on: Charity needed to find a friend, friendship is easy, it comes down to trustworthiness, Charity needed to get a promotion, this business was not going to fund itself, when would she be able to wire her next salary, Charity needed to start dating properly, she was too old to be playing. The torrent of complaints and demands poured from the locked mouth as if from an open spout.

Charity could not account for her life in London, not to her mother. She hated the idea of dating, it struck her as an almost literal word: marking a date, the passing of time, the marking of the passing of time. Better to bump bodies, hope for some pleasure, then vanish, or half-vanish – not gone but ghostly – letting the exchange of sex give way to an exchange of texts, LOLs and exclams, scratches on a wall. Charity had always cherished this simplicity, Human Relations as Human Resources: tit for tat, this for that. The clarity of reciprocity. But it turned out this kind of math didn't hold. Not even at work.

Her mother would be devastated when she found out that Charity had lost her job. On the screen, Mrs Kalabula's open mouth jerked twice, then fell back in step with the jumping beat of her speech, no longer divided unto itself. The molten ball rolling in Charity's stomach began to rise, and it hardened as it rose, as if her chest was made of ice, so that by the time it reached her throat it was stiff and cold. She had been right, goddammit. That man was not who he said he was. Before she had left her desk, she had checked the account, just to see. The item, The Lovers Bouquet, had already been tagged. Pending Review. Charity felt choked with unfairness.

Mrs Kalabula frowned. She had this witchy ability to see through the jumble of Skype, as if its pixellated mess were to her the clearest of windowpanes. Chi-chi-chi- – her voice stuck and drowned. Underwater, she droned glumly on – Whuut's. Goooing. On. Charity told the sorry tale, her voice catching on the splinters of the situation, hot tears slurring the sense. Her mother frowned at her, through a screen, across a world, through another screen. Charity snatched a tissue from the slitted box on her nightstand and blew her nose. She wiped her eyes. She gazed at her mother's face.

BaMayi? Hello? Are you there?

***

Mrs Kalabula said she would sell the flowers herself.

Mwanza had his work cut out for him. The doors would be taken off. The carpenters were coming. And then, thought Cynthia Kalabula, what a morning – fresh as if plucked from the soil.

What a gamble! What a leap! How nice it was to plunge like this into the morning, the air thick and soft and cool as a frangipani petal. It made Mrs Kalabula feel like something was about to happen. She paused at the Showgrounds exit, waiting for cars to pass. A smart woman, thought Mr Longwe, catching sight of Mrs Kalabula through a minibus window. A bit like a bird, a crow. Blue-black, alert, long in the body, though she was probably 50 by now, and had got fat since her eldest had gone to England. She roosted by the road, not seeing him, waiting to cross.

Having lived in Lusaka – how many years now? over 20 – you can feel, Mrs Kalabula was sure, a hush, a special pause just before a minibus accident. There! The metal crunch. First you hear a warning, the panicky honks. Then the collision. The shouting drivers circled each other now, insults dissolving in the air. Soon they would hop back in, carry on. Laugh and chat.

Foolishness, thought Mrs Kalabula, crossing the road into the petrol station. How quickly we forget bad things. Who knows why we love it, why we make it, break it, make it again. Life. Even the poor, those most dejected miserables sitting under trees. Even them, they love life. They can't be handled by government for that same reason: they love life too much. They enjoy. They will drink *chibuku* too much.

People's eyes. People shuffling, strolling, and trudging. The shout and uproar. Bicycles, cars, minibuses, trucks, lorries. Hawkers stringing their way through traffic and selling airtime through open windows. Clapping church groups. Singing church groups. The victory and the jingle jangle and the familiar groan of an aeroplane overhead – a reminder that Charity was abroad, making the family proud. Mrs Kalabula loved all of this. She loved life, Lusaka, this moment in March.

As she trotted across the feeder road into the Arcades parking lot, she shaded the sun from her eyes. It would rain this afternoon but this day would start with summer. She made her way around the cars scattered across the tarmac like sweets wrapped in plastics. The Customers wouldn't arrive for another hour. She scanned the stalls that had already been set up, searching for Mulenga. The blue tarpaulin between the stalls quacked and flapped and shuddered. It was striped with the shadows of marketeers setting out their wares on newspapers on the ground or *kachigamba* tables.

Mulenga was putting up her stall on the far side of the permanent canopy that ran down the middle of the parking lot. It would take time, and money, for Mrs Kalabula's stall to move from the outskirts of Sunday Market to this shaded corridor where the established stalls stood face to face like warriors, battling for customers' attention.

Mwa'uka bwanji?

Mulenga smiled at her with his mouth closed, which meant that he was running late. She stood over him, fists on hips, as he scurried around. The tarpaulin wasn't yet up between her stall, which backed onto his pickup, and Mrs Chisenga's stall next door. Mrs Chisenga was sitting on the ground, studiously ignoring her, reigning over her muddle of wares. There were wooden crocodiles and soapstone hippos and malachite frogs and wire giraffes. There were patchwork *chitenge* bags. There were copper cuffs and ebony bangles and beaded bracelets and twisted bands of elephant hair. Mrs Kalabula eyed all this with a sneer and turned away. Local goods. All the same.

Not like her flowers. Mulenga was carefully unloading them now, carrying them one by one from the pickup to a long table – bought from Kubu Crafts, imported from China. He cringed a little as he passed her, cradling each bag of soil like it held a baby. It's true. Mrs Kalabula bent over the table and rubbed a hairy Saintpaulia leaf between thumb and forefinger. Plants are just like newborns. They reach for warmth and water. They open and close their mouths. They grow.

Mrs Kalabula felt or heard a vibration in her handbag. That would be Mwanza, checking if she had made it to the market. She was doing his job today. She pulled out her phone.

Hallo?

Nothing. She looked down and turned the screen on. It wasn't a call. It was a Whatsapp from Chacha. She stepped toward the shadow cast by the canopy, out of the glare, to read it.

Hi ma we got cut off am comin home

Mrs Kalabula blinked at her phone. A car door opened and banged shut beside her, releasing a babble of American voices. Chacha coming home? Oh! Mrs Kalabula often told her church friends that, although she had been blessed with three wonderful daughters, she missed her eldest the most. So when the news of Charity's return came – first the warning, the urgent buzz; then the fell message – Mrs Kalabula's first feeling was joy.

Excuse me?

Mrs Kalabula turned around. The woman was even taller than her. Her companions were floating off into the market with their loud round voices. The woman wore shorts and an unironed shirt, her feet strapped into bulky sandals that should have just decided to be shoes already.

I was wondering if you might –

Mrs Kalabula smiled and guided the woman to the wooden table, inviting her to look at the lush riot of blossoms.

Oh, no, I can't take plants on the plane! You know, all those rules about produce and –

The woman carried on, her head and hands moving too much. Mrs Kalabula nodded, a smile stretching her cheeks. Her phone buzzed again in her hand like a big beetle. She frowned down at it. Another Whatsapp from Charity. She tapped it with her finger.

i was gonna tell you

Why did these messages come separate like this? Chacha had said that Whatsapp was better because it connected to wife or something like that. Mrs Kalabula didn't know what these technologies had to do with marriage, but she had kept her mouth shut, relieved her daughter was even saying the word wife. Now she wished that she'd asked for more explanation about Whatsapp.

Maybe she could ask this American woman, who looked like she would know about such things. She had a rucksack and wrinkles under her eyes. Her shins were ashy, her wrist wrapped in tattered ribbons. Her hair was straightened but there were patches of kink at the temples. Like a child and a gogo at the same time. Now she was pulling her bag around her hip and digging inside it.

I'd just love to just get a picture of you in front of your stall, your –

Another buzz. Mrs Kalabula thumbed her phone and read the message.

permit was denied

– fabulous, the colours are just divine against your –

Mrs Kalubula looked up again, her chest pulsing with a sudden heat. Denied? The woman was aiming a large camera at her. It squealed and fluttered like a bat as its head went in and out.

Yes, ah, no, no, said Mrs Kalabula. She stepped forward and raised her hand.

The woman stepped back and lowered her camera. Her eyes were blank as she said thank you, of course, sorry, and stepped over to Mrs Chisenga's stall next door to try her luck.

Mrs Kalabula's chest felt fit to burst, a hot pressure below her neck. Why had they denied Charity the permit? What had she done? What had she done wrong? Mrs Kalabula leaned on the table, which was now crowded with flowers. It rocked one way under her weight, then back again as Mulenga lugged the last fern onto it. He smiled at her cheekily, which meant he was finished.

Iwe, fix this table, it's wobbling. And I need a chair. Now.

Mrs Kalabula knew she was being unfair. The American meant no harm. Mulenga meant no harm. Even Charity, who had with three words – permit was denied – destroyed the day, even Charity had meant no harm. Mulenga hastily grabbed a plastic chair from the pickup and set it down in front of the table. Mrs Kalabula squeezed her buttocks into its narrow scoop. She tried to type a message back to Charity, but her fingers were sweating and her thoughts skidded off.

Everything hinged on this work permit. Without it, Charity would lose her job, would lose any hope of another job, would come home for good. And Mrs Kalabula would lose the funds for her business. She had been planning for a year to open this stall at the market. Not a normal stall – which needed no plan – and not the normal market, where people trade shouts, things, and cash. No, Mrs Kalabula wanted a proper stall. A flower stall. At Arcades, where tourists and expats and returnees wandered in the shade, buying carved and sewn and beaten things, no barter needed, no smells in the air or sewage underfoot.

It was foolishness, of course. Why would tourists buy potted plants? And why would locals come to Sunday market? But when she looked at her flowers, when she chose and touched and sniffed them, Mrs Kalabula felt like something cool and clean was pressing against her chest. She wanted to hold it out to people. She wanted to press that cool clean feeling into their hands and say, here, this is a piece of joy. Take it.

The market gathered bodies and noise. Sellers laughed with each other and called out lazily to customers. Yes, boss. Hello, madamu. Customers talked quietly with each other, hands on their wallets. *Zingati?* they drawled or stuttered in broken Nyanja. The tarpaulin lit the stall with glowing blue light. Mrs Kalabula could hear the American talking to Mrs Chisenga on the other side.

Who made these beautiful things? Who is the artist?

Ah, me I doh no. Mrs Chisenga giggled.

Ach, Mrs Kalabula kissed her teeth. Nonsense woman. Both of them. What had Chacha done? She tapped out a message asking for more details, taking the time to spell the words correctly. She still remembered the first time her daughter had corrected her English, the look on Charity's face. Like her mother's mistake were a mosquito bite. That small. That irritating. In the middle of her typing, the phone rang.

Muli bwanji, BaAunty.

Yes, Mwanza, what is it? What is going on on that side?

His voice came in and out like an old radio.

Carpenters… say costs… not enough… must pay…

Mrs Kalabula shook her head. This was exactly why you couldn't do proper business in Lusaka. These people. Mrs Kalabula's thoughts were divided among business calculations, as if her mind were a city, each part of the plan a building, lights inside going on or off as she thought. She had paid her stall fees yesterday. A man was coming tomorrow to bring soil and chicken waste to fill the wooden boxes being built today. She needed to hire another gardener. Meanwhile, tourists were strolling right by her stall, their eyes scanning her blossoms without commitment. Just looking.

Mrs Kalabula instructed Mwanza to send the carpenters away.

Ah-ah, he started to argue with her. But why?

Mrs Kalabula began to explain but Mwanza kept on complaining. How the carpenters had come late. How they were missing tools. How they had said yes but meant no. Familiar problems. As she listened to his ranting solidarity, his loyalty, Mrs Kalabula realized she might have to fire him. Mwanza, who felt the same way about plants as she did, who touched them the way she did. His hands sometimes brushed hers in the garden. His palms were rough like an old tree and they made hers feel smooth like a young one.

Maybe they were both too old for this business. This indulgence. Who needs flowers when people are starving? Why feed orchids when they can feed you, when their roots can put between your teeth the savoury succulence of *chikanda*? Maybe she should grow vegetables like everybody else. The very thought made her droop. How could Charity have failed them like this?

We must find other funds, Mrs Kalabula interrupted Mr Mwanza. We cannot keep relying on Charity.

Mwanza fell silent. He was no more ashamed of taking money from her daughter than she was. But etiquette kept him outside the begging circle. He was not family.

Of course, he said. Madamu, yes, please.

Tell the carpenters to go.

Mrs Kalabula hung up and stood up, looking around impatiently. Mulenga was sitting on the edge of the pickup, legs dangling, staring at his phone.

And what are you doing? Can't you be finding customers?

He jumped up, eyebrows and shoulders raised. He glanced around in a daze. *Heysh*. These gardeners were always high on *mbanji*. But she didn't want to fire Mulenga either. His eyes comforted her: brown and wide, tightly curled lashes clutching his eyelids. Mushroom eyes. He came and stood beside her and began rearranging the flowers on the table, beckoning to potential customers. Mrs Kalabula sat and thought. Then she began making phone calls.

She tried her business contacts first. She had been doing floral arrangements for weddings and meetings and funerals for years. But many of the phone numbers didn't work and hardly anybody picked up. When they did, she found it difficult to work her way around to the question of money. There were greetings to be exchanged, ailments to be sympathized, children to be asked after. The heat of the day thickened. Mulenga sold a purple geranium. Clouds stormed the sky.

Mrs Kalabula called her friends next. Mrs Kabwe, who sold vanilla cupcakes that she baked on the weekends. Mrs Bwalya, who sewed *chitenge* tablecloths. Mrs Ndeke, who managed four taxis. They all agreed it was a terrible situation. They all agreed something had to be done. They all said yes, of course they would help, but Mrs Kalabula knew well the sound of a yes that means no.

Mulenga cupped his hand up at the glooming sky. Under its shadow, tourists turned grey and shivered and put on their bright, ugly sweaters. Marketeers put out umbrellas imported from South Africa for sale. The clouds coughed some thunder, sneezed some lightning. As the first drops of rain trembled the petals and leaves of her abundant display, Mrs Kalabula finally called her sister.

Gertrude still lived in Eastern Province. She had set up her own business in Chipata many years ago at the lucrative crossroads of countries, roads, and interests. Mr Kalabula called her a *banamakwebo*, a wily trader. When Cynthia had first moved to Lusaka to marry that Bemba man, the sisters had lost touch for a while. But then mobiles had flooded the market, all those hard black chirping phones like a plague jumping right over the need for electricity and wooden poles. Now, with a touch of a button, Mrs Kalabula could hear her sister's voice.

Bwanji, sisi? How is Lusaka treating you?

Bwino pang'ono cha'be. Just a little bit okay.

Ah-ah, but what has happened?

Mrs Kalabula felt the full force of it now. Her forehead crumpled as she told her sister everything. Charity had lost her job. The money about to dry up. All these expenses still pending. Gertrude listened, grunting once in a while with sympathy or irritation.

Mrs Kalabula hadn't wanted to call her sister for this. Gertrude's shady business had helped pay for Charity's education. And Charity's training. Even her plane ticket to London. Charity didn't know this but the sisters did and it hung over their call. Cynthia stopped talking just as she reached the point of asking. The sisters sat in silence, present to each other through the sounds on either side of the line. In Lusaka, rain skittering on tarpaulin and marketeers yelling and car doors slamming. In Chipata, glasses chiming and voices murmuring and a TV telling the story of a football match.

When do you need it? Gertrude finally asked.

Soon-soon. For the carpenters.

Okay, I can send some now-now, so it comes tomorrow. *Zo'ona.*

Okay, *zo'ona*, it's fine. But how can it come that soon?

Gertrude laughed and explained. *Zo'ona* was the name of a new company. You could use it to send money with your mobile phone. You know those *tumabuildings ya* green?

Yes. Of course. The lime-green *kantemba* had been cropping up everywhere. At first Mrs Kalabula had thought the signs were a joke. The word wasn't even a word, more of an exclamation. *Zo'ona.* What you say when someone speaks the truth. A kind of amen.

My girls are working hard. It's a good time. Africa Cup. These men like to enjoy too much.

Mrs Kalabula closed her eyes. To ask had been humiliating. To talk about where the money came from would be too much. She knew Gertrude profited from the love of life that made men gather at her bar in the day and scatter into the rooms behind it at night with girls younger than Cynthia's youngest daughter.

Thank you, thank you, Mrs Kalabula changed the topic. I've been calling everybody. But at the end of the day, *wako ni wako*. Family is family.

Mmmhmm. *Zo'ona*.

They both laughed at the echo. They said it together again. *Zo'ona*.

✳✳✳

the boats stopped the winds dead they say we gotta wait for the water to turn or something the blue is forever here water and sky all mashed up with like no line between them the sun is superblinding and the sails white like my manipedi and the suns so hot the waters so flat Im so fuckin bored K talks and talks hes so fuckin boring but I like his gold his watch his buckle this bubbly I pick up my iPhone white with the rosegold back K dont care he know I need my Insta I scroll down see us at the airport us at the manipedi us at the hotel the bed so white and big and soft me lyin on the sheets my bikini flawless this tans gettin golder and golder I wanna go shopping I pout my lip he says fine of course whatever you want baby I love him iss true dont get it twisted but I gotta get my paper K say he want me to like him and not his money but I love his gold I love his ring and thass love too boo hes still talking he say he gotta fire some guy that work for him and I dont talk but he look at my lips and I look in his eyes and sometimes I think his heart is dark I say you gon fire me too boo? hes lookin older and older he surprised me at the airport hair all grey but age aint nothin I scratch his scalp my nail tips white in his grey hair this mani lookin flawless I got a french and he got a clear buff and after we had sushi and he says wanna teach me and he talks and talks but I dont talk I dont say I ate sushi since day one of this life I smile almost smile he only gets the big smile when I get the big money he think hes so slick but hes just a man with a dark heart and no game but his wallet but thass all I need I remember empty belly days and dry scab days and tiny room days judge me but you aint never live my life you aint never seen hunger like I seen hunger you aint never seen power like I seen power when I smile almost smile his eye sparkle he got ice in his eye when this boat move we gon go to the hotel swim in the pool then shower off and lie in the bed he like me layin on him my head on his chest my nails swirlin on his belly while he talks and talks sayin he gon leave his wife before she leave him but he gotta fire this guy first I aint listenin Im lookin at this hotel room so big the TVs the size my bed used to be curtains thin but supposed to be thin so the sun can come in make me golder the glass table with the flowers he sent the petals so open and so white and smellin like cologne when I got here yesterday K's Virgin flight was late so Jorge carry up my Louis V bags for me and he open the door and we stand there froze like whoah we both seen this room before but the flowers is new so big and so white like some kinda boat on the glass table me and Jorge we kick it sometimes when K aint here we smoke weed behind the poolhouse we just friends but yesterday those flowers was smellin strong and my Bulgari ice so chill on my neck and when I put a tip in his hand Jorge hold on and look in my eye and call me Little Flower and I start laughing cuz aint nobody own me yet and I drinkin my laughter down just drunk on it and Jorge close the door and he step to me and he brown like me he sprung like me he young like me my serpenti chain chill on my neck but my breasts warm warm in his hands and after we done Jorge ask me do I love K and I laugh cuz love is aint nobody own me yet cuz love is bling on my wrists and fingers and neck cuz love is a full belly and love is ice in your eye so I love my whiteman my blackman my anycolor man thass got that bling so yeah I say I love K yeah and Jorge laugh he says what you love is this life Little Flower and I say what you think yeah I love this life this room my own room I know you know iss good to own and own and own

Namwali Serpell is a Zambian writer and an associate professor of English at the University of California, Berkeley. She received a Rona Jaffe Foundation Writers Award in 2011. She was twice shortlisted for the Caine Prize for African Writing and won in 2015 for her story, 'The Sack'. You can read her fiction and nonfiction in *Bidoun, The Believer, n+1, Callaloo, Tin House, Public Books, McSweeney's, Triple Canopy, Cabinet,* and several anthologies including: *The Best American Short Stories 2009, The Caine Prize Anthology, Africa39, The Uncanny Reader, Should I Go to Graduate School?* and *Reader, I Married Him.* Her first book of literary criticism, *Seven Modes of Uncertainty,* was published by Harvard University Press in 2014.

The Caine Prize rules of entry

The Caine Prize is awarded annually to a short story by an African writer published in English, whether in Africa or elsewhere. (The indicative length is between 3,000 and 10,000 words.)

An 'African writer' is taken to mean someone who was born in Africa, or who is a national of an African country, or who has a parent who is African by birth or nationality.

There is a cash prize of £10,000 for the winning author and a travel award for each of the shortlisted candidates (up to five in all).

For practical reasons, unpublished work and work in other languages is not eligible. Works translated into English from other languages are not excluded, provided they have been published in translation and, should such a work win, a proportion of the prize would be awarded to the translator.

The award is made in July each year, the deadline for submissions being 31 January. The shortlist is selected from work published in the five years preceding the submissions deadline and not previously considered for a Caine Prize. Submissions, including those from online journals, should be made by publishers and will need to be accompanied by six original published copies of the work for consideration, sent to the address below. There is no application form.

Every effort is made to publicize the work of the shortlisted authors through the broadcast as well as the printed media.

Winning and shortlisted authors will be invited to participate in writers' workshops in Africa and elsewhere as resources permit.

The above rules were designed essentially to launch the Caine Prize and may be modified in the light of experience. Their objective is to establish the Caine Prize as a benchmark for excellence in African writing.

The Caine Prize
The Menier Gallery
Menier Chocolate Factory
51 Southwark Street
London, SE1 1RU, UK
Telephone: +44 (0)20 7378 6234
Email: info@caineprize.com
Website: www.caineprize.com